ATTRITION OF THE GODS

P.G. Burns

IP

Innovative Publishing

Attrition of the Gods

Printed in the United States of America

First Printing, 2015

ISBN 9780993451409

Innovative Publishing Ltd.
6 St Colman's Park
Co. Down
BT34 2BX
www.pgburns.com

Cover design by Apex media and print.
Book design by ORH Marketing Ltd.

P G Burns
Attrition *of* *The* Gods

Running nightclubs and organizing parties on the Island of Ibiza was far removed from PGs childhood growing up on a council estate in Coventry. He found the colourful life he craved when at the age of eighteen he discovered the Balearic isle.

Working as a DJ and later as nightclub owner and event organizer PG built himself a small empire and considerable fortune. Everything was perfect until he fell out with some locals who were envious of his success. PG says he could have handled the jealous rivals but when it was discovered he was involved with the top gangster's daughter it was time to make a quick exit. After the alleged slip from a twelfth story balcony which killed his friend and business partner the local police convinced PG to flee immediately with just the shirt on his back and he took the first ship out of there.

The ship docked in Casablanca and so began a yearlong "wander" around North Africa. "I was penniless but happy to be alive and well. I drew on many of the sights and experiences I had during this period when I wrote this book".

On returning to the UK he rekindled his relationship with fellow DJs from the clubs and bars of Ibiza and inspired by the late night party culture they joined forces, kicked the doors open of a disused warehouse, set up the lights, decks and amps; so began the warehouse party phenomenon of the early nineties. This developed into the rave scene and PG used his earnings to open bars and restaurants all over the UK.

"After a couple of spells behind bars and a near death experienced he embarked on his first grown up relationship, it lasted twelve years and although it ended in them both losing all their money and splitting up, she gave him the greatest gift ever, a beautiful daughter. "For the first time I wasn't the most important person in my own life". Enthused with a new sense of direction, PG returned to his ancestral home Ireland and although once more penniless he turned his hand to his favorite adventure- writing Attrition of the Gods

Associates

Published by www.innovativepublishing.co.uk

SEO online Marketing by www.seowebsitesuk.co.uk

Book design and Marketing by www.innovativemarketing.ie

Acknowledgements and thanks

My thanks to test readers, Bernadette McShane, Vicky Leahy, Elizabeth McDaid and Lorraine Gillespie, whose advice and observations were so valuable.

A special thanks to David Hughes a marketing genius who has been true to his word and helped me to get this story to you.

I am very grateful to both of my editors, Elizabeth (Lizzie) Wright and the brilliant Kelley Townley.

Also thanks to:

Nikki Mason, proof-reader.

Lukasz Skrzyniarz, Luke Corr, Joshua Neilly – OHR Marketing

Noel@apexmediaprint – graphics and cover

Thanks to Innovative Publishers for their belief in this book.

Attrition of the Gods is dedicated to Gerry and Bridie Burns for their support, especially during the last few years; thanks to you I have been able to get my life on track.

I love you both

Prologue

"Illusion is the first of all pleasures."

– Voltaire

Reuben Lupas looked a tall, gaunt spectre of a man as he strode through the dingy prison block. With dark eyes that contradicted his shockingly bright blond hair, he scanned the filthy corridor and lifted the hem of his monk's robes to step over the gullies that carried blood and excrement from the overcrowded cells.

He was accompanied by a man wearing a hooded robe, his face hidden from view. The two men trod carefully, wary of slipping on the wet stone steps covered in a slimy moss. Reuben was uncomfortable in these surroundings; he preferred a more palatial environment. He held his robe with one hand and a cloth to his face with the other. The stench of the cells threatened to overpower him, yet his companion seemed unaffected by the rancid environment.

Abel, the duty guard, ran over to greet the important-looking visitors. Reuben heard the screams of an inmate and his pulse raced. A smile invaded his face as the sound of the whip lashed time and time again. However, his mood changed when he realised the screams came from the cell holding the inmate he had come to see, the man who was a vital cog in his intricate plan. He turned to the guard.

"I assume the prisoner will survive the night?" The question was tinged with sarcasm.

"Yes," replied Abel. "Shay is just putting some manners on him."

Reuben shook his head in disbelief as the snap of the whip and another scream rang out. He turned to Abel once more but this time he was not so polite.

"Run ahead and tell this Shay that I will be wielding that whip on his back if the prisoner dies."

Eventually, after negotiating their way through a maze of declining stairways and thin stone corridors, they arrived at the door of the last cell in the damp squalor. Outside the cell was Abel and the gaoler, Shay, a thickset, extremely hairy mute with an unfortunate face, which now had the look of a child who had been relieved of his favourite toy.

Reuben addressed him, his voice low and sinister. "I expect this man to be capable of speaking. If he is not fit to speak to me then we will be executing two more in the morning!"
Both men looked at each other and peered into the cell, studying the prisoner.

"He is fine. Shay hardly touched him. See for yourself," said Abel. He then shouted into the cell, "A visitor for the King!"
Shay chuckled, amused by this remark.
Reuben pushed the guards aside and entered the cell. The two guards tried to follow.

"Leave us. I wish to speak with the prisoner alone," demanded Reuben.
Abel and Shay headed back up, leaving Reuben's companion waiting outside.

The prisoner stood naked in the cell, his body battered, bruised and torn and his face swollen. His hair and beard were matted with blood. Still he held his head up high and looked Reuben in the eye.

"My name is Reuben Lupas. We have met before, do you remember?"
"Yes, I remember."
"Good, then you know what I am capable of. I have come here today to discuss the possibility of your release."
He waited for a response, but none came.

"I am presuming you do want to avoid execution?" Still there was no response. Reuben impatiently raised his voice. "DO you want to live?"

There was a long silent moment before the prisoner finally responded in a gentle voice, letting the weight of his words sink in. "Everyone wants to live, yet I fear the price for my life will be too high a price to pay."

Reuben sat on the stone bench that furnished the cell and addressed the sorry-looking wretch. "Don't mistake me for one of those fools outside, baying for your blood. I do not ask for you to renounce your claims. On the contrary, I wish to help you confirm your status and cement it in history."

Once again the prisoner did not respond, barely making eye contact through hooded eyelids. Reuben accepted this as an indication to continue.

"I have travelled here with one of your loyal followers. A man similar in height, size and weight to yourself. He has agreed...no, he has insisted that he takes your place tomorrow. Now, I am pretty sure that, as you stand before me, battered and bruised and your face swollen, your own mother would struggle to recognise you. Our plan is for our friend, Shay, to give this man similar treatment. I do not anticipate anyone will notice. Do you understand what I'm saying?"

"I understand what you're saying but not why you would want to do this. Which of my loyal followers has agreed to such a thing?"

"He waits outside. Apparently guilt for something he has done to you is his motive. You can speak to him yourself. As for me, let's just say I'm a believer."

"And what would be expected of me once I am free? I am sure you are not a doing this out of kindness."

Reuben nodded. "First you will hide out in my villa. We will wait for the throngs of people who have come to town for the festival to leave and then we move you. You will have time to speak to your friends and family and to direct your followers and then you will say goodbye. I will arrange for you to sail far away across the sea. All I ask is that you never return."

"Why would I speak to my followers? What do I say when they see me alive days after witnessing my execution? Do they know of this deceit?"

"No. Only we three and the mute will ever know the truth. As for what you say to them, we will think of something. Now, I ask again. Do you want to live, Yeshua Ben Yosef, King of the Jews?"

The man history would depict as the Son of God, Jesus Christ, the Messiah, looked up to the ceiling with his hands apart as if asking for divine inspiration before answering, "Yes."

On hearing his master agree, the man outside stepped into the cell and kissed Jesus on the cheek.

Reuben laughed as he announced, "Behold, Judas, son of Simon, who will be known as Iscariot 'the false one'." His cackling laughter unnerved the two Jews.

June 1st 2146 AD

"Education is not preparation for life; Education is life itself."

John Dewey

The large auditorium buzzes with excitement as the new student's mill around. Ember Jones, a petite girl with flawless skin, long, blonde curly hair and stunning big, blue eyes, epitomises the Aryan race to which she belongs. Today she becomes a freshman here at the Reuben Lupas Temple of Learning – known as the RLT for short. She sits at her allocated seat amongst the throngs of first-day students and looks up to the domed ceiling that is decorated with the beautiful artwork of the great Angelo Abela. His paintings depict historical events such as the Verdi uprising, the Rapture and the return of the Messiah. As she scans the ceiling she sees scenes depicting the millions of deaths caused by the revolution in the twenty-first century and the terrible carnage that followed. Letting her eyes move further along she sees the events known as the Great Tribulation and the Rapture.

Ember has seen photos of the ceiling in books but she is not prepared for the sheer scale of the work. She knows its dimensions are the same as a historical work known as the Sistine Chapel but she imagines that even that painting could not match this for artistic genius. Between each of the thirteen pendentives that support the Dome is a depiction of one of the thirteen Djinn. Even the one known as "the traitor" is represented. Ember's heart beats faster and she can feel a tingling sensation all over as she realises that as of today she will be studying these events at this bedrock of academia.

Her eyes are drawn to the painting that is probably the most evocative of all the depictions: a beautiful young woman draped in a sheer veil that does little to hide her naked body. This is Amitiel, Ember's favourite Arc Hon. Ember was always drawn to her image when she studied this painting in books and, although fascinated by all four Arc Hon, she felt strongest towards Amitiel. Maybe because she was incarnated as a young

13

girl not dissimilar to Ember in appearance and age or perhaps because of the tales she heard of this young warrior. Ember needs to take a deep breath as she looks at Amitiel's image, the feeling of awe overwhelming her.

"Wow," she exhales, her hand resting on her chest.

At sixteen Ember is the youngest student to ever attend the RLT and she has achieved this honour by studying religiously every day. The fact her father is the Procurator of the Jinn City and Dean of the RLT has not in any way aided her achievement of gaining acceptance two years early, although many doubt this. This remarkable achievement would usually be major gossip but not today. Today she is overshadowed by an even more extraordinary student in attendance. Adam Costello is the first ever non-Aryan to graduate to the RLT. His recent acceptance into this, the highest of academic institutes has caused outrage amongst the Aryan Council and many of the inhabitants of Higher Jinn. Parents threatened to make their children boycott the classes he attended and, had it not been for Procurator Jones' intervention, the Aryan Council would have excluded the boy before he even arrived.

⊕𓇳𓂃𓇌𓆷𓏛

Adam, a squat, stocky boy made conspicuous by his short dark hair and olive skin, enters the auditorium and feels everyone's eyes on him. He looks for his name on a seat, positive that he will be placed in the worst possible area, probably with an obstructed view. A young girl whom he recognises as the Procurator's daughter waves at him and indicates a seat next to hers.

Shit, he thinks to himself, *they've sat me next to Conrad Jones' daughter? She is bound to be a right stuck-up bitch. Oh well, no one said this was going to be easy.*

Adam makes his way up to the seat, looking around at the sea of blond-haired sons and daughters of the master race. He hopes his feelings towards them are not as obvious on his face as they are in his heart.

"What a bunch of tossers..."

The other students point at him, murmuring to each other as looks of disgust cross their faces. He knows how unwelcome his attendance here is and can't help but imagine what they are whispering, although he doesn't really need to imagine; most do not even bother lowering their voices.

"Fucking Schwartskull scum," he hears from the group of uniformed lads.

"Yuck, he touched me," a plump bespectacled girl shouts, wiping her shoulder against the chair.

Adams feels his face get redder and redder as he climbs the steps to the seat. He does not know if it is embarrassment or anger causing this raised blood pressure or if perhaps it's the dread he feels at sitting next to the Procurator's stuck-up daughter. "She will be the ultimate bitch," he decides and prepares himself for a barrage of abuse.

"Hi, I'm Ember Jones." She stands, holding her hand out, a huge warm smile across her face.

Adam is momentarily stunned. *She is either taking the piss or she has taken a couple of DMTs*, he thinks to himself, tentatively holding his hand out too. He half expects her to retract hers and blow a raspberry, creating great hilarity amongst her fellow students. Instead she takes his hand and, with a noticeably firm two-handed grip, she warmly shakes it.

"I have been looking forward to meeting Adam Costello, the first Caucasian ever to graduate to the RLT." Ember's enthusiastic greeting surprises Adam so much he responds with a pathetic reply.

"It's an honour to meet you." Instantly realising how lame he sounds his face reddens even more.
Ember smiles awkwardly. "Really?"

"Sorry, I'm not used to Aryans talking to me."

The two sit down; looking around they notice that almost every student is watching them.

"See, you're a celebrity," Ember whispers to him, with a cheeky grin.

"More like a freak show," he replies.

The lights dim and a lone figure walks onto the stage. The auditorium contains a semicircle of seats rising thirty rows from the stage. Two giant smooth liquid crystal statues flank either wing of the stage. One is a representation of Reuben Lupas – also known as the Messiah, or sometimes revered as the Host – the other is Solfrid, the High Priestess and first of the Djinn. Their images stand either side of the stage almost touching a ceiling that moves like liquid. The venue seats over a thousand students. The stage is small, set high up with a black liquid screen behind it. Dallas Proctor, the world's leading authority on Old World history, is illuminated by a spotlight, giving him a celestial appearance.

"Welcome, students of the Reuben Lupas Temple of Learning. I am Dallas Proctor, First Scholar of the Templi and Historian to the Host."

The word *Host* prompts all the students except Adam to bow their heads and chant a sort of prayer: "One world a gift from the Host, One world to serve the Host."

Ember nudges Adam and he takes the hint and bows just as the rest lift their heads. Ember suppresses a giggle. Dallas Proctor looks for the source of said giggle and sneers when he sees the dark-haired filth he knows to be Adam Costello.

"Today we will give you an overview of the subjects that we will be covering during this first semester. You are going to learn about some very vile people. Some of whom are responsible for the slaughter of millions of innocent people. I do not apologise for the graphic knowledge we inflict upon you. You are entering adulthood...well, most of you are." He diverts a look directly at Ember. "Only by showing you the unsavoury details of our past can we ensure the same mistakes are not repeated."

With a dramatic wave of his arm the auditorium lights go out and the students' chairs recline back fully. The beautiful painting above their heads seems to melt and they find themselves staring at a three-dimensional picture emanating from a fluid ceiling. Once the paintings fully fade a bright light descends, enveloping the students and thrusting them into a virtual image experience. Ember feels an incredible sensation sweep over her as she and the other students are immersed into this computer-generated simulation. She looks ahead, startled, as the life-sized depiction of a man appears inches from their faces. He is wearing a black uniform adorned with a red badge displaying an upside-down crucifix. His face is blood splattered and his arms tattooed, the muscles like knotted ropes. His whole body seems to be criss-crossed with thick veins and a scar runs down his left cheek. His face is that of man who has killed many times; a man with hate-filled eyes and no remorse. He stands amongst derelict, bomb-damaged buildings, a swirl of dust covering a group of ragged-looking women and children that are cowering at his feet. Ember knows exactly who this man is.

"SHANE MILLS – the Antihost!" shouts Dallas over the noise of the gunfire and explosions that accompany the images. The image is complemented by the smells of the scene: a mixture of burning and rot. The image of dust is so real Ember instinctively covers her mouth with her hand.

The students' view moves from Shane to a small child whose tears create tramlines through the dirt on his cheeks. The small boy is no more than four or five and can be heard crying for his mum. Shane Mills walks over to the child, wipes his tears, then puts his gun to the child's head and, showing no emotion, pulls the trigger. Horrified screams from the other captives are soon drowned out by the sound of rapid gunfire as two other uniformed men and a woman with crazy eyes pump round after round of bullets into the bodies of the desperate mothers and their children until only two small girls are left alive.

The students recoil in their seats, a mixture of fear and revulsion overcoming them. Most subdue their screams but at least two can be heard crying as the image reverts to Shane's face. His image appears to be looking at each and every one of the students, as if they were to be his next victims. He lifts his infamous machete and with two heavy blows he beheads the last two children. The screams are no longer subdued and the image is so real only a brief shimmer in the picture reminds Ember that this is a virtual scene.

Many of the other youngsters struggle to remind themselves they are in fact safe in the confines of their seats in the RLT auditorium and that this is an image of a man long dead, a historical event. Dallas is aware they cannot detach themselves but persists with the simulation. Over the years he has witnessed many students scream, cry and even soil themselves while experiencing these portrayals of the Antihost. Only when one young girl vomits and passes out does he relent and end the programme.

The scene fades, the seats retract and the spotlight returns to Dallas Proctor.

"That may be the first time many of you have seen an image of the Antihost. Of course, it is by law that his image is banned in most places outside of this learning establishment. But here you will become familiar with not only his image but also those of his co-conspirators whom history has aptly called the 'Diabolicals'. You will endure graphic images of the horrendous atrocities that they were responsible for. Anyone who feels overwrought by what you have just witnessed may be better off joining the catering class down the corridor."

Dallas peruses the faces of the young people and a smirk grows across his face as he can see how disturbed and unnerved the new scholars are. Some shift uncomfortably in their chairs, not even conversing. The young girl who vomited gets up and leaves. Dallas revels in their discomfort and fails to suppress a smile. That is, until he catches the eye of Adam Costello who appears unperturbed; in fact he looks impressed at his first 3DVI experience. In truth Adam has never encountered such a high-tech video experience and is truly impressed but unlike most people he is already familiar with the image of Shane Mills from old-style TV footage he has watched with Raphael.

Dallas knows immediately that this boy from the Caucasian sector has little respect for Aryan ways. His joy at the other students' discomfort is spoiled and his lip visibly curls with disdain for this boy who had passed the entrance exam despite not having access to the Bibliotheque or any ordained tutor. How he managed to pass is a mystery. Dallas was not happy about teaching a "Schwartskull", but he is confident that he will dissuade the lowlife from continuing with his chosen subject very soon.

Adam feels the disdain coming from the lecturer. As a Caucasian he is very aware that his presence here is not welcome. Since he was a child Adam has obsessed about Old World history, especially the exploits of the Diabolicals, yet most books and footage have been banned. Of all the injustices his type have to endure this restriction of education on any subject was the one Adam resented most.

He had spent a childhood scraping around trying to find any books or films that related to the times before the New World Order and the rise of the Fourth Reich. Of course, the Grand Bibliotheque in the Aryan sector is bursting with books and research on this subject if you can get access. But being a lowly Caucasian, Adam was only granted a red chip and couldn't enter these places. It was a classic catch-22 situation – he could only learn about Old World history by getting onto the course at the RLT, which he could only do if he passed the entrance exam, which you needed to study for using books from the Bibliotheque. Adam had just about been resigned to a hopeless life of curiosity and ignorance when he met Raphael.

Thanks to Raphael's teachings he had access to all the knowledge he'd dreamed of. He spent hours every day at Raphael's listening to tales of world history, mainly about the early to mid-twenty-first century, the Revolution and its main protagonists, the Diabolicals, Leo Verdi and, of course, Shane Mills. For Adam it was like Messiah day every day, not that many Caucasians really celebrated the festival marking the return of the Messiah.

Adam's only concern was the authenticity of the knowledge that Raphael bestowed upon him. Many of the citizens of Ravensdale (Adam's sector) thought Raphael was a weirdo who made up stories to gain the company and trust of young men. Adam never believed this but still, on the day of the exam, he wondered if he was about to realise they were right and that all he'd learned from Raphael had been fairy tales. In fact Raphael had confused him over the last few months prior to the exam.

"To pass the exam you must learn untruths as well as truths," he had told him.

Adam lost track of what was supposed to be true and what was not, especially regarding Shane Mills. However, on the tenth day of the Autumn quarter Adam was awoken by the cheers of his sisters and his mother.

"You passed! Ninety-seven per cent! My son is a genius!" His mother yelled at him as she hugged him so hard he could hardly breathe. "My son is going to the RLT."
Adam's father, Aidan, showed no such elation. He feared for his only son's safety. The Aryans would not be happy sharing their school with a lower-class citizen.

Back in the auditorium the students recover and settle. Dallas decides to uncover what knowledge these students have acquired prior to attending his class. He always likes to separate the wheat from the chaff early on and he also hopes the Caucasian will be exposed.

"Who can tell me what is believed to be the catalyst for the Verdi Revolution?" Dallas asks the class.

The majority of the students look straight ahead, some nervous on their first day, most completely ignorant to the answer. Adam is tempted to show his extensive knowledge on the subject but decides this will make him even more unpopular. Ember Jones, on the other hand, is nearly falling out of her seat with her keenness to answer.

"Ah, Miss Jones, isn't it?" says Dallas.

Ember nods and spurts out her answer so rapidly that Dallas and the students worry if she will come up for breath.

"Shane Mills was incarcerated in prison for manslaughter. Before he went to prison he was described as a drunken thug with no affiliation to any political group or interest in world events. By the time he escaped four years later he was a dedicated extremist and anti-government activist. He caused havoc and promoted anarchy wherever he could. However..."

Dallas holds up his hand to stop her but Ember ploughs on. With her shoulders back and her chin slightly raised there is no question in her mind that she could be mistaken.

"However, the catalyst, as you mentioned, is thought to have been when Shane Mills murdered six hundred prison inmates and guards in order to escape from prison with the help of the Islamic extremist, Robert Price."

"Thank you, Miss Jones."

After a couple more questions, all eagerly answered by Ember, Dallas spends the rest of the class running through the areas that he will cover in the first term and finishes up with an assignment for the students.

"I want you all to present a thesis to me that will cover the period between the formation of the Diabolicals and the return of the Messiah. You will be working on this for the remainder of this first term and it will count towards your final results so make sure you get it right." Groans fill the room until Dallas offers up what seems like a small concession. "You will do the research in pairs but I need separate papers. Now pick your partners before leaving."

Adam immediately feels his face glow; he is sure he will be left out. A quick look at Dallas Proctor confirms this, his smug smile and raised eyebrow suggest this will be the first of many slights. No one will pick a Schwartskull.

"Well, shall we be partners?"
Adam turns to see Ember's open face smiling at him.

"Err, yeah, if you're sure? That'd be great."

Dallas looks furious. *What is she doing?* He thinks to himself. *Surely her father, the Procurator of this order, has taught his daughter about mixing with inferior classes? She can't mean it. She must be just humouring him...*

Ember suddenly grabs Adam's hand and holds it aloft announcing,

"Yeah, team freak show!" Adam shrinks back as everybody looks at them.

"Listen, Ember, maybe you should reconsider? I don't want to cause you any trouble."

"Fuck 'em," replies Ember, with a look of pride that proves she probably isn't used to swearing so casually.

Adam laughs at hearing this sweet, innocent, young girl curse and as they make their way out of the auditorium the sound of the heckling follows them.

"You are nothing like I imagined," he tells her.

Ember smiles; she is nothing like anyone imagines. She has been brought up and educated mostly by her father after the tragic death of her mother. Nobody knows this but her father secretly holds quite liberal views despite being a high-ranking official of the Aryan Supreme Council and he has taught her to question (again secretly) everything, including the belief that Aryans are the chosen and superior race. Ember has always disliked their caste type system even as a young child. She is wise beyond her years when it comes to understanding the purpose of it as social stratification and segregation. When she learned an actual Caucasian would be attending the RLT at the same time as her she was overjoyed and had made sure she would be sitting next to him on their first day.

Divide et impera

« Future cares have future cures, And we must mind today. »

Sophocles, Antigone

The two youngsters soon form a friendship that sees Ember disliked by the other students almost as much as Adam is. She doesn't seem bothered by it; Ember has always exuded a confidence instilled in her by her father. She is quite happy to spend her time exclusively with Adam as, quite frankly, she finds the others boring. Not only does he offer insight into a world she has never known, feeding her thirst for knowledge, but also only he can match her intelligence. The others respect her mainly for her status whereas Adam looks at her with eyes of intrigue. He makes her feel like something unknown rather than the foregone conclusion that she sees reflected in everyone else's eyes. Sometimes it feels like Adam's friendship is the only thing keeping her head above water. Not that she could ever let anyone know that. After all, what could the Procurator's daughter ever have to complain about?

Adam and Ember slip into a routine of going to the Bibliotheque after their lessons each day, both keen to maximise their research and make sure they do not give Dallas or the other students any ammunition to use against them. Without discussing it, each of them has decided they will submit the best dissertation at the end of term. Ember loves to see Adam so excited every time he enters this hallowed library. He looks like a kid in a Cybercandy market as he takes in the spectacular interior: six storeys of wooden balconies, solid carved oak and filled to the brim with books.

The smell of wood-polish and leather is one Ember has long associated with knowledge. Her father would sneak her in to the library when she was little, always keen to emphasise the importance of education and Ember had memorised the twists and turns well before she had reached her teens. When she had first brought Adam in he joked that she looked like she owned the entire building and all its contents. She had laughed it off but the comment had touched a nerve. Was that really how she came across? No wonder everyone else kept their distance. She watched Adam as he explored the library, seeing it through his eyes and trying to appreciate it, not just take it for granted. For possibly the first time in her life she has found her intellectual equal, although sometimes even she must admit his knowledge of the Old World is actually superior to hers, an accomplishment he tells her is credit to his tutor, a man called Raphael.

Adam is not sure what this friendship is. He definitely relishes the joys of exchanging knowledge and even looks forward to their often heated debates but he also cannot ignore just how beautiful she is. He's had female friends before but none as fascinating as Ember and none of them could ever make him think as much as her; she really gets into his head sometimes.

"I love this city," Ember says to Adam as they step out of the building into a sunny afternoon. She looks out at the gleaming lively Megatropolis. "I mean, sixty-seven million people all living in this one conurbation. Do you know it's the largest city ever constructed? It's even bigger than the cities people lived in before the Tribulation. In fact this whole place used to cross two whole territories of old Australia! This area around here was called Adelaide and..."

Ember stops talking as she notices Adam subconsciously shaking his head in disagreement. "What? You think I am wrong?"

Adam mentally braces himself for the beginning of one of their heated debates.

"No, I was just thinking that it's a pity more of them sixty-seven million can't live around here." He gestures towards the beautiful sculptures, fountains and monuments that adorn the courtyard they have entered. "I mean, look, free water!"

"Oh, well, yes. I agree it's a shame but still it's an amazing place, don't you think?"

Adam is careful, he knows Ember may be agreeing as one of her ploys to make him let his guard down and tell her what he really feels. If it was the plan, it works.

"I don't see how a city designed to keep people segregated into categories to allow certain races to have privileges over others can ever be described as amazing. Even the buildings around here have a hierarchical purpose. I mean, the higher up you live the more important you are. Do you really think that is okay?"

Ember shakes her head and Adam begins to rant, paraphrasing speeches he has heard Raphael make.

"Aryans rule. They have the privilege. Okay, that's fine, the 'Host' has decreed that they are the special ones but does that mean all others have to suffer? Thirty million Caucasians live in the industrial sector, which has none of the beauty and splendour or luxuries you have up here. Thirty million crammed into an area half the size of this exclusive fucking utopian home of what... seven million poxy snowheads?

"My dad works six days a week so we can eat and pay rent on our three-bedroom apartment. He doesn't complain because he was brought up to believe he was blessed. I mean the non-whites in the favelas and the slums are much worse off than us. They're not allowed to earn money, they are virtually slaves living in those shitty shanty towns but they don't complain because even they think they are better off than those who end up in Subterrainia, where God alone knows what goes on! It's all a very clever way to control the people and made possible because of *this* city. So no, I don't think it's amazing."

Ember waits before replying just to make sure he is finished. Adam looks to the floor half regretting his rant. He notices how her brow furrows and he recoils, expecting a sarcastic remark and some sort of put-down; he is not disappointed.

"Woo, reel ya neck in bad boy! I was just talking about the structure not the whole socio-geo-political situation. Chill out, matey, you know I'm not a fan of segregation. I'm just saying, and even you've gotta admit, the city is pretty impressive."

Ember's arms spread and she smiles playfully, trying to defuse the tension. Adam looks around from the steps they stand on and down into the sprawling city.

"Well, yes, the architecture is..." he stumbles over his last word, "...amazing."

He looks over to her sheepishly and bursts out laughing. Ember can't help but join in, playfully nudging him in the shoulder.

Adam jumps onto a podium and cranes his neck to look over the walls so he can get a better view of the city. In spite of himself he always does feel a sense of awe looking down at the Aryan part of the city.

Designed as a fusion of Ancient Rome and twenty-second-century architecture, it is a marvel of monuments, statues and magnificent buildings. An elevated simulacrum of Solfrid the First and the huge Sky Dome that hovers above it dominate the skyline. The neon-blue travel tubes that connect the corners of the Aryan section zigzag between the buildings, creating a network of tentacles running through the city. Behind it Adam can just see the tops of the buildings that populate his area, Midtown. This area is not so grandioso! Large grey apartment blocks and huge factories dominate Midtown, the home of said thirty million Caucasians and the industrial hub of Jinn City. Adam and his family live in Ravensdale, one of ten sectors down there.

Although he cannot see from here Adam knows that beyond his sector lie the ghettos and shanty towns that run right up to the ocean. These house the thirty-odd million non-whites, split into four racial groups: Black, Hispanic, Oriental and Asian. These people then fall under further caste definitions that, according to Raphael, are encouraged so as to keep the masses divided and dissuade any form of civil disobedience. Adam does know that they are heavily policed by a private security force known as the Mackies who rule with an iron fist and take full advantage of the lack of rights these unfortunates have.

Finally there is Subterrainia: a labyrinth of underground tunnels that are home to the rejected, undesirables and untouchables. No police force is needed down there as they are left to fend for themselves. The truth is, no one pays enough to risk policing this lawless domain.

"So how does a boy from Midtown feel about taking a high-bred Aryan to see his manor?" Ember is looking at Adam expectantly.

"Boy? I am eighteen. In my part of town you're a man at sixteen. We don't have our mummies looking after us until we reach thirty, like you Aryans." Adam says this with a cheeky glint in his eye.

"Okay, so how does a *man* from Midtown feel about taking me to his home?"

Adam is cautious. "Why would such a privileged girl want to slum it in Midtown?"

"Let us call it research. I need to get a feel for how the heart of this city beats."

"I don't think so. You won't like it down there, no marble pavements or boutique stores, not even a Y station."

"You still don't trust me, do you?" Ember's tone is light-hearted but Adam can't resist a dig.

"No. I don't trust Aryans. They tend to treat me and mine like something that they scraped off their shoe. I'm pretty sure that I've only been allowed to attend the RLT because your lot think I will fail and give them all something to laugh about."

Now it is Ember's turn to be defensive. She folds her arms tight and stands as if to attention, visibly hurt that Adam's accusations include her. On the surface she wants to keep the conversation light but no matter how much they try to avoid it they always come back to this. She adopts a firm tone.

"You know I don't think like that and nor does my father. He fought for you to be included when the other Council members wanted you disqualified."

"I passed the exam! Why would he have to fight for me? I don't need help from any fucking snowheads."

Recognising the hurt on her face he immediately feels guilty and a little ungrateful. He wants to trust her. He moves closer and lays his hands on her shoulders before saying. "Look, I'm not having a go at you or your dad

27

but let me ask you one thing, and I want you to look me in the eye when you answer, is that okay?"

Ember nods and holds her face close to Adam's, enthusiastically staring into his eyes. Adam steps back, a little uncomfortable. He looks back into her eyes and feels entranced, noticing once more how mesmerising she is. A shake of his head brings him back to reality. He concentrates. Raphael has taught him more than just history; he has explained how to read a person's face when asking a question, to know if they are telling the truth or not. He fixes his stare to hers before he asks, "Can I trust you?"

"Yes," she replies without hesitation.

He doesn't know if it's Raphael's teachings or Ember's angelic face or perhaps her sincere tone but from deep in his gut he feels he can trust her. It's as if he has known her all his life. If he is honest it has been like that since the moment they met.

"My mum is throwing a party for me next week for my birthday. I was thinking of asking you anyway, so how about we kill two birds with one stone and you come to that?"

Ember is slightly taken aback by the sudden change but also delighted. This is a true sign of trust. She knows when she has the advantage and pushes for one more act of trust and friendship.

"That would be great. I was going to ask you something as well." She pauses and shuffles in a cute, manipulative way before continuing. "Your mysterious tutor.....you mention him all the time but then when I ask about him you clam up. I mean, he sounds fascinating. Won't you tell me more, please?" Her bottom lip is pushed out as she attempts to use the look that has never failed on her father.

Adam looks at her unfazed; he's grown up surrounded by girls. Ember admits defeat and pulls her shoulders back to regain her proud posture,

"Okay, well, I'm fairly sure we can arrange some sort of information exchange instead," she says, with one eyebrow raised. "I happen to be privy to some pretty interesting stuff, you know."

Adam sighs, relenting, and soon he is relaying things to her that he has not even shared with his own family.

"Okay, so this guy, Raphael... he is a bit weird. A few years ago he offered to help me with my studies. He has a mind full of knowledge and he basically taught me everything I needed to know to pass the entrance exam. He never even charged me; he just asks for food and drink now and again, especially wine, but besides that he asks for very little. It's unbelievable what he knows and it all just comes out of his head. I hardly ever even see him with a book or VLD."

"Why do you say he is weird?"

"Well, quirky would probably be a better description. His clothes are strange, oddly old-fashioned and he almost always wears sort of greenish or bright blue..."

"Turquoise?"

"Yeah, that. And he's always saying 'holy moly'."

"Holy moly? Meaning what?"

"I've got no idea! I told you he's weird."

"Can I meet him?"

Adam looks away, not sure how to reply.

"He doesn't exactly come into High Jinn. I'm not sure what race he is but he definitely isn't Aryan."

"I guessed that! No, I mean when I come to Ravensdale with you."

Adam looks at her bemused, still not sure if she is serious about visiting his home.

The following week Adam and Ember leave the RLT early and set off towards the loop, an overhead magno rail system that links the sections of the city. Ember's excitement regarding visiting Adam's home and going to a party is evident from her lively chit-chat but she soon approaches the other reason she is excited about this trip.

"Will Raphael be there? Why don't you call him and see if he will be there?" she asks impatiently as they approach the loop station.

"Raphael doesn't have any coms. He doesn't even have a chip impla…" Adam stops himself, realising this may be a little bit too much information but Ember's curiosity is already roused.

"He doesn't have a chip?" she whispers. "But that is impossible! Everyone has a chip. Even the favelas have chips. How does he live?"

Ember looks at her wrist as she asks the question and Adam can clearly see she carries the latest version of an Aryan chip. Intrigued he reaches for her wrist to see the chip, his heart beating ever so slightly faster at the contact.

"Wow. It's tiny, more like a tattoo," he says.

"Daddy bought it… I mean… my dad bought it for me when I graduated. It has total quadro coms, limitless cyber storage and carries 2,300 credits." Ember looks up and sees Adam is not impressed. "What now?"

Adam ponders on whether to reply. He really doesn't want to get into another disagreement with her; still he can't just say nothing.

"Raphael says that chips became compulsory as a means to control people. They are just another form of segregation designed to empower the Aryans and enslave the proletariat."

Ember frowns. "But chips were developed long before the return of the Messiah and the Aryans were not even identified back when chips first were used. They are compulsory because they are needed. I mean, how would you propose people buy food or enter their homes safely? How would we travel or enter public buildings?" Ember swipes her wrist across the entrance to the loop, smiling as she proves her point. The door folds open and the noise from thousands of commuters cuts the conversation short. Ember points to a holo-screen showing the shuttle schedule.

"Next one is in two minutes," she mouths to Adam. "We'll have to run," he shouts back but she takes his arm and points at her wrist. "We just need a hover bullet."

Suddenly a tubular-shaped vehicle with two hollowed-out horizontal seats hovers next to them. Ember swipes her chip across a magnetic panel and with a sibilant sound the capsule opens. This time he is impressed. He has seen the local police riding around on these and witnessed a couple of Aryans riding them but he never dreamed he would ever get a go.

"Quick! Jump on!" she says.

The tube stands vertical, the transparent roof folded open and they fit alongside each other against its base. The roof folds back around them. The vehicle then tips up, hovering so they are face down but held by its gravity belt. Ember feels Adam trembling and is touched that he is scared, revelling in the opportunity to take him out of his comfort zone. Adam hopes Ember doesn't realise the trembling is caused by being in such close proximity to her.

Seconds later they are flying through the station.

"Yeeeehaaaa" shouts Adam, unable to control his excitement.

The hover bullet automatically dodges the throngs of people while negotiating the twists and turns effortlessly. Soon they are approaching the stairwell down to zone eight and the craft seems to hover for a split second before dropping like a stone, whizzing past the heads of others who are running for the Ravensdale shuttle. Adam prays someone he knows sees him as the drone comes to a stop, rights itself vertically and the two disembark gracefully next to the Ravensdale direct door.

"Fucking hell," is all he can manage to say.

Ember laughs at his wide-eyed look. "Guessing you're a speed tube virgin then."

She then leaps onto the first carriage, when she looks round at Adam, he is standing on the platform staring at her with knotted eyebrows. "Aren't you getting on?" she asks.

Adam points to the sign above her head.

Aryans Only!

Her face is flushed and she involuntarily chews her lip.

"We seem to be encountering lots of these *geo-social* issues you always mention," she remarks, exiting the carriage and, taking Adam's hand, she makes her way to the middle of the shuttle. As she walks she notices the disdain on the faces of the occupants of seats in the Aryan-only compartments as they look out at this young couple. She looks at Adam, hoping he is not too upset. She needn't have worried, he is still on a high from the drone ride and the feel of her touch. The two sit in a mixed section and when Ember activates a Micro data streamer via her implant Adam resumes his protest concerning the chips.

"Raphael told me that back in the day the chips were brought in under the guise of a convenient accessory to help people shop and stuff. He says they were like the latest must-have gadget – however, he believes the purpose was to make people so reliant on them that they would be helpless without one. You have to admit, people got on fine in the twentieth century without them. Now, as you say, we can't shop, travel, and even take a piss without one."

Ember's intense concentration is broken by this last remark.

"Eh, gross!"

"You know what I meant."

But she doesn't. She doesn't get it at all. To Ember the chip is pure luxury and convenience. "Well the way my father tells it is that when chips first appeared in 2014 they were a great idea, soon they were introduced by banks for contactless payment. Before long you could simply walk out of a shop with your shopping and not have to queue to pay. They were a revelation, no need to carry lots of bizarre plastic rectangles around anymore, did you know people had to do that back in the day?"

Adam shakes his head despairingly and is about to demonstrate but Ember carries on with her explanation.

"Also you would need to carry around tickets to go to music and theatre events, they couldn't store their own medical records, documents like travel or vehicle insurance would be on bits of paper, now all these things are loaded on to the chips, never left behind and never lost." She opens her arms out looks at him wide eyed, as if to emphasize how obvious her argument was."

Adam delays his response as he recollects Raphael's version of the chips introduction into human live. He told him that the uses were limitless and the Western world fell for the chipping idea, hook, line and sinker (all except the crazy conspiracy theorists, that was, and no one listened to them). The chips really took off when a tracking device for children was added and, after several high-profile rescues of abducted children, it was soon judged irresponsible *not* to have your child implanted. Within a decade seventy per cent of adults and ninety per cent of children in the Western world had implants. Many retail outlets started to refuse any other types of payment.

Then, what was known back then as the UK was the first country to input more official documents in the chip, like passports, visas and driving licences as a reaction to the horrendous Heathrow bombing by the Diabolicals. This eventually meant that everybody simply *had* to get a chip to function in society. Most people didn't really have a problem with this, it was terribly convenient after all. The telecommuting companies were not slow to react either. Soon the chip became your sim card and a small earpiece was all you needed for a call.

When Ben Starkey went on a killing spree in small-town America and then went into hiding, the LAPD tracked him down within minutes using the unique signal from his chip. A good thing really as he was a callous murdering bastard and everybody was greatly relieved, but when the same thing happened to a government whistle-blower, people became aware that each and every one of them was on the radar, so to speak. Some got their chips removed but they soon realised that it was very

33

difficult to survive in society without one. Without a chip it was hard to buy food, impossible to travel, drive or even enter a public building.

Then there was the luxury chip given to the rich and famous that allowed entry to areas that normal people could not go: exclusive clubs, expensive shops, VIP bars in nightclubs, Disneyland on special days. And thus a two-tier chipping system was born. And yet this was not the most sinister side of the chips, nor was the tracking application. Instead it was the sheer power of them.

Gerry and Bridie Hoey, an elderly couple from Australia, refused to pay a bill sent to them by a car hire firm. The firm claimed that they had returned the car with a scratch on it and wanted three hundred dollars to cover the work. Gerry was sure that there was no such mark when he returned the car but the car hire firm took him to court and the court found in the company's favour, ruling that if the Hoey's didn't pay the bill their chips would be deactivated. Gerry and Bridie still refused to pay. One week later, hungry, cold and scared, Gerry agreed to pay the bill plus five hundred dollars legal fees and a further two hundred dollars to have his chip reactivated. The chip was finally fulfilling its potential and most people conformed willingly.

Still there was reasonable resistance. When Senator Dan Cloud supported a proposal from NATAS (North American Technology in Analogue Science) to upgrade the chips with a shock application, the motion was beaten, albeit narrowly. The upgrade would have enabled the chips to administer a painful pulse through the person's body, thus allowing law enforcement agencies to subdue a suspect without pulling a gun. But then within twenty years this proposal was resurrected with bells on. Ultimately the chips would play a major part in the slaughter of billions of humans, an event known as the Tribulation.

Adam looks at Ember and decides not to relay his version he just nods and with a smile agrees to disagree.

On schedule, the train rolls into Ravensdale station and as they get off Adam is shocked to see a large group of people waving banners and flags at him. Ember is delighted.

"They came to meet you!" she says, raising onto her toes, unable to hide her excitement on seeing the banners with Adam's name written across them.

The people look strange to her. She has not really seen Caucasians in their own environment before and it strikes her how jolly they appear as opposed to the glum images she's used to, especially as they wave and cheer the arrival of their very own genius. Soon the crowd surrounds the two youths, friends slapping Adam on the back, women hugging and kissing him, men shaking his hand vigorously. Ember is very impressed. Adam not so much; he had pleaded with his mum to keep it low-key; he should have known he would have more success asking their dog to make the tea.

"All these people here for you... Wow, you're famous," remarks Ember, grabbing his arm excitedly. "Not really, my mum just goes overboard on the celebrations."

Many of the other commuters randomly join in the cheering. Then, even amongst the commotion, one or two of the group start to nudge each other as they realise this strange blonde-haired, blue-eyed Aryan among them is actually Ember Jones, the daughter of Procurator Conrad Jones. Whispers can be heard as the couple reach the centre of the group. Adam's mum grabs her son, pride beaming across her face and Adam introduces Ember. After a slightly awkward moment Margareta Costello catches Ember off-guard with a warm hug.

"You're very welcome to our little neighbourhood," she says and once more the crowd cheers.

"Thank you," says a startled Ember, unused to such affection; Aryans would never hug and kiss each other in the streets. She looks around at Adam's Caucasian friends and family, noticing the warmth they show each other. She likes these people.

"Which one is Raphael? Is he here?" she asks as they are propelled through the shuttle station.

"Oh no," says Adam. "He wouldn't be out with Joe Public. Raphael is not that type. I gotta be honest, I doubt you will ever meet him. There're people lived around here all their lives who haven't even seen him some think I made him up, like an imaginary friend." He laughs awkwardly and noticing the look on Embers face quickly adds "he's not"

Ember looks disappointed, she wonders if perhaps Raphael is actually a figment of Adams imagination, she decides to forget about meeting the enigma Adam has told her about and soon the fun and games of the celebration take her mind off it altogether.

As the group exits the station none of them notice the guy in the turquoise suit who is watching from an upper platform. "Holy moly, Miss Jones," he mutters. "You have come to us, just as the Antihost said you would."

"When a well-packaged web of lies has been sold gradually to the masses over generations, the truth will seem utterly preposterous and its speaker a raving lunatic."
– Dresden James

Shane Mills sits alone in the recreation room of D wing with his arms folded. He peruses the area, observing his fellow inmates. As a new arrival he is expecting the usual testing banter all inmates get on their first day in prison. Although this is Shane's only stint in a civilian prison, he has plenty of experience in military prisons and expects this to be the same except full of pussy civilian-pretend-hard-men. Ready to establish his place in this shithole he purposely sits upright, his muscular frame tensed in a deliberate display of masculinity. Shane is aware that today he needs to make his mark. He is prepared to bust some heads if required but he doubts he will need to. "Stand your ground today and let the others know you're not a pushover," he drills into his subconscious. "After that the next four years should go swimmingly."

It's not long before two inmates approach his table and stand either side of him. One speaks to him in a strong Geordie accent, "So you're one of the newbies."

Shane looks at the guy in the eye and decides to ignore him. The second male sits close by his right side. He speaks in a similar accent.
"Listen, we are just trying to be friendly."
Shane looks this wiry guy up and down. "I ain't looking for friends, and if I was it wouldn't be Ant and Dec."

"We all need friends in here," pipes up the other shorter guy, unfazed by the remark.
Shane studies a copy of yesterday's newspaper, completely blanking him out.

Undeterred, the guy continues, "Look, we really are trying to be friendly. Something is about to go down in here any minute and trust me, you don't want to know about it."

Shane folds the paper and looks the man sitting opposite him in the face. Six years in the army has taught Shane a lot but it was growing up on the mean streets of Dublin and Manchester where he first learned to read people. Both these men would look intimidating to the average Joe. One was small but stocky with unfashionably long curly hair and a certain menacing look. The other was a tall and heavy looking character with prison tattoos on either side of his neck. Shane notices both men's eyebrows flash as they talk and this plus their submissive stance leads him to deduce that neither of these men is a threat and he decides to hear them out.

"Okay, so what is it that's about to go down?"

"First things first, I'm Johnny, but everyone calls me No-Legs."

Shane shakes Johnny's hand while looking down at his legs. "Why do they call you No-Legs?"

"Well, if you look, I have disproportionately small legs compared to my torso and people say I look like an upright crocodile when I walk."
Shane looks again. It's true, Johnny's little legs dangling from the chair bring a smile to his face but he is impressed by the man's use of a word with more than two syllables.

"I'm Shane, Shane Mills."

"I'm Pete, they call me Big Pete."
Shane looks up at him and doesn't need to ask why they call him Big Pete, but he does shake his hand.

"So, you were saying something's going to happen?"

Johnny looks around before speaking. There are approximately twenty inmates in the room, two playing ping-pong, a small group are sat watching Deal or no Deal on the TV and three more sit on a broken pool table just chatting. One guy sits alone at a table, in his sixties, with small spectacles sitting on the end of his nose as he reads a small leather-bound book.

"See that geezer over there? The old guy?" Johnny nods his head in the direction of the lone man.

"Yes," says Shane. "He came in on the same wagon as me. It's his first day as well."

Pete lets out a laugh before he adds. "Yeah, well it's going to be his last."

Shane looks confused, "What, someone's going to clip the old guy? He can't have upset anyone that soon, it's been less than twenty-four hours. What's he done?"

"Don't know, don't care," replies Johnny. "Word is he's getting it and no one's to see or hear anything."
Shane's eyes narrow and he raises an eyebrow. "Are you here to warn me to behave?"

Johnny realises how this seems and quickly explains. "No, no, it's not like that, trust me. The two bastards that are about to clip granddad over there are no friends of ours. Thing is though, they would love for someone to interfere so they could hurt more people. Honest, we just want to give you the heads-up. They are a pair of right nasty cu…"

Just on cue, the "pair of right nasty cunts" walk into the room. The first one, Garfield Hilton AKA Big Bird, is a six-foot-eleven mountain of a man. Born in Birmingham to Caribbean parents he weighs in at twenty-six stone. His size and physical prowess gained him some notoriety on the nightclub doors of Birmingham's city centre. People loved to get their photos taken with this man mountain. "He's just a gentle giant," is the sort of remark punters made about him. They couldn't have been more wrong. Big Bird was a violent career bully whose main source of income was extorting money from bar and club owners in the West Midlands. He also acted as an enforcer for drug gangs and would often submit late payers to his own type of torture where he would experiment with how long it would take him to break nominated bones.

Two years ago an unfortunate Spanish student by the name of Paco Ballaguer, who was attending Aston University, found himself in a bit of financial trouble when his student grant was held up. He owed £136 for some blow that he had bought from one of Bird's pals, Kenny.

"There's that spic that owes me money..." remarked Kenny as he and Bird wandered home from a late-night blues club. Two hours later police found Paco's corpse. He had been punched so hard and so many times that at first the police were sure he had been run over by a truck. The imprint of the giant's huge gold signet ring in Paco's forehead was the evidence that convicted him. He was serving life imprisonment with a recommendation that he's not considered for parole for fifteen years.

The second man entering the room is Errol Christian. Errol may look small stood next to Bird but he is well over six feet. Born in Jamaica, Errol has strong connections with Yardy gangs all over Britain. He is an extremely violent psychopathic killer. Even Bird feels a little uncomfortable around Errol who is responsible for the murder of seven people. Working as a paid enforcer for Jamaican drug smugglers he would be called in as a last resort after all channels of communication had been exhausted. He loved his job and admitted to an almost sexual gratification when watching the lights go out in his victim's eyes. Despite his obvious mental disorder, Errol was professional. He always covered his tracks, stalked his victims and picked the opportune time and place to strike. He really never expected to get caught.

But fate changed all that when one of his bosses, by the name of Barrington, took a shine to Errol's girlfriend. Melissa never dared complain to Errol about his low libido but she was a virile young woman and so easily surrendered to most of Errol's friends, although he remained unaware of her indiscretions. Unfortunately for Melissa and Barrington, the contracted hit Errol was scheduled to carry out was cancelled at the last minute when the target paid his debt plus tribute in full. Errol returned home frustrated and angry. He had psyched himself up for this hit and the fucker went and paid up. His only option was to fuck Melissa's brains out and hope that would release some of his tension. He focused on all the positions he was going to take her in as he sat on the train home. This helped him to control his rage. He knew he could explode very easily and he could smash someone's face in just for looking at him wrong. As he got to his flat in Handsworth he ran up the steps. It wasn't yet midday so Melissa would not even be out of bed. Errol had taken his jacket off and was pulling his shirt over his head as he entered the flat.

"You better be up for it, 'cause I'm gonna fuck your brains out," he shouted as he opened their bedroom door.

A crime of passion was the defence attorney's claim. Twelve years was his sentence. Barrington Paisley would be in a vegetative condition for the rest of his life, tubes and a machine keeping him alive. Melissa was luckier, it took only forty-one seconds for her life to slip away as Errol squeezed his hands tight around her throat. He didn't feel nearly as much pleasure watching the lights go out in her eyes as the others he had killed but he had to admit, he did prefer it to a fuck.

As Shane watches these two hardened criminals enter the recreation room both Pete and Johnny scurry over to the TV and watch Deal or no Deal intently as Kat from Oxford thanks the banker but chooses not to deal. The young guys playing ping-pong decide they have had enough and head for their cells. A mixed-race guy sitting on the pool table walks to Bird, giving him a gangster hug while nodding over to the old guy sitting on his own. Everyone else except the little old guy and Shane join the crowd watching TV. Shane Mills still doesn't move even when he notices Johnny's discreet head jerks indicating for him to join them he just sits there. Errol and Bird spot Shane, look him up and down and then ignore him. They sit down, their attention clearly on the little old guy sitting in the corner.

"We got to make this look like an argument that got out of control," whispers Errol to Bird.

Bird nods. "No problem. Let's wind him up first. Have a bit of fun."

Errol nods. "Yeah, my man's taken care of the guards. He says we got ten minutes, so let's make the most of it."

They stand and head towards the poor wretch, smiles beaming across their faces.

Leo Verdi is a small, thin, bespectacled Italian Jew. He has tightly curled grey hair under his skullcap with a shirt and tie neatly worn under his prison issue. All these things make him stand out in this institution: a man who likes to keep up respectable appearance even while in prison.

Leo looks over his leather-bound book as the two thugs approach him. Aware of his impending fate his only thought is, *do not resort to begging and cowering when the time comes.* All he has left is his dignity. He should have known that the Djinn would get to him, even in here, but he had put his faith in Chamuel; the Arc Hon had said he would be safe in here. As a respected accountant and an upstanding member of the Jewish society he had brought disgrace on his family by stealing from a jeweller and assaulting a cop, all to be put in here to avoid certain death and yet here he was, facing certain death.

Over the last few years Leo's values have changed considerably. His eyes have been opened to a world of lies. He still remembers his resistance to the truth as the veil was removed. He wonders if, given the choice, he would return to ignorance. He knows the answer but to be honest it is irrelevant now, in a couple of minutes these two unsavoury looking characters are likely to cave his head in, ending any chance of him revealing the truth to others.

Any hope of rescue is pointless; the Djinn will have all bases covered. The guards will have been taken care of and the only other witnesses are the criminal underworld's incarcerated brethren.

He begins to mumble to himself, "Don't cower and do not beg."

"What yaw saying old man?" asks Errol with his exaggerated Jamaican accent. "Did you just call me a nigger?"

Leo does not respond as he stares into his book. He thinks back to the first day he met Simeon, the man (or whatever he was) who opened his eyes. He had not asked to have his eyes opened. No, in fact he was very happy walking around with them fully shut. What has anyone gained from this knowledge he was now privy too? Ever since he found out about the secret of the Djinn he had been hiding out, trying to avoid an untimely demise. Simeon told him that he had picked him for a reason, that it was his job to pass the information on to another, one who would become a great leader.

"You will know him when you see the beautiful woman on his arm," Simeon had assured him.

Leo had no idea what this meant. Plenty of men have beautiful ladies hanging onto their arms but he was pretty sure that he was not going to see any women in this place, on anyone's arms or otherwise. If there was one thing he has learned it is that everything is planned, right down to his imminent violent death.

"I said, what did you say old man?" Errol leaned over the desk and put his face right up to Leo's.
Bird stood behind him, holding a garrotte made from torn and twisted drinks cans. Errol upped the volume as he screamed into Leo's face.

"You're the fucking kiddie fiddler, aren't yaw? You de one that like fucking likkle boys, am I right?"

Leo is aware this disgusting jibe was just a way of goading him; however, it is also the worst possible insult to aim at a Jewish elder who has four beautiful grandchildren. A shadow falls across his face and anger builds up inside of him as he reflects that he will probably never see them again.

"You repulse me," says Leo, his voice shaking.
Errol looks impressed. He turns to Bird. "We got a brave blood clot here."

Bird laughs and becomes a little hysterical as he hears Errol cough up thick green phlegm from the back of his throat. He turns to Leo and spits, splattering it into his face. When the old guy attempts to reach for a handkerchief Errol restrains both his hands, leaving him powerless to stop the disgusting liquid running across his lips. Bird is now doubling over in cruel guttural laughter.

Errol continues his taunts. "What's wrong, yaw not like it? It not feels like the likkle boys jizz on yaw filthy Jewish face?"

A sudden loud thud distracts Errol and he turns around to look at Bird, but instead sees Shane standing in his place. Errol releases Leo's hands. He looks down and sees Bird, the six-foot-eleven, twenty-six-stone career bully lying at this new guy's feet, the spittle bubbling from his lips the only indicator that he is alive.

"What the fu…"

Errol doesn't finish his sentence as Shane Mills smashes his fist into his face. The end of the teaspoon Shane holds in his fist splits Errol's cheekbone near in half, the force and pain causing him to collapse to the floor. Shane then leaps behind Errol, placing his forearm under his chin compounding the pain. He squeezes hard enough to limit the air supply, being careful not to cut off his blood supply, thus rendering Errol unconscious but not dead. Leo watches in awe as this athletic-looking warrior saves his life. The elation of being saved, however, cannot distract Leo from staring at the tattoo on his saviour's arm – a beautiful woman and not just any beautiful woman. As a scribe to the Rabbi when he was a child Leo was fascinated by angels, so he recognises the tattoo of a woman holding a bow and arrow as Amitiel, the Angel of Truth.

Frankfurt, 1744

*"I want to be with those who know secret things or
else alone."*
Rainer Maria Rilke

The tall, distinguished figure of Isaac looked for the house of Moses the money-lender in the Jewish ghetto of Frankfurt. The town was quiet on this cold winter's night. His search ended when he saw the sign bearing a red shield above a shop door. *Finally,* he thought, *this is the shop I've been looking for.* Isaac knocked upon the well-constructed heavy wooden door.

Moses the proprietor was none too pleased as the unrelenting knocking on his front door woke his sleeping family. He wielded a wooden baton and had a bayonet tucked in his sash. A money-lender was often a target for desperate thieves and Moses was a cautious man.

"Okay, okay," he called from inside. A small peephole allowed Moses to see the caller but he did not recognise the tall, thin man standing outside. The fact that this man was wearing the robes of a priest did nothing to instil any trust in Moses. He shouted through a small crack in the door.

"Who is it? What do you want at this time of night?"

"I wish to speak with the man called Moses Bauer," replied Isaac. "I have a letter of introduction from the King of Prussia himself."

Isaac pushed a wax-sealed envelope under the door. Moses picked it up and broke the seal; concern washed over him as he recognised the seal to be that of Frederick II. He was wary but what could he do?

"Come in," he said, standing to one side as he opened the door.

Isaac entered and warmed himself next to the remaining embers that had survived in the large fire dominating the small but tidy room. He took off his gloves and placed them on the wooden table in the centre of the room and rubbed his cold hands together.

"What can be so important that a king would need a poor, hard-working Jew at this late time of night?"

"His Royal Highness has recently decided that he is destined to unite the kingdoms of Prussia."

Isaac made his statement, getting straight to the point, and then looked around the room nonchalantly.

"How does this concern me?" Moses looked puzzled.

Isaac continued to look around the rest of the house, wandering into the small back room where he could see that Moses conducted his business. Moses had a feeling that he was looking for something in particular. His hand fell down to the bayonet tucked under his tunic, as he prepared to confront this man on his true intentions. The cries of a child momentarily stopped Isaac's snooping.

"Ah, yes. I believe you have a new baby boy. May I inquire his name?" Moses felt even more concerned and with no desire to discuss his family with a stranger, he carefully pulled out the bayonet for Isaac to see.

"No you may not. Now, are you going to tell me what you want?" Isaac barely acknowledged the appearance of the weapon.

"The king needs money."

Moses paled.

"Don't fret. I can see you have little or no money."

Isaac casually picked up a small ledger that lay on the desk next to a catalogue of silks. Moses was deeply regretting letting this stranger into his home.

"As you say, I have no money. I cannot see what help I can be to his Highness," said Moses

"You will soon have money." said Isaac.

Confusion replaced the concern on Moses' face. Isaac's robes fell to the side revealing a tunic that Moses recognised to be that of the Jesuit order.

He continued, "Let me explain. As servants of the Lord Jesus Christ we are forbidden from charging 'usury' on the money we lend, or interest as you would call it. Yet many states expect us to fund them in some campaign or other: France and Spain want money to aid their war with Austria, Catherine in Russia wants to build another palace, Sardinia and England need to buy boats to defend their shores. All this costs money, money we have. My masters have no qualms in lending this money out but feel it is unfair to do so without the possibility of increasing our yield. As an astute businessman I am sure you see the injustice of this."

Moses nodded, saying nothing.

"Of course they offer tributes if they are victorious and many, such as the Spanish and Portuguese will convert thousands of savages to the Christian faith. But as a man of commerce you will understand this doesn't cover our costs or improve the welfare of the state. Papal policy says we should exclude non-Catholics from benefiting from our fortunate abundance of wealth, but us Jesuits, well, we believe all men are God's children. Still, we don't wish to upset the loyal countries or the bishops. Do you understand what I mean?"

Moses knew exactly what he meant. The Roman Church's concern was for souls but what use were souls if not to gain profit and power?

"So, what do I get for my soul?" Moses joked.

Isaac took off his hat and held it across his chest. "I am here to propose an alliance: we will underwrite loans that you will manage. For all intents and purposes the borrower will only see you as their benefactor. Our portfolio of, shall we call them 'clients', shall be passed to you. A position in the palace as Frederick's banker will lend credibility to your role. To keep it discreet you will only communicate with me concerning these matters."

Moses was not yet convinced and asked, "Why me?"

"I have looked for you for a long time, Moses. You are a fair man, an honest man, a clever man and a good father. If not for the cruel laws controlling Jews you would be a rich man in your own right. Now, I cannot promise that your life will become one of luxury but I will promise you this: the child who I can hear crying will have a great gift bestowed upon him, and his children will have opportunities that most Jews could only dream of. He will be in a position to pioneer a new kind of banking using stocks, bonds and sureties allowing them to be impervious to the tactics that have historically stolen hard-earned wealth from the Jews. What I will teach you will enable you to create a dynasty more powerful than all the kings and emperors on earth and will one day bring your people back to the Promised Land."

Moses eyed Isaac for a moment before going into the back room and returning with the good wine.

Over the next few weeks Moses met with Isaac each day, finalising strategy and rates. He received a letter from the Palace offering him a position at the Royal Court. Moses was still cautious but had begun to believe. He thanked God for this miracle, which would drag his family out of poverty. After years of struggle and strife perhaps he was about to be rewarded, and why not? He was a good man who honoured God. Isaac had suggested that he might need to change his surname to avoid any anti-Semitic discrimination. Bauer was a good name but Moses saw the sense in this. As a tribute to his ancestors Moses had always displayed the red shield above his shop. He decided this would be the new family name, Red Shield, or Rothschild as it is in German. After only six weeks Moses and Isaac were trading with the house of Hesse, secretly funding the Spanish and French alliance as well as their opponents, the British and Sardinians in the battle of Villafranca. The issue of whether this was morally right did concern Moses at first but his concern faded as his wealth began to grow. Moses soon learned that in most wars and battles the only true victors were the financiers.

With everything in place and months after their first encounter Isaac met Moses one more time. He handed him a leather-bound book embossed with a symbol that Moses at first mistook for a fleur-de-lis. On further inspection the symbol was closer to a three-leaf clover but even more curious was its title *Ledger of transactions* written in south-western Yiddish, Moses' native tongue.

"You read Yiddish?" Moses asked.

"Yes and I wish for all written transactions to be scribed using your dialect, is that acceptable?"

Still none the wiser, Moses simply nodded.

They said their goodbyes and before Isaac left he received an unexpected hug from the money-lender.

"From today I will conduct business through my agent. Her name is Emilie Du Chatelet. She will carry a parchment with this symbol on its seal." He pointed to the symbol on the book. "You must only use this ledger to record our transactions and always in your south-western dialect. I will return before your son's bar mitzvah and we will discuss the gift I promised for him. Do you understand?"

"Yes," Moses said but he really didn't understand; he just thanked God for his good fortune.

The streets of Frankfurt were bare and it was late. After leaving Moses for the last time Isaac headed out of the ghetto and into the main town. He made his way through the dimly lit streets, between the shops, up the cobble streets and past a tavern where a small light indicated some late-night drinking was occurring.

Isaac became aware of a form in the shadows following him. He reached down to his side feeling for the handle of his sword. Ahead he saw a narrow alleyway and decided it would be an ideal place to confront his stalker. Isaac sped up and pulled his sword as soon as he turned into the alley. He waited in the dark, sword in hand, but nobody appeared. Then a voice from behind startled him.

"Tut tut, Isaac, you are slipping."

Isaac spun, aiming his sword in the direction of the voice. In front of him a young girl, no more than sixteen years old, stood still, the sword pushed against her throat. With one look at his pursuer Isaac lowered his sword.

"Amitiel."

"Hello Isaac."

"I saw the comet last night, I thought that would be one of you Arc Hon."

He placed his sword back in its sheath. Amitiel pulled her hood down, revealing pale skin and bright-green eyes, her long blond ringlets accentuating her angelic appearance.

"We need to talk, Isaac." She indicated towards the street. "I noticed a light on in the tavern and I must admit to a thirst, shall we?"

They headed for the tavern and found the door unlocked but the place empty. A large barman looked none too pleased when the two entered his bar.

"We're closed," he said as they approached the bar.

"We are two weary travellers in need of a drink," replied Isaac.
The barman decided he needed to try a less polite approach. "Fuck off and rest your foreign arses somewhere else. I am closed."

Amitiel stepped out from behind Isaac. "You are very rude fat man. I have travelled far this night and I am in need of a drink. When I am in need of a drink my patience is very limited. So please, two glasses of wine and some wood for the fire."

The barman laughed at the young slip of a girl. "Over my dead fucking body. Now little girl, g..."

Amitiel's stiletto blade pierced the man's Adam's apple and exited the back of his head, cutting his sentence short. Isaac locked the tavern doors as she dragged the man's body behind the bar. She then took a bottle of red wine and two glasses and tucked a log for the fire under her arm. They sat at the table nearest the fire. The angelic face showed no remorse as she wiped blood from her blade before replacing it into a sheath tied to her thigh.

"So Isaac, I see you are going into commerce."

"Haven't you heard? It's the future. Anyway, why the interest? I thought *Watchers* only got involved when there is a breach?"

"I'm curious, just humour me. I have not had an intelligent conversation for some time. Living amongst these saps can be so boring. Come on, what's the plan?"

"The plan is to rule the world."
Both laughed.

Isaac raised his glass and Amitiel joined him.

"To world domination."

"So you think this Jew will help you win?" asked Amitiel.

"Well, I'm tired of nurturing and wet-nursing psychotic warmongers, emperors, and fucking kings who can't wipe their own arses. Even worse, religious leaders who think they are God's voice on Earth, for fuck's sake. So, I am ahead of the game. Reuben was right, this world is too big now. No one will ever rule through fear or retribution. The masses will only really worship one God and that's the one that feeds their greed: money!"

Amitiel nodded, impressed. "Yes, I believe you have a very cunning strategy there. It'll be interesting to see how Reuben responds. He is convinced whoever dominates Europe will become the Host."

"He's right but I doubt Zeb or Asher would agree. Don't tell them, will you? The longer they waste their time with the slanty-eyed fuckers, the better. Anyway, we have all night to exchange gossip now that you've convinced our landlord to be more hospitable. But my curiosity is getting the better of me… why are you really here, Amitiel?"

"Two reasons: firstly Simeon. We can't trace him. We think he may have gone native and renewed."

Isaac was shocked. "He what? Renewed…? Why would he do that? He won't know who or what he is!"

Amitiel refilled the glasses and sat back. "Simeon has developed some sort of perverted affection for the homo sapiens. He recently returned to Gheisthelm and appealed to the Council. He claims the humans should have their own champion, and that it was always the Demiurge's plan for mankind to rule the physical world, not Djinn."

Isaac gulped, nearly choking on his drink. "He has lost it! Tell me they refused."

"Yes, they declined after a certain amount of deliberation. A little bit too much deliberation if you ask me. Anyway, Simeon was not happy, he threatened to conspire with the saps and mentor a native champion, one who he claims will have the Vril from all thirteen in equal parts."

"What did he mean?"

"Well, if a human was to have equal Vril from all the thirteen it could give him certain advantages, but it is just a theory and thought to be near impossible, as the proverb goes, like finding a needle in a hay field."

"Haystack."

"Field is bigger. Chamuel, however, thinks differently. He has done his calculations and he thinks that by the late twentieth century one such person could exist. This is only a few hundred years away. We need to find Simeon before then and return him to the Corona, just in case Chamuel is right."

"But like you said, he may have renewed. If he has then he must have had help... free will and all that. He wouldn't break that rule. He would have had to find a mother prepared to allow him to possess her unborn child, which even for humans is a difficult exchange. If that is the case then none of us would be able to find him; that really would be like finding a needle in a hundred hayfields, a thousand."

"Exactly. He must have had human conspirators and he would have needed to reveal at least some of the secrets of the Djinn to them. Although we do not think he has renewed yet, only that he has threatened to do so."

"Yes, well, that is a mess, but if I'm right, it's your mess, not mine."

Isaac finished his wine and stood, ready to leave. He did not want to be dragged into anything that would distract him from the quest.

"Now, I best be off. Bullion to buy, wars to fund, you know how it is."

Amitiel grabbed his arm, pulling him in towards her with undeniable force. "I haven't told you the second reason for my visit."
Isaac relented and, sitting back down, poured out the last of the wine and handed her a glass.

"If you want me to listen to your problems, Angel, you will have to give me an update on the game."
Amitiel sighed then nodded. "What do you want to know?"

"Who are my main competitors? What are the rest doing?"
Amitiel let a smile escape her lips, took the wine and began. The fire seemed to reignite of its own accord and the two of them settled in again.

"I will tell you what I can." She looked around cautiously, as if worried that she would be heard in this empty bar.

"Asher and Judd are committed in the Orient. If one of them emerges victorious the rest of you should be worried. Asher is also aiding the whore-empress in Russia while Zeb was deeply involved with the Medici family. Like you, he was convinced the power is in banking here in Europe. Somehow this has all gone wrong for him, but I suspect you already know that."

A wry smile spread across Isaac's face.

Amitiel continued. "Levi seems to be using a lot of energy up on the Americas. He took the guise of a French immigrant, calling himself Marin Duvall. He has placed a lot of hope in the continent becoming the power centre of the world."

Isaac laughed. "It's just a bunch of savages and pilgrims who will probably kill each other. Anyway, the Europeans own most of the Americas already. What is he thinking? Does he expect to start a revolution?"

"Then there is Reuben, still championing the Holy Roman Empire."
Isaac snorted. "It is neither Holy, nor Roman, and definitely not an empire."
Amitiel laughed. "I will share that with a poet I know, if you will allow it?"
"Be my guest."
"Simeon was flitting between the French and the Spanish."
"Rather him than me."

Amitiel nodded. "And as I said, Simeon has gone native, Benjamin is persisting in Persia and then you have decided to finance the whole game."
Isaac detected a hint of scepticism in Amitiel's voice. "You don't think much of my new tactic."
"On the contrary, I believe it is a game changer. I only worry how Reuben will respond."

"He will probably invoke the slaughter of as many humans as possible; that seems to be his favourite ploy. I mean, he is slightly predictable. I often wonder if there will be an Earth worth winning."

"That's exactly what Simeon said. Now I have told you all I can about the state of play."

Isaac watched as Amitiel twisted her wine cup nervously. He sighed.

"And so to the second reason you are here?" he said.

"We think someone is murdering Djinn."

"Murdering Djinn? What do you mean 'murdering'? That's not possible. Djinn return, they don't die!"

"It's been three thousand years, but since the thirteen arrived here only Daniel has 'fallen'. And even he admits his return was his own fault."

Isaac chuckled to himself, remembering the circumstances. Amitiel scoffed and continued.

"So, anyway, Manasseh was disqualified, he ascended back to the Gheisthelm as expected. Nothing strange there." She went to get another bottle and poured another glass of wine, drinking it in one go as if she needed the courage to continue. "But then over the last sixty-odd years Gad, Naphtali and Ephraim have all 'fallen' and none have returned."

Isaac suddenly began to comprehend the seriousness of this conversation. "Three in so few years... You think they were murdered? Why not just ask them by whom?"

"You're not listening, Isaac. They haven't returned! Now Zeb has disappeared too, he was in the physical guise of Gian Gastone de Medici who was murdered. With no heir, his death has ended the dynasty he built over three hundred years. Zeb did not return to Gheisthelm. No explanation can be found."

Isaac shook his head. "Are you saying someone has removed their Vril? Are you saying they are actually, properly dead?"

Amitiel sat back down. "We believe so. The only way this could have happened is to remove or destroy the Pineal Amulet. Who else would know how to do this? It can only be one of the thirteen."

"You mean one of the remaining seven; six are gone, remember. I hope I am not a suspect."

"All of you are suspects and potential targets. Chamuel actually thinks it could be a human but that could only happen with the help of one of the Djinn. No human could know about the Vril or its location in the brain."

Isaac was not sure if being a suspect or a target was the most worrying.

"Well, it's obvious isn't it? You just told me Simeon's gone all native. If he renewed then who knows what else he is capable of. He may have a whole army of followers carrying out his bidding."

"Maybe, but can you really see Simeon killing one of his own? He is a fucking pacifist, he won't even kill these saps."

"Well, it must be Reuben. He kills for fun and no one wants to be the Host more than that bastard." Isaac thought before he added, "Or have you considered one of the Firsts? Or perhaps even an Arc Hon?"

"We have considered it could be one of the Firsts but we know it cannot be one of us Arc Hon."

Now it is Isaac's turn to scoff. Amitiel dismisses this as she adds, "Whoever it is, the Arc Hon will find them. We are all here and we will not leave until the perpetrator is caught. The game has changed Isaac: you are not only playing for this world but for your own lives. It has just got very real."

Adam Costello's house, July 2146

"The beauty of this day doesn't depend on it lasting forever."

Marty Rubin

The party at Adam's house is pretty low-key by the standards Ember is used to: a few home-baked cakes, some soft drinks and a bottle of whiskey held tightly by Adam's Aunt Maud.

"Hey, sorry about this whole lame party thing."

Adam has just got free of his uncles and aunts and is attempting to rescue Ember from the mob of curious cousins and friends who have hardly ever met an Aryan before, never mind one as famous as the Procurator's daughter.

"Why sorry? Your family and friends are lovely. It's so nice to see so many people all related to each other and I don't mean that in a piss-take way." Ember looks at Adam with those big eyes, reassuring him she is sincere in her admiration for his family.

"What about Raphael? You sure you're not disappointed he isn't here?"

"No, don't be silly. Anyway, your aunty was entertainment enough." Ember nods at the now snoring Aunt Maud and they both laugh.

"What time are you expected home?"

Ember looks at her chip. "Well, I suppose I should be making tracks soon. My dad can be a bit over the top if I'm late."

"Come on then, I will walk you to the loop. I don't want your dad sending the army out for you."

After Ember says her goodbyes to Adam's friends and family, they leave. Walking along the street the two kids feel very comfortable in each other's company. Ember links arms with Adam as they discuss the party. If she's honest she never really liked many of the Aryans she hung out with. They were all very superficial and shallow, not that she isn't a bit of a fiend herself when it comes to shopping and partying, but Ember craves the intelligent and challenging type of conversation she enjoys with

Adam. Only her father really had anything interesting to say and there is only so much you can discuss with your daddy.

"So… sex." She blurts out with no warning.

Adam chokes on the burger he has bought from a street vendor.

"What about it?" Adam looks startled and reminds her they were just talking about the effect of segregation on education.

"Yeah, I'm bored of that now… so back to sex. Are you a virgin and if not who was your first?"

Adam feels his face go red as he tries to look unfazed. "A gentleman doesn't tell."

Now he feels even more stupid, thinking to himself, "You are so sad, Costello". In an attempt to save his own blushes Adam turns the question on her.

"What about you? Surely you haven't, have you?"

Ember lifts both eyebrows and it seems she is about to confess all when a shuffling noise and the sound of footsteps disturbs them both. She stops talking, turns and finds a dark-haired, tall, tanned man dressed in a bright-blue suit with a bootlace tie and a Teddy boy hairstyle has walked up to them.

"Raphael!" Adam says. "What are you doing here? I was going to call you, but, you know, didn't know how." He taps his own wrist to highlight the reason. "Anyway, I got through my first month."

Raphael looks very proud. "Of course you did and you will get through the entire course and be the first Caucasian to graduate. Now, who is this young lady?" Raphael eyes Ember up and down.

In turn Ember is looking above Raphael's head. He knows why and pauses, staring back at her intensely.

"This is my friend. She was dying to meet you actually, weren't you?"

She doesn't say anything at first, too busy staring at what looks like some sort of smoke cloud swirling around Raphael's head. It forms the shape of a snake then disperses into a whirl of colours before reforming as a snake again. She catches Raphael's eye and instantly knows not to mention it, then it seems to fade.

"I'm Ember Jones," she says as they exchange long looks. Adam feels awkward.

Raphael takes her hand. "Holy moly, yes you are." He turns to Adam but keeps one eye on Ember. "Can I ask, have you two a few minutes to spare?"

Adam looks to Ember. She is looking very strangely at Raphael, almost as if she has seen a ghost. He decides it's best to take her home.

"Sorry, Raphael, Ember has to get home. I can come back though once I've walked her to the station."

"No, I need to show you both something."

Ember snaps out of her trance and holds her palm up as if to slow the conversation down.

"What is it you need to show us?" she says and Adam can feel her anxiety but wonders where it is coming from.

"I have a recording you will both be interested in. It's very rare footage from the days before the Tribulation. It should help you in the thesis you have been set. It is actually an eye-witness account of the Verdi Revolution."

Ember's bewilderment at the swirl she saw above Raphael's head is trumped by her excitement.

"Really? A recording from before the Solution? That's rarer than android shit."

"Indeed," smiles Raphael.

Adam has not felt uncomfortable around Raphael before but something is not right. Also, how does Raphael even know about the thesis?

"I can come, but Ember's got to go back to her sector," he says. "It's getting late and–"

Raphael interrupts. "She must come as well."

Adam frowns. "Why so urgent? Can't it wait 'til another day??"

"No time like the present," says Raphael. "I'll give Miss Jones a ride home straight after."

"Are you sure that's okay? I don't want to be any trouble."

"I insist," replies Raphael, smoothly taking her arm and leading her forwards.

Adam follows behind. Ember really badly wanted to meet Raphael and though Adam does trust him, she'd be cross with him for stopping her. Maybe he was being jealous; it was nice just the two of them. Raphael leads them to a Second World War army-style jeep sitting in a side car park and opens the doors.

"Who robbed the museum?" asks Ember.

"Don't dis the Raf-mobile," Raphael replies.

Ember laughs and looks at Adam. She raises her eyebrows and shakes her head with light-hearted disbelief, pleasantly surprised by Raphael's humorous retort. They drive to a large, detached, derelict house hidden behind some corrugated fencing near an old railway line in an area left over from the old city of Adelaide. Raphael pushes the unlocked door open and the two youngsters follow him through a side door and up some exposed stairs inside the building. They walk through a maze of doorways and end up in a dimly lit room.

"I'm sorry to drag you both down here like this but when you turned up with Miss Jones here, I couldn't miss this opportunity."
Adam looks at Raphael in confusion. "What opportunity?

"I was confident you two would become friends," mumbled Raphael. "But bringing her here so soon... I mean, holy moly!"

Adam is concerned as Raphael doesn't seem his normal self, not that he was ever normal but this is different.

"What do you mean? How could you possibly know I would befriend Ember? What has this got to do with anything?"

Adam looks to Ember for support but she is staring at the sparse room that contains just two chairs around a low coffee table, a filing cabinet against a broken window and a curious black rectangle device with a matching black box.

"Is that an old-style plasma television and an early twenty-first-century Blu-ray device?" she asks in awe.

Raphael laughs. "You know your historic tech."

Raphael goes over to the cabinet and pulls out a package. He turns to the teenagers and his eyes look a little manic. Sweat drips from his brow.

Ember finally shares a worried glance with Adam. Has she been stupid? She has just jumped in this man's car minutes after meeting him. A man who on first sight seemed to have smoke billowing around his head and yet no one said anything about this. She is now in some derelict squat in a part of town that her father has warned her never to go to with a guy who looks like he's on some serious drugs.

"Miss Jones, you look worried," says Raphael. "I'm sorry, don't be, you will understand in a minute."

The tone in his voice relaxes Ember a little. Adam smiles at her and then turns to question Raphael. "What's going on, Raphael? You seem a bit edgy."

Raphael places a package onto the table. "Yes, sorry, it all must seem a bit strange but trust me, my mood is driven by excitement. You will not believe how long I have waited to open this."

They all look down at a brown parcel no bigger than a book.

"What is it?" asks Adam.

"That is the last known correspondence from Shane Mills." The two teens look at each other, Adam wide-eyed, his jaw on his chest. Ember's raised eyebrows and slight shaking of her head expressed her scepticism.

"It is a recording he made over eighty years ago. Countless people have died protecting it, even though none have ever watched it. I have kept it for twenty years, hoping for this day."

Ember is even more disbelieving now. Adam looks stunned. "Why hasn't anyone watched it?" asks Ember. "Why would people die for something when they don't even know what is on it? Plus if it's authentic it would be priceless and highly illegal."

"Oh, it's authentic and they do know what's on it, Miss Jones," smiles Raphael. "*The Truth!* That is what's on it. The reason no one has watched it is because it wasn't for them."

He pushes the wrapped parcel over to her. Ember picks it up and reads the faded writing on the front.

For the attention of Miss September Jones.

It is signed in the same handwriting.

Shane Mills

Stoke Prison, present day

"Hear a lot, see everything and say nothing."

Since the events of his first day, Shane has had a comparatively quiet couple of months. Besides the two horizontal thugs, Errol and Bird, both of whom had been moved up to the high-security wing for some previous misdemeanours, he has not had issues with any inmates. Of course, the fact that he so easily dispatched the two most feared prisoners on the wing did not go unnoticed and all the lags give him the utmost respect: a type of respect that only comes from fear. But Shane has not exploited his new-found status and he has been just happy to be left alone. This has confused most of the others. In prison the toughest guys call the shots; they make the rules, they get all the benefits and extras. But Shane is not interested in becoming the daddy; he just reads his books and has kept his head down. An unlikely friendship with the old Jew he had rescued from the pair of would-be assassins is something else that puzzles the inmates. These two have become strange cell-mates, competing in daily chess matches and whiling away the hours in conversation.

Shane sets up the chess board as he waits for Leo to join him. He has learned some fascinating facts about the old man over the last couple of months. Leo Verdi was the personal accountant assigned to Pope Benedict XVI. Shane feels Leo is still sussing him out before he is prepared to confide in him why he would break into a jeweller's shop then wait patiently for the police to arrive, only to assault a young officer. Leo also avoids the issue of why he left the Vatican twenty-four hours before the Pope announced his retirement. Although Leo is shy when it comes to relaying information he certainly is not averse to asking questions. Shane gets the feeling that Leo is in some way interviewing him but for what he has no idea. Every game of chess turns into an inquisition. How? What? Where? Who? It is unrelenting. Yet strangely, Shane doesn't mind. He likes Leo and more importantly he trusts him. Shane has nothing to hide and although he's usually uncomfortable discussing his past, he eventually opens up to Leo, telling him all about his upbringing on the notorious Ballymun estate in Dublin and about his drug-addled mother who attempted to raise Shane and his baby sister Chloe.

To say his childhood was traumatic would be a gross understatement. His mother, Ainne, was addicted to heroin long before Shane was born and for a long time after. At first she managed to balance her addiction and live a comparatively normal existence but when Shane was three years old his sobbing mummy held him and told him, "Ya da has died. He's been killed."

His father, Tommy Mills, a well-known tough guy from north Dublin, was shot dead in a row over a missing car. On reflection, Shane lost both his parents that day. Without Tommy's income to feed Shane and more importantly her own drug habit, Ainne resorted to selling her body and with it, her soul.

Of course at such a young age Shane was not really aware of his mum's addiction or the trade she plied to pay for it. He was under the impression she was just poorly and had a lot of male friends. Ainne loved her little boy, and she would never have introduced Patrick O'Hagan into the family unit had she any indication of his schizophrenic personality. Patrick started out as a just another punter. Then after a couple of months he moved in with Ainne and Shane. It didn't take long before Ainne fell pregnant and within a year of Patrick moving in, Chloe was born. Shane didn't remember any trouble before Chloe was born but soon after her birth the relationship between his mum and Patrick became very volatile. Patrick would kick her out to earn money and then kick her head in for the way she earned it.

It seemed to Shane that every night he would be woken by his mum's screams as she and Patrick fought. He would wake up and go straight to Chloe, his beautiful little sister who Shane felt an overwhelming obligation to protect. She was a little bundle that would cry and cry unless her big brother held her and sang to her. She had big rosy cheeks and, although unkempt and often mucky, her cuteness shone through. Always either smiling or crying, she was a 'mischievous wee skitter' as their neighbour Fat Beryl described her.

By the time he was eight Shane was aware that his mother was a junkie and a whore: he just wasn't sure what that meant. Patrick was not a drug addict. His weakness was alcohol and when he had a lot he liked to believe he was either Elvis or Bruce Lee. Shane preferred his Elvis impersonation as the Bruce Lee one usually ended up with Shane being punched unconscious. Patrick completely ignored Chloe, and Ainne was generally either working or out of her head so Shane would change, feed and bath his little sister. Looking back, they were the happiest times of his childhood. Patrick would be unconscious from a late-night binge and Ainne would be shooting up before midday so that left Shane and Chloe safe and together.

Shane was a very extroverted and chatty little boy, always mucky like his sister and wearing hand-me-downs from people on the estate. They looked like they had walked out of an old war orphans photo. Everyone on the estate knew them and commented on how good Shane was with his little sister. Together they would spend most of the day out on the estate with Shane shoplifting any of the things he thought his sister needed. He would take her around to Fat Beryl's, the local matriarch, who would let him hang out and get warm. Beryl knew Shane and his sister's situation but still Shane would tell her, "Me Ma's not well so school have given me time off. She will be better soon."

As Shane told these stories in prison, Leo's eyes would widen in horror and pity but he really was a happy child back then, who loved looking after his baby sister.

It was two days before Chloe's third birthday that it all went wrong. Shane had nicked a small doll from the toy shop and was looking forward to seeing Chloe's face when he gave it to her. The two of them left Fat Beryl's at around 18:00. She had given Shane some tea and he had fed

Chloe. They entered the lift, which took them up to their seventh-floor flat but as Shane pushed the buggy out Chloe had cried, "Don't want to go home."

Shane understood what she meant; he always dreaded going home and just prayed his mum was straight and that Patrick was out in some pub. But on this day his mum was far from straight and Patrick was home and extremely drunk, even for him. Shane entered the flat and put Chloe safely into her room then sat on the torn settee praying that Patrick was Elvis tonight. He could hear him shouting at his mum.

"You fucking whore, you spent all the money on that shit."

The sound of Patrick slapping his mum no longer startled him. However, this was particularly loud and he seemed to be smashing the room up as well. After what could have been half an hour of screaming and smashing, the room went silent. Ten minutes later Patrick came out wearing his tracky bottoms and Ainne's kimono-style dressing gown. The bandanna wrapped around his head confirmed that tonight he was Bruce Lee.

To see this man mimic Bruce Lee would be funny for an outside observer. He would mouth words then say them in a terrible attempt at a Chinese accent. Then he would go through his efforts at martial arts patterns, which bore no resemblance to any real kung fu. Most the time he would fall over as he tried his version of the crane or the crouching tiger. Regularly he would use Shane as his punch bag. "Here, stand up, ya wee cunt, ya." Luckily Patrick was usually too pissed to actually hit him. When he did though, it was a fully grown man hitting a child and Shane had been knocked unconscious more times than he could remember. Still, not once did he cry or show the bastard any fear.

On that particular day, Shane thought he might have escaped the punches and kicks as Patrick seemed even less lucid than normal and not very interested in their usual "game". Instead he mumbled something under his breath and then went back into the bedroom. Shane didn't know if he should sit back down. Was it over? Unfortunately it wasn't.

Patrick leaped out of the room shouting his version of Bruce Lee's war cry, "aaaaayaaaay", with some recently purchased nun-chucks. Shane thought of running out of the flat but that would have meant leaving Chloe. He stood there as the sticks whistled past his head.

"Stop fucking moving, I won't hit you, I'm a fucking master," Patrick reassured him.

Shane closed his eyes and prepared for the pain of the blunt sticks hitting him.

"Stop it! Leave Shaney alone! Stop you, stop, bad daddy!"

Shane immediately opened his eyes and panic swept over him. Chloe had got out of her room and was standing in front of Patrick, scolding her daddy. Shane had told Chloe never to get out of bed when Patrick was "playing". He looked at Patrick and saw what was coming. Shane froze as Patrick quickly turned and smashed the heavy wooden staffs down on Chloe's head, caving in her tiny fragile skull. Everything happened in slow motion in Shane's eyes. He watched, frozen to the spot as Chloe's head crumpled, blood spurting from a wound, reddening her beautiful blonde locks. A loud crack followed as her skull smashed against a hard wooden table and then her tiny lifeless body flopped, her eyes still open, staring into Shane's, holding him in a trance. He snapped out of this state when he heard Patrick scream out a crazed warrior cry. He looked at him, no longer scared, just numb. Patrick dropped the stick and grabbed his jacket and ran out the door. Shane collapsed next to his sister as all emotion flooded from his body. He had held his breath, unable to function but eventually he had to let the air enter his body. His lungs filled, followed by a scream and then a heart-wrenching cry. His mother did not move, he could see her through the open door staring up at the ceiling. Shane shook his baby sister gently.

"Wake up, Chloe, he's gone now, wake up, WAKE UP!"

Paranoid schizophrenia, that's what people said Patrick was suffering from. "He is delusional, he is very ill." All Shane knew was his beautiful little sister was dead. Shane was taken into care and moved around several foster families in Ireland. All of them reported the same thing:

"Shane was very introverted and showed no interest in any activities". He spoke very little. After a year of moving from pillar to post Ainne's sister Maggie was granted custody. Maggie was a single parent, living on the dole in England. She would not be most people's choice for mum of the year but to Shane she was an angel. He only had his mother to compare her to and the fact she cooked dinners, cleaned his clothes and hugged him at night was enough to give her this status. Maggie's house was on a notorious council estate south of Manchester. She managed to get Shane into the local school and informed the headmaster of Shane's troubled past. With an Irish accent in an English school and in second-hand clothes, it didn't take long for some of the other boys to start picking on Shane. John Edwards was two years older than Shane and he was the school's worst bully. His family were well-known criminals but when he heard that Shane's mum was a brass he couldn't help but take his opportunity to inflict pain on a young pupil.

"Oi, pikey, I hear your mum's a slapper, ten pound for a blow job."

John had mimicked what he thought a blow job looked like and the four lads with him had laughed.

Shane had been at the school for four weeks. He had said no more than ten words in all that time. His only interaction with any of the kids was asking where the toilet was on his first day but he was about to interact for a second time.

Every bit of pain and frustration that Shane had suffered over the last twelve months went into the punches that pummelled John Edwards unconscious. The school headmaster said he was shocked that such levels of violence could come from someone so young. Shane had found an outlet for his anger and frustration.

For years to come people would not understand how a skinny wretch like Shane could knock people out twice his size. They could not realise that every punch he landed came all the way from Ballymun and every opponent he fought was paying for what Patrick had done. By seventeen he was annihilating doormen in Manchester's city centre. He was soon defined by his violent behaviour but to Shane it was a release valve for the pain he carried and the guilt he felt.

Known as the 'baby-faced assassin' Shane was enticed by a local gym that had heard of his prowess and soon he built a name as a promising amateur boxer. Later a stint as a professional boxer was cut short when Shane disagreed with the ref's decision and knocked him out of the ring before turning to his opponent and battering him to a pulp.

At a loose end and with no decent job prospects, the army seemed to be his salvation and when he was packed off to Afghanistan everyone that knew him feared for the Taliban. But Shane's lack of control saw him break Sergeant Stone's jaw and led to his first stretch in military prison. His reliance on violent conflict resulted in him behaving in the same way as a junkie, except that he had an insatiable appetite for breaking bones and removing teeth just like a drug addict or alcoholic he was trying to fill a hole that had manifested deep inside him.

But all this seemed to directly contradict another trait that defined Shane, one that was more difficult to analyse: his unwavering need for veracity and righteousness. Yes, Shane did commit many ferocious attacks but they were always linked to people who had a disregard or contempt for what was fair and right.

The CO of Shane's regiment fought hard to get him released, stating his bravery and popularity amongst his fellow soldiers as well as his ability and accuracy with a rifle. After promising to keep Shane under control, the CO got his wish and Shane was let loose on the Taliban once more. Unfortunately Shane soon found himself back in the slammer after he lost his temper with a new recruit who had jokingly asked Shane if he had a sister worth fucking. The new recruit's war was cut short and Shane was back inside. After six years in the army, three of which were spent in the nick, Shane was finally dishonourably discharged.

Back on Civvie Street, Shane became the scourge of doormen and licensees all over Manchester, abusing their hospitality and getting into fights all over the town. He had a group of friends who were more like hangers-on. They would start the fights and Shane would finish them. He thought of himself as a good guy. In his mind he never hit anyone that didn't either deserve it or whose job it was to fight. When Shane discovered cocaine, he loved it and quickly realised most of the dealers were scared of him so he took what he wanted and never bothered to pay. Shane was revolting against the world but he was doing it in his own way. Anyone who chose to be involved in the underworld was a legitimate target. Bullies of any kind would get battered, although Shane's definition of a bully sometimes got blurred.

When Mickey Brown, the local drug baron, decided that Shane had gone too far he called his friends in Glasgow to sort him out. Although Shane was out every night, he still hit the gym every day. The skinny little lad who had been knocking big men out was now a big man himself. Every morning he would spend at least three hours either on the weights or at the bags. The Glasgow firm knew exactly where to find him and when he left the gym to find four burly meatheads waiting by his car, he knew what to expect. He was admitted to hospital with a broken jaw and two broken ribs: the guys did a good job on Shane. Only respect for his courage and their own painful wounds stopped them from causing more serious harm.

Shane never held a grudge against his attackers. He knew from their accents they were brought in for the job and it was nothing personal. In fact, they did him a favour. While Shane was in hospital for three weeks the young doctor in attendance was Sara May, a kind and lovely-looking young woman. Shane had his pick of the type of girls who liked his troubled, hard-man reputation, but he had never spent any time with someone like Sara.

They instantly shared a connection and soon after Shane had been discharged they began seeing each other. Within a few weeks Shane moved in. Things moved quickly and naturally and his world seemed to have taken a 360-degree turn. For the first time in his life things were going right, though he feared it was all too good to be true. The next six months were the happiest he had ever experienced. Unfortunately his joy would not last.

Leo knows all this about Shane and still Shane knows very little about him.

"You're late old man," Shane says as Leo finally approaches the table.

"Yes, I'm sorry, I have had a lot of things to prepare," replies Leo.

"We're in prison. What the fuck do you need to prepare for in here?" Leo doesn't answer the question and instead turns his attention to the chessboard, seeing that it is set up, ready to go.

"Let's hope you do better today," mocks Shane good-naturedly.

Over the last two months Leo and Shane have played over thirty games of chess. Leo won the first game in less than five moves. He won the second easily too. The third game took over an hour and Leo commented on how much Shane had improved in such a short time. Then, after a five-hour marathon for the fourth game, Shane had his first victory.

At first Leo thought he had been hustled but he soon realised that Shane had barely known the rules of chess before the first game. As the days went by Shane beat Leo consistently and quite easily, with their last three games not lasting more than half an hour each. Even stranger was the fact that Johnny-No-Legs had played Shane only two days ago. Leo had watched the game and although Johnny was a competent player Leo hadn't expected him to last more than five minutes with Shane. To Leo's surprise Johnny beat Shane. How could this happen? As a lifelong member of the London Chess Society, Leo knew that luck played no part in chess. Shane assured him he didn't let Johnny win. Leo had played Johnny and beaten him many times. It didn't make sense, until Leo watched Shane play against Johnny for the second time. Shane had won with checkmate coming in less than eight moves.

It was then that Leo really started to believe. When the Djinn named Simeon had prophesied to Leo that he would meet a unique man with the attributes to lead and protect the masses, Leo often wondered if this man would be a warrior, or a scholar, or maybe a great orator who could stir up the consciousness of the people and open their eyes to the truth. Now he was seeing that Shane was much more than this. When Leo asked Shane what he believed was his greatest virtue, Shane thought for a long time before answering.

"I never tell lies. Well, not since I was a small boy. Oh, and I help old people like you and I am a great lover!"
Not impressed by the other two answers, Leo questioned his first declaration. "You never tell lies?"

"No. Maybe because I never felt the need to, or perhaps because of Chloe's death. I know that bullies thrive because of lies. Sometimes I wish I had told lies. I mean, even in court my brief did everything to stop me testifying. Some child psychiatrist once told me I was most likely autistic or something, like it's a disease to tell the truth."

When Shane says he never tells lies, he means never for his own personal gain. Leo was a good man brought up to believe in God and by honest, hard-working parents. He had worked in the Vatican, the epicentre of virtue. He had met many, many honest men and yet he had never met a man who wouldn't tell a lie for his own benefit. Leo realised how unique this was. Watching Shane play chess brought another realisation: Shane was not a great chess player, in fact he was barely competent. So how was it he could beat Leo, a very accomplished player, so easily? Shane was not conscious of his ability to read people, it was an instinctive action. Simply put, after the first few games with Leo, Shane was able to predict what Leo would do and use his own moves against him. Eventually he was able to work out in his mind every move from start to finish that Leo would play just from the first couple of manoeuvres. The same happened with Johnny, who was more predictable and was not an accomplished player.

This ability to calculate an opponent's moves had dictated events throughout Shane's life. When he boxed he often lost the first round only to completely annihilate his opponent in the second. His commanding officer in Afghanistan was convinced he had a sixth sense. Often he would listen in awe as Shane would explain to him what the local rebels' strategy would be next. One red-hot summer day Shane had lain out in the desert with no fear whatsoever of the enemy attacking him. "They won't attack today," he told Colonel Peter Quinn. He was always right and if the Colonel could have explained to his superiors about Shane's insight into the enemy's behaviour without sounding like a crackpot he would have. But what could he say?

Truth was Shane educated himself on the origins of the local tribes. He learned that they derived from people known as the Pashtun. He read all he could about their culture and beliefs. He discovered that the creed of the Pashtun is called Pashtunwali and they abide by this code of conduct to the letter. This and knowledge of the Deobandi teachings that the Taliban follow gave Shane a unique insight into their formidable adversaries. No matter what the outside world thought of these people, Shane believed that they were an honourable people who never strayed from their creed. He may not have shared their ideals but he did admire the conviction with which these tribesmen honoured their code. It also made them predictable and on that hot day the Pashtun celebrated Sheshbeeyeh, a festival almost unique to the tribes in this region.

Leo concludes that Shane truly is an exceptional person and the reason Simeon had singled him out was not because of his physical abilities or his near-unique skill with weapons – it was because Shane is an autodidact with an unbelievable attention to detail.

"What's one of them?" asks Shane, when Leo tries to compliment him.

"You told me you never went to school until you were eleven, yet you are obviously a clever man. You taught yourself to read Arabic. You beat me at chess, a game I am very good at. Your mind works differently from most peoples. An autodidact is self-taught, usually someone who sees things the collective doesn't. The way you read people, situations, and even strategy in chess. No one is teaching you this, you are self-learning. I think this is why Simeon picked you."

"Who? Picked me? What are you on about?" Shane stares at Leo, feeling both suspicious and puzzled. He doesn't know anybody called Simeon.

"It is time to tell you the truth, Shane," says Leo. "I hope you'll forgive me."

London – before Leo's enlightenment

"The best place to hide is in plain sight."

Life had been good for Leo Verdi: good family, good education and good job. He and his wife had recently returned from two weeks spent at their dream retirement destination in the beautiful Italian city of Rimini. At 62 years old Leo had planned to retire two years early but the opportunity to work for one of the world's most powerful leaders in the most iconic city in the world was too much temptation. Leo was not employed directly by the Vatican; instead the work he was required to do was outsourced to his company: the Verdi Accountancy Firm. His wife, Regina, understood why he continued but she was hoping that they could soon pack their bags and finally move to the Adriatic coast for good.

When the very modern and smartly dressed man called Simeon had first approached Leo at his office in London, Leo assumed he was some sort of music mogul or perhaps a film director with his mop of well-groomed hair and the stylish sunglasses he wore even when inside. He was surprised to hear that he was, in fact, an envoy from the Vatican and was offering him the opportunity to work for the Pope. Leo was very excited. He rarely went into anything before dotting all the i's and crossing all the t's but Leo shook Simeon's hand there and then, committing to work exclusively for the Pontiff and preparing a report on world economic strategy. Apparently the Pope had been invited to speak at the World Economic Forum in Davos, Switzerland and wanted to brush up on his knowledge. Leo was curious why they didn't use their own experts or at least a Catholic accountant. "His Holiness has his reasons," was the only answer he received.

The report was quite simple for a man of Leo's ability and he received a letter from the Pope himself thanking him for the accurate and easy-to-follow format. The report translated the global economy and its economic systems into layman's terms. The Pope addressed some of the world's leading industry and business academics and the general consensus was surprise at His Holiness' knowledge of current global finance. Leo was well paid for his work and treated Regina to a new sports car, ready for their retirement to the Adriatic coast in six months. Then Simeon visited Leo at his London office a second time.

"His Holiness wishes to employ your services once more," remarked the dapper, thirty-something Italian who, as on the previous time they met, was wearing sunglasses inside?

"That's great but I must tell you I will not be able to work on any reports myself; my nephew Fredo is taking over the firm from next week. I will, of course, make sure he follows the exact format I used for the previous report and…"

Simeon held his hand up to stop Leo mid-sentence. "The Pontiff wishes for *you* to fulfil this task. It is not a report he needs this time." Simeon pulled out a sealed envelope and handed it to Leo. "The Bishop of Rome asks that if you decide to accept this commission all correspondence should go through him only via myself or face-to-face."
Leo's curiosity was aroused. "Face-to-face with the Pope? You mean I will be meeting with His Holiness himself?"

"That is his wish, yes," replied Simeon.

Even though Leo was a devout Jew he had always been fascinated with the pomp and ceremony of the Roman Church. The chance to meet the top man himself was very intriguing and most likely the job would be fruitful financially and very exciting.

Although Leo moved to London with his parents when he was a young boy, he was born in Venice. He was fluent in his father's tongue and still thought of himself as an Italian; maybe this was why he was favoured by the Pope. Then Leo reminded himself that the Pope was a German.

Leo opened the envelope and read, quickly needing to sit down. "He wants me to audit the Vatican accounts?"

"Well, if you read carefully, the required task is to audit the books from the last millennium or so."

Leo stared at the letter. He shook his head in disbelief. How could he turn this down? The job entailed five months working at the Institute for Works of Religion. It included an apartment in Rome and all expenses paid and a very generous financial package. He was to have access to all areas. For someone like Leo this was like a backstage pass to the best gig ever. Of course he would have to discuss it with Regina. She was expecting to be moving to Rimini next month so she had the last say. After all the late nights and missed holidays she'd had to put up with over the last thirty years, that was the least she deserved. It was far too big a decision to make without asking her...

"So, will you accept?" asked Simeon.

"Yes."

Two years on and Leo was still trailing through different ledgers and ancient records. By now he knew that the Pope was looking for something specific but he was not told what. He'd realised very quickly that the Vatican Bank or IOR was a very complex organisation; the Vatican itself was a unique state. Leo discovered that it's only real declared earnings or financial support came from a voluntary payment dating back over a thousand years. These donations were called 'Peter's pence'. The IOR's remit is to serve the global mission of the Catholic Church by safeguarding the assets of institutions and individuals related to the Holy See. However, its profits and assets are not the property of the Holy See.

In plain English, it has all the benefits of a charitable organisation, the authority of self-regulation and the opportunity for officials to hide behind diplomatic immunity if the need arises – and all these things were an invitation to corruption and fraud. If the Pope was looking to clean up his house then Leo was the man. After the first couple of months exposing one indiscretion after another Leo was called for an audience with the Pope. This both excited and worried him. He was aware of the privilege and status that came with working for the high priest of the Romans but to be called to the court was to follow in the footsteps of Michelangelo. His worry, however, was that perhaps he had failed in this puzzling assignment, an assignment that he did not really understand and so led him to constantly doubt his performance.

Leo was escorted by two guards to the Pope's private office. He waited by the entrance as the guards assumed a stance of honour then the doors opened and a middle-aged, stern-looking nun appeared.

"The Holy Father will see you know, Senior Verdi."

Leo walked in, looking around like a child entering a Disney shop. He realised beads of sweat had involuntarily appeared on his forehead. Pope Benedict was sitting behind a large, hand-carved wooden desk. He was dressed in his papal robes, leaning over while writing a letter. Without looking up, he addressed Leo.

"Please, Señor Verdi, sit."

Leo hesitated.

The Pope continued to speak as he wrote his letters. "I am aware that the institute I am head of is riddled with corruption, money laundering and numerous other misdemeanours. What I wish you to find is something far more important."

His tone was punitive and Leo instinctively adopted a defensive tone.

"It would help if I knew what I was looking for." Leo took a deep breath, trying to both assert and calm himself before continuing. "I mean, if I am not here to keep you informed on such things as theft or fraud, why do you want me to investigate the finances of the state?"

The Pope finally placed his pen down on the oak desk, looked up and gestured to the still standing Leo to sit. His face had softened as he began to explain himself.

"Forgive my reluctance to tell you exactly what I am looking for or why I have asked you to carry out this task. I am sure you are frustrated with the little information I am giving you, but you must believe me, it is for your own good."

"But your Holiness, I don't know how to find what you're looking for if you can't tell me what it is."

"I don't want you to feel insulted by this process, it is just that I am looking for something very specific. What it actually is even I do not know yet but when you find it I believe I will. Therefore, I want you to report any irregularity that you find and feel is significant. I may dismiss most of your findings as irrelevant but you must not feel your work is fruitless."

Leo left more confused than when he went in. Still, he knew from the tone of the conversation that the work he was doing was important and that the Pope had faith in his ability to complete this quest.

Over the next six months Leo reported payments to non-Catholic organisations, contracts traced back to companies with dubious history, even monies paid directly into a certain cardinal's personal account. Simeon took Leo's findings to the Pope but time and again he was told to look elsewhere. When he discovered that the IOR purchased banks all over Eastern Europe at a knock-down price after the Second World War he was sure this was what his benefactor was looking for. Simeon thanked him but asked that he research the Holy See finances prior to the formation of the IOR. Leo dug deeper and the months soon became a year. He found himself wallowing in the archives relating to the administration of the property of the Holy See.

Once again Leo found evidence of illegal and immoral behaviour. Money laundering to American-Sicilians, collusion with fascist dictators, even a mortgage document that proved the Holy See was the landlord to most of the properties in Paris's notorious nineteenth-century red light area. Still the Pope thanked him but asked Leo to dig deeper, maybe go further back.

The historic archives delighted him: the Papal State is the oldest political chancery in continuous operation in the world, its records go back centuries. Although Leo's labours were seemingly unappreciated, he still relished going to work every day. Aside from the constant nagging by Regina about their retirement plans, Leo loved his assignment. Numbers and history were his two favourite things (outside of his family) and he had access to probably the world's wealthiest store of knowledge on these subjects. He sometimes wondered if he really wanted to find the illusive information the Pope sought – retirement was beginning to look boring.

A comparatively benign event from 1748 caught Leo's attention but he doubted the Pope would have any interest in it. He dithered on whether to bother Simeon with it at all. It appeared a Jesuit monk by the name of Isaac received three payments of quite significant amounts directly from the Pope of the time, Benedict XIV. It seemed that this Isaac was acting as a go-between for the Pope and the Chinese Empire, which at the time was ruled by the Qing dynasty. The sum was paid in gold and brokered by a Jewish lender. No real documents seemed to explain the transaction, just a note in the Pontiff's own hand saying: *Ledger held by MB*. Leo followed the paperwork and discovered that this book was used to enter many more transactions right up to 1945. Strangely there was no pattern to the deals. Some were to organisations, some to companies and some to countries. Even the broker changed. Early on they seemed to use Rothschild, then James Barclay or Barings, later Warburg and Morgan. These were large sums of money but it all balanced as far as Leo could see. He also noted that at the end of the trail in 1945 the promissory and the book were supposed to have been kept in the Vatican vaults but he could not locate them.

He doubted that the current Pope Benedict would be interested in this information as it all seemed completely above board and he should probably not mention it until he had traced the ledger, which had probably just been misplaced, but it had been a quiet week and he needed something to justify the thousands of Euro's he would be billing Simeon so he included it in his weekly report with a footnote saying he would look for the ledger the following week.

Tired and a little frustrated, Leo went home to his apartment in Rome. It was an upmarket place that the Vatican had provided, just two hundred metres from the Piazza del Popolo in an executive block. The flat itself was very modern, furnished in white leather and clear glass with marble floors that led to plush carpets and both bedrooms contained sunken baths and shower rooms. A cleaning lady and a cook came as part of the deal. Leo had commented to Regina that they now lived like film stars but she was not impressed, finding the flat sterile; all she really wanted was to get out of Rome.

On this evening Regina was back in London visiting their oldest daughter. Leo realised she was unhappy and he was ashamed of the way he felt about her indifference. He had always strived to make Regina happy but now he almost resented her for not wanting to be part of this great adventure. She had taken to visiting the children at any opportunity and Leo knew that she preferred to be anywhere but here in Rome. Tonight though, Leo missed her. He wanted to see and hold her; something told him it was important. He phoned his wife.

"Hello. It's me."

"Hi. How was your day? Did you find the Holy Grail yet?"

Leo laughed at his beloved's remark. In an effort to avoid Regina's interrogation about his role for the Pope he had joked with her that he was searching for the Holy Grail though he now realised that task would probably have been easier. Leo was not a great man for phone conversations but to Regina's surprise he continued talking well into the night, telling her every detail of his week and even more unusually, telling her how much he missed her and wanted her with him. Still, this didn't prepare her for his final words.

"I love you Regina. More than I ever have or will love anyone or anything."

His words invoked concern in his wife. She told him she would be home the following day and as they disconnected a feeling of foreboding fell over her.

When Leo hung up he felt bad that for the first time since they met over thirty-five years ago they wanted different things.

He was so happy here. Fifty miles of books and manuscripts fill the Vatican library's shelves. Packed with knowledge. Millions of books and scriptures. It is the world's greatest repository for medieval and renaissance manuscripts as well as many incunabula collected or stolen from cultures over the first half of the millennium. The machine that is the Roman Catholic Church owned works of literature and art, science and maths, priceless documents, even parchments that were written before Christianity existed telling of a history forgotten by the world. This fountain of knowledge was Leo's utopia yet unbeknown to him the adventure was about to escalate and the fun was about to end.

The next day Leo was up and about at the crack of dawn. It was Friday and Leo hoped to get into the office before 07:00 so he could finish early and meet Regina off the plane. She was scheduled to arrive at 15:00 and Leo was looking forward to seeing his loving wife. When he got to the Vatican Sister Bernadette, the nun who looked after the admin at the small office out of which Leo worked, met him at the door.

"You are to go straight to the Papal office," she told him. "His Holiness wishes to see you."

Leo was slightly alarmed; the sister had sounded anxious as she hurried him up. Although Leo met with Simeon at least once a week he had only met with the Pope three times during his assignment as the Pope was a very busy man.

Normally Leo would wait for a Swiss guard to escort him but today the nun was insistent that he go straight to the Pope's personal library. As Leo made his way through St Peter's Basilica, the greatest of all churches in Christendom, his gaze was drawn to the huge central dome and he was once more overcome by the gravity of his place of work. Leo could not help but be impressed by the Catholics but he also wondered how they could pretend to be the church of the people and the descendants of Christ when they surrounded themselves with such ostentatious architecture. He wondered what the man who threw the traders from his father's home would make of all this grandiosity.

Eventually he averted his gaze, remembering that he was about to meet with the Holy Father. Quickly he tried to recount his rehearsed explanations for the lack of progress in his search for whatever it was he was looking for. Head down and mumbling to himself, Leo reached the exit of the great church, headed up the corridor that led to the library and walked straight up to the guards who stood at the entrance to Benedict's apartment. The head guard waved him past, he was obviously expected. As he approached the grand library he could hear the Pope's voice and that of Simeon, the loyal servant. The discussion was about some book.

"You asked to see me, Your Grace," Leo said, addressing the Pope.
To his discomfort it was Simeon who answered, still wearing the damned sunglasses.

"Did he fuck? I wanted to see you!"
Leo recoiled in horror and surprise. Did Simeon just curse in front of the Pope? Leo looked at the Pope, the man who is God's representative on earth, the man who commands over 1.2 billion Catholics across the planet, the most famous man on earth, who was now cowed like a schoolboy brought before the headmaster.

"Sit down, Leo," ordered Simeon.

Leo immediately recognised an authority in Simeon's voice that was absent before. He looked again to Pope Benedict.

"Is that okay, Your Grace?" he asked.

The Pope nodded. Leo noticed a look of trepidation fall across the elderly priest's face. Simeon spoke again.

"The last report you sent mentions a transaction from the Vatican to China."
Leo felt uncomfortable. He noticed that as well as authority, Simeon's voice was bearing a certain menace.

"Well?" asked Simeon, his voice raised.

Uncomfortable was now an understatement, especially as Simeon was acting as if the Pope was a secretary awaiting instruction. Leo gathered his courage and inquired to the Pope.

"Is everything all right, Your Worship?"

Simeon sighed. "Trust me, he is fucking fine. He shits in a golden latrine and gets blow jobs off the nuns so don't worry about him. I need you to focus, Leo. The Jesuit and the Jew, what paperwork have you found on them?"

A mixture of outrage and fear prompted Leo to stand suddenly. His mind raced: *What is going on?* he thought. *Is this some sort of prank? No, of course not, you fool. Perhaps it's a test. Well, I've failed if it is. What if Simeon has flipped? Could be drugs? No, he doesn't look drugged, does he? I can't see his eyes with those confounded glasses on, I need to get out of here.* Eventually he had a clear thought. *Of course, Simeon must have had some sort of breakdown and the Pope is playing along. I must alert the guards!*

"It's okay, Leo," said the Pope. "Take a seat."

Leo hesitated as he watched the Pope get up and offer Simeon the chair at his desk.

"Thank you," said Simeon, slipping into place. "Now I understand that this is a little strange, Leo, but let me explain." He opened a drawer in the desk and pulled out Leo's report before nodding to Benedict who turned and left the room, closing the doors behind him.

"What I am about to tell you is a secret that only a handful of men and fewer women have ever heard. This secret goes back three thousand years. I am a part of this secret and the first thing I must tell you is that my name is Simeon, Utrillo, Santa Cruz and I am not human."

If someone tells you he is an alien your first thoughts will probably be ones of pity towards them or perhaps fear as you naturally conclude that the person is either on drugs or mentally disturbed. Of course, if the person claiming to be an alien is sitting opposite you in the Vatican library and has just dismissed the leader of the Roman Catholic Church with a nod of his head, then the feelings you are likely to have are ones of utter confusion and possibly an unease. However, the thing that bothered Leo most about this encounter was that the man talking to him was not moving his lips.

"You are wondering how you can hear me," smiled Simeon without opening his mouth. "I am communicating through a connection we have via a gland in your brain. Don't panic, everything will become clear soon."

Leo felt he should be panicking but he really wasn't. The voice in his head had a calming tone that relaxed him in a way he imagined meditation would. As well as the monotone vibration that carried Simeon's words, pictures seemed to be forming in his mind. Simeon began to explain.

"I am one of a delegation that came to this place thousands of years ago."

In Leo's mind he could clearly see a ball of intense fire sitting in a crater of its own making. The sands of a desert surrounded the scene. A group of a hundred or so nomads were curiously looking into the crater, their faces portraying their awe at this mystical fireball. Then thirteen of the tribesmen started to walk towards the fire that burned within as their friends and family screamed at them to stop. The thirteen seem to be in a trance and ignored the remonstrations. A small man was knocked to the ground as he stood in front of his brother, trying to withhold him. Undeterred the thirteen walked into the crater, no longer pursued by their fellow tribesmen as the heat became unbearable. Leo could almost feel the heat himself. The thirteen men continued into the white flames. Huge blue shafts of light shot from the sphere and a loud noise resembling a thunder clap encouraged the observers to run away. Only one young boy stayed as witness. The boy watched the men enter the fire and burn in front of him. First their clothes and then their skin melted from their bodies. Not one of them screamed with pain, no cries could be heard at all. The men stayed standing even though only bones remained. The boy stood to gain a better look. The brightness of the sphere increased, as did the heat and soon the boy had to retreat as it grew too intense. He ran behind a dune and peeked over the top. As the light expanded so did the searing heat.

The boy could see the other tribesmen running and clambering aboard their camels, speeding away as fast as possible. A large explosion sent debris and sparks flying past his head. Camels and horses stampeded, throwing off their riders who then ran after their steeds, determined to escape. The young boy tucked his head down safely but did not move.

Then silence fell, the heat receded and the light faded. The boy stood up and tentatively walked back to the crater but before he got to it the thirteen men appeared, climbing out of the pit. They stood in front of him, naked except for an amulet around each of their necks. Solomon looked at the faces; they were identical to the men that entered the fiery sphere but he knew these were not his tribesmen. They looked at each other and then at the boy whom Leo instinctively knew was Solomon, son of David, who would become the last king of the United Monarchy of Israel and Judah.

Leo snapped out of his trance-like state and was thankful to see Simeon's lips were moving again as he told Leo, "What you have just witnessed was our arrival amongst you and our first assimilation into human form."

"Who, or what, are you?"

"We are the Djinn, a race that has existed on this planet alongside yours for all time. The Djinn collective exist on a different frequency to that of humans. We evolved from a very similar sapient form to you, although we exist in a state of non-biological dependency. We have a very different view and perspective of this world to you."

Somehow Leo knew that what Simeon was telling him was true but still he could not comprehend it.

"You claim a whole other race lives alongside us? Surely we would have noticed?"

Simeon nods. "In some ways you have. Many of your stories of ghosts, vampires and all those things that science cannot explain are caused by the occasional interaction with us. But please, I will try to explain as much as possible over the next few months. First we must address the matter at hand, this book."

Leo was shown photos of a brown leather book. It was obviously old and had a species of clover embossed on the front.

"What is that?"

"This is the ledger mentioned in your report about the Jesuit and the Jew."

Leo reached out for the pictures. "May I?"

Simeon pushed them towards him. "Yes, go ahead."

Leo was looking at two pictures: one of the book's cover, the other of an inside page and so he realised why he, a Jewish accountant with no links to the Roman Church, had been picked.

"This writing is south-western Yiddish dialect!"

He didn't know why he'd studied this practically extinct language when he was younger but he did know he was one of a small minority who could read it fluently.

"It is important we find this book, Leo. It will help us to defeat humankind's worst enemy and you are the key."

And so Leo listened as Simeon explained that the Jesuit who created this book was one of the thirteen Djinn who appeared out of that crater. His name had been Isaac but he had disappeared, believed to have been killed in 1944, and his murderer had been trying to get hold of this book ever since. Simeon had specifically worked his way into the inner circle of the current Pope so as to get access to the Vatican, where he was sure Isaac had hidden the book prior to his death. The Popes throughout the ages had historically been great allies of the Djinn, Simeon explained. "Hiding our true identities and much more."

"They have always known?" asked a shocked Leo.

"Yes, often guided by another of my kind though," said Simeon. "Not someone I would trust with such power. I fear this Pope is also in league with him and I think I will have to get rid of him."

Leo's mouth dropped open. "You... you are going to kill the Pope?"

"Oh, no," said Simeon. "I don't think we need to do that. I'll just make him abdicate."

"But, no Pope has left the post alive since 1415!"

"True, it is generally easier to kill them, they're normally so old anyway, but I'd rather not."

Leo shook his head. He did not understand what Simeon was saying. Once more, Simeon's lips stopped moving and his words vibrated through Leo's mind.

"Do not be alarmed. This pope, like many of your leaders and their predecessors, is a pawn in a game. He has supported a Djinn called Reuben Lupas, the aforementioned 'mankind's worst enemy'. I will replace him with a more benevolent and less accepting man, someone who is not aware of our presence, if I can ever find one is this den of iniquity. So, back to the book."

Leo's mind seemed to transcend from his body as he witnessed a new scene.

"This is 1944 and Italy has recently signed an armistice with the Allies." Leo saw a tall man with tight black curls sneaking through the streets of Rome. He carried a parcel under his arm that Leo guessed must be the book. The man entered St Peter's Square, looking around as if worried he was being followed.

"This is Isaac," Simeon explained.

Isaac entered the church and shouted, "Raphael, are you here?"

From behind the altar stepped a man wearing a very loud turquoise zoot suit, a fedora hat and French-style pointy shoes.

"Shush, we will be heard! You know the rules. I shouldn't be meeting with you and this place is full of Reuben's spies," said the strangely dressed man.

"As if you don't stand out enough," said Isaac as he looked Raphael up and down. "I have a book. You must hide it." Isaac pulled the book from the parcel he carried.

"What's in it?" asked Raphael.

"This is an account of transactions and loans I have made with countries all over the world, financing wars and revolutions, industrial growth and loans to both sides in this skirmish."

Raphael laughed at Isaac calling the Second World War a mere "skirmish".

"Amitiel told me you had a network of Jews running all that for you. She says you were on the brink of winning the Host."

"Yes, very nearly, but now Reuben has his little dictator slaughtering every Jew in Europe. He is gassing millions to make sure he wipes out anyone allied to me. Surely you must interfere?"

"Killing humans is not against the rules, Isaac. You are in danger of sounding like Simeon."

Leo frowned. Simeon? The same Simeon as the man in front of him now? And what were they saying? Discussing the near extermination of the Jews as if it was a mere petty violation of rules in some perverse game!

"However," continued the turquoise-clad Raphael in the church, "I agree that six million Jews killed to assure he gets the handful working for you could be considered overkill – in the truest sense of the word. But I suspect he may have an alternate reason for this genocide, a suspicion I cannot share with you at this stage. I guess your claim is that he will have too much of an advantage if he has your book."

"The book. What was so damned important about this book," thought Leo.

The vision seemed to pause and as if in answer to his question Simeon cut in. "Let me explain. Over the last two hundred years Isaac has used his knowledge and bloodline to create the world banking system as we know it. In that book is not only the location of tons of gold, but also numbers that correlate to accounts in Switzerland and South Africa. By 1936 Isaac controlled fifty per cent of the gold and diamonds in the world. Every nation, every international company, every bank owes Isaac money. The Allies and the Axis have funded their war by borrowing money from one institution or another, all owned by Isaac.

"Isaac has a great mind but still he can't remember everything, so he needed a record and certain people to keep it. By 1936 he'd created the 'global collateral account', which governs the world's wealth so he could then undermine a whole country's economy simply by calling in a debt.

He uses corporations such as the central banks, the Crown and, due to a shaky alliance with Reuben, the Holy Roman Catholic Church to elicit his operation."

"But how could one man, or whatever you call yourselves, have that power and remain anonymous?" asked Leo.

"For any of us to operate without revealing ourselves the Djinn have had to recruit, and sometimes create, secret societies that have been doing our work for centuries. Most famously the Templars and the Freemasons."

Leo asks, "Like the Illuminati?"

"Ah yes, the Illuminati, the 'enlightened ones'. They were actually a group of learned men who discovered clues of our existence. They opposed us and tried to save mankind so we used our propaganda tools to turn them into the evil puppet masters. I suppose they played a part a long time ago but they haven't actually existed for two hundred years. Still, it keeps the conspiracy theorists off our backs.

"We call these groups our brethren. We select one or more senior members to be our contacts. These brethren are pawns but they are well rewarded to follow instructions and front our operations. Isaac used the Jewish Zionist brethren as his chosen people to run his financial institutions.

"Keeping secrets is easy within a secret society, especially one with a secret language or at least an ancient language only understood by a select few. Isaac allotted code numbers to each operation. These codes and other data would reveal vast stores of wealth, such as gold dumps storing over 360,000 tons of the stuff, in hidden tunnels all over the world. Then there are many promissory notes signed by kings and emperors. He has land deeds for whole territories, even priceless artworks and other plunder from wars, all in the book.

"But since Isaac disappeared sixty years ago these debts have lain idle and the people running the societies have started to believe the debts are void. That is a problem on its own but what will be worse is if one of the surviving Djinn gets their hands on the book. With the codes and accounts they could control the whole world's economy. I need to find that book and then you need to help me decipher the codes so we can get hold of this wealth."

So far Leo had not seen or heard anything that would lead him to willingly assist this man to acquire such extreme wealth.

"Surely you are one of the Djinn you talk of? I have no desire to help you obtain this wealth!"

"Trust me, I have no use for the money, but you want to know why you should help me, Leo? I will show you."

A short sharp flash plunged Leo back into the vision. Raphael and Isaac were still talking about the book and Reuben Lupas.

"What he has done to root out my brethren is beyond belief!" said Isaac "I put up with his pogroms and ghettos but this extermination is vile. He must be stopped."

"You really are beginning to sound like Simeon," sighed Raphael. "They are only humans after all."

"Maybe Simeon was right, this game is becoming a farce. It should have ended centuries ago. Humans are different now. We can't treat them as insignificant."

Raphael looks disapprovingly at Isaac.

"And how many died throughout the Crusades when you aligned with Reuben to wipe out Ben's tribe?"

Isaac shakes his head. "I am not saying I'm a human lover but they deserve better than this. If you could see what my eyes see you would understand."

Isaac and Raphael shared a vision, one that Leo was also privy to. The pictures in Leo's mind focused on a macabre event. He was witnessing two nurses and a doctor operating on beautiful twin girls no more than three or four. The girls were unconscious, side by side on the same bed. Leo assumed these would be victims of war and he prepared to witness horrendous injuries. He took in a deep breath and then... his fists clenched; a far worse scenario was unfolding. The two perfectly healthy and formed children were having their arms amputated, one her left, the other her right. The surgeon then sewed the two bodies together at the open wounds, creating a Siamese-type join. It was an experiment even the surgeon did not understand the purpose of but he seemed happy enough to follow the instructions of the man known as Reuben.

At this point Leo realised who the surgeon was. Chillingly average looking, a dark-haired man with a small gap between his teeth. He would not be recognised by everyone but Leo had his face engraved on his memory by his father's teachings, a man he referred to as the Angel of Death. This was the infamous Joseph Mengele.

As if his mind had a fast-forward mode Leo now saw these poor children post op, screaming in pain as the stitching that fused them together pushed poisonous pus from the wounds. Still, Leo felt someone else close by was in even more pain. A scan of the room showed a distraught woman tied to a chair, forced to watch her children suffer without the chance to offer comfort. A young nurse entered in a white uniform with shoulder-length hair and lovely blue eyes. Leo guessed she was mid-twenties, quite pretty really, and hope rose in his heart that help was at hand. The nurse looked at the children, inspecting their wounds. She smiled at them, and it was a kind smile, before she filled out the board by their bed. She then turned to leave.

"Why? Why are you doing this to my babies?" pleaded the woman. Her words were barely audible, but she managed to speak loudly with her eyes and they were begging.

The pretty little nurse with the blue eyes sneered at the pitiful mother.

"Filthy Jew, your snivelling, selfish kind deserves everything they get!" Her words spat out; her face, no longer pretty, was contorted with absolute hate.

The image thankfully faded away and Leo tried to speak, to beg Simeon to stop, but he was still in the first vision with Raphael and Isaac. It was obvious Raphael had witnessed the scene of the twins for the first time as well as he shook his head in disgust.

"Okay, I see. Reuben must be reeled in. But it has to be within the rules."

Isaac was aghast. "Reeled in! For fuck's sake, are we actually demons? Reuben thinks he can create some sort of mutant human for him to occupy. I have heard he plans full-scale dehumanising, even crossbreeding! And along with these sick experiments there is the mindless slaughter!"

"These things are regrettable and unsavoury but not against the rules," remarked Raphael, sounding embarrassed.

"Okay, well, I am also sure he took Joseph's amulet and then killed him... and he must have killed the others too. Surely killing Djinn is against the rules! This must stop! You are a Watcher, you can remove him."

"I am an Arc Hon. I can do anything. Can you prove that he took it? Or that he is the one killing Djinn?"

"No, of course not, but you know it is him. He is killing Djinn and stealing their amulets so they don't return to testify. I always believed we made up the myth of Satan to scare the humans but now I think maybe he really is amongst us."

Raphael was pondering. Leo realised he was obviously no fan of this Reuben character.

"Amitiel told me of Simeon's plan for a human competitor," Isaac continued. "I believe he was right. Only a few Djinn remain and we will all surely suffer the same fate as the rest. Simeon was smart enough to renew and now I understand why."

Raphael looked concerned. "Surely you are not thinking of doing the same?"

Isaac didn't answer; instead he lobbied Raphael. "Will you do this for me? Will you hide the book?"

"Yes, okay, I will," replied Raphael and in return handed him a small star-shaped gem. "Here, you will need this when you want it back. I will hide the book well."

"Thank you, Raphael. I am to head for Venice. I can only hope Reuben does not break with our sanctuary rules."

The vision passed and Simeon spoke out loud to Leo again. "The gem he passed to Isaac is called a *spell*. It is Djinn technology. I am guessing it will be a divining tool to find the book, or maybe a key to open the place it is hidden. We need to find that gem."

Leo was beginning to feel a bit hysterical.

"You keep saying *we*. Why am I involved? What has all this got to do with me?"

"The thirteen came here to compete in a game. The victor could stay and rule humankind, lead them into enlightenment as the Arc Hon led us. I realise how this sounds but we are eons more advanced than you. We looked upon humans the same way you look at animals."

Leo felt anger stir in him. "Yes, I can see that."

"I understand how you feel and as time went on some of us realised our mistake. I am not trying to convince you that I am any different, but trust me, we need to stop the Djinn known as Reuben Lupas. If he wins the game and becomes the Host it will bring more misery and pain to the human race than they have ever known. You have seen what happened the last time he made his play, which is nothing compared to what will occur if he ever triumphs.

"I realised this centuries ago and proposed that your race should have an opportunity to win the game themselves. I was denied then but you've just heard Isaac second that opinion. With two Djinn agreeing to it, the High Council and the Arc Hon have had to allow this. The humans now have a chance to win their world back but it may be too late if Reuben gets that book."

Simeon paused to look at Leo intently. "Can you really say no to helping me?"

And so this was how it began. Leo was sacrificing everything he had in life: his home, his marriage and his family. He knew that soon it would also be his freedom and one day his life. But the more Simeon taught him about the Djinn and the Arc Hon, the more he knew he had no other choice

Stoke Prison

"The truth is rarely pure and never simple."

Oscar Wilde

Shane has been listening to Leo's fantasies for nearly six months now. He is amazed at the old man's imagination: Djinn, amulets, global conspiracies! Shane never questions the stories that Leo spins; in fact, he enjoys listening to them. As far as he is concerned everyone in the slammer seems to be a bullshitter so he might as well listen to good bullshit. Not that he thinks it is all bullshit; he knows Leo genuinely believes what he is saying, but by the fact he is here at all it's clear he's had some sort of breakdown and lost his grip on reality. Shane knows that the bit about working for the Pope is true. He is also aware that Leo was a very intelligent man, who spoke several languages and was some sort of maths genius, although surprisingly not too good at chess. But the stories were definitely becoming more far-fetched.

"We should write this all down in a book," says Shane. "Get it published and make a few bob."

The otherwise perfectly sane Leo loses it. "Are you fucking crazy?" Leo screams at Shane, jumping out of his chair and accidently throwing the table over, chess pieces spilling all over the room. Shane leaped up, startled by the old man's sudden wrath.

"Wow, hold on there, bald eagle! I was just joshing with you. Fucking hell, calm down."

The guards walk over but Shane waves them away as he tries to calm Leo.

"Don't panic, just a little misunderstanding."

The two guards nod, leaving the men to sort out their dispute. Leo sits timidly as Shane picks up the chess pieces.

"I know you think these are the ramblings of a madman," says Leo. "But one day, probably soon, you will know what I say is true. I pray that it will not be too late for you when your eyes finally open."

"I don't think you're mad, old man, well, I didn't until this little sissy fit, but look, I'm sorry, I wouldn't purposely offend you."

Leo accepts the apology and offers his own. He is truly sorry and knows it is a lot to ask of Shane to believe these outlandish accounts without the evidence he had seen first-hand. He is aware that Shane is just humouring him, too polite to tell him that he is a mental case. However, Shane does listen and can repeat every event Leo describes. This is the best Leo can expect for now at least when the time comes he will have some idea. That is, once he recovers from the shock that it is all true.

Shane decides he must be more considerate with what he says. He likes the old man and doesn't want to upset him. Anyway, who knows, it might all be true... He thinks for a minute then makes a note to himself: *You got to start hanging out with some other dudes.*

But he didn't. Instead he began asking questions. If he was going to listen to the old man he might as well test him.

"How is it that these Djinn guys live all these years? I mean you're talking thousands of years in human form? They got to have a face like Keith Richards' ball sack, if you know what I mean. All fucking wrinkles and that!"
Shane laughs at his own joke in a juvenile display, his shoulders bouncing involuntarily as he holds his side.

Leo ignores his childish giggles. "They possess different human bodies. The Djinn may seem magical but really it is just advanced science. They are sentient beings with no carbon form so to live among us they take over a male body...."

"Does it have to be male? I've always wondered what it would be like to be a woman for a day. Imagine the possibilities!"

"They choose males because men can sire more children in a lifetime than a woman can give birth to."

"Why are they bothered about having children?"

Leo rubs his face. "It appears that part of the game is to spread their DNA as far as possible. If you carry Djinn DNA in your bloodline then they have a certain amount of power over you."

"So they just fuck all our women, spread their seed and rule our minds? That's how they win this game? Jesus!"

Leo smiles at how Shane simplifies things. "Yes, in a nutshell that seems to be it. And the boys need to be pre-teen, between ten and thirteen."

"Really?" says Shane. "Because that is starting to sound a bit dodgy."

"Not really. Simeon told me this is because the Djinn life-form is contained in the pineal gland of the body it possesses. Apparently this is where the human connection to the metaphysical life force resides. Under ten they would be too immature to retain the Djinn memories and over thirteen they enter puberty, which causes certain changes in the gland, such as calcification, making it inhospitable."

"Yeah, nobody wants to live in a lime scaled house. So then what happens?"

"The Djinn will keep the body until it gets too old or becomes ill or perhaps they just get bored of it, then they simply transfer to another. Simeon says it is actually rather a complicated procedure, one he couldn't really explain to me. Strangely, though, he did tell me that the rules specify that the body must be offered by the child's parents."

"Why on earth would someone offer up their kid?"

"The Djinn have recruited many human followers over the years by offering fortune, fame or whatever they desire in return for service and sometimes their own children. Simeon said I would be surprised how little a price some humans put on their own kin. This is what he believes lead men to coin the phrase 'selling your soul'. Some followers are deluded and believe they are following a higher being, but most are just greedy."

"No decent father would sell his child," says Shane, moving his rook.

Leo is happy Shane is showing so much interest, even if he knows most of it is feigned.

"Checkmate," says Shane.

Leo shakes his head; he barely gets going in their chess games nowadays.

As Shane leaves the table, Leo notices that a couple of new inmates have joined the wing today. One is a small white male who seems very effeminate, the second is a large well-built black man who sports the long full beard that can be associated with Islam. Leo knows he is paranoid but any new inmate could be a plant from the Djinn to complete the task Errol and Bird had started. Who better to kill a Jew than a Muslim? Leo calls Johnny-No-Legs over to enquire about the new guy. No-Legs looks at him in disbelief.

"That's Robert Price. The media call him 'Al Qaeda Bob', don't you read the papers?"

Leo reads papers from back to front, just not the sort of papers that give people titles like "Al Qaeda Bob".

"What's he in for?" asks Leo.

"He's the guy that was out in Syria training with the ragheads. He was arrested getting off a plane, they say he was plotting a terrorist attack over here."

That wasn't exactly true: No-Legs had merely read the headline and filled the rest in himself. Robert Price, aka Al Qaeda Bob, was born in Coventry, England. He grew up on the Painter's Corner council estate. Robert was pretty much like every other British kid on the estate, in and out of trouble but nothing too serious.

When the a family called Mustapha's arrived they were the first Muslims on the estate and were often taunted and called "Pakis" as they walked down the street. Robert was as guilty as anyone else in not being very welcoming. Robert never steeped to the depths others did but he did join in the laughter when jokes were made. Then his life and views changed.

He wasn't even aware of the eldest daughter, Rain, until she turned up at his secondary school. Rain was special. Although she wore the traditional headscarf associated with Muslim girls, she never acted as Robert imagined Muslim girls did, or in fact any other girl. Rain played football, she was funny, and, boy, was she pretty. Robert expected a lot of ribbing from his friends when he began dating her but to his surprise they all seemed happy for him and probably a little jealous.

Soon Rain was accepted among many on the estate and it followed that so was her family. The main problem for their relationship was their parents. Rain's father was not a strict Muslim but he did attend the mosque and she feared he may insist that she stop seeing the non-Muslim black boy. Robert's mother was of West Indian descent and was a strict evangelist who attended Mass at least three times a week. She had nothing against any other religion but hoped her boy would meet a nice Christian girl. However, after a few months of grief, both sets of parents relented and accepted the couple. Rain never tried to persuade Robert to convert to Islam but after three years together he asked her to marry him and volunteered to convert, suggesting it might soften the blow for her family. Robert's mum had passed away so there was nobody to upset at his end. Personally he was not at all religious but he was respectful of Mr and Mrs Mustapha, Rain's parents. So when he took the decision to convert he studied at the mosque and learned as much as possible about the Quran. Still, he would have to admit, it was his undying love for Rain that motivated his worship and not his belief in either Allah or Muhammad.

Everything was great. Rain fell pregnant within a year of the couple's marriage and Robert had found full-time employment driving buses. A very normal life.

Soon after they announced the news of Rain's pregnancy Mr and Mrs Mustapha asked her to come with them and visit her grandparents in Algeria before she became tied to a family in the UK. Robert had heard his wife mention disruption back home in Algeria but he wasn't really aware that the country was at the peak of the worst civil conflict in recent history.

Regardless of this, the Mustapha's travelled home to visit their relatives in Rias, a small village outside Algiers. On the second day they were away Robert tried to call his wife but was not too disappointed when she didn't answer. She had warned him that her village had barely entered the twentieth century so not to expect technology to work there.

The ITN news never actually mentioned the Rias massacre. The first Robert heard about it was when Imam Shahid from the mosque called at the door.

"As salamu alaykum," Imam Shahid greeted him.

Robert hated trying to speak any Arabic, even this simple greeting. "Eh, Alaykum err s-salam," he replied, hoping it didn't sound too wrong.

"May I come in?" asked Shahid.

"Yes, yes, of course. I'm sorry about the mess. My wife is away this week in Algeria."

Robert showed the Imam into the house, worried that he had been reported for not fasting last Ramadan or the times he may have had an alcoholic tipple.

"Hussein and Ariadne have also gone," he added trying to make small talk. "They have gone to have our baby blessed by the village elders back in Algeria. It's tradition apparently."

People of authority had always made Robert nervous and he realised he was babbling.

"I know," replied the Imam, his tone very sombre. All of a sudden Robert realised this was far more than a pep talk on how to be a good Muslim.

The Imam continued. "I am so sorry to be the bearer of such tragic news." He paused as Robert sat down. "A terrible thing has happened."

The Imam held his hands as if to pray and he averted his gaze, then reluctantly re-engaged. His brows furrowed as he bit his bottom lip, preparing to pass on the grave news. Robert's stomach turned. He somehow knew whatever came out of this man's mouth next would change his life forever. He wanted to stop him from saying anything.

"Last night armed gunmen raided the village that the Mustapha's visited. We have been informed that Mr and Mrs Mustapha were killed."

"What about Rain? My wife?"

For what seemed like a lifetime Mr Shahid looked down at the coffee table. Eventually he looked back up. "It seems the leader of the raid told the others to round up all the pretty women and then shoot everyone else."

Robert didn't have to ask why they would round up all the pretty women. The breath caught in his chest and he began to weep. His beautiful wife, they would abuse her, they would force her to do things.

"Oh my god, our baby is inside her," he cried out, rocking and holding his head. "Who has done this? Who are these men?"

The massacre of Rias village happened in August 1997. Robert would not find the answer to his question until the twelfth of July 2002.

Immediately after the tragedy that befell Robert and his family, he tried to fly out to Algeria. Obtaining a visa was very difficult; the bloody civil war meant the government strongly advised against UK citizens travelling to the North African state. By the time he arrived, the funeral of his in-laws had already taken place. He tried to find out what he could about the raid. Over eight hundred people were slaughtered from a village, whose population had been barely a thousand. Most of the survivors had packed up and left.

He managed to speak to two men who witnessed the horrific event. It seemed they had totally different views of what happened. Tariq, a goat herder, watched from a hideout on the hills as what he called Islamic fundamentalists killed the villagers. He overheard the killers telling the villagers it was their punishment for not sending food to the GIA, an anti-government Islamic revolutionary army. But Malik, an old Imam who survived a bullet that entered the roof of his mouth but stopped short of his brain, told Robert that as he lay down pretending to be dead he saw the men remove their garbs to reveal government troop uniforms underneath.

But that was as far as he got. The task of finding his wife was near impossible. He could neither speak Arabic nor French and as a Black English man he was on a par with cancer in the popularity stakes. The only place he could have expected any help was her village, which was now decimated and the authorities couldn't have been less helpful.

In one of the most sensitive and volatile places in the world he was going round like a bull in a china shop. Frustrated at the lack of help from the police or soldiers at the nearby army camp, he would end up hurling abuse at the unhelpful officers. He was trying to hold it together but the fear of never seeing Rain again was driving him insane. He was changing. His regard for his own safety was diminishing rapidly and he couldn't do anything about it. Luckily the locals didn't really understand much of what he said. On the other hand, certain words had entered international tongue and were understood by anyone who had watched a Scorsese movie, so when he called the commanding officer of the barracks "a motherfucker", he found himself at the wrong end of a rifle butt and had to stagger home bleeding heavily.

Robert had been in Algeria for four weeks staying in a town called Larbaa near Rain's village. Life was cheap in this region and no one was looking out for him. Many locals had begun to place bets on how long the 'big Negro would last.

He wasn't stupid, he knew his life was in danger here, but fear was a thing of the past. He simply would not leave until he either found his wife or he found the people who took her. These thoughts constantly raced around his head, knowing that the longer he searched the less chance there was of finding her alive. Desperation was driving him to act recklessly. As time passed he knew his time was coming to a close. The local police had had enough of his accusations. The leaders of the rebel forces had heard how he was telling anyone who understood English that they were a bunch of rapist cowards and the local drug smugglers were tired of his outbursts bringing attention to this small town where tons of South American drugs were stored ready to flood the Spanish and Italian markets.

When a local villager witnessed him being bundled into the back of an old Volkswagen campervan by three masked men, he ran to the local coffee house to collect his winnings.

Not that Robert had gone quietly into that campervan. He fought tooth and nail with his abductors, throwing one against the door of the van and taking hold of the second man's face so he could gauge his eye out. Only the sound of a gun cocking and the feel of the barrel pushed hard against his back calmed his resistance.

Reluctantly he let them pull a hood over his head and force him into the VW. He attempted to sit up straight, saying nothing as his abductors pulled a string to tighten the sack over his head and tied his hands together.

A sharp instrument was pushed into his throat and the guttural shouting from one of his attackers made Robert realise that the one whose eye he had popped moments before wanted to kill him there and then. A thump to the side of the head dazed him slightly but it was the blow to his abdomen which left him reeling and gasping for breath.

He fell to the floor of the vehicle as kicks rained in around his head. Unable to protect himself he gritted his teeth and embraced the pain, promising himself he wouldn't die, not today. "I must survive until I find my wife."

He heard more shouts as if they were arguing between themselves and struggled upright again. They drove off at a relatively fast speed. The panic in their high-pitched voices led Robert to believe that these were young men and not experienced kidnappers. They drove for an hour or so before pulling up. They spoke to him in a mixture of French and Arabic. With his hands still bound and the sack over his head he stumbled out of the van and felt the heat from the midday sun. Half expecting another blow, he tensed his body. One assailant grabbed his arm, pulling him to his knees. Robert began to pray, not from fear but from desperation. Waiting for the sound of gunfire, expecting to be executed any second, he asked Allah to save him so that he could find his wife or revenge her death.

The sack was removed. Robert's eyes burned as the sun's glare hit them. When eventually he could see, he looked around. A man dressed in the robes of a nomad with a large white turban stood in front of him. They were in a desert wilderness. Robert looked him in the eye.

"What do you want of me?" he growled.

The man replied in perfect English, a hint of Oxbridge to the accent. "You are causing quite a stir in Larbaa, my friend. Lots of people are not happy to have you around."

Robert's eyes showed no fear. The man looked impressed.

"Someone murdered my family. They took my pregnant wife. I will not leave here until I find out who. Now, you can kill me if you want but I will haunt that fucking town and I will haunt you, your kids and their kids."

He turned and looked at the young men who had brought him here. "And I'll fucking haunt you little cunts as well," he screamed, veins exploding out of his temples, his eyes popping out of his head.

He meant every word. The men cowered.

"My name is Abu Abdallal," said the well-spoken man. "I am not going to kill you. I am going to help you."

Abu dismissed the three stooges, cut the ropes from Robert's hands and invited him to follow as he walked. They were in a desert and, although not sad to see the men drive off in the wreck of a van, Robert did wonder how he would get out of there. The man led him to a small mound of rocks where a fire burned and a small animal was roasting. Two large cushions were placed nearby and a woman dressed in a hijab appeared from behind a dune carrying water jugs. The woman bowed to the robed man and poured two cups of water, giving one to Robert and the other to Abu. It was all very serene.

"Are you familiar with the proverb: the enemy of mine enemy is my friend?" asked Abu.

Robert looked at the white-robed man carefully. "I've heard it. It's from *The Godfather* or something like that, isn't it?"

Abu laughed. "No its not from the Godfather, but where it's from is not important. What it means is that we – me and you – are friends because we have a common enemy. The men that attacked the village are traitors. They have sold their souls to the devil."

Robert's heart leaped. Did this man really know who did it?

"They call themselves rebels and Islamic warriors but they have long since allowed this corrupt government and its Western allies to infiltrate and use them. I am their enemy. I have created a new rebel force, one that will operate with our brothers throughout the Muslim world, one that will infiltrate our enemy's strongholds. I tell you with grief in my heart that I cannot rescue your wife; my sources have confirmed she is already dead. Murdered." Abu bowed his head in a respectful pause before he continued. "I promise you this. I will one day stand next to you as judgement is passed on the men that are responsible and you shall have your justice."

Tears streamed down Robert's face as he finally accepted his beautiful wife's fate. Abu knew the right words to comfort his new prodigy.

"They will pay, rest assured that we will make them."

Hours later Robert and Abu extinguished the fire with a plan hatched. One that would lead to Robert operating as a covert sleeper in the UK, helping to recruit Jihadists from young British Muslims. He would keep his Western name so as not to draw attention to himself. Thanks to Abu and his organisation he would eventually discover the man who ordered the massacre of the village and the kidnapping of his wife: a high-ranking officer in the Algerian armed forces.

In July 2002, five years after this meeting, Robert presided over a kangaroo court in an Afghanistan cave with this officer and three other captured men. He found them all guilty. With encouragement one of the men finally confessed to being involved in the gang rape of a pregnant villager who was visiting from England. He explained that she died in the back of a van after she miscarried during the rape. Robert felt neither shame nor glory regarding what followed next. As promised Abu was in attendance at the cave. Robert was fiercely loyal to his mentor by this stage and he appreciated the unwavering determination with which Abu had helped him track down the men who had inadvertently changed his life forever. Abu had also guided Robert on what punishment he must carry out.

"Respect can only grow where fear is installed," he said. "You must let the world know that no mercy will be shown to those who harm us or betray us. These men have done both and should pay for both."

Robert carried out the sentence himself. The cave they were in doubled as a place of execution. Of course the four condemned men all protested and pleaded on hearing the death sentence being passed on them but after witnessing the first execution all they could do was whimper and cry.

Robert chose Ahmeed Rassam, the captain during the raids on Rias, to be the first to die. Two mujahedeen soldiers removed his robes and dragged his naked body to the hard stone floor. The captain begged forgiveness between prayers to Allah.

Robert was not concerned that he lacked the technical skill to carry out the penalty: it hardly mattered in the end, the man's fate was sealed. One of the guards roughly pulled at Ahmeed's genitals as the second tied a length of binding string around the base, so as to give space from the pubic bone. Even with both hands and feet tied the two strong soldiers struggled to hold Ahmeed when he saw Abu hand Robert a blade and flat stone. Every fibre in the man's body spasmed and like an eel he thrashed about in a hopeless attempt to get free. Eventually his energy was spent and with a last minute panic he forced his face to the floor and shuffled to Abu's feet, kissing them as he begged for his life. Abu pulled him back to his knees and fixed him with a stare, which calmed the man. The other condemned men watched Robert tuck the stone under the separated genitals and as Ahmeed's high-pitched squeal rang out he chopped down on to the target.

His first hit was not accurate and he only severed the end of his penis. One of the watching soldiers laughed, one of the prisoners gagged. Robert brought the blade down once more, this time hitting all the genitals. The cut was not clean, the parts hung from his body, held there by sinew and skin. The captain witnessed his own castration before passing out. A soldier threw freezing water over his head to wake him so that Robert could take the blade to his throat and began hacking and sawing his head off. The process took over ninety seconds. The blade was purposely old and blunt so Robert had to rely on his weight and strength. Gurgled screams rang out from the three remaining men and Robert repeated the sentence on each one, driven by the anger and pain he had kept close for the last five years. He showed no mercy.

The cave was a blood bath and Robert was drenched. When the last connecting tissue was severed from the final man's neck, the deed was complete. Robert looked to Abu, dropping the blood-covered blade. It was only later that he remembered a small black man in Western clothes standing next to Abu, who seemed to be calmly eating boiled sweets from a paper bag throughout the entire event. Too much was going on to worry about such a strange anomaly. But some years later Robert met this man again when Abu requested he meet with an important associate, a trusted man. This small young black man would change Robert's world view for a second time.

At the meeting Robert was recruited to be involved in a plot where he needed to purposely get caught carrying anti-West propaganda into England from Pakistan; this was the first part of his mission. His cry of loyalty to Al Qaeda and his refusal to recognise the UK courts resulted in the tabloids labelling him "Al Qaeda Bob". He was sentenced to six years.

When the authorities offered to put him on a protected wing in case he was attacked by hostile prisoners, he refused. He managed to get himself transferred from four prisons in his first three months for various reasons. Finally he ended up here in Stoke Prison and on his first day he knows he is in the right place when he sees the man he was sent there to kill.

Jinn City, 2146

"A lie can travel half way round the world while the truth is

Putting its shoes on." Anonymous

"But I don't understand? How it can be for me? It must be some kind of mistake."

Ember is examining the package that Raphael has pushed towards her. She looks to him for an explanation.

Raphael gives her a sympathetic smile. "It's true. Jones was a common name from Celtic descent and admittedly a popular name in that culture for centuries but it is not a name that survived the Tribulation and September is very rare. Put them together and it's unique to you."

"What? You're saying I'm the only September Jones on the planet?"

"You are the person who this package is for, trust me," confirms Raphael.

"Raphael?" Adam interrupts, sounding annoyed. "What are you talking about Ember is just a friend I brought to meet my family she has nothing to do with the anti-host, that's crazy"

Raphael drops his head momentarily. He knows he must explain things to Adam but there are more urgent things to address.

"Adam, I'm sorry, you deserve an explanation but first, Miss Jones, the disc. I believe it contains a very important message for you. A message that you will be tasked with spreading amongst all the people of the world. A message that will bring down the Aryan overlords and the abomination that calls himself the Host."

There's an awkward silence before Ember raises one eyebrow and gives him a look of defiance, showing her young age. She is fighting the urge to either laugh in his face or punch him out. Her feelings of excitement at meeting Raphael have gone through uncertainty and out the other side into definite unease. Adam is still looking confused and hurt but Ember is not some easily duped Midtowner. She is the daughter of the second-highest ranking Overlord in Jinn City. Ember has overheard Council meetings at her home where they've discussed a revolutionary group known as the Sons of Verdi. The High Priestess Solfrid herself has called them terrorists and warned they must be hunted down before they cause chaos in the city. Well, this Raphael is obviously a sympathiser, or more likely a member. She decides she wants no part of this.

"Am I allowed to leave?" she asks, with her head held high and she tries to show no fear.

Raphael looks perplexed. "But, but… what about the disc? You must watch the disc. I've been waiting so long…"

"Here, you watch it. I give it to you." Ember pushes the disc back to Raphael. "Now can I leave?" She looks from Raphael to Adam. Adam's face reflects the anger he is trying to control. She knows this is not aimed at her but the whole situation is making her feel increasingly anxious.

Raphael looks desperate. He opens his mouth to attempt to sway her but Adam speaks first.

"Well, can we leave or are you kidnapping us?"

Raphael's body tenses, his hands opening defensively showing his hurt at the accusation.

"No, no, of course you are free to leave. I am sorry. In my eagerness I have gone about this all wrong. I see I have frightened you. You are not my prisoners and you may leave whenever you want. I will be here, I will keep the disc. You can come back whenever you want to see it, okay?" He turns to Adam. "Please, if you escort Miss Jones home, I will meet with you later to explain."

Adam says nothing but takes Ember's arm and the two youths quickly leave the room.

"Oh my god! That was well on top, wasn't it?" Ember's statement is followed by a nervous giggle.

The two friends are making their way back out through the labyrinth of corridors and stairways that run through the old warehouse, the tension finally releasing from their bodies at the prospect of going home.

"I'm so sorry, Ember," Adam says. "He is not normally like that, I know he is weird but all that stuff about the disc and bringing down the Aryans… I didn't have a clue, honest, Ill speak to him later….sorry"

111

Ember is just relieved to be getting out of there. "And what does 'holy moly' even mean?" she laughs trying to lighten the mood, Adam finally smiles. The sun has gone down and they exit the warehouse into a now dimly lit alleyway.

"Where is this place anyway?" asks Ember, putting on a brave face.

"It's just wasteland," Adam says regarding the pretty run-down part of town; most of the buildings seem derelict and Ember takes Adam's arm as a feeling of impending danger surfaces between them. A startling noise in the distance doesn't help.

"Let's hurry," says Ember.

"Yes. It's this way to the station." Adam has not been around here before at night and the whole area seems to have taken on a sinister identity. Ember convinces herself that they are being paranoid and tries to think of something to talk about to relieve the tension but the only thing she can think about is Raphael.

"This might sound strange but did you notice anything weird about Raphael tonight?"

"Weird? Are you kidding me?" Adam feigns disbelief at Ember's question.

Ember laughs and shakes her head. She'd been thinking about the snake shaped swirl she'd seen over Raphael's head and now, come to think if it, she'd be the one sounding weird if she brought it up. She searches her mind for a more light-hearted conversation, then smiles as it comes to her.

"So... you were rudely asking me if I'd ever had sex before Raphael showed up earlier and I didn't get a chance to answer." She grins mischievously, looking to the floor then raising her head, clearly ready to tell all.

Adam feels nervous for some reason, waiting for her answer. He realises he wants her to say no, she's never been touched, not that it should matter. Ember's mouth opens but she stops; all of a sudden her face is fearful. Adam frowns then follows her gaze behind him. A group of men are running towards them, barely two hundred metres away. The bouncing lights of their torches indicate there are at least ten of them.

Ember is gripped with fear. She recognises the uniforms of the Protection Squadron who are notorious for treating any non-Aryans as shit on their boots to enforce "justice" on the streets. They will not go easy on Adam; she must let them know he is with her.

"Put your hands in the air. Do not move," calls out a young squadron officer, raising a very real gun at them.

Adam obeys immediately, his raised hands shaking. The officer sneers at him and then looks at Ember whose arms are not raised. Instead she tries to explain.

"I'm Em..."

The officer swipes at her with a leather strap. "Put your fucking hands in the air, I said!"

Ember stumbles, more from shock than due to the force of the blow. She raises her hands with rebellion, her mind playing out the punishment her father will dish out to this pig. The rest of the troop surround the two shell-shocked teenagers as a higher-ranking officer walks to the front, facing Adam and Ember.

"What are you doing here?" asks Captain Peter Cameron, his question directed to Adam.

Adam, reluctant to mention Raphael, makes up a poor story.

"We were just exploring the old buildings," he explains. "My friend here, Ember Jones, has not been to this sector before so I was showing her around." Adam desperately hopes someone will soon recognise Ember, apologise, put their guns away and beg her not to tell her daddy.

Captain Cameron turns to Ember. "And you, Miss Jones, why are you here? I assume your father has no knowledge of your whereabouts?"

Knowing the captain recognises her, she lowers her hands and lays into her inquisitor.

"I tell you what I'm doing, I am finding out for my father how the PS behaves when it is outside the Aryan section!" She walks over to the officer who struck her and takes a note of his number. "I will have a lot to tell him."

The sound of laughing disturbs her and a small, fat Aryan woman appears from the shadows. She is dressed well but has exceedingly thin hair that you might even call balding, tiny, discoloured teeth and an upturned nose. She is instantly recognisable and Adam curses under his breath. Ember also recognises the woman: her curse is not so subtle.

"Ember Jones!" the woman trills. "Your behaviour and language is beneath you."

Freya Mortensson is one of the most prominent members of the High Council. She is the high commander of the PS and feared by even the most powerful Aryan lords.

"Apologies, Madame Mortensson," Ember backtracks. "I was startled." Freya looks her up and down and then looks to Adam. Ember is confused by Freya's manner. She has met her many times; in fact, only recently Ember and her father dined at Freya's house.

"Where is the man known as Raphael?" Freya asks Adam.
Adam looks to Ember for help. He is not sure if he wants to say anything but he knows if the "pig" woman, as his people call her, is involved this is serious. His thoughts race as he tries to keep his composure.

"Who?" he says unconvincingly.
The sudden and instant scream of pain that leaves Adam's mouth shocks Ember so much she jumps and stumbles. Her gaze is directed to the glowing chip in the back of Adam's wrist and the swelling that has sprung up around it. At first she wonders what has happened, then she notices the CF controller in Freya's hand; she must have released the pulse.

"Stop it, you will kill him!" Ember cries. "The guy, Raphael, is back there through that alley in the old run-down house."

Freya orders most of the officers to search the area as she taps the screen on her handheld control pad. Adam collapses, almost lifeless. Ember tries to go to his aid but Freya grabs her arm.

"He will be fine," she tuts. "I only dispensed a tiny dose. Now, little miss perfect, come show me exactly where this 'Raphael' is and on the way you can explain what a High Aryan's daughter is doing in the company of a traitor."

As Freya manhandles Ember along with surprising strength she turns to the only officer remaining.

"Take this piece of filth to the favelas gaol. Let him stew in there for a while."

"Leave him alone, he hasn't done anything! The crazy man, Raphael, he tricked us into coming here," Ember says in horror as she watches Adam being marched away. "We didn't know about any disc."

Freya suddenly goes very still. "Disc? Did you say 'disc'?"

Ember didn't think things could have got worse. But they did.

Freya's eyes bulge and she screams at the top of her voice, "Did you just say 'disc'?"

Any pretence of bravery is ebbing away; this is not good. Ember tries fighting back her tears. As much as she tried to act grown-up there was no denying that she was still very young, and never before had she been treated in this way.

"He... he had a disc he wanted to show us but we left."

Freya shouts down the street. "Bring the boy back! Ellis! Bring the boy to me!"

Adam is staggering pathetically as the officer curses and rants at his inability to control his body and turn it back around. Eventually he drags him, scraping his knees along the hard concrete. The pain Adam feels is momentarily forgotten due to the great relief at not going to the favela's gaol; however, this is crushed when he realises Ember must have mentioned the disc. People have been executed for having tiny old newspaper clippings about Shane Mills and now they were connected to a disc that may have a message from the man himself on it.

By the time they reach the back room, Raphael has already been restrained by the guards Freya had sent ahead. The officer dragging Adam's sorry form is coming up behind them.

"Target apprehended, Ma-am," says the pompous Captain Cameron. "Thank you, Captain. Well done. Now while we are waiting for the young man to join us, I believe you have a disc recording of some sort for me?"

Ember feels guilty as Raphael glances at her sadly. Freya sighs and pulls out a gun and puts it to Ember's head in an effort to persuade him.

"You would shoot an innocent girl, one of your own…" remarks Raphael, more as a statement than a question.

"I would. Now the disc, hand it over." Freya holds out her free hand.
Slowly, Raphael reaches inside his drape jacket and pulls out a brown package. He hands it to her. All the officers look on curiously as Freya reads out loud: "*For the attention of September Jones.*"

She visibly gulps when she sees the faded signature: *Shane Mills.* The officers huddle to get a look but Freya pushes them back with a stern stare. A very groggy Adam is then pushed into the room; he falls near Ember and she instinctively tries to help him up as Freya wanders around the room, but his toxin-riddled body is non-responsive.

"What is this bullshit?" she says, looking first to Raphael then to Ember. Ember tries to plead her innocence but Raphael interrupts.

"Those are the words of Shane Mills. It is the message that will free the people from tyranny and slavery, bringing down the Fourth Reich and freeing the world from sick bitches, like you."

Freya gently places the disc inside her tight-fitting military jacket and then, like a giant, fat toddler, she throws a tantrum, smashing the antique TV set and kicking the Blu-ray box across the room. She pulls her gun back out, walks up to Raphael and squishes the barrel hard into his cheek.

"You are going to die. You do know that, don't you?"
While Ember is so scared she's worried she might soil herself Raphael merely laughs. "You probably can't even squeeze the trigger with your fat piggy trotters!"
Ember's breathe catches in her chest. Raphael just laughs louder and makes a pig's snorting noise

Embers instinctive blink means she misses the exact moment Raphael's head explodes and his brains splatter against the back wall like some morbid art but she can feel the wet slime of bits of skull and grey matter sliding down her cheek. Losing control of the contents of her stomach she violently vomits. Adam is helpless on the floor as he tries in vain to avert his gaze from the bloody mess that is a hole in Raphael's head. Freya stands over his dead body, calmly wiping blood from her tunic.

"Let me explain what happened here, Captain," she says. "We followed the fugitive known as Raphael into an abandoned house after reports that he and his accomplice had kidnapped the Procurator's daughter. The kidnappers opened fire, we returned fire." She looks at Adam then walks over to Ember, still recovering from her sickness. She lifts the shaking girl's head by the chin before speaking directly into her face, close enough for Ember to smell the rancid breath exhaling from her foul mouth. "Tragically we were too late to save her. The criminals had cut the poor girl's throat before doing who knows what to her," Freya smiles before adding. "They also bashed the girl's pretty little face in before killing her."

Ember blinks rapidly, desperately trying not to weep. *This cannot be happening,* she thinks.
Freya turns back to her captain. "I will let you decide if she was raped during the kidnapping." Adam stiffens and Ember feels a cold clench of raw fear strike her insides. The captain looks momentarily bemused. Maybe he is disgusted by the old bitch's intentions and will come to her rescue? Any hope fades as his face settles and he starts to undo the buckle on his trousers.

"Oh yes, it would be rude not to," he says, looking Ember up and down.

"Well, I have better things to do than watch you violate a young virgin." She looks at Ember with distaste. "You are a virgin, I hope? I don't want my boys catching any nasty diseases."

Ember can barely speak but she manages a weak, "Please don't do this." Tears are streaming down her face now. "Please, my dad..."

"Oh, do shut up. I am doing you a favour. I mean, you don't want to die a virgin, do you?" A nasal laugh snorts out from Freya. "Now boys, I have to go. Have fun and clean up after yourselves." She hands the captain a grenade. "Oh, and it looks like one of the kidnappers had a grenade and before we could stop him he blew everything up."
A genuine smile spreads across the captain's face. "Yes, Ma-am."

Freya leaves and the officers all look to their captain. A particularly young man, probably a new recruit not used to their ways, says, "Sir, are we really going to do this?"

The others mock him. A tall, thin officer nearest to Ember pulls her roughly towards him, "Fucking right, we are, kid." He licks her face.

Ember is trembling, all her strength dissolving in fear of what is about to happen and her inability to stop it. She struggles to breathe as a panic attack takes hold.

"Sweet little virgin pussy," the officer adds, pushing his hand down and forcing it roughly between her legs. She suddenly recovers her senses and bites down hard on his exposed cheek. In reflex he lets go of her and she uses all of her tiny frame to push him away. The other men all laugh at his discomfort.

"You fucking little whore, I will rip your cunt apart for that!" He hurriedly undoes the buttons on his trousers to reveal a semi-flaccid penis, aggressively playing with it to make it harder quicker. With the situation quickly deteriorating Ember's bravery fails her and she starts to go into shock. The captain appears, pulling the panting man away, but any hope this gives Ember is short-lived.

"I believe the highest-ranking officer goes first," says the captain. "The rest of you can strip over there. First one ready can follow me. I'll break her in for you all."

The captain pulls out his gun and Ember can't even cry any more, her mind falling into a sort of horrified trance. The other officers' frantically undress, racing to be next; no one wants to be last and fuck a corpse. As the severity of what is about to happen overwhelms her, Ember crumbles to the floor, just a little girl who wants her daddy.

Adam still struggles on the floor. He has been trying to sum up the strength and courage, looking to somehow protect Ember but what could he possibly do? He can barely lift his body and there are more of them and they have guns. It is utterly pointless.

Regardless, Adam uses a surge of effort to get to his feet and stand between Ember and the captain.

"Leave her alone, you bastards!" he cries out.

He sways and his legs buckle as he attempts to throw a punch before crashing back to the floor. "Poor Adam," thinks Ember, all their hopes for a better world being brutally crushed. She sees the captain's face; a rough-looking beard covers it, his teeth are stained from tobacco and a scar runs from his eye to his neck. Ember's disconnected mind wanders. She is a virgin, she has never even kissed a boy, and now the only touch she will ever know will be the sick perversion these men are about to commit. She knows what awaits her but she decides she will take control. She would rather take her own life.

Ember looks around. There are small shards of glass left over from Freya's tantrum. She makes a mad grab for the nearest but the sweaty hand of the captain catches her first. She is lifted from the floor like a rag doll and forced into the corner of the room. The captain presses her tight into the corner and nuzzles into her neck. Ember turns her head in pure distress, waiting for the gross act to begin. The man brings his mouth to her ear, his hot breath coating her as he says, "Don't worry."

Ember can see something else now: a cloud-like swirl of colours forming a snake sits upon this man's shoulders. He gives her a brief nod before turning his back to her, shielding her from the others who are in various stages of undress, slobbering with anticipation. Those ready and waiting watch him, a little bemused as he raises his firearm, pointing it right at them.

There's a burst of gunfire and the men's bodies dance as they are peppered with bullets. Their faces have little time to show the fear and confusion they feel as their trusted captain slaughters them. Ember looks over his shoulder mystified. The captain stops firing once he is certain all the guards are dead. He walks over to them to make sure, then walks to the prostrate body of Raphael. To Ember's utter bewilderment he strips Raphael's body of his blue Teddy boy jacket. He inspects it, frowning at the spots of blood before putting it on. He then walks to a drawer and pulls out another small disc and places it in the inside pocket. He looks down at the two stupefied children.

"Holy moly! That was some buzz. Come on kids, we have to go."

Acre 1270 AD

"We have enough religion to make us hate but not enough to make us love each other" Jonathan Swift

Six men ride across the barren land that leads to Acre. They are dressed in the garb of Turks and carry the banners of Baybar, the fourth Sultan of Egypt. The lead man in this group is Baybar himself and he is followed by four head tribesmen known as Caliphs and one lowly slave.

A large tent sits in the middle of the wilderness. From the east rides another group of six: one wears the royal armour of the Kingdom of Great Britain, two wear the white surcoat adorned with a red cross as worn by the Knights Templar, two wear plain black robes and the last is conspicuous by his grey large-brimmed hat denoting him as a chaplain.

Standing at the entrance to the tent is a man adorned in a turquoise tunic and purple cape. Inside awaits King Hugh, the king of Jerusalem, and his general. Both groups arrive at the exact same time. A summit is about to take place that will bring an end to the Holy Crusades that have destroyed lives and land in this area for over two hundred years.

First to dismount is Jacques de Malay of the Knights Templar, followed by the Grand Master Thomas Bernard. The two sergeants dressed in black robes hold the horse of Edward, the Prince of Wales, to aid his dismount. They all look over suspiciously at the Arabian contingent.

Baybar waits for the Christians to tie their horses up before he instructs his men to dismount. Prince Edward looks at the Sultan. He is surprised at the blonde hair and blue eyes of this infamous warrior. Baybar returns his stare. He had heard this son of the Western king was a giant. He is tall, but he is no Nephilim.

The turquoise man at the entrance of the tent greets the honoured guests. Baybar and his generals remove their swords and enter the tent.

The slave remains to tie up the horses and then takes out a bag from one of the saddles before settling beside a campfire outside of the tent.

Prince Edward, the two knights and the two sergeants make to follow Baybar into the tent. The elaborately dressed turquoise man welcomes them and, speaking in French, explains that they must leave their weapons at the door. The chaplain waits outside and joins the slave by the campfire as his party disappears inside.

Raphael adjusts his turquoise clothes and closes the heavy drapes sealing inside Hugh, King of Jerusalem, who is hosting this meeting between the Sultan of Egypt, the four Caliphs of the great Muslim empire and the soon-to-be king of England with two of the most influential men in Christendom. This great event will decide which of the two most powerful forces on the planet will gain control of the Holy Land.

It is to be held around the campfire outside of the tent. Raphael throws his cape over his shoulder as he makes his way to the small fire where the slave and the chaplain sit waiting. Raphael sits down cross-legged, turning to the slave first.

"Holy moly Benjamin Ocdar, you're acting as the Sultan's servant? This is a new low for you, at least you were a court guard with Saladin."

"I prefer to call myself an attendant."

The Djinn known as Benjamin has had many guises over his two thousand years on this physical plain. He knows the lowliest slave is the one who has the best access to the highest power.

Reuben Lupas is in the guise of the chaplain, he pulls at his clerical robes, exposing the marks where they irritate his neck.

"This fucking material."

Raphael is amazed that in each incarnation Reuben always looks the same: pale blonde hair, a bony face and almost transparent skin. Why, when he can choose from thousands, does he always favour this appearance?

123

"So, you wish to agree to the Christian retreat from the Holy Land?" starts Raphael.

Reuben looks at the bright-blue Arc Hon, then to his fellow Djinn.

"First," says Reuben. "I wish to have a ruling on these hand canons the savages have 'all of a sudden' discovered."

Benjamin is quick to reply. "Are you accusing me of intervening with technology? That is rich coming from you."

An argument breaks out as the two Djinn vent their grievances to Raphael. Eventually Raphael calls for quiet.

"Do you want the lords and masters inside to hear you?" says Raphael. "Now, we investigated the hand canons and found no reason for action. This man, Baybar, is indeed an exceptional general and has developed new warfare and weaponry all by himself."

Reuben scoffs, but concedes in the end.

"So, on to the surrender," says Raphael. "Are you agreed, Reuben, that continuing is pointless? Benjamin's side has defeated the Christian powers as well as Zeb's Mongols so I think it's only right that you pay the concessions, agreed?"

Reuben looks none too happy. "What is the concession?"

Raphael looks to Benjamin who answers. "Well, there is the pre-agreed reparation of gold but I also wish for a man you have under your influence."

Reuben is outraged. His normally controlled face glows as a vein throbs on his forehead. He knows who the man Ben wants will be.

"Well, tell me, who?" he says stonily.

"Thomas Aquinas." Benjamin smiles when he says this, knowing the upset it will cause Reuben.

Indeed Reuben leaps up and stomps around, kicking over a water bowl. He addresses Raphael while pointing an angry shaking finger at Ben. "He must have used the Almanac! How else could he know about Thomas? I have invested a lot of time in that man, I will not be handing him over to this arse-fucking slave."

Benjamin calmly interrupts. "You say I used the Almanac but I have no access to it. Only the Arc Hon can allow such a thing."

"Then you have forced your will upon one of my brethren using Vril. It's the only other answer," declares Reuben.

"Who was it that entranced the Caesar Constantine?" counters Benjamin. "Who is it that revealed our secret to the Knights Templar and showed them Vril?"

Again Raphael calls for calm but the two rivals are riled now. The occupants of the tent come out to witness the slanging match.

"What about you?" bites back Reuben. "Creating this religion, appearing to the Quraish! You started this fucked-up religion just to wage war on the Christians. You can't tell me you did that without using Vril to inveigle their precious Muhammad?"

Raphael notices the onlookers from the tent. Prince Edward is aghast, Sultan Baybar seems confused. The two Templars look wary.

"Enough!" shouts Raphael. He looks to the delegates and shoos them back into the tent as if they were kids. Then he turns to the two Djinn. "First of all, using Vril to enter a dream is not strictly breaking the rules, it is only a violation when the human is fully conscious, which by the way, we know you did with the Roman, Saul, Reuben, as well as a few others. The Council are concerned about you flouting the rules and what seems to be a perversion for blood! So I recommend you agree to Ben's request and clean up your own act before you start casting these aspersions at your fellow competitors, agreed?" He then turns to Ben. "As for how you discovered the name of Reuben's protégée: we are aware of your alliance with Levi since the sacking of Constantinople. That alone does not break the rules but you know you cannot have influence over any who don't carry your pedigree."

Ben explains, "I don't want influence over Aquinas. I just want to kill him."

Reuben is still raging. "Well, you can fuck off! You say I have a blood lust?"

Raphael is aware that this meeting is going around in circles. He decides to make a ruling.

"Reuben concedes the Holy Land and he will pay the gold tribute. As for Aquinas, he will remain with Reuben for two more years, then he will be sent to Ben. I suggest, for convenience, that Paris is the best place for the transfer. He is not to be killed, only retained. That is my final decision. Now recruit your ambassadors and let's get out of this godforsaken place."

Raphael wipes his brow and wonders why these two ever fought over these barren lands in the first place; they are his least favourite place on the planet. He is also curious as to the high value both Djinn put on this Thomas Aquinas. Still, it is not for him to ask.

The two disgruntled Djinn take their place in the respective cavalcades as Raphael rounds up the dignitaries.
As the groups leave, Hugh, the king of Jerusalem, asks Raphael, "Have you agreed what is to be done?"

"Yes," replies Raphael. "If I were you I would return to Cyprus. The war is won, this land belongs to Islam. I must take my leave."

𓀃𓃰𓏏𓀫𓀃𓏲

Raphael mounts his steed and rides out to the wilderness. He drives his horse as fast as the Arabian stallion can gallop. Out into the distance he can see what he is looking for: a bright light. As he gets closer the light becomes clearer. It is a cascade of blue and white electric bolts crashing against each other, covering a spherical space. The phenomenon emits a large clattering sound as Raphael gets nearer. The animal is stuttering as Raphael holds the reins fast, forcing his horse to ride straight into the electric storm. As they are about to enter, the light grows brighter and the noise louder. Raphael kicks his heels in and they both disappear through the bolts.

As the horse's tail is swallowed, the electric bolts peter out until a spark no bigger than a Chinese firecracker dances around the sand and eventually dies.

The horse and rider appear on the dark terrain of the corona, a neutral zone between the frequencies inhabited by Arc Hon and Djinn. Dark red skies are punctuated by a bright white light setting in the horizon. The beautiful black stallion collapses as soon as he enters this strange world, gasping for air as its very bones crumble and the hide from its back melts away.

Raphael walks away from the remnants of the horse and sits on a marble seat. He looks around uncomfortably as he awaits the arrival of the Council. This place is not his favourite either. Not too different from the Levant, he observes; however, it is a plane that both Djinn and Arc Hon can exist in while still in human form and so is ideal for Council meetings. But it is a soulless place, a land left over from times forgotten even by someone who has lived as long as Raphael. If magic ever really existed, it was here in this nether world that it was spurned. Many times the Arc Hon, and more recently the Djinn, have called upon the corona's unique power to aid the governing of the game, especially the arrival of the thirteen that marked the inception of the quest.

Raphael was not one for hocus pocus but this barren void that contained no living thing, not animal, insect or bacteria, even though it had all the necessary components to sustain life, gave him a sensation he believed was akin to man's emotion of fear. He reflected that perhaps it was that he didn't actually understand what this place was and how it came to be that caused this emotion or perhaps the eerie fact that any living thing that arrives here without the symbolic invite suffered the same fate as his horse did just moments earlier. But he knew what really freaked him out about this place was that even knowing that it was void of life, he always felt he was being watched, and not by a friendly gaze.

A buzzing noise tells him someone else is coming. He can see in the distance a dramatic swirling of a swarm of insects heading towards him at high speed. As the millions of bugs cluster around the seat next to Raphael they transform into a small black male.

Chamuel bows to Raphael who returns the greeting. Neither talk but Chamuel makes an exaggerated gesture of wiping his brow and flicking sweat, which amuses Raphael. Michael arrives next. A huge geyser erupts, spurting hot liquid over the terrain. The liquid rises up and covers the third seat, transforming into their leader, the high Arc Hon.

Each Arc Hon politely bows to the others but still no one speaks. There are still three seats unoccupied in the hexagonal stone courtyard. A wind rises and encircles them as glistening debris whirls at great speed. With a whoosh it stops and two Djinn are revealed. Not from the thirteen who are competing to become the Host of the human world, however, but two of the first to enter the physical plane and gain knowledge of its many alien ways: Solfrid and Baal. This is a rare meeting of the joint councils of the Djinn and the Arc Hon. Raphael is not sure exactly why this one has been called.

The High Arc Hon, Michael, speaks first. "My fellow Arc Hon, Amitiel will not be attending so we can begin."
Solfrid, red haired, blue eyed and ivory skinned, speaks next. "How goes the challenge? Who is in place of the Host?"
They all look to Raphael. "It is not conclusive," he says. "Reuben has lost ground against Benjamin, so too has Zeb. Levi has changed his alliance from Reuben to Ben. Simeon and Isaac have joined together to defeat Asher who has influence on the north and east. Daniel has set up the house of Solomon in Ethiopia and…"
Solfrid taps impatiently. "Yes, yes, but what of the bloodlines? Are they of pedigree, are the Djinn controlling the purity of the bloodlines?"
"Well," says Raphael, "the humans tend to copulate with whatever is about but, yes, there are clear bloodlines with enough pedigree to rule. I only fear for the likes of the southern tribes as their progress is slow."
Michael concludes, "We are happy with things in general. No real violations. Reuben and Naphtali do bend the rules a lot and Gad seems to make little or no impact anywhere. Besides all that though, there is the matter for which we are all gathered."

A picture develops in the centre of the courtyard. All of them recognise Amitiel as she sits in a market square talking to a young man who looks besotted.

"This young man goes by the name of Marco Polo," says Michael. "He has appeared from nowhere and claims to be the son of Nicoli Polo, a man who has no son. His aura shows he is Djinn but we have the locations of the thirteen, so he is not one of them."

Baal and Solfrid exchange a look.

"Am I right in assuming you have called us here while Amitiel keeps surveillance on this man, expecting to prove that one of us has taken this guise?" says the somewhat rotund Baal.

"Actually to disprove it," says Michael. "Now that we are left with no doubt the question remains: who is this Marco Polo? Only you two and the thirteen have entered the physical plane as far as we are all aware. We all know the energy needed to open a new gate and any Djinn crossing over and taking physical form would have to first undergo the metamorphosis here in Gheisthelm. This Marco Polo has already crossed into the land of Zeb's Mongols. We believe he plans to make his way into the Orient and even down through the southern continents. It is like he is mapping the progress of each of the Djinn.

"Why don't we simply enquire of him what he is doing?" asks Baal.

Chamuel responds. "It was only by coincidence that we found him. Levi was with Amitiel in Constantinople when they both sensed the presence.

"Expecting Reuben or Ben to appear, they were both shocked to see this strange young man race around the corner followed by two guards who seemed to be trying to apprehend him. Amitiel has since learned that he is planning a trip around the East with his so-called father. I shall meet with this traveller myself. Incognito, of course. I will get to the bottom of this before he leaves for the East, if we are all agreed?"

Chamuel shrugs as his sign of agreement; Raphael nods then looks to Baal who also nods in agreement, even though his face doesn't show it.

"Excellent. Now if you have no further business I will call the meeting to a close."

Stoke Prison

1913 – President Woodrow Wilson publishes "The New Freedom", a collection of speeches in which he reveals: "Since I entered politics, I have chiefly had men's views confided to me privately. Some of the biggest men in the U.S., in the field of commerce and manufacturing, are afraid of somebody, are afraid of something. They know that there is a power somewhere so organized, so subtle, so watchful, so interlocked, so complete, so pervasive, that they had better not speak above their breath when they speak in condemnation of it."

Shane sits alone, hunched over a letter that he holds loosely in his hand. He contemplates the events that have led him here, in this bastard prison with only the ranting of a madman to keep him amused.

Shane has been avoiding Leo today. Well, not just Leo; he is avoiding everyone. It is exactly a year to the day that his reaction to something left him serving this six-year sentence. He should have known at the time that life was going too well and something was bound to happen to fuck it all up. And something did.

◦🏃🏃🏃🏃

After meeting Sara, Shane had gone from drinking and fighting in the roughest bars in Manchester to attending charity galas, book launches and theatres together with this beautiful, intelligent, and fun young woman. Shane was very happy and very content with his new life. It was like he was finally leading the life he ought to be living. Sara had somehow tapped into another Shane, the little boy who loved looking after his baby sister, who played out for hours with friends from the estate and found so many things funny.

Not only that, but Sara could relate to his grief too. Even though she had been only six at the time she remembers crying so hard she couldn't breathe when her mother died. This beautiful woman who loved her unconditionally had suddenly become poorly. But people usually got better when they got sick and the young Sara always believed that her mummy would soon be up and about again. Unfortunately the monster called cancer did not let her mother get better. Instead it left behind a six-year-old girl, alone and vulnerable with no one even to wipe the tears away. It was her hatred of cancer that drove Sara to study medicine and she hoped she could save every little girl's mummy so that those little girls wouldn't have to grow up with the same sense of loss that Sara had.

Amazingly Sara managed to get Shane to open up about Chloe. He realised that since she'd died he hadn't spoken to a single person about her. Not because he didn't want to but because no one had ever cared enough to ask. There were a lot of tears when he finally let loose his pent-up feelings and again he pondered that he'd never before cried for the person who he'd loved most in the world, not one tear. Somehow this eventual release of emotion seemed to stabilise his mind. The anger and frustration he'd felt all his life slowly diminished and was tucked away in a little corner.

It was replaced by joy, something Shane had not experienced in a long, long time. Although he didn't have any proper qualification, Sara helped him find work in a tattoo parlour owned by a friend. Shane loved exploring his artistic side, a talent that the parlour owner commented on often. "Never seen anyone create art like that one," he would tell his clients.

Soon word got around about the amazing tattoos Shane created. Some people would be dubious when realising it was the nutter who they use to avoid like the plague when out on the town, but after sitting with him as he decorated their bodies they soon found him to be a polite, well-spoken and funny human being. Who would have guessed such a big change could occur in such a short time? Nowadays Shane hardly drank, never took drugs and had not had a cross word with anyone since the day he met Sara. Even when a burly Hell's Angel walked in calling Shane every name under the sun for beating up his brother a few years back, Shane had politely apologised, offering the man a free hit or a free full-colour forearm tat. Thankfully he took the tattoo and was so impressed by the artwork that he insisted on paying.

Sara worked late hours so Shane learned to cook. He wanted to look after this person who had transformed his life. When she came home it was all he could do to keep his hands off her. Not that Sara minded. She was just as happy as Shane with the transformation in her life and, besides the occasional whispers behind her back about the psycho she was dating, only good had come from her meeting him – or so she thought.

Sara was a high performer. She had passed all her exams a year early at school, got top grades in her A-levels and passed her medicine degree at Manchester with a first. As well as this she was also a concert-level violinist and a talented skier too. She was even asked to represent Great Britain in the 2002 Winter Olympics but she turned it down to follow her passion in medicine.

She had dark brown hair, green eyes and pale porcelain skin. "You're an English rose with fantastic tits," is how Shane answered her when Sara once asked "What do you see in me?" Shane saw so much more in her though, he loved the way she looked, the way she smiled, the way she moved, but mostly he loved the fact that she cared, not just about him but about things, people, the world, even animals. To top it all she was fun, not the sort of fabricated fun Shane had grown to depend on, but pure unadulterated joy. She laughed and made everyone else laugh. Shane loved her, really, really loved her.

Sara also genuinely loved Shane. He was not like any man she had met before. She could admit to herself that most, if not all, of her previous relationships involved doing what was expected of her. Yes, she'd had a couple of "fuck buddies" while at university, but then her "proper" relationships were all set up by friends and colleagues and seemed to fit a preordained narrative that a professional girl like her should follow rather than what she really wanted. Shane was not in the script at all, she knew her friends and family would object to everything about him.

Just like Shane was instantly attracted to her, Sara was drawn to Shane from the moment she first laid eyes on him. She was on duty the night he was admitted, battered and bruised, his face a purple and black ballooning mess, his torso torn and several broken bones and teeth for good measure and yet she was somehow smitten. It was while another doctor stitched a wound in his abdomen without anaesthetic in case he was drunk that Sara hung around and took his hand, hoping to comfort him through what she was sure would be unbearable pain. She fully expected this powerful-looking man to squeeze the life out of her hand but instead he ran his thumb gently across the soft skin behind her knuckles and looked at her as the stitches went in, smiling as if only the two of them were there.

"What's your name?" he asked.

"I'm Sara, erm, I mean... Doctor May."

"I prefer Sara."

That was it. He smiled and throughout the whole operation fixed his eyes on her with not even a grimace of pain, just a look of wonderment. Sara too just stared, hoping the nurses and doctors didn't cop on to her childlike infatuated gazing.

As he got better Sara would look in on him and at first stayed professional when he made his remarks and obvious advances because a doctor must not engage romantically with a patient. However, after a few weeks Shane was released and Sara had no doubt they would meet again.

She was actually a little panicked when she did not bump into him during the first couple of weeks, but then at the gym while she was coming out of her yoga class covered in sweat with no make-up on and her hair bunched on the top of her head like a pineapple, there he was. Sara wasn't sure whether he had seen her and was in two minds whether to hide from him or jump on him. She remembered her midriff showed between the sports bra and leggings she was wearing. *Damn, why did I eat that bowl full of ice cream?* she asked herself.

133

Shane spotted her the second she left the studio, beads of sweat glistening off her glowing skin, gorgeous curly locks and what a body. He knew she had seen him and for a moment feared she was going to ignore him. Then finally she came over.

"Hello Shane, I didn't know you were a member here."

"I am a member here... and every other gym this side of town."

Sara looked puzzled at his reply, not sure if he was trying to crack a joke.

"What do you mean?"

Shane was nothing if not observant and he'd known straight away that this girl must go to a gym, not because of the slim athletic body – that could be genetics – instead he'd observed the concave back and straight shoulders, the pert gluteus and flat stomach; every bit of her taut and toned. These things need work, and yoga was the most likely form of exercise to achieve this condition.

"I have been joining gyms all over town looking for you," he said. "This is one of five I attend every week hanging around outside yoga classes hoping you'd be at one so I could casually bump into you."

Shane was aware that by confessing this he was actually ruining this marvellous plan and possibly making himself sound like a bit of a stalker. He could hear his own voice telling him to shut up but still he rambled on.

"There are lots of classes at different times. In fact this is the sixty-seventh class I have waited outside." *(SHUT THE FUCK UP!* he screamed in his head.)

Shane looked at Sara, determined not to speak again until she did. There was a moment of awkward silence before she looked to the ground then back up to him.

"I am on Facebook."

"Yeah, that probably would have been easier."

Shane gave a childlike smile and Sara let out an uncharacteristic girly giggle, then they both laughed.

"So can I buy you a drink?" he asked.

"Well, I suppose after sixty-five classes it would be rude to say 'no'."

"Sixty-seven."

From that very first night any worries that Sara had about this being a "bad boy makes the heart beat fonder" syndrome were completely put to bed. They went to a quaint jazz bar called Misty's and soon relaxed in each other's company. Shane listened intently to Sara, genuinely interested in her job, her loves, her hates, her hobbies... just everything. Sara had never felt this comfortable around anyone. She found herself opening up, telling him everything, even her most intimate secrets. However, she was aware that anything she had to say was not going to compare to Shane's confidences, which she sensed would be deep and dark and best left for now. After the bar he walked her home and gently kissed her cheek goodnight, not attempting to make a play. He asked if he could see her again. For a moment Sara felt she was in one of her favourite movies, she was Audrey Hepburn, he was George Peppard. It was only when he turned to leave that she went out of character – not for Hepburn, but for Sara.

"Why don't you come up? It's still early."

By the time they'd climbed the four flights of stairs and crossed the threshold they both were caressing and kissing wildly. She felt any thought of virtuous resistance melt as his hands clasped either side of her waist and lifted her with ease, her beating heart pulled against his chest. Moments later she was pointing the direction of the bedroom and with his usual enthusiasm Shane crashed through the door, tearing at his clothes as she pulled her dress off, losing a couple of buttons in the process. He pushed her naked body onto the bed as he removed his final items of clothing. He paused for a minute, taking stock of his unbelievable luck then he collapsed down on her.

Shane had been with many women and believed he knew how to please them; his sheer animalistic aggression and physical stature seemed to do the trick with his previous encounters; no one had ever complained. Sara's words were not really a complaint but she knew what she liked and she was not shy about telling him.

"Slow down, let me show you."

Sara guided Shane and showed him a slower way to enjoy the passion. Soon she was swaying on top of him, her hair falling down across her face as she followed a rhythm that would bring them both to the plateau of carnal pleasure. Shane was both surprised and comfortable with the feelings he was experiencing. This act he had taken part in many times was suddenly taking on a whole new level of intimacy. He felt powerless against her will but he was savouring every moment.

All his previous sexual encounters had involved woman literally bending over backwards to please him but these paled into insignificance as he became the student learning from her knowledge. Sara was teaching him the difference between having sex and making love. She was taming him.

She took control but when the crescendo of lovemaking reached its finale, it was time to let him free. He placed his strong powerful arms around her and effortlessly turned her, not a beat missed. She lay face down on the crisp white sheets, lifting herself up and down and writhing as she felt the beginning of her inevitable orgasm. She thrust herself back hard into him and he instinctively took hold of her outer thighs, unleashing the power and vigour she had earlier sought to control. She left no doubt as to when she had climaxed: "Oh! Fucking yes! Oh yeeeeeeeeeeeeeeeeeeeessssss!"

Shane held her even tighter as she forced him further into her, not moving, just waiting as she gently pulsated and eventually collapsed face down.

"Wow, you really have recovered, Mr Mills," she joked before turning over to face him, welcoming him with a huge beautiful smile.

She looked down and observed he had not finished yet. The smile got even bigger.

"I still need some looking after, Doctor May," he smiled.

As they lay in each other's arms, both fully satisfied, Shane stared up at the ceiling. These feelings of contentment were totally alien to him. He had never felt emotion like this before.

"What are you thinking about?" asked Sara, with a hint of mischief in her voice.

"You, me, everything really. Who would have thought that bunch of psycho jocks who put me in the hospital were actually doing me a huge favour?" He turned his head to look at her. "What will the hospital say? Are there rules about this sort of patient–doctor intimacy?"

"Strictly speaking we haven't broken any rules but I'm sure if they ever found it would be the juiciest gossip for a week or two."

"So is this a one-time-only thing, Doctor May, or will you want to be seeing me again?"

"I prefer Sara and I am not quite ready to discharge you yet."

There was no awkward conversation the next day, no wondering if they would see each other again. It was all that was said, the rest was known. They were together and very happy. Sara loved Shane and Shane loved Sara.

Unfortunately so did Eric Temple Lloyd. Eric was the head practitioner at the clinic that Sara interned at two days a week. Eric and Sara had had a drunken grope at the 999 party the previous Christmas and as much as Sara regretted it she was always polite when Eric mentioned her red stockings. Sara was aware that Eric had a crush on her but had no idea to what extent.

Eric was the only son of Sir Richard Temple and his wife Caroline, formally Caroline Lloyd of Lloyd's medical suppliers. The joint wealth of his parents ran into tens of millions and Eric knew in his own mind that he was a great catch for any woman, especially a low-paid intern who drove a ten-year-old VW Beetle. Eric first heard the rumours about Sara dating an ex-patient shortly after Shane moved in with her. At first he dropped hints and sarcastic remarks but when he saw the loved-up couple kissing and cuddling outside his office one day he saw red.

He researched the rules on this sort of thing but was disappointed to find that as the relationship started after Shane was discharged, technically they had broken no rules. Eric's interactions with Sara soon became hostile and he began treating her as a skivvy. At first Sara was naive to his motives but Elsie on reception put her straight.

"It's 'cause he wants to get in your knickers," she told Sara over coffee in the staff room one day. "He's heard about your soldier boy and he's jealous."

"Don't be daft," dismissed Sara.

"I'm telling you," Elsie said. "He is obsessed with you, always asking 'Is Sara in today?', 'Will Sara be in later?'. He could not be more obvious. He, err, even hinted to me and Mary that you two had sex at the Christmas party last year."

Sara's face glows red; half through embarrassment, half with rage.

"Sex! The cheeky bastard...! He only groped me and stuck his tongue down my throat and tried to stick his hand up my skirt. Fortunately I was sick before we got any further."

Still Elsie raises her eyebrows and the reality of the situation hit Sara as she accepted what Elsie was saying.

"Oh my god, how could I be so blind?" she said, more to herself than Elsie. "What am I going to do? That's basically sexual harassment! If I say something I'm liable to flip out but if I don't I'll be Cinder-fucking-rella for the rest of my time here."

Elsie shrugged. "Eric may be a prick but he is the prick boss. It's not worth causing a fuss. If I was you I would just suck it up. You've only got a few more months left and then you don't have to see him ever again."

Sara thought for a second. "Yeah, you're right. I can last for a few more months." The two women nodded in shared pain and then Sara said, "You guys didn't believe I'd had sex with him, did you?"

"Oh no, dear, of course not. Apparently he had you swinging from the chandelier in pure orgasmic delight!"

They shared a glance and then both dissolved into hysterics.

The next few months were tough for Sara at work as Eric became even viler towards her. She coped with the hassle, knowing her term with him was soon over and because she had Shane at home to wine, dine and make love to her each night. Sara had discovered a very sensitive and intelligent man. She could feel the power in his arms and knew what he was capable of and guilty of in the past but she honestly believed that this was the best man she could hope to meet. She was also amazed at how clever he was.

"If you had had a proper education you could have been a doctor or anything you wanted," she often told him, meaning every word.

Up until she met Shane, Sara had only had one tattoo which comprised of five tiny stars on her foot. But after seeing some of the tattoos Shane drew she begged him to ink her shoulder, trusting him to decide what to do. After six hours of surprisingly not overly intense pain he finished and showed her his work in the mirror.

"Wow."

She was truly gobsmacked, it was beautiful. It was not until she looked closer that she cried, emotion building as she fully took in the scene. A little girl, who Sara identified as herself when she was a tot, sat in the hands of a beautiful angel. It was when Sara recognised her mother's face that the tears fell. The detail and accuracy was startling, the compassion it portrayed was overwhelming. She held Shane tight as the tears ran down, ignoring the burning pain from her shoulder.

"I love you, Shane." The first time he ever heard those words from a sober woman.

"I love you too." The first time he'd ever said those words to anyone.

One month before Shane and Sara were due to go to Majorca for their first holiday together, the staff of the clinic were all invited to attend a gala dinner after being awarded a government citation for work in the community. Sara was not that keen to go, she'd not enjoyed the last three months very much and was looking forward to leaving it all behind but Elsie and Mary begged her to come. "It won't be any fun without you," they moaned.

Still Sara wasn't sure. She was concerned about Eric's behaviour although she hadn't mentioned anything to Shane, knowing he may revert back to busting heads if he felt she was being mistreated.

When Shane found out about the event he told her she was stupid not to go and even suggested he drop her off and pick her up if she wanted so she could just relax and have a good time. With everyone pushing her to go, she relented. Maybe she would have fun after all and Shane would be right outside.

The dinner was at the Parkside Hotel in the centre of Manchester. Shane noticed that Sara was quiet on the way. He also noticed that, for her, she was dressed very conservatively. He guessed she would be meeting some toffs and didn't want to look slutty.

"Everything okay?" he inquired as he pulled up outside the foyer.

"I'm fine, just don't like mixing business with pleasure." She played with his collar. "And I miss you already."

Shane stuck his fingers down his throat and Sara gave him a playful slap.

"I will wait down the road with my book," he said. "I'll be five minutes away."

Sara felt better. "Good, because I won't be staying long." The couple kissed as the queue of cars beeped at them.

"Love you."

"Love you."

Sara entered the large function room and located the girls. A feeling of nausea came over her as she saw Eric and another young doctor sitting with them. She thought about turning and heading back to Shane.

"Sara, Sara, over here!" called Elsie. Too late.

Sara sat next to Elsie but Eric made a point of sitting the other side of her. He leaned close to speak.

"Sara, I want to apologise for the way I have treated you lately. It's a tough business this one we're in and it would do you no favours if I didn't show you the down side as well as the ups."

Charming, she thought, unsure if he was telling the truth or not. At least she felt less awkward now the elephant in the room had been addressed. She looked at the pathetic excuse for a man and accepted his apology. Dinner was great and the entertainment surprisingly good but Sara was still careful not to drink.

"Why aren't you drinking? You scared you won't be able to resist Eric?" Elsie whispered to Sara, followed by a cackle of laughter.

"I would need to mainline heroin for that to happen," replied Sara. The girls laughed a little too loud and she hoped Eric didn't hear, but then decided that actually she didn't give a toss if he did or not; this was nearly the last time she would ever have to see him.

A little after ten-thirty Sara texted Shane: *Meet you in the foyer at eleven. I've had enough xxx*
She smiled at the thought of the tough man waiting in the car with his book for her and then felt eyes on her. Eric was watching. Even his eyes were grubby, she thought.
Eric raised his hand and had champagne delivered to the table.

"Raise your glasses," he said as he poured out a glass for everyone at the table. "A toast to the best clinic in Manchester and a fond farewell to Sara!"
Sara wasn't that fussed when the drink ran out before he'd filled her glass.

"Not to worry," she said. "I'll toast with water."

"We can't have that, can we?" Eric said loudly and everybody around the table agreed. "Anyway, it's okay – I have another bottle here."

Sara's mistrust of Eric raised her suspicions but when he produced a small 187ml still-corked bottle of Korbel brut – her favourite tipple (the prick obviously remembered) – she thought, *what the heck,* and popped it open to join in the toast, knowing she was leaving soon anyway. They raised their glasses and cheered to their success and Sara's future career.

Maybe it hadn't been so bad at the clinic after all, she thought. She might even miss it a bit.

First her neck and cheeks became hot and then the room began to tilt ever so slightly. She looked at the time on her phone but had trouble reading the numbers.

"You all right, love?" asked Elsie.

"Yes, I just need to go," she muttered.

Maybe she'd drunk more than she thought? Or maybe she was coming down some sort of virus – damn it! Not for our holiday! Knew I shouldn't have come tonight, she thought and with a quick goodbye she left and walked across the dance floor past some tables.

Her vision had become tunnelled and the tunnel was getting smaller. Sara told herself, *just make it to the foyer, Shane will be there and everything will be all right.*

As she staggered out of the glitzy room she was suddenly afraid she was suffering some sort of colloquial brain attack. All she could think was, *don't have a stroke in front of all these people!*

She exited the function room into a corridor that led to the foyer. She could see it, nearly there! On the left a lift pinged opened next to her and she vaguely made out an older couple exit. Then a hand took her arm and she felt powerless to resist as she was guided into the lift.

It was like she had no control over her own body and the sudden and horrifying realisation that she has been drugged did little to stem the effects. The lift rose, the doors opened and the corridor was spinning. Doors then more doors, the hand was tightening around her arm. She saw a man in some sort of uniform walking past. *Why doesn't he help me?* she thought.

"She's just had one too many," said the owner of the hand, guiding her. She knew that voice. A door opened but she couldn't feel her legs. She was carried inside, numb from top to toe. He laid her on a table and started to undress her. Her chin banged against his head as he pulled her top over her head. "Stop, please stop," she said but the words were not forming.

Eric was having a great time as he pulled off her boots.

"Laugh at me, will you, you fucking little prick-tease?" he said, gleefully pushing her bra up and cupping an exposed breast. He was out of control, shaking with anticipation, sweat dripping from his brow as he fumbled at removing her knickers before positioning himself to mount her.

"Come now, Sara, we both know why you came here tonight."
Eric's mind was rationalising. He wasn't a bad man, she wanted this. He didn't even need to drug her really, that was just a kindness to help her get past the guilt of picking him over that Neanderthal thug.

"You want this bad, don't you?" he said, pulling her legs apart and forcing his fingers up inside her. A wide grin spread across his face. "Oh, we're a bit dry. Let's get this cunt moist."

Deluded, he believed his fumbling was arousing her. He sucked on his bottom lip as his eyes rolled, revealing his own arousal was already near climax.

"You like that, don't you? I bet soldier boy doesn't know his way around your sweet pussy like I do. Well, we've waited long enough. Christmas was a long time ago. Let's get down to the main event, little miss perfect."

Sara couldn't even feel her body. Her mind was a swirling blur. She could just make out Eric's form floating above her. She tried to focus, seeing the glistening forehead drip sweat down his nose and the foam from his mouth like a rabid dog that was attempting to mount her. Beyond horrified it was all Sara could do to move her lips. Eric took this as an invitation and invaded her mouth. His slobber slipping down into her unresponsive throat.

The noise coming from him barely formed words. His main concern was not to come before he entered her. Still he continued to poke at her with what felt to her like a shitty stick until he successfully entered her. It didn't take long, a few jerks that banged her into the table and then his whole body went into spasm as he ejaculated. She was thankful her body had no feeling but the pure violation made her want to curl up and die.

143

The sick pig grunted as he collapsed on top of her, wet with gratification, his already limp penis barely inside her. Through the horror she became aware of someone else behind Eric, a menacing shadow. She could hardly see who, but somehow she knew.

The force with which Eric was pulled from his victim gave him some indication of what was to follow. Shane had been trained to kill. He pulled Eric up by the hair, exposing his throat. He then smashed his fist into it, full power, collapsing the windpipe. Shane dropped him and went to Sara, turned her on her side and held her close to him. He covered her up as two security guards rushed in. One spoke through his walkie-talkie, "Ambulance required." He looked at Eric, "Make that two." The two men looked more concerned about Eric than Sara. Shane wiped her brow trying to comfort her.

"Sara, can you hear me? Sara?" Shane hardly noticed that the guards were desperately trying to resuscitate Eric.

The defence lawyer would claim that in the heat of the moment Shane had lashed out, not aiming for anywhere in particular, his only intention had been to protect Sara from the monster that was raping her. It came out in the trial that Eric had tainted the drink he'd given Sara with rohypnol using a syringe through the top to avoid breaking the seal so Sara would not suspect anything.

The prosecution called expert witnesses that confirmed that Shane was a trained killer and his blow to the throat was a "kill blow" and that was the intention. The jury found him guilty of manslaughter, rejecting the prosecution's argument that it was fully intentional. But they had got it wrong, Shane was well aware he was pressing the off button. Still, justice was done and "Eric the prick" died, with trousers round his ankles, gasping for breath.

Given the chance would he do it again? Would he and Sara still be happy and together if he'd just knocked the vile piece of shit out? Was it even worth thinking about? What was done was done.

Since his incarceration Shane has not received a single visit, not even a letter from Sara. He doesn't blame her; after all it was he who had insisted she forget about him. But still.

"Mills, the Governor wants to see you," shouts Officer Goodwin. "Come on, quickly."

Shane puts his auntie's letter away. "What does he want?"

"I don't fucking know. Do I look like his fucking secretary?"

Goodwin is a prick and everyone knows it.

No-Legs is nearby and can't resist a good jibe. "No, you got bigger tits than her plus she doesn't suck the Governor's cock as often as you do!"

Everybody laughs except Goodwin.

"I will sort you later," frowns Goodwin. "Come on, Mills, move it."

They head out of the wing and through the north yard into the admin building and up the stairs to the main offices. Governor Byrne is a good man from what Shane can deduce. Goodwin knocks.

"Come in."

Shane enters and sees the Governor sitting at his desk with a smartly dressed woman in her late forties or early fifties beside him. The woman is quite striking with platinum hair and tanned skin. She radiates class. Shane is surprised at the attractiveness of such a mature lady. "She must have been something in her day," he thinks to himself.

"Well, come in, come in," repeats the Governor.

Shane enters and Goodwin leaves, closing the door behind him.

"Sit down, please, Mills."

Shane sits down in the chair opposite the three people wondering what this is all about.

"This is Solfrid Gjerde," says the Governor.

The attractive woman greets him with a smile that knows its power over men and in a strong Scandinavian accent she says, "I am sorry to drag you up here."

Shane is bemused. "Well, so long as I don't miss playtime," he grins.

She smile again and Shane notices her perfectly shaped teeth, all sparkling white.

"I am here to ask," she says, "if you would like to have better conditions? For example, a bigger cell with a TV and shower in it? And the possibility of up to two days a month of supervised outings, leading to tagged release one year earlier than the recommendation."

Shane raises his eyebrows. "Wow. Who do I have to fuck to get that?"

Shane and the woman called Solfrid share a flirtatious glance and the Governor shifts awkwardly in his chair.

"No one needs fucking," she says. "Your government have asked me to set up an experimental facility based on the detention units we use back in Sweden. In Sweden we have reduced the amount of re-offenders by over fifty per cent leading to the closure of six prisons. This at a time when here, your country is choked full of prisoners and needing to build new facilities."

As Shane hears the words he is making a note that he must visit Sweden if this is what the old ones look like.

"The unions won't be happy with closures," he jibes. "However, if you want to offer me a TV, a shower, and some early release," he winks. "Then I accept."

Governor Byrne coughs. "The facility is not here you understand. You would have to transfer to a unit specially adapted for the project. It's up near Blackpool."

"We have adapted an old air force base to accommodate forty prisoners," says Solfrid. "You have been selected from over eighty-five thousand eligible inmates. I feel this is a great opportunity for you. The plan carries on after your release as we have a two-year 'back to society' package, which will include setting up jobs and accommodation if needed. What do you say? Sounds good, yes?"

"It sounds fucking great, but why me?"

Solfrid shrugs. "I'm not sure, you must fit the criteria set out by the company."

Shane looks around suspiciously. He's never believed in blind luck before and the belief has held him in good stead so far in life. Something Leo said also occurs to him: "They will probably try to separate you and me if they think I am telling you these things so don't tell anyone." Shane doubts this is what's happening now but still, he knows if something sounds too good to be true then there is usually a catch.

"Can I think about it?" he asks.

The woman looks surprised. "What is there to think about? Surely you don't want to stay in this archaic dump?"

Solfrid's comments are not appreciated by the Governor, who tells Shane, "It is your choice, of course. We will give you twenty-four hours. How does that sound, Miss Gjerde?"

Shane picks up on the sudden change of atmosphere in the room. This beautiful mature lady looks different, her eyes change from sparkling to piercing.

Eventually she relents. "Very well. I will return tomorrow. You have until then or we will pick another for this great opportunity."

Shane nods. Just as he stands the phone rings.

"Hmm, must be important," the Governor says, picking it up apologetically. The look on his face tells everyone something serious has happened.

"Stabbed? Who? Leo Verdi! Why would anyone... Never mind." The Governor bangs the receiver down and shouts, "Goodwin!"

Goodwin rushes in, "Yes, Gov?"

"Guard Mills. I've got to get down to C wing immediately. There's been a stabbing. Heaven help us, one inmate is dead!"

Shane sits back down in shock.

Leo is dead?

As Leo watches Shane being led out by Goodwin, he asks Johnny where he is being taken.

"Governor wants to see him," answers Johnny. "Don't know what for though. You know how helpful fatty Goodwin is."

Leo hates the fact that he relies on his big, tough friend to protect him in here. His fear has grown ten-fold since the Black Muslim arrived. Leo has noticed Robert Price watching his every move. Even the other Muslims on the wing seem wary of this guy and rumours of how he kills his foes do nothing to calm Leo's worries.

With Shane off the wing, this would be a perfect time to carry out a murder. Leo's fears are exacerbated when he notices Robert watching Shane leave and then look over at him. Leo decides there's safety in numbers and heads down to the recreation room, hoping there is someone he knows down there. When he gets there no one is about. *Damn*, he thinks, *not even a witness, I have made it easier for him.* In a panic he looks around for a weapon. He almost laughs at himself. *Who do you think you are? You would need a shotgun to stop this fella.*

Leo sits in the middle of the room facing the entrance, waiting. Someone is coming. To his great relief it is Graham, the gay hairdresser guy that arrived the same day as the Muslim. Leo feels guilty involving this new guy whom he has only spoken to once before but has no choice. "Graham, come over here," he calls, hoping a witness will deter his assailant.

Graham prances over. "Hi," he says loudly.

Leo pulls out a chair. "Would you join me?"

He is not very familiar with homosexuals and hopes Graham does not think he is trying to pick him up.

"Of course, I would love to. Just got to get some chocolate." He points to the vending machine behind Leo. "Do you want anything?"

"No. No, thank you."

"Oh, you're sweet enough, hey?" Graham taps Leo on the shoulder playfully, and then walks to the vending machine.

Leo's heart then misses a beat as he spots Robert Price enter the room. This time the man his fellow prisoners call "Bob the Beheader" doesn't even bother to disguise his stare. He looks Leo in the eye then past him to observe Graham. Leo hopes that seeing a possible witness will at least delay any action until someone comes to help him. Robert pulls a six-inch blade from his waist and Leo's heart sinks. Once more, he contemplates his imminent death as he sees Robert come hurtling towards him. He hopes Shane will know the truth and at least he'll have fulfilled his role. Graham's hand falls on his shoulder and Leo is gripped by guilt, knowing this poor, gentle man will be terrified. In what he thinks is his last act on this earth, Leo does not try to protect himself, but instead turns to comfort Graham. But Graham looks different. His face is contorted. He holds a large blade in his left hand and is pulling it up, ready to plunge it into Leo's neck. Everything is blurred as the blade hits his collar bone, filling him with a sharp pain as suddenly another force hits him, knocking Leo right out of his chair. In a surreal moment of possible concussion he sees Robert thrusting a blade into Graham's heart. With Leo slipping into unconsciousness Robert releases Graham and rushes over to him, ripping his shirt off and packing the wound in Leo's neck with it.

"Come on, old man, you can't die on me now!" he shouts as the guards flood in and take over. Robert is led away through the wing. He can guess what they are all thinking.

⚱𝍐𝍕𝍖𝍐𝍒𝍕𝍮

Shane paces up and down the Governor's office. He has heard a lot of commotion and knows from the phone call that Leo was involved. *Fuck,* he thinks to himself. *He told me that this type of thing would happen at the first chance they got. Shit! Wait, what am I saying? The old man's mad. Who knows what's actually happened.*

Still, something about this Solfrid has unnerved him and it's not the fact that she is over fifty and still fuckable. He is sure he noticed a smile when she heard the words dead and Verdi in the same sentence.

Fuck, I'm losing the plot here. Stop jumping to conclusions. Shane, and just find out about Leo.

Shane remembers Leo warning him that the big black guy with the Bin Laden beard was watching him and he was sure he was up to something. Well, if he has harmed Leo he will soon learn all about decapitation and castration, only there will be no blades involved this time.

"Okay, Mills, boss says normal service is resumed," says Goodwin after a quick phone call. "You're going to need to find a new chess opponent though." Shane's stomach turns. So it's true... "Well, at least for a week or so," adds Goodwin.

Relief floods over him. "Leo, is he alive?"

"Yep, which is more than I can say for the wee Nancy boy who came in recently."

Shane is puzzled. "You mean Graham? What happened?"
Goodwin was not usually one to talk to prisoners but these events were curious enough for even him to elaborate.

"Well, no one is confirming anything but I would guess Graham tried it on with the big silverback, Price, and didn't realise shit stabbing is punishable by death in Islam."

Shane mulls over Goodwin's non-PC statement and decides that was not what happened. As he enters the wing the recreation room is closed and most of the cons are milling around Johnny's cell and gossiping. Shane pushes by.

"Here he is, misses all the action, this one," says Johnny.

"What the fuck happened? I was gone twenty minutes."
Johnny shoos the other inmates out. As soon as they all leave he tells Shane what he knows.

"The big black guy that came in a couple of weeks ago, I think he may have tried to kill Leo, and unbelievably gay Gray seems to have come to his rescue and got a blade in the heart for his troubles."

"How's Leo?"

"Well, he wasn't looking too clever but I think he is okay."

Shane spots a guard passing the cell. "Mr McEnery! Can we have a word?"

James McEnery enters the cell. Shane likes this polite and honest screw.

"I guess you want to know about Leo's condition?" he says. "He's fine but we are concerned about his mental state. The doc says he is rambling."

Shane assumes this will relate to the Djinn conspiracy theory.

"What's he saying?" he asks, fearing the worst.

"Well, he claims he and Graham had a row and it was Robert who was trying to break it up. Leo is claiming that it was him who killed Graham in the struggle."

Shane's jaw drops "Leo killed him and the black guy broke it up? Bullshit."

McEnery shrugs his shoulders. "Problem is the CCTV went down just before the incident so we can't check."

Shane thinks back to the last time Leo was attacked. He was expecting an extra six months for knocking those two cons out but apparently the CCTV had been down then too and no one even asked him what happened.

"How fucking often do the cameras go down in this place?" he says. "Is that privatisation at work?"

McEnery frowns. "Don't start. I've been here since before it went private, in fact, it'll be twenty years next May, and in all that time the cameras have only failed twice that I know of."

"Yeah, both times when Leo Verdi happened to be attacked." Shane sits down, his mind racing. Too many coincidences

𝄞 𝄢 𝄪 𝄪

Besides an almighty pain in his shoulder, Leo feels surprisingly good. He is amazed that once more he has cheated death and although he was knocked senseless when Robert collided with him to get to Graham, he is well aware that the man he believed was his would-be assassin was in fact his saviour.

151

It had been the least he could do to take the blame for Graham's death and he had also calculated that he would almost definitely be put in solitary for it, which will make it harder for the Djinn to get to him. Unfortunately he doubts he will be able to see Shane any more so he has to hope that he had shared enough knowledge for Shane to be ready when the time comes. The big guy had been released back onto the wing within a couple of hours of the incident; with Leo claiming to be the killer there had been no reason to detain Robert. He has barely spoken one word to anyone since arriving and it is doubtful that will change in regards to him elaborating on what really happened. Shane is pleased to see him back though.

"I'll get the cunt to talk," he tells No-legs and Big Pete.

The prisoners are wise to the fact that these two formidable inmates are likely to clash in the near future and bets start to be placed. Shane will wait for the right opportunity to arise; he is a patient man. The Governor had warned him when he officially turned down the Swedish woman's offer that he had best not be planning a revenge attack in his prison.

Shane knows the screws are on alert. Through the grapevine Shane has heard that Leo is in solitary on D wing and awaiting transfer. Shane has tried in vain to contact him. Leo has also tried to contact Shane but he has only been allowed access to his solicitor, a wet-behind-the-ears just-out-of-university useless intern. Nice kid but one who has no idea about the system. Leo is certain his number will be up as soon as he is moved anywhere else but as long as he is here in solitary he can sleep, knowing he will not be disturbed. Leo finds time to reflect on his meetings with Simeon.

Rome, before Leo's incarceration

"It must be said that charity can in no way, exist along with mortal sin."
Thomas Aquinas

After Simeon's revelation to him in the Vatican library, Leo worked tirelessly, traipsing the corridors containing the archives that ran throughout the Vatican City. Over fifty miles of shelves held thousands of years of knowledge, much of which was stolen during Crusades. Leo noticed only a small proportion actually had anything to do with God or religion but that just made it all the more a treasure trove. The problem was Leo no longer enjoyed the task he was carrying out. Regina had grown impatient and after many tears and their first fight in thirty years she had packed her bags and left for Rimini.

"You know where I'll be when you finish playing your game," were her parting words.

If only he could tell her what he was really doing.

I am working with a mysterious entity who is a member of a race called the Djinn. They come from another world... no frequency, that's it. They come from the same world but they exist on a separate frequency. Anyway, this Jinni and I, we are trying to prevent other entities from dragging the human race into slavery.

It was hard enough explaining it to himself. Besides Leo was also sure Regina and the rest of the family were safer away from him, for now at least.

On the twelfth of August Simeon asked Leo to travel to Venice and meet him there. Leo was relieved to get out of the vaults, which were starting to feel a bit claustrophobic, and to visit the beautiful city of his ancestors. He met Simeon in a café bar in the Piazza San Marco. It was a warm summer's day, just the type of day to receive bad news.

"The game is up my friend," said Simeon. "It seems Reuben has already obtained the book and is instigating a debt request with the intention of causing a world financial crisis."

Leo had not even managed a sip of his espresso yet. "How do you know this? Has he contacted you?"

Simeon roared with laughter, sounding like a madman. "Reuben and I do not have 'little chats', my friend. In fact, he would pay dearly to find me and have me killed." He waved a copy of the *Financial Times* at Leo. "No, I use this as my almanac and trust me, the clues are easy to spot when you know what to look for."

Intrigued, Leo examined the paper but saw nothing out of the ordinary.

"What? I can't see anything. Some stocks are up, some down."

Simeon pointed. "Here, the article about the American mortgage boom."

Leo read the headline: "Sky high investments and growth over the last decade".

Simeon explained, "If you read the article you will see." He pushes the paper to Leo's side pointing to a article.

WASHINGTON – The U.S. Department of the Treasury announced today that it priced a secondary offering of all Citigroup trust preferred securities (TruPS®) received pursuant to the Asset Guarantee Program (AGP). The aggregate gross proceeds from the offering, all of which represent a net gain or profit to the taxpayer under the AGP, will be $2.246 billion. The closing of the TruPS® sale is expected to occur on Tuesday, October 5, 2010. The entirety of Treasury's proceeds from this sale represents a profit to taxpayers, because Treasury did not incur any losses on the Citigroup assets it guaranteed in exchange for these TruPS®.

Leo was none the wiser so Simeon continued. "Financial institutions run by bankers have used a false stability enabling them, in recent years, to loan huge amounts to US financial companies, thinking the money was tied up in a fiscal pool of long date securities. They believed the origin of the collateral was long gone so they used it as their own little piggy bank – just like I said. Then the origin re-emerged, I suspected this was Reuben using the book and the debts were called in, that's what caused the recent worldwide crash, the article proves that Reuben has moved to the second stage in his plan and he must have the ledger.

In other words Reuben has used the book to near bankrupt the world. If I'm correct he has gleefully torn down the pillars that held the financial world aloft. The banks, the insurance companies, large corporations all toppled like dominoes. He will use the collapse of these institutions as an opportunity to obtain them at knock-down prices, the market will steady in one or two years before he collapses them once again, only this time all his newly acquired companies will topple too, causing the end of first world prosperity and the beginning of a class system reminiscent of ancient times. Eventually Reuben will appear as a saviour and the world will bend its knee. That is his game plan: the people of the Western world fear nothing more than losing their luxuries, now even the once communist of the east have the same fears."

"So, we are too late?" Leo felt guilty at his relief that he could finally go home to his wife and await the consequences of the world falling under the influence of a psychotic evil dictator. "At least we tried", will be his defence when reckoning is asked.

"No! Of course not!" exclaimed Simeon. "We must act to reduce the impact, I suspect Reuben is struggling to deceiver the Yiddish dialect or he would have recalled far more resources. Since I noticed the warning signs of this financial crisis I have channelled my own resources. Hopefully, with a monetary and fiscal stimulus I can avert his planned second crash, and halt the world's economy from spiralling into chaos. I can only soften the blow and slow his rise but this will buy time to prepare the human champion."

"Damn, here we go," thought Leo. Then, out loud, "Who is this human champion? Please tell me it's not me."

"No," Simeon chuckled, "but you will meet him – you will know him by the beautiful woman on his arm. I will mentor you and then you shall mentor him."

Leo drank his espresso. He knew he was not going home to his wife. He doubted he would ever go home again

155

From that day on Leo would meet Simeon at four or five times a month as he was told everything he needed to know about the contest and how it was played. They would meet in strange locations, sometimes in steam rooms at the back of a Masonic establishment, sometimes in bars or cafés.

"Why here? Why Venice?" asked Leo one day, curious that they were in the town where he was born.

"When the game began we nominated neutral zones, sanctuaries where no wars or epidemics could be purposely inflicted. Venice is one such zone and I hope that Reuben is not too far gone as to break that rule."

Once or twice they met in an upmarket brothel. Simeon may not have been of this world but from what Leo had witnessed he certainly enjoyed its pleasures.

"How are you able to take human form?" Leo asked after listening to Simeon talk of all the exploits he and other Djinn had been party to over the centuries.

"It is called anatomical assimilation. The arrival of the Djinn that you witnessed, with Solomon and the crater, that took more energy than would run this planet for a millennium, a complex process beyond man's comprehension but let's just say quantum physics would be like basic arithmetic in comparison.

"However, once we had taken human form things became much simpler. First we synthesised an organic chemical called Vril that runs through our bodies. It works as a carrier that transfers our life force into others by a simple process similar to a blood transfusion. The Vril then travels through the person's bloodstream into a tiny gland you call the pineal gland and our consciousness takes over the vehicle that you know as a body."

"What happens to the person? Their personality? Their soul?" Leo said with a hint of accusation.

"We don't take the life, they are still alive in there." Simeon pointed to his head. "But instead of the driver, they are now a back seat passenger, witnessing things they would only dream of in a normal life. But we're only talking one person here – hundreds, no, thousands of humans die in your world every day. And we have given as well as taken."

"Really?" said Leo, unconvinced.

"Look, Vril transfers our intellect but also extrasensory capabilities: telekinesis, telepathy, astral projection. Each Jinni has the ability to access these plus Vril makes us immune to disease and boosts all our body's natural healing processes. As we have sired many children, our Vril has made its way into the majority of human descendants and with that came a leap in your intellect and physical health. Perhaps there is the possibility of humans also achieving the other ability's. As of yet few humans have evolved sufficiently to access them but I believe there are some examples: Houdini, Karl Marx and Darwin would be the most famous recent to show such characteristics traits, however you could go all the way back to Buddha."

"You said you only take children... that they have to be offered to you by their parents? I find that hard to believe. It must be done under duress. I mean what sort of parent gives away the life of a son and what gives them the right?"

Simeon's voice was calm. "You have too high an opinion of your fellow man. Over the years people have traded the lives of their children for wealth, power, love, even revenge. After all, if you have five children and all are starving would you not give up one to save the rest? Of course once we were established it was even easier. Almost every powerful family or dynasty that has risen over the last three millennia has done so through a deal with one of us and they will also most likely be direct descendants, all can trace their genes back to one of us.

"You have heard the myths of the genie of the lamp, no doubt, who grants three wishes? Well, all myths have some truth. We cannot explain to these parents the full extent of what we need of their child, only that we will not kill them and that they will be part of something very special. To be honest though, most never ask." Simeon pauses to gauge Leo's reaction to this information. "I can see from your expression that you are concerned about this process but let me assure you we are not able to force our Vril onto any human without the birth parent giving up the child. It is one of the rules even Reuben cannot break."

"So, do I carry some Djinn DNA?" Leo asked bitterly. "Am I a descendant of one of you Djinn? Are we related?"

"The Jewish people come from Isaac so, yes, it is likely that you carry some of his Vril. Indeed, Jews tend to be of a very high pedigree."

"Pedigree? You mean like a dog?"

"Not at all. We deeply value our descendants. The stronger our bloodline, the more powerful we become. Each child that we spawn will carry our genetic marker and will be connected to us through neurotransmitters within their pineal gland. The same will be true of their children and that child's children and so on. Now, if the bloodline is corrupted by that of another Jinni, which is often the case, then it weakens our control so we thrive on what we call pedigree species.

"Remember, Djinn do not wield much power ourselves, we merely nurture and mentor others. As I said before, almost everyone throughout history who has ever been in a position of high authority was put there by one of us and would be as strong a blood relative as possible. For instance, the royal families of Europe are mostly direct descendants of either me or Reuben. They have kept it in the family, so to speak, so they will always predominantly carry our genes.

"And through the ignorance of religion you humans have kept mainly to yourselves: Isaac's Jews as I said stick to their own, as do Benjamin's Muslims, Hindus and all the other believers too, thus keeping the bloodline strong and enabling the controlling Jinni – or father if you like – to progress well in the contest. Daniel had controlled his bloodline through skin colour and instigated many issues of prejudice to keep it that way."

"You invented racism?" Leo started to understand that the Djinn had not only controlled the direction of the world but even influenced people's feelings to their own ends. "Why though?"

"Why what?"

"Why are you here, playing this game and fucking with our lives?"

For the first time since Leo met Simeon he saw a flicker of real emotion. It could be regret or perhaps embarrassment.

"I could say research or even experimentation… the Arc Hon claim it will help mankind's progress and evolution but I believe the real reason was simple, we envy you, that's all I can say. I am not trying to excuse what has happened but you have to keep in mind although we are vastly more advanced and evolved than you we craved the simple things you had. I know this comparison is likely to invoke confusion but even though humans are viewed by Djinn the same way you would the view animals in a zoo, deep down we desire the physical form we once had, even your mortality is coveted by us which lead us to resent you, even despise you."

There was genuine feeling in his voice when he added, "However, some of us realised we were wrong and as people advanced and became capable of creating magnificent works of art, music and so much more, we grew to see you humans for what you are: a race not unlike ours who deserve to be treated with respect and not just as pawns in a giant game played for the amusement of the Djinn.

"As I told you before I was the first of the thirteen to attempt to halt the game. I believed we should fix the wrongs we had done and then leave you to your own fate. The Assembly of Djinn rejected this idea so I suggested a radical addition, to allow a human competitor to enter the game. The idea was apparently so abhorrent that Reuben and Levi petitioned to have me removed and the Council agreed. I was disqualified and sentenced to return to the non-physical plane."

"So how come you are still here?"

"I renewed."

"Renewed?"

"It is easy enough to hide from other Djinn, as you can imagine. What with us changing at least once every generation, tracking me down was not easy. But there are other entities involved, you may have heard me mention the Watchers?" Leo nodded. "Well, they are the adjudicators, they are not Djinn nor are they human. They are in fact Arc Hon and they are the ones responsible for upholding the rules. So when it was decided that I should be removed for 'going native' as they called it, and I simply refused to leave, going underground, it was the Watchers who were tasked in tracking me down.

"The Arc Hon can identify Djinn by using an aura defining device, which can give them our general location, and then they send the hounds in, so to speak. I was on the run for years but they would always find me and I would have to flee over and over again. Eventually I realised the only way to escape from them long term was through a process called assumption, which removed my aura and brought me to the base existence of a human."

"And how does this assumption work exactly?" asked Leo warily.

"By assimilating with a developing foetus."

Leo looked visually sick.

Simeon nodded. "It is totally against the rules but I was already disqualified."

"That's all right then," mocked Leo, trying to work out if it was better to take over the body of someone who has lived for thirteen years or someone not even born yet. Simeon sighed.

"So I was reborn as a human and remembered nothing of who I was, I was what we call renewed."

"Yet here you are," said Leo, trying to hold in his feelings of disgust.

"The memories weren't lost, just locked away," said Simeon.

"And what mother would give up her unborn baby?" Leo asked.

"Susanne," Simeon said with reverence. "She was an astonishing woman, an artist and my lover. I confided in her about everything and together we hatched the plan – she only had one condition, I could not father the child. So I had to involve another of my brethren, Pierre-Cecile Puvis de Chavannes, to get Susanne pregnant." Simeon paused, looking at Leo as if he should recognise the name.

Leo was too busy reeling in shock: Jeremy Kyle would have a field day.

"So Susanne gave birth to me and brought me up as her normal human child. I left behind many writings to help remind myself of everything that

I had previously known. Quite a complex situation, as you can imagine, but it did the trick and the Arc Hon lost my aura."

Leo was tempted to ask if mother and son had reignited their love affair but decided against it. Instead he shook his head. "And you want me to relate all of this information to a complete stranger who I will know because of the beautiful woman on his arm? He's going to think me a complete lunatic!"

"It doesn't matter what he thinks of you, it only matters that he listens."

Leo sighed. "What exactly are the rules of this game?"

Simeon took a breath and ploughed on. "There are many but I will explain the main ones and how we have bent them to suit our situations.

"Rule one is Djinn are not permitted to kill one another. However, they may cause the death of another by influencing events around the said Jinni's physical incarnation. If his human form is killed, the Jinni will be removed from the game and return to their former state back in our dimension. This has sometimes led to millions being slaughtered in the pursuit of removing an opponent. Also, killing the people around each Jinni reduces the power of their bloodline. I am sorry to say that genocide is not against the rules."

"Like Reuben did against my people during the Holocaust?" Leo said coldly.

"Technically against Isaac's people."

Leo pushed up his spectacles and rubbed the bridge of his nose. Enough was enough. How could he even think about helping this man who had been complicit in the sort of violations he had just described? Tomorrow he would go home to Regina and be dammed with Simeon and the fucking Djinn.

"I must retire, I am tired," he said politely, rising to his feet.

He never did go home to Regina, of course. How could he when there really were these entities using mankind for their amusement? Simeon seemed to have had a change of heart, like a Djinn version of an animal rights activist, considering they see humans in the same light as animals.

But what was the reason for Simeon's change of heart and how could Leo trust a man who, by his own admission, was part of this cartel of non-humans, responsible for mass murders, infanticide, genocide and who knows what other atrocities?

"Before I can continue I need to know why," Leo told Simeon the next time they met.

Usually when they met, alcohol was prevalent. Simeon had a love for red wine, beer, whiskey – everything in fact. The more they talked, the more he seemed to sink into a depression and the more he drank. It was with a large glass of wine in his hand that Simeon answered him now.

"Why what?"

"Why did you change your mind and decide to help the humans?" They were in a trendy wine bar in the middle of Venice's late-night quarter with hundreds of people enjoying the pleasant evening.

"Just so you understand," said Simeon. "We originate from the exact same place. The Djinn are sapient just like you are, just thousands of years more evolved."

Leo did not understand why he was receiving this explanation from Simeon. Was it because he was worried that he was about to be judged? His answer soon followed.

"The reason I am saying this is because I need you to understand that a Djinn falling in love with a human is not some sort of perverse a-bomb-in-a-tion." The final word came out in five distinct syllables, with closed eyes, as practised by many a drunken man.

Is that what it came down to? Love? Leo felt he was about to be burdened with an awkward confession. He was not equipped for this type of heart-to-heart conversation, especially with a non-human. Still, it was he who had asked.

"Susanne," he guessed.

"I fell in love with her after seeing her image in a painting by Renoir," Simeon said, looking into his glass reminiscently. "Renoir was a good friend. He was part of my close-knit group who helped me hide out from the Arc Hon. Of course, they didn't know exactly who or what I was but in those days Paris was very trendy and to be involved in the occult and have secrets was all part of the excitement amongst the bohemians.

"Susanne was a model at the time, but she was so much more than that. She was ambitious, rebellious, flirty and promiscuous, traits rarely found in women in those days. She was also very clever and talented. I fell in love! Properly in love." Simeon became animated once more, his fingers pointing, then his arms flaying as he slurred out his words. "I'd been hiding from the Watchers for a hundred or so years during which time I drank a lot and had relationships with many females. I was spiralling in a human like descent of self-pity until I met her." Simeon looked into his glass his mood becoming calm as he reflected. "Susanne was different. It was like a scene from one of my own plays." He looks up at Leo. "Did I mention I was a playwright in a former life?" A hiccup punctuated his sentence and he stared off into the distance again before continuing. "When I realised that I had fallen in love and that this beautiful woman was the most important person I had ever met, I allowed my feelings of guilt towards the human race to grow and I became more than a conscientious objector. You see I realised that I must now side with her kind. I had to save them. So I told her everything about the quest, about the Djinn and the Arc Hon."

The last drop of wine was consumed and Simeon looked around for the waiter. With a shake of his head he continued, only this time his voice carried a pang of guilt, or perhaps sorrow.

"As I have told you before, the two of us planned the renewal together. I was reborn as a human with no knowledge of my real identity and Susanne was now my mother. She was only 18, such responsibility, but she brought me up as best she could. She named me Maurice and I grew up surrounded by the most wonderful art and artists! Never before had I felt such a connection to the universe. Unsurprisingly though I had a troubled life and was in and out of mental institutions as my past memories began to re-emerge. We had agreed that I would not receive the notes I had written to myself until Susanne had passed away as my reaction could not be predicted."

Picking up Leo's glass, Simeon took a large swig. Leo feared that he was about to burst into tears, an action that would render Leo useless, as his wife could testify.

"Are you okay?" asked Leo once the silence became unbearable.

"Sorry, I was just thinking," slurred Simeon. "Anyway, before I read the notes I was a somewhat accomplished artist myself, but still the truth came as a bit of a shock. I spent the next twenty-odd years as a recluse trying to deal with the truth and then I began planning my next move and how to honour my lover and my mother's memory. That's why I became a traitor to my own kind. Love: what a cunt it is."

Again Simeon stared aimlessly into the table in front of him. A waiter passed, asking politely in broken English, "Any more drink?" Simeon replied, "Yes, a large bottle of J-fucking-D, pronto!" Leo was concerned that this was the most drunk he had ever seen Simeon and worried they would draw attention to themselves. He was right to be concerned, Simeon was very drunk. The drunken Jinni looked around the bar observing the vapid groups of revellers, disdain etched across his face as he listened to their pathetic babble. He pondered on what he had given up for these pieces of meat. He took a slow deep breath to calm himself, then he remembered Susanne and with a sip of wine he focused. He held both hands up to signal he was calm and ready for Leo to continue with any further questions.

Leo was nervous now but he still wanted answers. "Why fight for a human competitor? Why don't you try and win the game yourself and then put things right?"

"Didn't you listen? I am disqualified, remember! I only suggested a human competitor before to rebalance the scales. Then after I met Susanne it all became more vital."

Leo pondered this and came to his own conclusion.

"Redemption," he nodded. "You're seeking redemption for yourself and the abominations that came with you, the demons who have brought evil to this earth." Simeon's face changed from a man struggling with guilt to a man feeling anger: gritted teeth and an intense stare left Leo in no doubt that he had hit a nerve.

Simeon slammed his fist down on the table, startling Leo and attracting even more attention from their fellow patrons.

"Do not for one minute think that mankind is not responsible for its own problems! We use the tools that are free to us, such as man's greed and indifference to each other. Mankind has an ability to do things to each other that we couldn't even dream of, things so bad it never ceases to amaze me. I told you the Djinn have a rules that even Reuben has never broken and one is we can only influence, not command. 'Only by free will'. Everything that has happened on this plane was done of your own free will. No threats, no mind control, no torture, just persuasion or at worst coercion!"

Leo looked sheepish; maybe he had been a bit quick to judge. There must be thousands of incidents where humans have committed horrid acts without any Djinn interfering.

"I will give you an example," said Simeon, "of how stupid you humans can be. Over the years we have invented many untruths to control and manipulate the masses. One of the most successful of these is the virgin birth. A myth we didn't use just the once, but at least ten times: Krishna, Christ, Dionysus, all concocted from a story Solfrid and Baal came up with during the First Visit many, many years before we arrived, where they propagated a myth about a child born after his mother fornicated with a phallic instrument. Horus was the first incarnation of the virgin birth and we used him again when Egypt rose to a great empire and we didn't even change his name that time.

"When Reuben came up with Christianity he didn't even bother coming up with an original line. There was no need, humans were so desperate to have a messiah that he could come up with any old story so long as there was a virgin birth. He was clever though, he used some old myths as well that he'd heard from Solomon when we first arrived. Then with the help of a few scholars he elaborated on the story of a local radical from Nazareth. He put both books together over a thousand years and, hey presto! The first world were all following the book called the bible. This gave him the lead in the quest and one he has held on to for a long

165

time, until Isaac discovered there was a religion even more conducive to controlling man: wealth."

Simeon slumped in his chair. Leo was aware that this was one drunk, angry Jinni getting loose-lipped around religion. He decided to take advantage of his new buddy's inebriation and ask the question any devout Jew would ask. "What about God? Did Reuben or one of the others invent him?"

Simeon laughed as he sipped his drink, choking in the process. "Leo, the Djinn are a highly developed race, we know things you don't but we don't know everything. God is man's name for the creator and yes, there was a creator, but he doesn't sit in the clouds watching over us all and judging us. He left. He was probably a little embarrassed with how his creations turned out. Anyway, I believe he has other things to do, other worlds, other races, countless living beings that he has created." Simeon fixed Leo with a pitiful look and addressed him in a sincere tone. "It's only you humans that are so self-absorbed to believe that God belongs to you." He poured one more drink and Leo joined him as his last ounce of faith disappeared

"We believe it because you trick us into believing it. You say that you don't use mind control but surely that is mind control."

"Cognitive bias. Do you know what that is?"

Leo did not know but was sure he was about to learn.

"It is the weakness in your thought patterns that has allowed us to convince humans to believe certain things are important when really they are not. We thrive on your inability to reach bounded rationality. Your fear of loss is the strongest of these irrational patterns and loss of existence is the ultimate motivation. By creating religion we reinforced all of these biases daily. There are people throughout history who have chosen to die to prove to themselves that they will live eternally and no matter how irrational these religions are, you just keep on following them. All religions thrive not because of man's love for each other but because of their greed. One life is not enough for you. You believe you are so significant that some God who created everything is just waiting for you to snuggle up to him at his place."

Leo was deflated, but felt the need to defend his species. "That's easy for you to say; you have lived thousands of years as one of us and however long as whatever you were before."

A group of Italians sitting on the next table looked over curiously.

Simeon shrugs. "Maybe you are right but trust me that when threatened with your very existence. It is then that all peoples of the world will plead with world leaders to deliver them from this evil. The one thing every man fears is the unknown. When presented with this scenario, individual rights will be willingly relinquished for the guarantee of their wellbeing granted to them by their world government lead by the new messiah."

𓍹𓃾𓇋 𓃾𓏏𓆰𓏥

Taking his solitary daily walk around the prison yard, Leo suddenly understands what cognitive bias is. "Why do we give a fuck what anyone else thinks, mostly people we don't even know?" Leo laughs out loud, becoming hysterical. The guard becomes concerned as Leo collapses. He has no idea what is so funny but he cannot stop laughing. The guard calls for assistance. Two more guards come and take Leo by the arm, leading him back to his cell.

"It's all over, do you understand? The Djinn will rule we are all just God's Toys," he screams out in a crazed rant, no longer fearing that people will think he is crazy.

After examining Leo the prison doctor calls for Samantha Beresford, a psychiatrist who deals with incarcerated patients.

"He is babbling about some spirits that possess men and he claims that the royal family and presidents are all part of some conspiracy started by a superior race of beings. Plus he just keeps laughing. All the time laughing," the doctor tells Samantha.

She meets with Leo twice over the next couple of days. It is not uncommon for felons who had carried out murders to imitate insanity as some sort of excuse and so she is always thorough and never overreacts.

"He is mad as a fucking hatter," she explains to the prison doctor. "He is not fit for trial, or any sort of stress at all."

Leo is to be held on a special wing for at-risk inmates until a place for him at Rampton can be found. His family are contacted. Regina feels relief that the reason for his behaviour and abandonment has been due to what the psychiatrist has described as a slow deterioration and loss of stability of the mind leading to delusions and an eventual complete breakdown. For the first time in over eighteen months Regina goes to visit Leo. She cries from the minute she arrives until the moment she leaves. When she enters the small private room where Leo is waiting, her tears turn to sobs. The man she had loved just stares, mumbling to himself, then laughing, then crying. It is as if he has never known her, or that she is not even there.

For over an hour Regina tries to speak to him but it seems he is lost altogether. She is glad she hadn't allowed Megan, their daughter, to come along. This man sitting in front of her is not the kind, loving, hard-working, family man she had fallen in love with. That man has gone and in his place sits a bumbling mess, a wreck who had purposely got caught stealing, then assaulted a poor police officer and had now killed a young man for no other reason than because he was gay. She accepts that this is an illness but still she feels anger towards him. Why now? They should be enjoying their retirement, sunning themselves in Italy, awaiting visits from their children and grandchildren. Regina feels robbed and angry.

"This is a waste of time. You can't even understand what I'm saying, can you?" she says to Leo as he reads from an imaginary book. Regina stands. "I'm going to leave now, Leo. I don't think I will be back." She turns, knocks on the door and is released.

"I'm sorry, my beautiful wife," Leo whispers as the door closes behind her.

STOKE PRISON PRESENT DAY

"As flies to wanton boys are we to gods."
King Lear, Shakespeare

When Shane hears the news that Leo is to be committed to the Rampton mental institution for the criminally insane, he has two trains of thought. First, that it is probably for the best; the old guy is proper mental. The second is concern about how close he has become to believing everything Leo has said. He'd even turned down the chance to go to this experimental holiday camp up in Blackpool due to his paranoia around these fucking ghosts that Leo had told him about.

Still, he feels no resentment to the old guy; he just feels a little stupid. Shane also had to question if the Black Muslim guy was guilty of anything other than being part of Leo's illusions, and maybe he did only break up a fight between Leo and gay Gray after all. Whatever it was, it is over now and Shane wonders if there is a way he could be reconsidered for the Swedish hotty's project.

Robert is not sure of his next move. He had been sent here to protect the old Jew and was told that he must make sure nothing happens to this Shane Mills as well. He is certain that Shane is not his biggest fan and some of the other prisoners had told him to be careful as they had heard Shane was looking to take him out. This was going to make things difficult as Chamuel had insisted that under no circumstances was he to kill this white boy. Anyway, until he hears from Chamuel there is nothing he can do, so best not to over think it. If the soldier starts a fight he will just have to defend himself without causing too much damage. Although, from what he's heard this guy is a pretty formidable fighter. Robert hopes that Chamuel will contact him before the two clash.

Leo had been sorry to mislead Regina but the sudden epiphany he'd had in the yard has left him believing something is about to happen and he needs to stay within these walls and stay alive, at least until he fulfils his mission. Convincing the head-shrink he was mad had been easy; he just told her the truth about the Djinn. But now it is important that he gets a message to Shane. He is sure that he has read the signs right and that Reuben is about to attack. He tries to remember what Simeon had told him once when they were sitting outside yet another café bar in the Morano district, a beautiful group of islands connected by a series of bridges just outside Venice's centre.

"There are many logistical problems in contacting someone when you have little idea where they are, or even who they are," said Simeon. "So when we Djinn wish to make alliances with each other we have used different methods. A favourite of mine was hiding symbols in cultural art and by using semiotics I'd communicate with other Djinn without alerting mankind to our existence. Many historical books, writings, plays, musical compositions and paintings carry messages that the Arc Hon or Djinn can interpret. Lately a few of the human intelligentsia have begun to decipher the meaning behind some of the symbols. Then you have the conspiracy theorists, seeing signs where there are none mostly but actually uncovering many of our messages."

Simeon saw from the blank expression on Leo's face that he had no idea what he was talking about so he pulled out a tablet from his bag and brought up some images.

"Rembrandt," said Leo, pleased with himself.
Simeon nodded. "Isaac and I had many an alliance during the previous four hundred years. We used paintings by mostly Dutch artists, this way we knew the messages were for us and we had our own code.

"If you see this one, titled *Belshazzar's Feast...*" Simeon enlarged the image of a very detailed oil painting depicting a group of people at a feast looking on in horror as an unconnected hand writes on the wall behind them. "This was my communication to Isaac that Reuben had persuaded Ferdinand, the current emperor of the Holy Roman Empire, to attack the French on 18th September 1635."

Leo looked at it, waiting for the explanation.

"You see, the writing on the wall is the date. Translated it means *nine plus nine of the nine*. The man wearing the robes is Belshazzar but it's actually a portrait of me or how I appeared in my first incarnation. The spilt wine is a symbol for bloodshed." Leo had no time for this bullshit. Simeon and he had been talking like this for eighteen months. Time, for the long-living Djinn, may feel different but to Leo it felt like he was quickly running out of it.

"You keep telling me that I will need to mentor a champion to win this game for the human race. I need to know more useful stuff. What of the opponents? Who are they?"

Simeon nodded. "You are right. I am prone to nostalgia. To my reckoning there are only four, perhaps five, Djinn left, out of the original thirteen. There is Levi who is pulling the strings in America, Judd is prevalent in the Orient and then Asher controls the Politburo and the Middle East. I will tell you all about each of them but there is one in particular you must be aware of."

Leo was well aware of the one he was talking about.

"You mean Reuben."

Simeon nodded. "However, all of them must be eliminated. When the thirteen Djinn first arrived we stayed for thirty years in what you now know as Israel. We needed to acclimatise and get used to having a physical presence. We spent the time planning our journeys. Each of us took a name from one of the tribes that lived in the lands. When the time was right we left the hospitality of the then king, Solomon, who we rewarded for helping us. Each of us had nothing but a small guard and a harem and some gold.

"Benjamin stayed in the Levant, Reuben headed for what we now call Italy, Levi went to Egypt, I went to Greece, Zeb to China, Judd to Persia, Daniel went to Ethiopia, Naphtali crossed to South America, Isaac went to Iberia, Asher headed for northern Europe, and Gad, he headed to the North of Africa. Oh and Ephraim went to the Indian subcontinent and

Manasseh crossed to North America. On the day we left we all took oaths and each of us was assigned one of the four Watchers."

Leo had brought out his pen and some paper. "Who got which Watcher?"

"Okay, let's see, Amitiel was assigned Isaac, Gad, and Ephraim; Chamuel would be mine, Naphtali's and Judd's; Raphael looked after Ben, Daniel and Levi; the others, Reuben, Manasseh, Zeb and Asher, were Michael's."

Leo felt like a reporter getting the scoop on the greatest revelation ever, still writing as he talked. "So am I right in assuming you all then built your empires from these original locations?"

"Well, the first part was to send us out into the world, so to speak, so we could settle in before the game really got going. Remember, all we had was the small guard, the harem of women and some gold. We were on our own in a dangerously savage world with only our wits to guide us. The rules stated that we pitch our tents in the chosen destinations. The first part of the competition required us to stay there and build our tribe over the next couple of hundred years. We could not contact a Watcher or each other for this period. Then after two hundred years the game began. Those first years were both terrifying and exciting at the same time."

Leo could hear from Simeon's voice that these were memories of a time he had enjoyed.

"I was fortunate to have picked a comparatively civilised part of the world and I set myself up as a scholar. In fact my first student was the epic poet Homer. My next move was to create one of the strongest tools known to man."

Leo knew he was meant to ask. "Which was?"

"The written word! Using symbols I developed what you know as the Phoenician Alphabet. I didn't invent it but let's just say I helped make sense of it. This simple process propelled my chosen tribe towards being the world's leaders in all aspects of communication and academics."

"Then once the first two hundred years were over, we could go wherever we wanted, but obviously for most of us we used these original hubs as our strongholds. For instance, if you follow Reuben's trail he discovered Rome then built its empire slowly but surely over centuries. It was a steep learning curve for him. He was the first of us to realise that to win this game you would need more than a large army, as he witnessed barbarian rabbles overrunning his highly trained armies and knew that chaos could easily prevail.

"Reuben was inspired by the Jewish religion from Israel that Isaac had adopted and devised a plan to create a worldwide religion that everyone would buy into. So he found a young ideologist he met in Judea, chucked in a virgin birth, a faked death and there you had it: Christianity. So while his first great empire crashed around him, he rose another. Later Isaac, Levi and I all infiltrated this religion in various attempts to divide it and reduce its power from within. Reuben was very nearly defeated but unfortunately off the back of the Frankish empire he continued his domain under the name of the Holy Roman Empire.

"This was the first Reich. Eventually this sham of an empire was also torn down, defeated by Napoleon's forces under the mentorship of Levi, who had moved north from Egypt and had concentrated his efforts on Europe, although he still had a soft spot for his original country.

"Reuben didn't accept defeat, of course, instead he slowly developed his Aryan plan. He had a brief revival in Germany under Bismarck, his second Reich. He brought the empires of Germany and Austria together and started the First World War, a war he always intended to lose, by the way. This was the master stroke – by losing he created a powerful mix of injustice and outrage that allowed him to create the largest military force known to man: the Nazis and the inception of his Third Reich."

Leo shook his head thinking how ironic it would sound to people to know that both Christ and the antichrist evolved from the same source.

"Isaac, Levi and Asher joined forces to defeat Reuben, of course," said Simeon. "It was touch and go for a while but they did it in the end. The defeat should have been the end of Reuben but he wasn't ready to give up, not by a long shot. By bending the rules and killing Isaac he adopted, or more accurately stole, the tactic of financial dominance. Now he has risen once again to be the leading Jinni in the quest to be the Host and soon he will attempt to create the fourth Reich. His New World Order."

"I get that the prize is to be the Host but what does that actually mean?" asked Leo.

"Whoever is dominating the challenge as judged by the Watchers is termed the Host. It's a temporary title but will become permanent once all the others have been defeated."

"When you say defeated, do you mean killed? None can remain?" The reply he received was not straightforward.

"In some cases a Jinni is disqualified, like I was. You can also be disqualified if your tribe yields the least influence and their pursuit has become untenable. Manasseh was the first to go; he was unsuccessful in bringing the North American indigenous people to any real power, unlike Naphtali in the South American continent, who successfully mentored the Mesoamerican dynasties such as the Mayans, Incas and Aztecs. Once Manasseh was removed then all the others could compete for his territory and so the United States was born. After a Jinni is disqualified the Watchers remove the individual from the game and send them back to our space in this world, Gheisthelm."

"When you say your space, is that like, a different dimension or a different planet…?"

Simeon sighed. "Not really, you see a dimension describes height, width, depth. We Djinn occupy the same space, just on a different frequency."

Leo was none the wiser but nodded as if he understood. Simeon carried on.

"Over the last four hundred years, six of the Djinn have disappeared and not returned to our home. The only explanation for this is that one of us is killing other Djinn and removing their amulets so they cannot return to Corona and give evidence against their murderer."

Leo still found it difficult to sympathise with the death of a handful of Djinn who themselves were culpable in uncountable atrocities.

"We never envisaged Djinn killing other Djinn so we had no contingency plan for this event. The conclusion I have come to is that Reuben will set up his Aryan-Christian kingdom on earth and remain as a god-like deity, to be worshipped and served by an enslaved human race."

"That's it? That's his grand plan – to sit on a throne and lord over a bunch of what he considers animals?" Leo said, confused. "What is the point?"

"There is more," said Simeon. "The coming Nibiru that we suspect will carry the Demiurge…"

"I cannot cope with more," said Leo. "Not right now."

"You must listen it was never the intention of the game – to rule over humans," said Simeon. "The Host is supposed to bring the same enlightenment to humans that the Arc Hon brought to us, you see…"

Those were the last words Simeon said to Leo before the shooting.

Leo had noticed the two young men on the scooter pull up opposite the café that he and Simeon were sitting outside. As Leo listened to Simeon tell him about the Rapture that was to befall the human race he was aware of the passenger on the scooter pulling out what looked like a sub-machine gun. Even after all that had happened Leo didn't fully realise the situation. It wasn't until the man pointed the gun directly at the table where they were that the reality hit: this was an assassination attempt and he was at best in the way, at worst the target.

Simeon noticed the panic on Leo's face, and spun round just as the shooter opened fire. Simeon was no stranger to danger and always picked tables that were tucked out of the way by a wall or behind a pillar, and with plenty of alternative escape routes. Leo instinctively dived under the table as glass and wood splintered with the impact of the bullets that sprayed around him. Screams of customers caught in the crossfire were drowned out by the noise of the guns and Leo looked on in horror as the shooter confidently came closer still, reeling off bullets. The fact their eyes met clearly confirmed to Leo that he was one of the targets.

Simeon had jumped behind a concrete flower cradle. He sat upright, his back to the shooter, looking at Leo as the fire stopped for a second. Leo was sure he saw him smile before he jumped to his feet and ran full pelt at his attacker. He remembered his surprise at the agility and speed that Simeon showed as he leaped over a table, rolled and then sprang to his feet, still careering towards the shooter. At least two bullets hit Simeon, slowing him down but not halting his momentum as he dived into the midriff of the gunman. To his shame Leo took advantage of this distraction and crawled to the open door of the café. When he felt he was covered by enough onlookers he got to his feet and ran through the diner and out of a back door. Leo kept running and running until he reached the town centre, where he flagged down a taxi and made his escape back to his apartment. Once there he had packed his bags and headed to the airport. He was getting out. Simeon was most likely dead and he had no idea what he was supposed to do next. He was an accountant, for the love of God! He wasn't equipped for this type of thing!

From the gunman firing his first shot to Leo boarding a plane to Birmingham airport was less than five hours. Birmingham was the first flight out of Venice and Leo had a second cousin living in nearby Coventry; for now that would have to do. Leo caught a bus from the airport straight into Coventry. He called at his cousin's home in a council estate on the outskirts of the city. The address was 85 Raphael Close. How ironic, he would later think.

"Nah, mate. No, Peter here. This is my gaff now," said the large, rough-looking young man who answered the door.

Leo's face dropped and he meandered off as he contemplated his next move. He had less than a hundred euros in his pocket and was reluctant to use a card, knowing that Reuben had control of many security agencies and could maybe trace his location. How true this really was, Leo did not know, but nothing resided outside the realms of possibility any more.

At the end of the path Leo shuffled to a halt and looked around. He hadn't noticed on the way here how run-down this estate was: boarded-up empty houses, a pack of three mongrel dogs parading around, cars with bricks for wheels. It was also getting quite late. Leo felt pangs of anxiety build up inside of him but where on earth was he going to go?

A black kid appeared and Leo swallowed nervously.

"Listen, Leo, come with me."

Nothing surprised him anymore.

"Where to?" he asked the boy.

"Just come with me," said the boy. "You need a friend and it won't take Reuben long to find out you came here. Boiled sweet?"

The young guy offered up a brown paper bag containing boiled sweets then nodded his head indicating for Leo to follow him. Not exactly convinced but at least happy to have a plan of action, Leo followed.

They crossed the road and walked to a sporty-looking ten-year-old BMW. "This will do," the kid remarked and then pulled out a tennis ball that had been cut in half. He placed the rim of the half ball around the door lock and pressed it to form an airtight seal. He whacked the ball with his hand, the air forcing the locks to pop open.

"Come on, Pops. This is probably the local drug dealer's car, we best get going before he looks out."

Leo looked around and, with one of the most uncharacteristic actions of his life, climbed into the passenger seat of the stolen car. The young boy expertly started the car and they drove off. Leo's first question was not who are you, or why are you helping me, but rather, "Are you old enough to drive?"

The boy laughed. "Mister, we just robbed this car. I just coerced you into grand theft auto and all you want to know is how old I am?"

They spent the rest of the journey in silence as they drove out of Coventry and twenty miles up the road to Birmingham. Leo saw a sign for the jewellery quarter. The car pulled up outside a florist that sat in between two jewellery shops. The young lad jumped out.

"Come on, old guy."

The odd couple headed into the shop. A lady preparing a bouquet looked up as the shop door opened.

"Hi, Chamuel," she smiled.

Ah, so that is who he is, thought Leo, one of the Arc Hon. As surreal as the situation was, Leo did not question what was occurring. They walked through a small kitchen at the back of the shop and up some steps into a small flat. A little settee and an old-style TV occupied the room.

"Take a seat, old man," instructed Chamuel.

Leo sat and stared at the TV, wondering if this Arc Hon would ever stop calling him "old man" – especially ironic since the Arc Hon was goodness knows how old himself.

"So, I guess you have a few questions," said Chamuel, sitting on the arm of the settee. "Let me explain. I am going to help you out, and hopefully save your life. My name is Chamuel..."

"Yes," said Leo. "I know who you are. Although I thought you would be older."

"Old man, ya really got issues wiv youff, ain't ya?" the boy cackled.

Leo resists the compulsion to correct Chamuel's grammar. "The only thing I don't know is why you are helping me. Simeon told me that the Watchers 'watched' and didn't really get involved."

"Yah blood, that's true but we got to get wiv the programme on dis un."

Leo was struggling to decipher this coded lingo. "Are sure you are an eternal entity who has existed for eons, because you sound like some chavvy kid."

"I am an urban renaissance man. Check dis out..."

To Leo's amazement Chamuel burst into a rap.

"Mister you dissing an immortal being,
Ya wanna be careful ya know I'm supreme.
I is Arc Hon. I can do powerful stuff.
If you like how I'm talking, I ain't said enough."

Chamuel clicked his fingers, pleased with himself. "Yeah man, I got tunes."

Leo had recently experienced many surreal moments but this topped them all.

"Okay... may I enquire as to why are you helping me?"

"Man, that Reuben, he gone and fucked up. He is one bad fucker. He broke all the rules and now he gone and kicked off in a neutral zone. That fascist-making, child-murdering cunt has pissed me and the other Watchers right of. He want to fuck with us, then we gonna to see who is the man, ya understand what I'm saying, blood?"

"Not really," said Leo, but he got the idea. "So, you are going to eliminate Reuben?"

"No, man! Did Simeon not tell you nothing?" Chamuel began to pace around the room. "Reuben has gone all Colonel, Walter E. Kurtz on us."

Leo stared blankly. "He has gone what, on whom?"

"Man, you never watch films? Marlon Brando... Colonel Kurtz... *Apocalypse Now*??? He goes AWOL and starts his own game. No? Fuck's sake man, what you being doing with your life..."

Leo's continued blank stare betrayed the fact he had no idea what was going on.

Chamuel sighed. "Reuben is disqualified but he ain't playing by the rules no more. We fink he has killed most the other Djinn and when he gets the rest he is gonna enslave the human race, ya understand me?"

Leo had heard this prophecy of doom from Simeon and their belated concern angered him.

"Isn't that what all the Djinn were trying to do? I mean, we humans are just insects to both of you, right? This is just a game, isn't it? And we humans are just pawns. I mean what's the difference? Whichever of the damn Djinn win, the human race is fucked!"

"Stand down, Gramps. For a start us Arc Hon ain't nothing like the Djinn. In fact you humans are more like the Djinn. They is you, just a bit further down the evolutionary road, that's all. When we first came across Djinn they had limbs and heads and shit, they were just like you, organic,

179

pushed out of their mother's vagina, skin-covered motherfuckers. We watched as their race nearly became extinct. You see they was smart but they was weak, ya know what I mean?"

Leo shook his head in frustration. "No, how would I know what you mean?"

"Fuck man, what has that Simeon taught you? I mean, I know he renewed so maybe he ain't sure what's going on himself, but he must have talked about the ascension of the Djinn and shit... Please tell me he has told you about Nibiru and the coming of the Demiurge?"
Leo looked away. He'd had enough history lessons, thank you.

Chamuel took his expression on board. "Well, we ain't got time for that shit now anyway. We need to execute the plan."

"What plan?" said Leo hopefully.
He was pleased there was a plan. Chamuel whispered something under his breath about Simeon being a "useless hillbilly actual motherfucker", then began to explain. "Okay, so, you are going to prison."

Leo imagined this was a slang term for somewhere that was not really prison. He waited for a more accurate explanation of the plan.
Chamuel gave him an apologetic smile. "Seriously, prison is the safest place for you, man. I'm gonna put a friend in there who's gonna watch your back."

"Are you serious?" Leo said, surprising calmly. "You think I'm going to prison? What for? Why? How?"

"Listen to yourself: how, what, why! You got to stop asking and start doing, man, because if Reuben finds you he is going to fuck you up. He doesn't like Jews at the best of times so he is going to go all Spanish Inquisition on your ass. Anyway, there is another reason." He looked embarrassed. "One I can't tell you."

"Of course," thought Leo as he watched his life spiral hopelessly away from him.

"So basically we gotta get you to commit a crime. Nothing too serious, we don't wanna go clipping some white dude." Leo was relieved until he heard the next idea. "Maybe just armed robbery or something?" Chamuel paused for thought as he looked out the window. "Yeah...armed robbery, that's the trick. We can break into one of these jewellery shops downstairs. How does that sound?"

Leo had given up on being rational. "Great."

Within the hour Chamuel and Leo case the Gold is Us jeweller two doors down from the flower shop.

"Yeah, we do this one. He got a wicked Rolex in the window that'll look mighty fine on this wrist."
Leo looked confused. "But when we get caught they will take it off you, so what difference does it make?"

Chamuel revealed a big toothy smile and shook his head, looking at the floor then up to Leo before informing him. "'We' ain't getting caught, mister, 'you' is getting caught. I'm too pretty to go to prison. They be thinking their entire mother fucking Christmases come at once if they see my cute black ass in the shower."

⊸𓂀𓏏 𓈖𓂋𓏏𓈖

The crime was over in less than five minutes. They had a brief problem when Leo refused to go in armed so they agreed that he would have to at least assault a police officer while resisting arrest. As they entered the shop a tall man, early twenties, smiled at Leo asking him if he needed any help. "Plenty," Leo thought drily. When Chamuel followed him in carrying a holdall the man's attitude changed to one of caution and he returned behind his glass counter.

"Racist motherfucker sees a black man and thinks he's about to be held up!" remarked Chamuel. "Well, he is about to be held up." replied Leo.

"Yeah, well let's see his face when he realises Woody Allen is heading up the heist."

Despite the situation Leo laughed, albeit it slightly hysterically. Chamuel pulled out a machete and screamed in his best Hollywood tough guy voice. "OK Ishmael, fill this bag full of the sparkly shit or I'll cut your fucking head off."

The young shop attendant pressed an alarm under the counter and ran into the back of the shop, locking the door behind him. Chamuel randomly smashed the display cases and filled the holdall. He went to the shop window where the watch was displayed, reached in grabbed the Rolex then turned to Leo, handing him the holdall and a bag of boiled sweets.

"Enjoy and keep in touch."

Chamuel opened the door just as a cop car pulled up, and quick as a flash ran down the road. One young female officer ran after him as the male PC moved to apprehend Leo. Leo closed his eyes as he attempted, for the first time in his life, to assault another human being. The ineffectual punch caught the cop off guard, and as he stepped backwards he toppled off the pavement and fell to the road.

Shocked, Leo realised he could easily make his escape as the cop was slow to recover. *Fuck, what now?* He thought. Fortunately another squad car could be heard approaching. The only thing that Leo could think of doing while waiting for them to get there was to give it to the copper. He politely kicked the young PC, wondering how this lad would cope with a real villain as he curled up in a ball to protect himself. Soon Leo's ordeal was over as the second car screamed to a stop and two burly coppers wrestled little Leo to the floor.

"Fuck you, pigs!" he shouted unconvincingly. When questioned at the station he refused to cooperate and name his accomplice so they threw the book at him as he hoped they would.

🕯️👤⚰️🔌

Leo lies on his bunk and smiles at the absurd memory of being dragged away by police outside the jewellers; the look on the shop assistant's face had been a picture, as Chamuel had predicted. "Wow, that seems like yesterday and yet like a lifetime ago," he muses.

182

Leo is aware he has only bought himself a few weeks with his crazy act but he also knows that the signs indicate weeks are probably all he has left anyway. Now he needs to get in touch with Shane and somehow escape or die trying. If he's right the black guy, Robert, was "the friend" sent in by Chamuel and he has a vital part to play in the plan.

Vienna, 1910

"One does not establish a dictatorship in order to safeguard a revolution; one makes the revolution in order to establish the dictatorship." George Orwell

As arranged Chamuel and Amitiel waited for Reuben outside the Theatre An Der Wien in the Mariahilf district of Vienna. Chamuel had recently discovered the pleasure of boiled sweets and he took two from his pocket, offering a slightly fluff-covered yellow one to Amitiel. She declined.

"So, is he out of the game?" Chamuel asked his fellow Arc Hon.

"What do you think?" said Amitiel. "I mean, he was the last one to see Benjamin, he can be connected to all the other disappearances and we know he is responsible for slaughtering far too many humans unnecessarily. Whether he is the one doing all the killing or not, he is definitely out of control. We intercepted these only last week."

Amitiel showed Chamuel four black-and-white photos depicting mutilated gypsy children.

"Ah, I see you're appreciating my artwork." The tall, gaunt, pale blonde Reuben appeared behind the two Arc Hon.

"Humph," said Amitiel, unimpressed. "Every form you take looks the same. I assume you have worked out that I am Amitiel and this is Chamuel. We have not met for a long time and I don't think you two have ever had the pleasure."

Reuben looked at Amitiel. Her current form was a teenager of angelic beauty and he had trouble dragging his eyes off her delicate features. He then directed a disgusted stare at Chamuel, a skinny black ragamuffin.

"No... I tend to avoid the western Oriental gentlemen. I'm not very cosmopolitan," he commented.

Reuben pulled out some keys and opened a side door into the theatre.

"All these years I have only had dealings with the big guy, why am I now relegated to the lackeys?"

"Michael prefers that we deal with this issue," Amitiel lied.

"Come in, we won't be disturbed," said Reuben. "I suggest we go to my office to conduct this business. I need to open the theatre in an hour so I hope this won't take too long."

Amitiel and Chamuel looked at each other and both shook their heads at his casual manner. They followed him up some stairs and into a plush first-floor office that looked out over the street.

"Take a seat." Reuben stood behind his desk as he waited for his guests to sit. "Now, what can I do for you?"

Chamuel spoke first. "We are investigating several accusations of misconduct and rules being broken including the very serious disappearance of several Djinn. We have information that leads us to believe that you are responsible for their demise, and the fact they have not returned to their former states."

Reuben looked unconcerned and gave a nonchalant shake of his head; his face was calm and open. He reached for a brandy bottle and three glasses.

"Are you old enough for one of these?" he joked as he poured each of them a measure. "Now, I assume you will be presenting evidence of these accusations."

Chamuel stood up sharply. "We are the Watchers, Djinn, and we don't need evidence. If we believe the charges, which we do, then it is for you to prove otherwise. Our intention in coming here is more of a courtesy call, to give you twenty-four hours to get your things in order before we return you to Gheisthelm."

"You say several Djinn."

Amitiel nodded, wary.

"And you assume that the same murderer killed all of them?"

She nodded again.

"May I inquire who the last to die was?"

"Benjamin," said Chamuel. "Coincidentally just two days after you and he held a summit on the alliance between his Ottoman empire and your Prussian kingdom: an alliance he refused."

Reuben smiled as he began his defence. "He did indeed and I was quite upset that he was so stupid; however, I did not kill him over it and I can prove it."

Chamuel sat and gestured for Reuben to continue.

"You say yourself that this happened only two days after my last meeting with Benjamin. I will take this as a fact seeing as you have stated it, although I am curious how you are able to pinpoint this event so accurately?"

"Benjamin was under my council," said Chamuel. "He contacted me and asked that we monitor his aura as he was concerned that due to meeting with you, his existence was in danger." Chamuel smiled as he delivered this information.

Reuben sipped his drink. He licked the liquid from his lips and made a slight purring sound before offering his defence.

"Obviously you didn't watch it well enough. Now, I admit to a heated argument with Benjamin; however, I am devastated that he would have considered me a threat. I have nothing but admiration for Benny boy."

Chamuel sighed at Reuben's attempt at innocence. "Reuben, we are not human simpletons that you can manipulate with your bullshit. You need evidence and it needs to be solid."

"It is. I can prove that I was nowhere near Benjamin during that period of time and I have a witness."

Both Amitiel and Chamuel laughed. "We have not told you where he was when he died, so you cannot possibly say that you were nowhere near," said Amitiel. "We have questioned all the remaining Djinn so we know none of them are your witness and we do not accept human witnesses. So please, can you stop wasting time here? As you said, the theatre opens soon."

A bell rang from downstairs.

"Ah, that will be my witness," Reuben said and exited the office to answer the door.

Chamuel and Amitiel exchanged concerned looks. They waited patiently as they heard muffled talking coming up the stairs.

"My dear Watchers, may I present my witness."

From behind him Solfrid, the first of the Djinn, entered. Chamuel and Amitiel were stunned.

"Hello," she said. "I am sorry to cause you to waste time but if you had informed me of your action against Reuben I would have told you he was at a pogue with me. I was with him acting as his visor. He was in a meditation chamber during the period in question and for the following six weeks. Unless you are mistaken about the dates, I'm afraid you have made a terrible mistake."

Chamuel's head reddened. He felt the human emotion of embarrassment and the even stronger one of contempt, as he noticed Reuben's wry smile in his direction. Solfrid was the very first of the Djinn to cross into the physical plane – she was highly regarded by all, as the humans might revere a queen. Not only that but she was the original architect of the game and basically invented the rules. The Arc Hon might have been invited in as referees but she was the one with the final say. Chamuel stood and walked to the window, trying to control his anger, knowing the charge would have to be dropped. He stared outside at the street below noting how peaceful it all was down there: people enjoying the sunny day, street performers entertaining the crowds, a small tramp selling his painted postcards to a young family, while a tall man waited with a rose in his hand looking anxious. A well-dressed gentleman sat at the corner of the fountain and took out his lunch. Two police men patrolled the streets and seemed to be about to move the postcard-selling tramp on. Amitiel could no longer bear the long, embarrassing silence.

"Well, in that case I think our work here is done," she said out loud, hoping to re-engage Chamuel. He turned suddenly as if he had just had an epiphany and his face lit up.

"Although we have not met before, Reuben, I have followed your progress with great interest. Your methods are ruthless but, I must admit, effective."

Unable to see past Chamuel's skin colour Reuben dismissed the praise and opened the door to let them out.

"I also believe you claim that you could do anything the others could or, if I'm correct, you could do better." Reuben closed the door again.

Chamuel readied himself, as if he had just had a tug on his line and he did not want this one to get away. "You may have heard of the wager that the Arc Hon Raphael had with Zeb?"
Solfrid narrowed her eyes but this time Reuben was unable to hide his interest.

"Yes," said Reuben. "Raphael waged that if Zeb allowed him to pick his next protégé and found success with said person he would allow him access to the Almanac, which, may I add, has given him an unfair advantage over the rest of us."

"Well, it would have, but he was one of the unfortunates that was murdered."
Reuben shook his head sadly. "What is the world coming to?"

"Strangely enough he was also the only one tortured, as if the murderer was after information."

"Tsk. Well, surely that is further proof it was not me. I would have tortured all of them."

"Mmm, so back to the wager." Chamuel smiled without humour. "I propose a similar challenge with you. I will pick you a new protégé and if you can rise with the nominee as your protégé and, let's say, get your Prussian empire back on track before the middle of the century, then I will give you access to the Almanac."

Amitiel gave a little gasp of surprise but Chamuel was happy with his proposition. He couldn't help but think that Reuben had already got hold of all the information contained in the Almanac (how else was he doing so well?) but he could never admit to this. And if he refused the challenge he would look weak in front of the others, another thing he could never admit to. No right-minded Djinn in the game would refuse an opportunity to look at the Almanac but for Reuben, it would surely only slow down his carefully laid-out plans.

"Well, that's an offer I can't refuse." Reuben's irritated tone betrayed his real feelings; he knew he had been tricked and must take the wager.

"Come on, then," said Reuben, coming over to the window. "Which of the simpletons will I nurture for greatness?"

Chamuel stared out the window once more. He saw the man holding the rose still waiting. Perhaps he had been stood up. Well, his fortune was about to change, not necessarily for the better, but it was going to change.

"There, over by the park. That man standing alone."

"Where? There is no man alone?"

Chamuel looked back and saw the expectant girl had arrived, a bubbly, gay young thing. He considered confirming the target when the young tramp came into view with his dog in tow.

"That one there. The guy carrying the paintings with the little dog."

Reuben's face betrayed his loathing. The man was not only a small, insignificant-looking reprobate but his jet-black hair left Reuben suspecting he could be Arab, or worse, a Jew!

"He will be your next and only assignment, only via him can you compete. Agreed?"

Both Amitiel and Solfrid looked to see the pathetic wretch whom Chamuel had allotted to Reuben. Reuben was still straining to hide his disdain. "As you wish," he said through gritted teeth.

Amitiel smiled at Chamuel, Solfrid looked bemused.

"Now, we don't want to keep you, I'm sure you need to get the theatre open and of course you may want to feed your new protégé."

As Amitiel and Chamuel left she commented, "That was cruel but funny. You think it will slow him down?"

They walked to the park and were surprised to see the young tramp had set up pitch only a few metres from where he had been moved on from. Chamuel felt a pang of guilt and thought to himself that the guy had balls so he went up to him and gave him ten times the value of the postcard for a painting of what looked like a local building. He was a bit taken aback when he received no thanks but was, in fact, ignored. The tramp, however, did walk up to Amitiel and handed her a picture of the theatre. "This is for you. Keep it, I will be a famous artist one day, more famous than Mozart or Beethoven."

She looked at the picture then glanced at his signature:

Adolf Hitler.

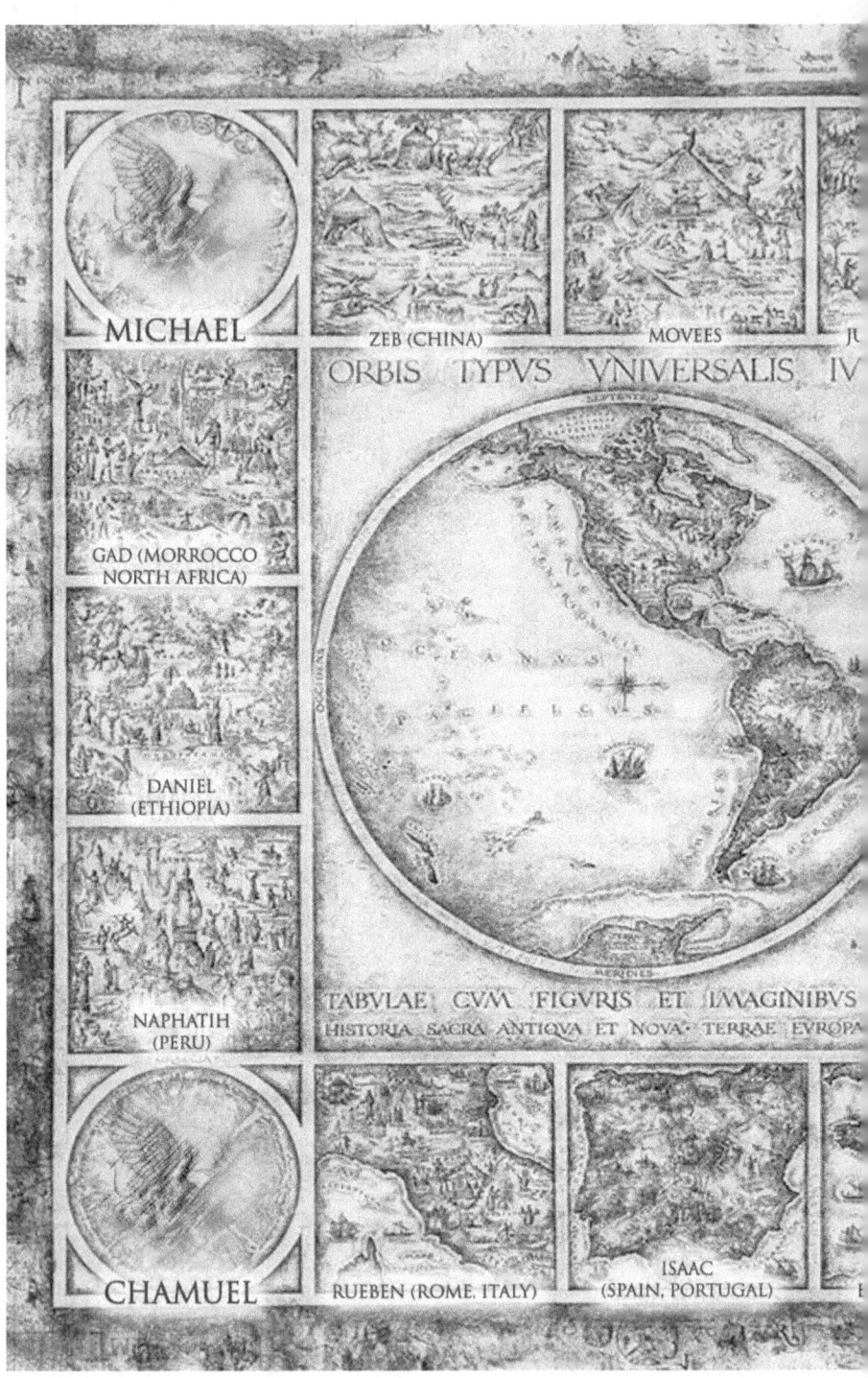

MICHAEL

ZEB (CHINA)

MOVEES

J[

ORBIS TYPVS VNIVERSALIS IV

GAD (MORROCCO NORTH AFRICA)

DANIEL (ETHIOPIA)

NAPHATIH (PERU)

TABVLAE CVM FIGVRIS ET IMAGINIBVS
HISTORIA SACRA ANTIQVA ET NOVA· TERRAE EVROPA

CHAMUEL

RUEBEN (ROME, ITALY)

ISAAC (SPAIN, PORTUGAL)

LEVI (EGYPT)

ASHER (SCANDANAVIA)

AMITIEL

TORICORVM TRADITIONEM·

MANASSEK
(NORTH AMERICA)

BENJAMIN
STAYED IN THE LEVANT

MVNDI VSQVE NOSTRVM TEMPORIS·
INTERPRETATIONES METAMORPHOSES ET SIMBOLA·

SIMEON (GREECE)

GERMAINIA

SHARK (AURA)

RAPHAEL

2146 AD

Raphael's derelict house, thirty seconds after the Protection Squadron officers are slaughtered by their own captain

"We must hurry," shouts the captain. "Freya pig-face will be back soon."

Adam and Ember remain frozen in fear and shock. Adam struggles once again to get to his feet. Ember snaps out of her trance enough to help him. He smiles at her groggily.

"Let's just get out of here, yeah?" he says, distress still clear on his face.

Ember just nods, too scared her words will tremble if she speaks. They follow as the captain runs up an old metal staircase and leads them through a labyrinth of corridors. "Where are we going?" Adam asks as Ember helps him hobble along.

"Out of here. I will explain when we get to the Jeep."

"No!" Ember declares. "I am not going anywhere with you! Who are you? What has just happened?" Ember is close to hysterics; her head feels like it's about to explode. What is going on, is this some crazy reality prank show she has stumbled into? Are there hidden cameras? No, she has brain splatter on her clothes and there are dead bodies and blood everywhere. She needs answers before she goes anywhere.

"Why did you just kill all those men? You are one of them, you were about to rape me!" Ember's eyes narrow as the fear and anger rise again.

The captain stops to turn and look at Adam who looks both terrified and confused at the same time. He asks, "Do you not recognise me, my young grasshopper?"

Adam's jaw drops. Grasshopper was Raphael's nickname for him, a name he says originated from the greatest TV series ever made. Adam never asked what this meant but liked the reference to an extinct insect.

"How do you know what Raphael called me?" Not waiting for an answer he leaps at the captain whom he has just witnessed aid in the killing of his mentor and friend, and then who for some reason saved both him and Ember from the Protection Squadron. "You killed him, you shit!" Adam surprises himself as he rains blows down on the man, screaming out loud, "You even stole his jacket, you bastard!"

Raphael laughs, the groggy punches having little effect on him.

"It's great to know you care so much, grasshopper, but I am not dead. I just body swapped."

The man restrains Adam then addresses both the youngsters. "If I explain everything to you both, then by the time I am finished we won't have time to get away. Ember, you can see it's me, I know you can."

She nods slowly as she watches the smoky snake dance around his head. Adam opens his mouth to ask her how but a loud scream startles him. All of them recognise Freya Mortensson's voice.

"Whoa? Already? We'd better go." Raphael pushes a side door open. "Quick, this way."

More scared of Freya than this guy, Ember and Adam glance at each other with a resigned look before following him down a set of rickety stairs and out into a courtyard. Ember vaults up an eight-foot wall then reaches down to help pull Adam up, the recent adrenaline surge pushing the remains of the toxin through his system faster. Raphael looks down at the fat belly he has just inherited and with a groan runs at the wall and manages to grab the top before scrambling up.

The Protection Squadron officers can be heard crashing into the yard. The three fugitives leap to the other side and sprint down a narrow alley. Two shots are fired then one guard shouts, "The captain is with them, hold your fire, radio for the dogs."

Adam recognises their location when he spots the jeep. They have come out the back of the building and circled around to the front. Raphael leaps into the driver's seat, Ember and Adam jump in the back. Dogs can be heard gaining on them as Raphael attempts to turn the key.

"We won't get away in this old thing," Ember shouts.

"I told you, don't dis the Raff-mobile!" replies Raphael, as the motor turns and the car's wheels spin away from the attack hounds.

A police Volkswagen S690 with a top speed of 230mph and armed with CSV net technology, two hyper modules and an ultrasound drum, approaches at high speed and is soon hanging on the tail of the jeep. A Superfly Aircopter dives from the sky and hovers above them and up ahead two more VW S690s block the road.

"Pull over or we will be forced to fire upon you," the amplified voice yells to them.

"We can't escape, pull over," Ember advises Raphael. Adam looks at her like she is bat-shit crazy but every instinct in her body is screaming out for them to follow instructions, to get back to the safety of her father and the world of comfort and luxury that she knows so well. She never knew she would yearn for conformity quite so much.

Instead Raphael says, "Hold on tight!" as he floors the accelerator and points the surprisingly rapid old banger at the blockade ahead. Ember screams and Adam freezes as they see their lives flash before them. They both have a feeling that this is only the beginning and that their comfortable childhoods are definitely coming to an end.

The car hurtles towards the road block and the four PS officers standing behind the cars scurry away, realising the inevitable collision. Raphael has a manic look on his face as he focuses on the task of hitting the red switch at the very same time that the jeep hits the two VWs.

"Hold on and don't die!" he cries out.

The observing officers witness a massive explosion on impact. The Aircopter is thrown around by a disproportionately powerful aftershock, the pilot struggling to regain control. Freya Mortensson's vehicle pulls up next to the smoking carnage. She exits the VW and walks as close to the scene as possible. Heat slows her progress as she tries to ascertain the damage. Clearly all occupants of the old car will be dead. Freya is sad that her captain is dead, sad because she will not be able to torture him while seeking an explanation of why, after years of loyal service, he turned on his own to protect enemies of the state. She is glad she broke protocol and played the disc though and has seen some idiot boy from the twenty-first-century singing some song that just repeats the word 'baby' instead of the message from the Antihost, Shane Mills, otherwise she would not have returned and seen the prisoners escaping with her captain.

Freya frowns as the smoke clears. Her expression changes to one of utter confusion as she sees only the two VWs smashed up. She looks around frantically.

"Where the hell are they?"

𝕬𝕬𝕬 ⚏ ⚎

"Are we dead?" asks Adam, as he looks at the bright white light surrounding the three of them.

The jeep seems to be melting away and they are being carried by pure light over Jinn City. He feels disembodied, as if he is dreaming. He knows that Ember is next to him but cannot see her. He also knows that Raphael is with them. He hears Ember ask, "What is happening?" A whirling prism of colour veils the scene below, then stillness. Everything freezes. Adam feels calm as he imagines he is stuck in a still-life photo, then, for a few seconds, they gently drift.

Suddenly the sensation of dropping seizes him and as if woken from a deep slumber, fear takes over. A building is hurtling towards him. They will surely smash into the rapidly nearing ground! He hears a clunking sound and can see the components of the car reassemble around him, only this time it is an electric-blue 1950s-style Chevy. He looks down at his hands. They are half formed with tiny shards of light emanating from them. He sees both Ember and Raphael in their seats but they are made up of colours still swirling, gradually becoming solid and then another shift sees them all regain full physical presence. A shooting pain slices across his back and Ember's screams of agony confirm they are awake and thankfully alive. The car is now complete around them, and, as if it had just driven down a bumpy steep ramp, it throws the passengers about before landing fully formed on a long stretch of road.

"Holy fucking moly! That was awesome!" cries out Raphael.

Adam holds on to the side door, breathing erratically and experiencing his first panic attack. He feels as if there is no oxygen. As if he is emerging from beneath the sea, his lungs fill several deep breaths and he frantically looks around for Ember. She too is gasping for air, unable to speak. He looks at Raphael who seems more interested in checking his car's metamorphosis

"You gotta love a Chevy."

Eventually Raphael looks around and checks his passengers are also okay. Both sit staring at him with their mouths open. Shock has taken over. Raphael slowly drives into a side street then gets out, opening the back doors.

"Hurry, we need to move," he tells them. "Be careful though, you've just passed through a vortex wormhole and your bodies will need time to realign."

Dazed, both teenagers follow his instructions without question as they struggle to gather their thoughts and find they can barely walk.

"Bambi on ice," remarks Raphael as he takes Ember's arm to prevent her from collapsing. "Take deep breaths and close your eyes. It'll all be fine in a few minutes."

As promised, Ember feels her faculties return and Adam looks steady.

The two follow Raphael down a side street and into a dingy-looking bar. Adam suspects that they are in the Oriental sector of the city, but can't fathom how they got here; this part of the city is at least an hour away from the road block. They continue past the bar area and out the back through the kitchens, the staff appearing unconcerned. A door at the back of the kitchen leads them into a candlelit room. Both the youngsters are instantly aware of unfamiliar but pleasant odours.

A very fat, tattoo-covered man who is of East Asian descent sits smoking from a large multi-stemmed glass pipe. Several differently coloured plumes of smoke pour from its many ports and each seems to carry its own essence, creating a strangely calming environment. He looks up casually as the door opens and nods towards Raphael. The room has the appearance of a small Buddhist temple and there is a bench attached to the wall. The large man points to the seat and indicates for his new guests to sit.

"Hello, Raphael. I was not expecting you."

"Hello, Baal," responds Raphael. "We need your help."

As the two men become locked in muted conversation, Ember and Adam look at each other, trying to think of what to say, where to start.

"Are you okay?" asks Adam foolishly.

She stares at him, wide-eyed for a moment. "Am I okay?"

Adam instantly regrets asking and is about to backtrack before Ember cuts him off.

"Let me think." She is animated, channelling all her fear and exhaustion into her tirade of abuse at Adam. "I don't even know if I'm alive or dead! I have no idea what the hell has just happened. I was planning on completing an assignment for school, not becoming part of some weird messed-up cult or whatever the hell is going on here. So in answer to your question, am I okay? No, I am far from okay. I may never be okay again! I have been beaten, nearly raped and murdered, chased by the law and crashed head on into a blockade at full speed." Ember taps her hands around her body. "I seem to be none the worse for wear physically but my mind is reeling. We're sat here with your mate, Raphael, who has possessed that captain's body and is now in a conference with Buddha..."

Ember bursts into laughter but all too soon it turns into tears. She begins to shake uncontrollably. Adam stares for a moment, completely taken aback by Ember's response. He moves towards her awkwardly and contemplates putting his arm around her. The large man stands and walks over to the overawed girl. He places his huge hand under her chin, raising it so she can see into his eyes.

"Shush, you have had a traumatic experience, little bird, and you are right to be upset. But you are safe now. I will protect you." A warm smile beams across his face and somehow Ember feels she can trust him. Baal gently squeezes her shoulder and then turns to Adam. "You need to sleep, the both of you have just passed through a collider formed vortex wormhole, and this is a hard thing for a human's physical form. You need to rest. Come with me."

Baal opens a trapdoor beneath the altar and leads them down some steps into a luxurious-looking chamber with floating hammocks. Happy to finally leave all responsibility in the hands of this big, warm stranger, the two teenagers follow willingly. Neither Ember nor Adam can keep their eyes open and almost on contact with the pillows, they fall into a deep sleep. Baal returns to the small room where Raphael waits.

"But we haven't viewed the disc yet. She could have slept later," complains Raphael.

Baal opens the door back to the noodle bar and the two make their way to a window seat.

"The message is for her. She has had a long and traumatic day and she needs rest. Heaven knows what will be required of her once she sees it. Let her have this one last night as an innocent," suggests Baal.

Raphael nods in agreement and pours tea from an urn that has been placed on the table.

"So, it seems the Host is on to us and will soon know about the disc. He will move heaven and earth once he realises what it is and who Ember really is."

Baal takes the tea and replies, "Yes, we must be careful. We all know what he is capable of. I will take the two of them to Chamuel but you will need to create a distraction."

The chambers of the High Council of Jinn City

Freya is not a woman known for her nervousness. She is steely and strong, never showing any emotion. This is how she rose from the fat, ugly kid who was bullied at school and whose attempt to kill herself was thwarted by the Host Himself. That was forty long years ago. Now she is the one who is feared, she is the one doing the bullying.

Freya is not sure how her lord and master will react to the news about the Procurator's daughter and the events of today. She knows even mentioning the disc could mean her death, but she is going to face her fate and tell him everything. If he chooses to exterminate her then so be it; her life is his to do with as he wants.

Freya enters the temple through the corridors that link to her own office in the security hub. Even as she approaches what could be her doom, Freya feels awestruck by the grandeur of the temple. Huge halls draped in the red and black banners bearing the symbol of the Crucifix and Eagle. Oak doors almost reach the ceiling and reveal the entrance to the great hall, which occupies the centre of the temple, giant steel sculptures of the Host adorning the four corners. Freya notices in the distance at the end of the hall the Host sits on his throne. He wears the golden robes and crown that he favours.

"Come, dear Freya," calls the voice of Reuben. "What news have you?" Black conjoined twins sit at his feet. One boy and one girl connected perfectly asymmetrically, something not achieved by nature. A small blonde girl, who is perhaps four or five years old, sits on his lap.

Freya slaps her hand across her chest in salute and bows. "My Lord, I bring grave news. During our surveillance of the reprobate known as Raphael we were alerted to the fact that he had made a new acquaintance, which made us suspicious of his actions."

Reuben dismisses the three children who are led away by an old woman. He holds his hands steeple to his chin and leans forward in his chair, his curiosity piqued.

"Who was this new acquaintance?"

"We saw Raphael enter the old warehouse with his Caucasian apprentice, Adam Costello. Also with them was Ember Jones, the Procurator's daughter."

Reuben pulls a stiletto blade from his cloak and casually picks at the long nail that protrudes from his forefinger. "And what, pray tell, followed?"

"Master, I ordered that officers apprehend the three suspects and question them. However, when we came across the two youngsters I discovered that Raphael had retrieved a disc. I was concerned this may be the message you warned me of and my first thought was to acquire the disc and eliminate any witnesses."

Reuben nods in agreement.

"I killed the traitor Raphael myself but unfortunately, for some reason that I cannot fathom, Captain Cameron turned his gun on his own guards and aided the two teenagers in escaping."

Freya looks at the Host expecting to see anger reflected in his face.

"Continue," he says calmly, still using the blade as an instrument to manicure his nails.

"We pursued the captain and the two delinquents as they attempted to escape in the old car that Raphael was seen using. I did not foresee any problems in catching them as they were in such an antiquated vehicle. A road block barred their way and several of our vehicles surrounded them. The driver of the car seemed to deliberately crash it into the blockade causing an explosion. When I searched the debris for any remains of the car and its occupants, there were none, not a speck was left. Only the wreckage of two SC90s remained."

Freya is tentative as she looks for Reuben's reaction.

"Raphael has incarnated using his Geist and he is now the captain. His old body must have been ended for him to do that. So...do you remember what I said about Raphael?"

Freya looks at the floor as she remembers Reuben's frequent demand: "I want Raphael alive."

"I do, Master. I succumbed to his taunts. I am weak. It was like I was back in the playground and the kids were taunting me. I failed you."

Freya kneels, her head bowed as if awaiting the axe.

"No, Freya, you are the strongest woman I have ever met. Raphael is a skilled Arc Hon. He would test anyone with his mind-fuck ways; he obviously knew which buttons to push when goading you. Don't worry, we will catch him but first we must call for the Procurator and find out all about his daughter, this Ember Jones."

Freya lifts her head, fear subsiding as she feels happy to be back on side. She straightens and resumes a stance of confidence. "I have taken the liberty of having him picked up by the PS. He should be here any minute," she explains. "Very good, my beautiful muse. Come here, sit at my side," Reuben says, pointing to the small bench next to his throne.

Freya tries to calm her breathing as she moves closer to her master. He takes her hand and every inch of her body tingles, her heart racing. Without encouragement the blood flows between her thighs and her face flushes red as he pulls her close. His arms embrace her and she squeezes her thighs together, involuntary hip movements and a sigh revealing her true feelings for her master. Freya feels she is on the very edge of orgasm before her master releases his hug. Reuben is aware of the effect he is having on his loyal servant and he enjoys toying with her emotions, even though she is a repulsive woman.

She coughs and splutters as she tries to compose herself before she stutters out her question, regaining her professional composure.

"May I ask, Master? Raphael... you say he incarnated? Does this mean the captain did not betray us?"

Reuben nods. "Your captain has gone. He is dead and in his place is Raphael. The Arc Hon are complex – they are like a spirit that attaches to a human form. They can attach to any living form within a certain distance. This is why, when you kill an Arc Hon, you must make sure they are *confined* and *alone*."

Freya bows her head at what she fears is a dig at her failure but is soon reassured.

"You did not know this and I should have instructed you more clearly. I am sure next time you will be more successful." He kisses her cheek, taking her face in his hands. The heat between them builds again and sweat begins to drip from the brow and neck of the vile woman, adding to the stale biscuit odour that she omits.

She takes a deep breath, trying to control her panting and slow her beating heart. "May I ask what is on the disc he was carrying? It was signed by Shane Mills."

Reuben is aware of her infatuation and leans over so she feels his warm breath on her neck before he answers.

"I don't know exactly. My spies have reported that it is a message from that cursed Shane Mills himself, supposedly a message to the 'Celestial One', a legend, a myth that cannot possibly exist." He looks Freya in the eye. "But this message can cause us all grief. A story that gives those ungrateful shits hope of a future where they will rule their own destiny could cause chaos if this recording is not recovered and this pretender left free."

He places his hand high on her thigh, gently rubbing it, enjoying her ridiculous reaction. Freya is quickly close to orgasm once more. She bites her lip and thinks hard of some sort of distraction.

"Is this Raphael the Celestial One?"

She realises from Reuben's manner that she may have asked too many questions. He removes his hand from her chubby thigh, then looks away, exhaling loudly, bored of this game.

"No, he is an Arc Hon. Keep up, Freya. I assume that one of the two youngsters will be the pretender, the bringer of false hope. Now, where is Procurator Jones?"

As if on cue Conrad Jones, a stout, powerful-looking man with an air of dignity around him is escorted in by two PS guards. He looks concerned. He kneels at the feet of the throne after first giving a filthy look to Freya.

"You may stand," directs Reuben.

"Thank you, Master. May I inquire why I have been dragged unceremoniously from my own home with no explanation or reason given?"

Freya's sexual frustration only adds to her contempt for Conrad. She hates the disrespect that Conrad displays in front of the Host. How dare he? Reuben on the other hand quite enjoys it as he recognises the balls it takes for Conrad to do this. However, today is not the day to try Reuben.

"Where is your daughter?" Reuben asks.

Conrad is caught off-guard and shows real concern now. Freya cannot hide her delight in his discomfort as her smile exposes her tiny yellow teeth. Conrad shakes his head as he responds. "My daughter, you mean Ember?"

"Do you have another?" intercepts Freya in an aggressive tone.

"No, sorry, I meant… Why do you ask of my daughter's whereabouts? She was with a fellow student completing some sort of assignment. I had expected her home by now. Has something happened?"

Freya coughs out a short laugh, savouring her moment. "Your daughter, Procurator, has been involved in a major incident today. One that resulted in the slaughter of six Protection Squadron personnel and damage to several company vehicles. We have reason to believe that she is in cahoots with a terrorist group led by a man you will know as Raphael."

Conrad looks stunned. His first question does not please Freya. "Is my daughter hurt?"

Freya shifts her feet as if ready to launch herself at the Procurator. "She is a traitor! What worse fate could become her? I have lost six men today and all you care about is your lowlife, treacherous slut of a daughter!"

Conrad is not sure which of these insults tips his scale but without any thought for his own safety he storms towards Freya and squares up to her. "My daughter is no traitor. You have got this wrong. I ask again: is she hurt?"

Freya does not relent and keeps her eyes firmly fixed on Conrad. "I witnessed it with my own eyes, Procurator Jones! See for yourself. We have the drone record downloaded."

Conrad looks up at a screen that appears from Freya's handheld unit. He knows this is the bird's-eye view from the PS drone that records all of their operations. He has no doubt it will have been edited just like all the others he has seen. The first image shows the suspect Raphael approaching his daughter and the Caucasian student, Adam Costello. Conrad is already regretting allowing Ember to go to this part of town. Several minutes later they all enter an old derelict house. A little later he sees Ember and Adam leave. A bit of distortion on the recording breaks as Ember, Adam and the captain can be seen fleeing the building and getting in the old car. The next thing he sees shakes him to the core: the car they are in crashes into a road block and the tape distorts as the explosion seems to engulf the drone.

Freya smiles at his horror. "She's dead? My daughter is dead?" He asks. Freya's chuckles invoke a reaction not befitting the Procurator of the High Temple. He hits her, a crack on her jaw. Freya falls back over the steps behind her but as if on springs, the woman regains a vertical posture and runs her hand around her jaw while still smirking.
Reuben holds up his hand to stop any escalation. "Stop this, the two of you. Freya stop goading him. Conrad, sit!" Both Freya and Conrad reluctantly obey, watching each other like school children pulled apart at playtime.

"Now, Conrad, Freya lacks decorum in these matters but there is great cause for concern here. Firstly from what we can gather your daughter is probably not injured."

Conrad's relief is evident and he attempts to ask how that can be possible but Reuben cuts him short.

"Trust me, she is safe. She and the two insurgents escaped Freya's officers this afternoon. I believe she will be holed up with them at this very moment, most likely in the ghettos of the Oriental District."

Conrad again attempts to speak but Reuben's raised hand tells him not to interrupt.

"It may be that she was taken by force or coerced by some means. It may be that she was misled or forced into helping them. Whatever the reason, I am sure the one thing we all agree on is that we need to get her back home."

Now Reuben invites Conrad to respond with a raise of his eyebrows.

"Yes, Master. I can only think that she is a prisoner of this Raphael. My daughter has not a rebellious bone in her body. This I know." Freya scoffs but is tamed by Reuben's stare.

"Well, you are one of my most loyal servants," he says. "So I will give you the task of finding her. You have twenty-four hours after which I will have to delegate the task to Freya and her PS guards. Do you understand?"

Conrad exchanges another dirty look with Freya before replying. "Yes, thank you. I will have her back in half the time and I promise all the confusion will be cleared up."

As Conrad storms out of the court he's already talking into his communicator. "I need you and ten of your best men to meet me at the gates. Also liaise with the Mackies. Tell them we will be on the ground in their district in thirty minutes." He is giving these instructions to Red, his loyal captain in the Civil Guard: highly trained men who come under his jurisdiction and not Freya's. Conrad is more than aware that this is now a fight for survival and he needs to stack the cards in his favour. He will make sure the Civil Guard takes the lead in this investigation and, to the best of his ability, keep Freya's PS lackeys away. His concern, however, is with the Mackies, a private police force who patrol the non-white areas of the city. A group he does not hold in high regard and has chastised publicly many times for their heavy-handed approach to keeping law and order. If Ember is truly in the Oriental District he has no choice but to liaise with these cowboys but he will make damn sure he makes the calls. Reuben stated but didn't explain to Conrad Raphael's transformation to the PS captain, exacerbating his confusion over the whole situation.

As Procurator Jones exits, Freya looks at her lord and master inquisitively, her face screwed up even more than normal.

"Don't fret, my pet. The girl will run to her father. Then we will have her and the others ready for your questioning." Freya smiles once more.

As Conrad finishes his call he is desperately trying to hold it together, the fear and worry for his only child causing his heart to beat out of his chest as he heads for the armoury. Conrad does not like to carry weapons but he knows how dangerous the ghetto can be. Recent reports estimated over three per cent of the population there have removed their chips through self-mutilation, which means a few thousand non-white anti-establishment rogues are roaming those streets.

While walking Conrad tries to contact Ember's chip and his worry only increases as it fails to connect. He has taught her how to "code red", which will disable a chip temporarily while sending him a link to her last location – this is highly illegal and she knew only to do so if ever she was in serious trouble. It was not on his mind that she would ever have to but he always put her safety first, even ahead of the High Council and the Host. If she'd done this, why hadn't she sent her location? The only explanation he can think of is that she has been kidnapped by these Raphaelites and her chip has been disabled by them. He pauses as his concern for his only daughter overwhelms him. With a quick check to see that no one is watching, he squats down, holding his head, tears beginning to appear. Then a cackle of static from his coms shocks him into action. He must be strong, he must find her before the Host lets that fat bitch loose.

"Pull yourself together man, your little girl needs you," he says to himself before standing tall and marching towards the Aircopter station. Conrad meets Captain 'Red' Carter at the Aircopter station.

"Your craft is ready to go, Sir," he says.

"Thank you, Red. Are you piloting?"

"Of course, Sir, we need to get that little lady home safe and sound."

"Thank you." Conrad feels genuine gratitude to his loyal friend as he seats himself, the safety harness automatically engaging.

The Aircopter takes off vertically then accelerates at breakneck speed towards the Oriental District. The city below him speeds by and within five minutes they are landing on top of the Central Admin building, part of a large barracks where the Aryan curator, Alan Mackie, administers his control over the millions of non-whites that live here. The Mackies are a formidable family-run security agency, founded by Alan's father, Dermot Mackie, to keep order in this region. They rule with an iron fist and quickly crush any subversive actions.

Curator Alan Mackie awaits the arrival of Procurator Jones with anticipation. He is not a supporter of this man who may be his superior on the Grand Council, but not in this district – *his* district. Alan relishes any opportunity to undermine this liberal jerk. Freya Mortensson herself has told him to be vigilant as she suspects the Procurator may be compromised due to his daughter's suspected involvement. However, Alan Mackie is always professional and greets his superior with the courtesy expected.

"Procurator Jones, it is an honour to receive you into our zone, circumstances aside of course." He hides his pleasure at Conrad's unfortunate situation. "My men are searching the whole sector. They will soon find the traitors." He glances at Conrad and decides not to apologise for his reference.

Conrad takes control, maintaining steady eye contact. "The Host wants them alive. Make sure no harm comes to them."

"Of course, Lord Procurator. My men have been instructed to treat your daughter as a victim until we discover any evidence to the contrary. Now, if you follow me I will take you to our operations room."

Conrad and Red are led to an elevator, which takes them directly to a busy control centre full of officers monitoring screens. "You can observe the whole district from here if you wish. My brother Colin and his men will apprehend the trio." Conrad's furrowed brow betrays his obvious distrust of this man. "I wish to be involved at ground level. Where is the most likely place for them to hide out?"

Mackie projects a map. "Raphael and his supporters have often been spotted here in the Chinese quarter and my spies say he frequents a couple of places, mostly in these roads here." Conrad rubs his chin as he studies the map. "Right then, I will go there with a small team. Once more, thank you."

Alan nods. "My brother Colin is already at the Chino gate. He will meet you there and act as your guide. No one knows those streets better than him."

⊕𝍖𝍕𝍓𝍒𝍗

In the noodle bar Raphael and Baal sit drinking tea.
"We must assume Reuben has been watching you for a while," says Baal. "If the sow woman was so near when you took Ember to your den then it makes sense that you were also spied on during your visits to China Town."

Raphael acknowledges Baal's wisdom and throws back the rest of his tea, preparing to leave. "They will soon be searching around here. I will let the two youngsters rest while I throw them off track."

Baal laughs, "I hope you are not thinking of driving around in that old nail again?"

A smile catches the edges of Raphael's lips, "Actually, that's exactly what I'm thinking of doing."

苟 苟 鬯 鬯

Conrad arrives at the gates that act as the entrance to the Chinese quarter. Colin Mackie is waiting for him as expected and after they exchange pleasantries Colin begins to inform Conrad about this sector.

"China Town is over fifty per cent of the Oriental District. We keep strict control over the inhabitants' movements using the locators on their chips. Like most of Midtown, all of them must be back in their zone by seven o'clock each evening, unless special permission has been granted, of course, which is rare. These electronic gates record who comes and who goes so it's easy to see if any persons are missing and also if any non-Chinese are in the area. We should be able to pick up a reading from your daughter's chip but for some reason the tech guys can't locate it, nor the Costello boy's. We suspect the third one, this captain or Raphael character, has somehow deactivated them but he would need some pretty advanced equipment to do that."

"He has a car that disappears into thin air and he has morphed into someone else so I guess he may have access to such things."

"Maybe, which is why I suggest we use this..."
Colin pulls out a handheld device which fizzes with blue sparks as he presses the button.

"A Banshee gun? That won't be necessary yet," Conrad explains, aware that his motives of protecting his daughter are obvious.

"No, of course not, Procurator. I was only thinking as a last resort as it is the only non-lethal option we've got that works on the non-chipped," explains Colin, unconvincingly. Conrad dislikes this brother more than the other. He has heard of the savage beatings he dishes out regularly to the locals for petty crimes; stories of public floggings, gang rape and hangings without trial have too often been attributed to him. Conrad had once advocated that a judge be sent to investigate the Mackies, in particular Colin, but his suggestion had been ignored – the methods being too effective at controlling the rebellious masses. He was also aware that this had made him very unpopular with these mercenary Mackies and now he was almost regretting his earlier move. Today he would need every ounce of the diplomacy he was famous for.

"Shall we begin?" says Colin. "This colony is home to millions of Chinks, half of whom don't even speak English. I don't think you always appreciate the difficulties we have here, Procurator, but they can be less than cooperative and sometimes need persuading when it comes to doing as we tell them. It will not be easy to locate the traitors in the catacombs these locals call streets. I fear we may not beat the deadline set by Commander Mortensson before she brings in her PS officers." Normally Colin would see any interference by PS on his patch as an insult but he perversely enjoys adding to the stuck-up Procurator's fears.

"Well, we don't want anyone claiming you are not capable, do we?" retorts Conrad as he jumps in the driving seat of an aerocar. "So we'd best hurry."

Red jumps in behind him, followed by ten more Civil Guards. Begrudgingly, Colin gets in with Conrad and points to a golden owl statue sticking out into the skyline a mile ahead.

"Head for that big bird, it will take us to the middle of China Town."

Conrad has to admit to never visiting this part of the Oriental District before. He feels guilty, remembering when he was first honoured with the post of Procurator of all Jinn City, how he'd told himself he would reach out to all the people and visit all the city states. That was a long time ago and he'd soon found out that his role was more honorary. He had very little real influence on anything and was merely a ceremonial figure. He rarely finished one pompous occasion before he was whisked off to another. His role seemed to be to act as entertainment manager for Jinn City.

Still, he is Procurator and in essence he is in control of the best armed forces and the largest budget on the planet. He also has the ear of the Host and is the only courtier with the guts to question Reuben at Council meetings.

As he looks around the Chinese quarter he is amazed at the sheer number of people who must live in such a small area. Every building is at least twenty storeys high and some easily over sixty; not bright, cleverly designed skyscrapers like in Upper Jinn but dull, sad-looking buildings. To combat congestion there are conveyor bridges that join the tops of many buildings, spread like a spider's web, available only to the higher caste, local dignitaries and others who are rewarded for loyalty to the Host. This also means any high-ranking visitors never need touch the ground of the lower cast area.

As a member of the High Council Conrad is also aware of the tunnels of Subterrainia that run directly under this part of town and are home to Jinn City's most undesirable inhabitants. Even here in the poorest areas there is a hierarchy, the better-off living up in the sky, the lower caste on the ground and the untouchables below.

As the aerocar hovers above the town Conrad can see the cramped, narrow streets packed with street vendors and stalls of the night market. Even this high up he can smell the spices from the many food hawkers. He spots many of the makeshift clinics that pepper the side streets that sell cures for every ailment. It all seems very busy he thinks to himself. From his view it resembles a beehive with these specks darting in and out.

A message comes across the shared coms interrupting his observations. "Sir, we have spotted the captain. He is driving an old Chevrolet and he has just bumped a squad car then sped off! All cars! The vehicle is heading south down Hong Kong Drive towards Shanghai Avenue."
Conrad looks at Colin. "Is that far?"

"Nope," says Colin. "He is coming right this way. We need to get down there. We'll need to block his exit, he must be trying to get out of the section," he says as they descend and glide back down to the street. Both Mackie's men and Conrad's Civil Guard take position.

Conrad addresses the men, reiterating, "No one is to be killed. We want all three alive."

The streets are busy with mostly hoverpeds and small old-style electric cars. Soon he hears what, in this day and age, is the unique sound of an eight cylinder combustion engine approaching. People can be heard screaming as they dive for cover. The Chevy crashes through the labyrinth of packed streets as the Mackie police cars chase after it either blatantly ignoring the "no kill" order or otherwise not privy to the instruction as they can be heard firing their tube guns at the car.

"Tell your men to stop firing!" orders Conrad as the alarming noise gets closer.

Colin radios his men to cease fire and just guide the ancient Chevrolet towards Peking Square where they are ready and waiting. Soon the old car can be seen in the distance. A cluster of smoke and debris is left in its wake, women pull their small children off the roads seconds before it roars past. Conrad witnesses a stallholder leap up a stairwell as his makeshift small pitch is smashed into a million splinters.

"Here they come," shouts Red. "Hold your ground, men, and do not shoot. I repeat, do not shoot! We need these suspects and the hostage alive!"

Conrad is grateful to his captain. He studies the unfamiliar-looking car approaching. It hurtles down the long narrow street, barely missing any other vehicles on the road, almost as if on purpose. Soon there is just a few hundred metres between the Chevy and the new blockade.

Raphael ponders his next move. The authorities had moved much faster than he anticipated. He had hoped to get to the Black District before he was spotted and so the search would be concentrated there, giving Baal an opportunity to sneak the youngsters out. Now he's in a predicament. The car cannot pass through another vortex wormhole again so soon, as the juice was all used up. If he hands himself in the cops will still look for Ember and Adam in China Town. If he stops to fight... well, he is heavily outnumbered.

He decides he must cause as much havoc and confusion as possible, he must go for plan B. The screech of the breaks is immense as the car grinds to a halt a hundred or so metres from the road block. He looks across at all the roads running off this main square but, as he guessed, the steel auto barriers are being raised. The trap is well set and he is forced to face his opponents. The Mackie jeep pulls up behind him around fifty yards away. He hears a voice come over the street PA system.

"Turn off your engine and step out of the vehicle – everybody."

Raphael is thankful for his tinted windows, recently mocked by Baal. He winds his window down a tiny bit and shouts out.

"I have the Aryan girl, Ember Jones. If anyone comes near I will shoot her!"

Conrad is aware of the clench of his heart as he continues on the PA. "No one needs to die. We will listen to grievances. Let the two children go, then come out with your hands up."

Raphael sets the high explosive under his seat. He holds the detonator switch in his hand and then plays his card. "I will only negotiate with the commander of the Mackies. Is Alan Mackie out there?"

Colin takes the hand com off Conrad. "This is Colin Mackie. I am heading up this operation. You negotiate with me."

Perfect, thinks Raphael, as he shouts out, "I will hand the hostages over to you. Come down the street and I will release them when I am certain it is you."

Colin looks worried. He wonders why the traitor wants to identify him. He knows it won't be through any hope of fair treatment. Still, he cannot show fear in front of his troops and the bastard Procurator.
He turns to his aid. "Get me a double HP high velocity." Conrad objects. "We want them alive remember, all of them!"

Colin, in fear of his life, gives up on any false respect. "You want your daughter home, Sir, and with all due respect I want to go home to my son, so I will decide if there is reason to kill or not, okay?"

He tools up and makes his way down the now deserted street. Like a scene from a twentieth century western he strides towards the car. When he gets around fifty feet from the car he hears Raphael say, "That's far enough." Colin stops. "Where's the girl?" he asks, trying to see inside the car through the tiny gap of the open window.

"She is here," replies Raphael as he finalises his plan. He knows this will hurt more than the shot in the face. Why did he have to plant the bomb right next to his balls? Oh well, too late now. Still, he needed to goad this scumbag outside some more. Technically he was not allowed to kill himself, according to Arc Hon law, so he still needed Colin to take the shot, but he was fairly sure how trigger happy both the Mackies were. Once he'd angered him he was sure Colin would take the shot thus hopefully killing Captain Cameron's body and allowing his Geist to leave at the same time as he releases the detonator and then bang! The explosives were enough to kill him but would hopefully be contained in the car; it was important that Colin Mackie's body was not damaged as Raphael was planning to inhabit him so needed to keep him intact.

By the time they discover only one body is in the car, Baal would have got the kids out. His Geist will link to Colin Mackie's body, giving him the added benefit of insight into any plans. He congratulates himself on his ability to adapt, it was a near perfect plan.

Before his plan can play out, however, a speeding poison-tipped dart enters the small opening in the window and hits him straight between the eyes. The poison leaves him completely paralysed but he knows the precision and accuracy of this laced projectile can only be the result of one person's skill. Powerless to even release his finger from the dead man's switch attached to the explosive he watches the shooter approach the car. You bitch, he thinks.

Solfrid stands in full assassin regalia: a loose cape secured with a cloth belt, dark leggings and her head covered by a silk scarf that also covers the bottom half of her face but permits her intense blue eyes to be exposed. Raphael has not seen them for almost two centuries, yet still he recognises her piercingly stunning gaze. Solfrid removes her scarf, a smile revealed as she does, and instructs the guards to follow her as she opens the door and carefully takes the detonator from Raphael's paralysed hand, making sure the switch stays depressed. Raphael's petrified body is dragged across the road and into a detention van. Conrad is as perplexed at the scene as everyone else. He runs to see if Ember is in the car.

"Ember!" he shouts, the panic obvious in his voice.

As he gets nearer his panic rises. He sees Solfrid is walking away from the car and telling everyone else to clear away. She holds up the detonator and turns to look at the desperate Conrad who can see what she is about to do. He shouts again, this time a long drawn-out cry of anguish. Solfrid merely smiles and releases the switch. The car explodes. Conrad stumbles and runs towards the wreckage, panic stricken and rambling. He only falters when the heat from the explosion becomes unbearable. He turns to Solfrid aggressively. "What have you done? If my daughter was inside..."
Solfrid speaks matter-of-factly. "Relax. The car was empty."
Conrad is not convinced. "How do you know? What about the boot?"

Colin reminds him who he is talking to. "Solfrid, the High Priestess, does not answer to any of us. Have the actions of your daughter messed up your brain? Now we have the ringleader it should be a simple task to find your daughter and the Caucasian."

𓀀𓏏 𓏲𓏏𓀀𓏥

In the back room of the noodle bar Baal sits back in shock after witnessing the whole event on the monitor that hacks into the Mackies' security footage. He realises that he must move Ember and her friend immediately.

"Come quick! We must go," he shouts down, waking the two friends.

Ember stirs slowly; Adam leaps to his feet.

"What's happened?" he says.

"Raphael attempted to lead the search to another section but he has been captured. Solfrid is with them so they will be all over us soon. We must go under."

Adam looks at Ember, quickly guessing she does not understand what "going under" means as she does not look too concerned. He decides not to tell her, lest she panic and runs. He has never been under himself but he's heard stories. His father had been a food distributor when he was younger and had spooked Adam with tales of how dark and deep the underworld was, how millions of unfortunate souls were punished and cast underground where they were out of sight. No food, no housing, no sanitation or medicine. They were never able to come above ground again as their implants were adjusted to react to sunlight, causing a fatal shock to the nervous system the instant it detects solar rays, even those reflected by the moon. He also heard that over the last few years the underworld inhabitants had had to resort to cannibalism to survive. He assumes Ember is oblivious to this horror-filled place but she knows more than he imagines.

Her father had always schooled her on the history and creation of the New World, especially that of Jinn City. She is familiar with the architecture, the people, and its past, both the one the media portrayed and the less savoury truth.

Jinn City is the New World's capital, biggest of the six megatropolises, running along the coast of old Australia. Ember has learned that it was on these lands that the final battles were fought and it was here that the Host first appeared to the masses before saving mankind from the revolutionaries. It is because of these momentous events that Jinn City was built here and became the hub of all that happens in the New World, even to the point of the Host himself setting up residence there.

When her father taught her about the unofficial things that happened within the city he would make her promise never to repeat the information. It was dangerous. He taught her these things hoping they wouldn't get lost to history, with people repeating the same mistakes, hoping she would be part of a generation to make them better. Now it seems she will need this knowledge for a whole different reason.

She remembers her discomfort when he first told her about the strict apartheid rules, not explaining why, nor giving his views, just educating her and always allowing her to form her own opinion. He'd said, "Jinn City is purposely built to allow the easy segregation of Aryans from inferior races. Caucasians are then separated from non-whites, these include Blacks, Asians, Orientals, Semitics and Mongols. Jews and Muslims are thought to be extinct but anyone displaying either gene or who follow the teachings are terminated immediately so they cannot pass it on. Jinn also has an underworld better known as Subterrainia, or the Pitts, where the lowest of the low inhabit. These people are not allowed to breed, they cannot come up to the ground level and they may be killed on sight with no charge to the killer."

Ember remembers distinctly that her father's tone while tutoring her on this subject betrayed his obvious disapproval of the conditions and methods. She was always confused how someone as great and good as the Host would allow this and once questioned her father.
"This doesn't sound right. How can this be the will of the Host?"

Conrad rarely scolded Ember but he was sharp with his reply. "We are not fit to question the Host. If he says it is to be then there is reason." He still looked unconvinced as he summarised. "At the time when mankind faced its worst enemy and near extinction the Host returned and saved us. He is the light and we the chosen ones must follow him without question." He looked to the ground as these words tapered off, then, changing the subject, he returned to his matter-of-fact tutorial on the city's inhabitants.

Ember read between the lines when he tried to explain about the inhabitants of the Pitts: convicted criminals, the mentally ill, and the poor, the sick and any political opponents to the Aryan Council. These inhabitants scavenge their food from the waste that is excreted from the city sewers. There are also many criminals who were disfigured and mutilated as punishment before being sent down there. Some rumours also exist that the mythical Humanzees and other such hybrids escaped from labs and live down in the Pitts. Some charitable Caucasians have tried to help these unfortunates but the resulting deaths of many of these people at the hands of the very people they are trying to help has all but ended this practice. "Hell on earth" was how Conrad described this place to his daughter.

☥ ꜣ ⸗ 𓎛

Ember feels Adam's eyes on her, knowing what he is thinking: how will the spoiled little rich girl cope? All her life she has faced this opinion. People see her for what she has, not who she is, and automatically assume she is blind to the nastier truths of the world. To some extent she has played up to this image. People would then leave her to her own devices if they thought she was only interested in dolls, clothes and make-up. It is so much easier to go unnoticed when everyone around you thinks they know everything about you. But the more time she spent with Adam, the more important it became for her to become the person she truly was and not hide behind the expectations of others. She knew she was strong and she'd damn well show it when they went down into the Pitts.

Baal decides that they will enter the Pitts via a tunnel known as Purgatory Gate. As they arrive he is glad to see the grey dull building is deserted. They enter the wide open doorway, activating sensors and a recorded voice that warns only security one chips are accepted for the pods and informing anyone entering the Pitts that the likelihood of violent death and the possibility of being eaten is high. It also warns you that there will be no emergency services past this point. Ember is surprised to realise that up until now she's not considered her implant. She checks it, expecting to see a million calls from her father, then notices the constant light is no longer visible under her skin. What happened? Did someone deactivate her? Freya? Raphael?

"Adam? Is your chip working?" Adam looks down and frowns. Obviously not.

Baal explains. "When you passed through the vortex wormhole in the car with Raphael all Nano tech would cease to work. So you are, in fact, totally free."

Ember doesn't feel free. She was happy with her implant. It allowed her access to all areas and gave her a generous allowance for all the luxuries she was used to. To not have an implant was unthinkable. It was needed for medicine, food, drink, transport, school. The implant was her link to her friends with its communication and magazine applications. Ember looks around her and realises that none of those things were any use to her at the moment. She so wanted to contact her father, he would sort everything out. This was one hell of a very strange day but she had not really done anything wrong – but then Ember gets the feeling that things are not going to be sorted by her father; he is probably in serious trouble himself. Her heart hurts at the thought.

As they pass through the gates several signs warn them of the dangers. To actually get down to the Pitts you must enter a descent pod housed in the station. The three cram into a small pod meant for two. Ember looks out of the gate entrance and feels tears flow down her cheeks as she realises this is goodbye to her father and her old life. Baal has made it clear that they will be killed if caught and after her encounter with Freya she believes him. She knows this is the point of no return. Half of her is terrified of losing that comfortable luxury life but strangely a part of her is almost excited for this chance to be who she really is. Almost.

Adam also wants to weep; he wonders what fate could be so bad up here that would make him follow Baal down to the Pitts. He knows that his life is worthless up top and this is their best chance to avoid capture. Baal has promised that they won't have to stay down here but they need to meet with some other contact who will take them to a safe place elsewhere in the city. Still, he wonders if this will be any better. His eyes keep returning to Ember, terrified of how she will react to the underworld that she has never experienced. An automatic grill drops down in front of them and a voice recording plays.

"To activate please engage your security one RFI."

Both the youths look at Baal who stands waiting serenely.

"Oh! Right," he says, patting himself down.

"You don't have a security one chip?" says Ember.

"How are we gonna...?"

A sudden rumble announces the imminent arrival of a vehicle outside of the doorway.

Just as they look to the skies a Civil Guard aerocar can be seen approaching. Panic sets in as they look back to Baal to warn him but are mesmerised by what they see.

Baal has casually pulled a dismembered hand from his cloak. He looks up at the nearing truck but seems very calm as he swipes the hand over the contact point. Next he takes a magno grenade from his pocket and throws it at the steel sign above the entrance. It attaches and the red light comes on. The truck lands outside and men, some wearing Mackie uniforms and others Civil Guard ones, exit it. With a start Ember recognises her father, just as the pod drops through the floor. She is caught halfway through a yell which turns into a scream as she is shocked by the speed of their descent and the noise of the grenade exploding up above.

After the stomach-churning drop the pod grinds to a halt and the grid rises again to let them out. Baal casually exits, apparently unfazed by the prospect of entering this deadly underworld. All they can see at the moment is darkness but a warm breeze flowing through it wafted a stench that overpowers the two youngsters. They all disembark and Baal turns on a handheld light. Ember and Adam gasp as the light exposes the huge underground tunnels.

"We have to go back, that was my father! He will help us!" shouts Ember as she attempts to re-enter the pod.

Baal grabs her arm and pulls her away, just as the debris from the explosion lands firmly on top of the pod, crushing it and any hope Ember had of getting back to her father. Ember stares at it in disbelief and horror. Adam puts a comforting hand on her shoulder, a look of discomfort on his face too; no one wants to be trapped down here.

Baal tilts his head sympathetically and then leads the way, heading into the dark, damp Pitts.

All too quickly any thoughts of her father vanish from Ember's mind as her eyes adjust to the darkness. Good God! Her father was right, but nothing could have prepared her for this. The Pitts are the results of excavations to mine materials during the building of Jinn City. It consists of a labyrinth of alleys and tunnels that lead off a main fifty-foot-wide ramble. The ceiling varies in height from thirty-odd feet to only four foot in some places. At her feet, what she thought were rocks and boulders turn out to be people, bodies strewn everywhere, some sleeping, some pushing their way round. Groans and moans are punctuated by the odd scream. Adam listens intently for some sort of conversation or language but there is none. Random fires appear with groups huddled around them as the tunnel opens up and then stretches on as far as they can see. Hunched broken people, cleanliness not a priority, dressed in mixtures of discarded clothes and homemade garments from litter.

Adam taps Ember's hand and with a nod directs her stare to a decrepit old woman bent over nearly double as she walks, a huge twist in her spine leaving a hump across it. She drags the remnants of what looks like a dead dog behind her. On closer inspection it is indeed a dead dog: some sort of poodle whose original owner must have loved it, as it was still wearing a pink studded collar and leather lead. Adam imagined this was to be the old hag's dinner. If only he knew. She was in fact the twenty-nine-year-old daughter of a scientist who had failed in a task issued to him by the Host himself. His punishment was to watch as his previously beautiful child was broken and rebuilt in front of him; bones fused so as to twist her into this unrecognisable mess.

As an act of compassion the Host allowed her to take her beloved poodle with her when he sent her down to the Pitts. She'd gone quite mad over the ordeal and hadn't even noticed when the pampered pooch had quickly died of the conditions down here. She still slept curled around it. The scientist would not fail again; he had three other daughters.

Many of the other inhabitants have deformities as well, burns and missing limbs mostly, all at the request of the Host. As the inhabitants turn to look as the owners of the torchlight go past, Adam sees they are startled and scared. Baal knows they are probably concerned that this is a patrol from the Mackies. Many recoil in fear, a few, mainly newer ones, take an aggressive stance. Baal finds a path and takes Ember's arm and he tells her to take Adam's. Soon their eyes adapt to the very dimly lit territory and Baal turns off his torch.

Some of the people down here have carved out meagre alcoves from the sides of the rock, some have built makeshift homes from paper, cardboard and plastic bottles, just about anything they can get their hands on.

"I never knew... I mean, I knew there were people down here... but so many!" says Ember.

"Estimates are that one and a half million people exist down here." Baal explains.

"The Pitts are a state on their own. Jinn City has no actual prisons, you are either put to death or mutilated and sent down here." Adam feels uncomfortable as Baal does not attempt to lower his voice as he discusses those around him, even pointing at people as he elaborates. "Some are simply innocent survivors of the Host's sick experiments.

"What about the Humanzees," asks Adam. "Are they real?"

"Mmm, maybe. I've never seen one but the rumours are rife. They are believed to be part of Reuben's devolution project: an attempt at creating a hybrid human and chimpanzee. There's even rumours of other hybrids with humans. Most residents of Jinn believe the stories of the hybrids to be myth but I know Reuben from old and, trust me, it is very likely they do exist."

Ember shudders she feels for these poor unfortunates who are discarded and treated as less than animals.

"But what do they do all day?" says Adam as they pass prone body after body after body. "Do they just lay down and wait to die?"

"Oh no," says Baal. "Would you? No, there is a whole sub-society down here: traders, builders, medics... The place even has a council of sorts and their own police force. But the situation of starvation and illness is rampant. These tunnels here are the ones most frequently visited by outsiders and so are mainly avoided except for by the truly desperate."

"Even the underworld has a caste system," Ember says sadly.

Even knowing what to expect, Ember is still shocked by what she sees and Adam begins to wonder if Baal is intent on hiding down here for the foreseeable future; he begins to wish he'd taken his chances up top.

"Where are we going?" asks Adam.

"We need to get to the avenues at the end of this tunnel," Baal explains, giving Ember hope that there was at least a plan of sorts.

"I have friends there who will be able to sneak us out of Jinn."

"Out of Jinn??" Adam chokes. "But nothing can live outside the city! What about the pollution and radiation caused during the rapture?" Baal just shrugs. With a shake of his head and both arms out wide he looks at Ember for her reaction. His jaw drops as she smiles and he notices she looks relieved.

"If Baal says it's okay then it has to be better than staying here," she says.

A huge gully carrying raw sewage from the city appears, carrying several makeshift boats and rafts.

"This is the main form of transport through these tunnels," says Baal. "The people literally wade through shit to get about."

Baal waves down a small half-inflated raft that seems to have some form of crude motor, an adapted old farm machine that sucks up the sewage then forces it out.

"This is the luxury travel of the Pitts," Baal tells them as he flags down the woman manning the boat. It also contains a hand operated up and down mechanism to steer it. There is one cushion for comfort. The tall, thin, dark-skinned woman slides the raft over to them. Ember stares at her, trying not to as she notices her left foot is missing. She does not notice, however, that this unfortunate woman has also had her left breast removed. This was her punishment for allowing a drunken Aryan soldier to "dirty his dick inside her foul black snatch" as the soldier's wife politely put it when she and her mates conducted their own kangaroo court. This was another reason why the Pitts were so heavily subscribed, many just fell foul of racist Aryan citizens who would happily take the law into their own hands like modern-day lynch mobs.

Ember says nothing as they board her carriage, even as the woman stares at her suspiciously and Ember feels very conspicuous with her Aryan features and intact limbs. "We need to go to Deep Hole," says Baal. "Just drop us as near as you can." Adam detects a look of trepidation on the woman's face at the mention of this place. He tries to assure himself that surely it cannot get worse.

੧ æ ੧ ᚼᚼᚼᚼ

Up above, back in Jinn City, Procurator Conrad Jones has ordered his man to clear the rubble from the blast that caused a collapse at the gate entrance. He is sure he saw Ember in the escalator just as the explosion occurred. She is alive at least, but she is entering a world she is not equipped to handle. He fears the Pitts will be too much for his delicate little girl – too much for any girl, or grown man for that matter. Still, at least she is alive he reminds himself as he watches his men remove the debris while Colin Mackie and Solfrid watch on.

"You are wasting your time," comments the High Priestess.

Conrad is no fan of Solfrid but he must admit to being impressed by her skill with the dart. Still, he knows she would not think twice about killing his daughter if she felt it was the best action.

"We need to enter via a different gate," she sighs impatiently.

There are four official entrances into the Pitts: Purgatory Gate, Black Gate, Thomas Gate and the Espino Tunnel set in the first favela. Conrad estimates that even with a siren blaring and total free airspace it will take thirty minutes to get to any of them.

"Are there no steps down or a service entrance?" he asks Colin.

"Service entrance?" laughs Colin. "No. Only the descent pod, which unfortunately your daughter and her friends have blown up."

Red instinctively puts a hand on Conrad's shoulder to stop him saying anything he may regret. "He is not worth it," says Red. "We need to find your little girl and then you can deal with that bollocks over there, okay?"

Conrad nods. He tells his men to carry on digging as he, Red, Solfrid and Colin get back in the lead vehicle and head for the Black Gate.

ᚨᚱ

The boat taxi pulls to a stop at their destination and lets the three passengers off. The tall, thin black woman holds her hand out for payment. Ember explains her chip is not working so she can't give her credits. Baal laughs and the black girl screws up her face with a look of disgust.

"You can't spend them down here anyway," explains Baal as he pulls out the severed hand he used earlier and gives it to her. The girl is not impressed but takes it. As the raft leaves, Adam and Ember both notice a hum from the distance. Baal walks off and they follow to see a distinct bright red light ahead. As they get closer the tunnel opens out to a Citadel of underground stone buildings. The noise of music and the smell of alcohol confirm that this is a place of recreation.

A sign reads: Welcome to Gomorrah, Sodom all.

There are people everywhere. Unlike the rest of Jinn City every race, creed and colour seems to be represented and most are drunk or stoned. A fight breaks out; not the clumsy fist fighting Adam may have seen in his street, nor was it anything like the tournament fighting Ember watched the day she sneaked into the temple. This was violent, bloody, bone-snapping, skin-tearing brawling.

Baal takes them into a tavern with a hanging carpet as a door. The place has a bar, tables, lots of occupied seats and even a stage. There's a forlorn-looking man covered in welts on the stage, tied to a post so that people can throw stuff at him. Adam is more distracted by the naked women, most badly mutilated, parading around the room, getting grabbed at by random men who molest them.

"Sex and violence is all that they have left." Baal says quietly as they sit at a makeshift table. "Don't you worry though, no one in here will harm you. You are with me. Now we need to wait for my friend to come meanwhile you may witness some of life's more sinful behaviour. This will not kill you, so try not to be too offended."

Ember watches the activities with curiosity. She realises very soon that although there is a lot of rowdy activity, the majority of people were actually enjoying themselves, even the girls didn't seem too averse to getting molested up against the bar while their suitors pulled them around by their hair. She is mesmerised by it all: hands and mouths all over each other, bodies writhing and screams that Ember can't work out if derived from pain or pleasure. She witnesses an abundance of naked flesh but it is not like the beautiful carved figurines at the museum or even the old-fashioned photographs she'd found of naked men and women in her dad's room that day. No, this flesh is covered in puss-filled sores, welts and burns, matted hair and caked in dirt. She can't look away but the scene is beginning to make her feel nauseous. Adam also feels he should look away but can't either. Ember occasionally looks at him but his eyes are elsewhere, his mouth open. Her mind thinks back to their shy and immature discussion of sex earlier and she blushes at her naivety.

Eventually three huge black guys enter the bar, amidst them a small black boy who wears a trilby hat and carries a small paper bag. Baal waves and the boy dismisses his entourage and joins the trio.

"What'cha Baal, my yellow nigger," says the boy and Ember watches curiously as the two men enter into some sort of ritual handshake. "Boiled sweet?" he asks her, sitting down.

"Oh, no. No, thank you," she says, looking dubiously at the colourful contents of the paper bag.

"Chamuel, this is Ember Jones," Baal says to the boy. "She has been compromised and the Mackies are tracking her down."

The boy, Chamuel, looks Ember up and down. He can't be more than eighteen, she thinks.

"Girl, you looking just like ya mammy." He smiles warmly at her.

Ember is shocked. Ridiculous! Firstly how could a young black boy have ever known her high-born Aryan mum? Secondly she knows she does not look like her mum, quite the opposite. In fact she barely resembled either of her parents. "We found you under a tree," her mum would often joke to explain this.

Before she can question Chamuel, Baal interrupts. "We need to get these two out of the city now and get them to the camp. Raphael has been captured. I witnessed it. Solfrid was there. She took him down."

A sudden look of anger appears in place of Chamuel's smile. "That no-good, blonde daughter of a bitch. Why does she not fuck off and die?"

He stands and calls over the three black men, whispering into the ear of the largest, then he turns back to the table. "Okay kids, time to rock and roll. Baal, you wait here, they will probably track you to this place so you're going to have to take one for the team. We will move faster without your fat ass holding us up anyway, so you stay here and hold them off. My boys will help you and I'd guess most of these good people will come to your aid as well. Motherfuckers love a fight. You

231

two," he says to Adam and Ember, "are coming with your Uncle Chamuel, so let's get de fuck outta dodge."

Baal reaches for Chamuel and slips him the disc. Chamuel places it under his hat. They leave with this new stranger in a hurry, Adam and Ember once again looking at each other as if for reassurance.

Chamuel leads them through a maze of alleyways, often strewn with people fighting and copulating, eventually getting back to the path running alongside the sewer channel. They jog down the track for a mile until the number of people dwindles to nothing and then they reach a weir with several outflow pipes. The waste water can be heard picking up speed when it enters these pipes, suggesting a steep drop on the other side. Chamuel hunts around for something in the dark behind where Ember stands. He makes a triumphant noise and returns with two elongated fibreglass oval boards.

"Ah, me old surfboards! I knew you'd come in handy one day." He kisses the bigger of the boards then explains what must be done. "Right, we need to take the third waste pipe; it should open soon. Ember, you get on old faithful here with me. Adam, you take the small one. We'll tie them together and I'll lead. Now don't be flash or anything, just lie belly down and paddle to that tunnel."

"Which tunnel?" says Adam, looking a little daunted.

"That one on the right. Not that one. And definitely not that storm drain on the left-hand side," Chamuel says. "There will be a current so stay behind me and you should be fine. Okay, get on your board."

Adam is hoping that he has misunderstood but knows he hasn't. He is expected to get onto this thin floating bit of plastic and paddle through the shit and waste of the city, then direct it to the entrance of a waste pipe, hurtle down said waste pipe – which is also full of shit – to god knows where while holding on for dear life, hoping he doesn't fall into the shit!

"No fucking way am I getting on that little thing and going down through one of them fucking death traps! Are you mental?"

Chamuel seems unfazed as he places his board in the water and gently slides across from the bank so that he is now kneeling on it.

"Look mate, shit is shit," says Chamuel. "And twenty-second-century shite is just the same as twenty-first-century shite and believe me I've waded through that too. Now, it ain't pleasant, but if you don't follow me you will be caught and I promise you, you will beg for shite in your hair if those Mackies get hold of you."

Ember is already sliding onto the back of Chamuel's board. Adam groans but relents and places his smaller board in the shitty water.

"Okay, we are not travelling first class any more, people," says Chamuel. "Make sure you go down the right hand tunnel. Do not go down the pipe on the left! I repeat, do not go down the left-hand one. Understand?"

Adam's question on what is down the left pipe is ignored as Chamuel continues with his instructions. Ember, who has resigned herself to do whatever it takes to get out of this hellhole, very gingerly slides across and kneels up behind Chamuel. This morning she would have been questioning every step of this but somehow it just seems easier to accept her fate and trust these bizarre strangers. At least she isn't alone, she thinks to herself, looking at Adam as he struggles to mount his board without falling.

Adam is not looking convinced.

"Get on, Adam. We have no choice." Ember asserts herself, knowing Adam will not leave her to face this peril alone. He is just about the only thing keeping her sane and stopping her from completely losing her cool at this point. She looks him in the eye, lips tight, and he knows not to question. He finally settles onto his board.

"Take the ropes tightly," says Chamuel. "If you fall in, keep hold, and the board will at least pull you along. Now we need to shimmy these things out into the water." Chamuel dips his hands into the putrid water and paddles out towards the middle. "I christen this boat Solfrid," he declares, "as it's as flat as her tits and stiff as her bony ass!"

Ember can't help but feel horrified at this mocking of the High Priestess she has revered all her life, but maybe it's time to change. Instead she worries that the pipe is not wide enough. She imagines them blocking the entrance, causing a dam of waste water, which will envelope them and for certain kill them. What a way to go, she thinks, drowned in faeces.

"Huddle up, it's going to be a tight fit," Chamuel says, confirming her anxiety. "And don't forget to hold your breath."

The sudden surge catches Adam off-guard and he has little control though Chamuel skilfully directs the boards towards the right pipe. Ember closes her eyes and holds on for dear life as Chamuel squats down low, preparing to enter the black hole. Behind them there's a rush of air. Chamuel looks back, worried.

"Uh oh."

"What?" says Adam, also looking back.

"Incoming," says Chamuel going ashen.

There's a roaring noise and then a torrent of water can been seen hurtling towards them.

"Paddle!" Chamuel shouts.

Quickly all three dip their hands in and scoop like mad. The roar of the coming water increases and just as the first board is about to enter the pipe Adam's board gets jack-knifed as the sudden wave hits. He crashes against the wall with a cry of surprise and tumbles off.

Ember screams for Adam but as soon as they enter the right-hand pipe they are plummeting down, rattling from side to side. Her head bashes against the metal pipe around her and her arm grazes along rusted walls. No words are possible as it picks up more and more speed as they ride the crest of the wave but she is sure she hears Chamuel shout out a childlike yelp of excitement. Then with a sudden whoosh they launch into another underground river. Chamuel quickly reaches out to an exposed tree root that hangs above and steadies the vessel.

"Wahoo! Back in the day people paid good money to go on a ride like that," Chamuel enthuses in a high-pitched scream. He looks back and his childish state changes, "Where's Adam?"

Ember is shaking. "He came off right before we entered the tunnel. Maybe he will be here, he can't be far behind..."
They both look up expectantly. A heavy weight forms in Ember's stomach as she keeps her eyes on the exit, willing Adam to appear. Chamuel paddles the board to the side of the river, guiding it to the embankment so they can disembark.
"Don't worry. He's tough cookie. He'll be fine," Chamuel says, not wanting to lie but needing to calm Ember down. The crazed look in her eyes makes him nervous.

As the realisation that she has just lost Adam hits, she borders on hysterics. The only thing keeping her feet on the ground is Adam. They were in this together. Without him she has no idea what the hell she is doing.
"No. He won't," she cries. "The excess water would have dragged him towards the left-hand pipe. What's down there? Where does it go? Tell me!"

⚓️🕯️🕯️🕯️

Adam's board is lost. Not a strong swimmer, he struggles vainly to swim against the tide which is now dragging him towards the left-hand pipe. Desperate to avoid this he kicks hard and grapples with the wall, his fingers catching a small ridge. He holds on for grim life but then a second surge hits him and pulls him from the wall, dragging him right into the mouth of the left pipe.

Desperately holding his breath Adam feels like he is being spun in a blending device as he whirls rapidly around the wrong pipe. It descends at a sharp angle and seems to go on for an age. He doubts the destination will be any better than the trip but he needs to get out of here before he runs out of air and limbs. A particularly brutal tumble smashes his ribs into the wall of the pipe and any remaining air is knocked out of him. Suddenly, though, he is airborne, gasping for breath before he plummets down into an underground lake.

He is underwater again, rolling, not knowing up from down. Then the waters calm and he can see flickering light in one direction. He heads for it as his throat burns and his ribs spasm in pain. He breaks the surface, delighted but terrified. Chamuel never did say what was down this tunnel. He half swims, half floats to the water's edge where he can see he is in a large cave, courtesy of hundreds of flaming torches placed around the walls.

'Fire means people, surely,' he thinks. 'Is that good or bad?'

In the distance Adam can hear some scrambling. It sounds like some sort of animal noise and a stampede getting closer and closer. He looks for somewhere to hide but cannot make one out. The din is getting louder as whatever it is gets closer. Panicking, he swims to the edge and scuttles behind a rock in the darkest space he can find as his ribs pulse with pain. A hundred or more shadowy figures are entering the huge cave. He watches as they scurry around the edges of the lake, excitedly gathering the many bits of litter that have arrived with the rush of water.

Adam lies flat trying to avoid detection. He is on the far side of the lake and notices the figures don't seem keen on getting too wet as they pull objects from the pool with long stick-like hooks. Adam feels a slight sense of hope. He assumes these are a nasty gang, remembering Chamuel's warning about not wanting to end up flowing down the left pipe. Also the sounds coming from the group are not what he would associate with a friendly welcoming party. Adam struggles to make out any individuals but can see they are working in unison as they scavenge through the waste. "How bad does it have to be to have to survive off shit that has already been cherry picked by the other inhabitants?" he asks himself.

The answer soon becomes clear as a larger member of the group climbs up on a rocky parapet next to one of the flamed torches. Adam gulps as he can see exactly what he has stumbled upon and why Chamuel was so reluctant to travel down this side.

With thick leathery skin that covers his large forehead and an elongated bottom jaw, the beast is distinct. His powerful limbs hold his body, covered in a down of rough hair. Upright and wide shouldered, the figure is revealed to be an emaciated and decaying, but fearsome-looking, Humanzee. Its cold eyes strike fear into Adam's heart. He recoils in a sudden panic and rising to his knees staggers backwards, dislodging a rock as he moves. A splash as the rock hits the water alerts the beast, who turns, looking towards him. A prayer is all the young man can muster. "Please God, don't let him see me."

A snarl from the beast causes its large, fierce-looking teeth to unfurl as it points towards Adam's hideout, screeching to the others who all turn to look. A moment's silence is broken by a cacophony of screams as the pack seems to go into a frenzy, running in then out of the cold water, none daring to go above their depth, but seemingly desperate to reach him. Adam's relief that they cannot cross over to him is short-lived as three or four figures carrying tall objects come into view. They are large poles and the beasts are pushing them into the ground. He looks up and his terror is compounded as he can see the labyrinth of tree roots hanging from the cave ceiling. The poles will reach them easily and then the agile-looking beasts will effortlessly swing from one to the next, transporting themselves to his little sanctuary.

The first attempt fails as a small member falls into the water while trying to reach the roots. His aids drop the pole so he can scramble out and back to the shore. A second and third attempt also fail and Adam allows himself to hope once more. The figures seem defeated and have gone quiet, then suddenly more pandemonium ensues as a larger pole arrives and two of the pack lodge it firmly into the mud, holding it steady, then tipping it towards the roots. It easily reaches and Adam decides he must take flight. He looks around but there is nowhere to go. He looks back up and can see three Humanzees now climbing the pole.

A noise behind him reveals he is no longer alone and an unseen assailant grabs him, clasping his head under their arm and pulling him into the lake and below the water. Petrified, Adam can see nothing. Powerless to resist the firm grip around his neck, he is dragged further and further down. Certain he is about to die, one flicker of a thought gives him some hope. "Those Humanzees can't swim so how is this one dragging me down into these depths? It can't be a Humanzee."

⸱𝕀𝕄𝕀𝕄𝕀𝕄⸱

"Humanzees... they live out there, don't they?" Ember is still trying to extract information from a reluctant Chamuel.

Eventually he relents. "Yes, but believe me, if I am right, which I always am, there is much worse than them down there. We got to keep moving, Ember. I am sorry about Adam, really I am, but we can do *nothing*. I have to get you out of here and follow the plan. We have a mission and nothing can stand in the way."

Ember's mind is going round in circles as she tries to process everything she has gone through. And now she has to do it without her partner in crime, on her own, without even the prospect of her dad being able to help her. She can feel the heat of tears behind her eyes and is desperately trying to stop them from pushing through. She knows as soon as those tears start to fall she will completely lose it.

What other creatures could be down there? She tries not to think about what might be happening to Adam but all sorts of vile and terrifying images flash through her mind. And then Chamuel's words sink in. A mission? What mission? The panic fades as she begins to think things through: the disc and everything Raphael had been saying was all leading to something. The possibility of purpose sharpens her mind and she looks at Chamuel with focused eyes.

238

"Wait...What do you mean... mission?"

Leo's notes...

Thirteen Djinn left Levant with gold and harem?

Reuben went to Italy - He is our main worry, seems to be evil personified, definitely doesn't like Jews. Mainly in Europe now, Possible based in England

Levi Egypt Still in play Simeon thinks he is controlling both the US and Canadian governments.

Simeon Greece Now part supporting humans and recruiting new champion. Seems to have a serious drinking problem!!

Zeb China Believed to be still in play either China or Russia

Judd East Asia Believed to be still in play either China or Russia.

Daniel Ethiopia First of the Djinn to return to their home after death caused by an accident in Africa

Naphtali South America Dead I think he returned as well?

Isaac Iberia? Spain/Portugal - Seems to of been a victim of whoever or whatever is killing these Djinn and taking their amulets. He has not returned to Djinn dimension.

Asher West Asia - Assumed to still be active

Gad North Africa Dead not returned

Ephraim India Dead not returned

Joseph North America Dead not returned

Benjamin ??? Stayed in the Levant = Middle East Persia? Iran? Unknown believed dead not returned

Four Arc Hon = Amitiel, Raphael, Chamuel and Michael. Unsure whose side they are on seem to be on Simeon beliefs Michael was victim of the same assailant that has been killing the Djinn.

Baal and Solfrid first Djinn to assimilate as humans thousands of years before the thirteen arrived.

The Demiurge, creator, absent God?

Human champion has beautiful woman on her arm?? No idea what this means

Stoke Prison

Leo is grateful to the prison Governor for granting him permission to meet with Shane each day for their chess game. Leo had been a model prisoner before the "incident" and the routine of the chess games could only add to the stability of his mental state so the Governor told him he would ask Shane if he was willing.

At first Leo had wondered if Shane would accept. He wouldn't blame him if he didn't. He realises that the tiny crumb of credibility his stories ever had with Shane is probably long gone now that he has been banged up in the loony wing and diagnosed with delusional disorder. Still, he needs to try to warn Shane of the event that is surely going to happen. Faith has been in short supply lately but Leo needs to at least have faith in Shane. The thought that he might fail to convince Shane that he has been telling the truth is his biggest fear, as he knows this could lead to Shane being unprepared for the coming attack the Djinn most definitely have planned. He also knows his idea to escape from the prison will not be met with approval from Shane. Leo decides not to panic. He has to believe in fate, even though he knows even fate is controlled by the Djinn.

Shane had pondered the idea of turning down Leo's request for special visits. The Governor told him there was no pressure if he wanted to decline; he explained that Leo's condition was called delusional disorder and caused him to imagine things. Shane had only begun to settle into a normal prison existence since Leo's episode. He was curious though since so many things didn't add up. The cameras failing on the two occasions Leo was attacked, the involvement of Robert Price, the lady called Solfrid, even the attempt on Leo's life at the exact time Shane was off the wing. So he agreed to the visits in the end and the two reignited their chess tournament.

"So they finally clocked that you're a fruitcake," remarks Shane on seeing Leo for the first time in months. Leo smiles and hugs his friend. They set up the game and begin to play.

"Do you think I'm crazy?" Leo asks him.

Shane looks away. "I don't know, man."

Leo is encouraged that it's not an outright "no". He decides to plough straight into it.

"You must plan an escape." Shane gulps; he hadn't thought Leo would embark on his normal crackpot conversation so early on.

"Escape? Why would I want to do that? I will be out in less than eighteen months."

Leo sounds very concerned as he replies, "You won't be alive in eighteen months, maybe not even in a month if you stay here."

A sigh from Shane betrays his impatience at Leo's ramblings. "Listen, old man, I agreed to these meetings because you're a genuinely nice guy and I enjoy the tales you tell but if you think for one minute you are going to coerce me into some crazy fucking escape plan, you can stop now. Can we not just play chess and do our time?"

This time Leo is irate. "Fucking hell! Are you blind? I have spent the last twenty-odd sodding months trying to enlighten you on what is going on out there. I have explained that you are an important part of what is about to happen. You saved me from my first assassination attempt, for God's sake! Do you think it is a coincidence that the minute you're not around a second attempt is made on my life? Do you? I am past concern for my own life; however, I have been given the unenviable task of trying to educate you on the facts."

Leo tries a lower tone, reminding himself not to panic or throw a wobbler.

"I know, I'm sorry, I also resisted the truth in the beginning," Leo says. He looks at Shane's face and sees there is no belief, just pity. Now he feels panic, his tone rises again and the thin veil of calm quickly falls. "I know I had Simeon to show me but still... All the things I've told you? Shane, you are now bordering on the retarded scale? Why

Simeon and Chamuel ever thought you are something special is beyond me. Fuck, fuck, fuck!"

The guard looks over, concerned at Leo's erratic behaviour.

"Calm down, old man. You got to sort that temper out and the language is not befitting! I was just saying…" Shane leans in so the guard cannot hear, "…what's the plan then? How are we getting out?"

Leo knows Shane is humouring him and he regrets his outburst. That was not the best way to prove to someone you are not crazy.

Cumisky's Casino, present day

Three men are meeting in the plush office at the back of Kieran Cumisky's Casino in London's West End. Standing outside the office are two heavily armed Serbian gangsters, an equally armed man who is Kieran Cumisky's personal bodyguard, he regards the other men warily, and a young man with many piercings and long hair with a fringe covering his eyes. The men inside the office are seated around the table.

Kieran Cumisky, casino proprietor and one of the East End's most notorious villains, is facing his two guests: Jovan Ramaska, a Serbian drug and prostitution provider, to his left and to his right Reuben Lupas, a blond-haired, pale gaunt man who reminds Kieran of a seventies horror film star.

"Well, I hope you had no trouble finding the place. I feel I should do the introductions as it's my gaff, but to be honest I don't know who you are," says Kieran, addressing Reuben, "so that makes it awkward."

Jovan scoffs. "Well, I know who *you* are Mr Cumisky and I am sure you know who I am." He turns to Reuben. "But I have no idea who the fuck Starsky here is." Cumisky laughs, then corrects Jovan, "You mean Hutch, the blonde one was Hutch."

Reuben says nothing as the two murderous and dangerous gangsters amuse themselves taking the piss out of his appearance.

"I think he looks more like a skinny Donald Trump," adds Cumisky. Jovan agrees, laughing even louder. "So Donald, why are we here? You're not a policeman, are you? Because you would be the most obvious copper I have ever seen."

He laughs one more time, this time alone as Cumisky scans Reuben's face for signs of nerves just in case he is with the law. Reuben returns his stare and suddenly Cumisky feels a little uncomfortable.

"My name, gentlemen, is Reuben Lupas. I have a proposal that will benefit all three parties: the Serbians, the Cumisky group and, of course, myself."

Jovan is struggling to take the weird-looking guy seriously. He is pissed off that his so-called superiors back in Serbia have insisted he come to this meeting without telling him what it was about.

Jovan is laughing to himself when he makes his next comment. "So how is a faggot like you going to help two well-respected businessmen like myself and Mr Cumisky?" Jovan flicks Reuben's blond locks and blows him a kiss chuckling to himself. Then with a spark of inspiration, he lifts his left arse cheek and farts in Rueben's general direction, laughing hysterically at the discomfort he is inflicting on the man.

Kieran Cumisky watches curiously as if watching a mouse caught by a tomcat. He has no pity for the weird-looking guy and wonders how someone so ill-equipped to handle the type of people in the underworld ever expected anything else but ridicule, or worse, but he catches Reuben's gaze and once more feels discomfort.

Reuben looks unfazed by Jovan's aggressive and unfriendly attitude. He stands and walks to Cumisky's drinks cabinet.
"Aw, have I hurt your feelings?" laughs Jovan.

Cumisky thinks to tell him drinks are not complimentary but then sees he is not looking for a drink. Instead he opens the secret draw under the cabinet, pulls out the gun hidden there, turns, and blows the Serbian's head off.

Kieran Cumisky jumps back, struggling not to topple the furniture. "What the fuck?" He looks at Reuben who replaces the gun into the drawer. A disturbance can be heard outside the door but no one enters. The hardened West End criminal sits back down and listens to Reuben politely.

"As I was about to say," says Reuben, "I have a proposal. It is regarding your brother, Phil Cumisky."

Now Kieran is confused, his mind races, he struggles to look composed. "My brother is in prison, he won't be out for a long time." Reuben nods and lights up a cigarette. Cumisky thinks about explaining the recent legislation regarding smoking in a workplace but decides this guy has little time for rules.

"And how do you feel about your brother's internment? I believe you two are very close."

Kieran is understandably suspicious of this man who somehow knew the location of the gun he hid so well that two previous police raids had not uncovered it, a man who then blew a hole in the face of the leader of one of the most violent gangs ever to operate in London as if he was a lame horse.

"What is this all about? I would appreciate it if you got to the point before our friend here starts to stink the office out."

"Of course. I wish to join forces in a common interest. I will assist you in organising a prison break. I also have someone in the same prison and I have a couple of inside men who will aid our mission. I have an excellent plan and a relocation strategy as well."

Kieran asks the obvious. "So why do you need me?"

"Manpower. its common knowledge that you command a small army of your own and that you have good relations with other mob bosses."

Kieran looks at the Serbian's body. "Well, I did have."

Reuben chuckles. "Don't worry. I will clean up this mess. Jovan here has been skimming profits from his overlords back home; they requested that he be eliminated. They will announce a new London boss today, one that I will introduce you to. Together you will have a very lucrative relationship." Reuben smiles at the awe in Kieran's face. He is glad he took the opportunity to kill two birds with one stone when he killed Jovan here. He has terminated the target and cut out any doubt with his new partner that he is a serious and well-connected man.

Once business is agreed and the next stage finalised the two men shake hands and Reuben leaves. Jovan's two henchmen enter the room, saying nothing as they place Jovan in a prepared body bag. Then the young dogsbody wheels in a cleaning trolley as soon as they leave and proceeds to remove any smaller parts of Jovan still remaining. Twenty minutes later the office is spick and span as if nothing had happened.

Once he is alone, Kieran walks to his drinks cabinet, checks the hidden drawer where he concealed the weapon. It is locked. He delves into his pocket and pulls out the key. He pours a drink, sits down and reflects on the most bizarre meeting he has ever had.

Stoke Prison

Back in Stoke Prison Shane has managed to calm Leo down. Convinced now that the old guy has truly lost his marbles, Shane rethinks his decision to spend his recreation time listening to ever more ridiculous stories and prophecies.

The fact that the guy is a fruitcake doesn't stop Shane from liking him though, so on returning to his cell he decides to play along with Leo's scheme. He has to admit, loon or not, he was definitely the most interesting person in this prison. As if to reinforce this Johnny and Gary come to his cell raving on about their new favourite TV programme. As Shane pretends to listen he is disturbed to see Robert Price appear at the cell door. Shane looks up at him, preparing for an attack. Johnny and Gary both quickly attempt to get out of the way of any potential conflict.

"Can I speak with you, man?" asks Robert, in a low non-intimidating way.

Shane points to the chair opposite his bunk, inviting him to sit. Robert makes his way to the seat, looking Johnny and Gary up and down.

"It's a private matter, if that's all right?" he adds.

Johnny and Gary look to Shane for instruction. He shrugs. "Give us a moment, hey lads?"
The two men wait until they are alone before they begin.

"So what can I do for you?" asks Shane.

"How is the old man?" The genuine concern in Robert's voice surprises Shane.

"Why are you so concerned about an old Jew? I mean, if I'm not mistaken you're a follower of Islam and from what I've heard an enthusiastic Jihadist."

Robert is not thrown by Shane's candidness and answers honestly. "I have discovered the Gnosis. I know about the Djinn. I am a Muslim and he is a Jew but we are just men with a common enemy."

Shane has to wonder how two people can be suffering from the same delusion and end up in the same fucking prison.

"Listen, I put up with the old man's bullshit because I like him but he is a fucking space cadet. I don't know how you have come across this fantasy about the master race of spirits or whatever they are, but if that's what you came to talk to me about then I got to tell you I have had it up to here with it. I live in the real world, not some paradox where the planet is a giant game and we are being manipulated by some sort of fuckwit aliens or whatever they're supposed to be."

Robert takes no offence and nods, not in agreement, more in empathy, before he perseveres in an attempt to convince Shane. "I know it's a lot to take in but we ain't got much time. I was told that Reuben would first set the Muslim world on fire. He has done this and then he will bring Europe to the brink once more. Man, you heard what's going on in the Crimea?"

Shane looks at Robert with a blank expression.

"He is picking his foes off and setting the seeds for his plan. Some of his competitors' most valuable brethren have disappeared. Planes have disappeared, for fuck's sake. These are all distractions, that's how he works and he is planning a distraction here in this prison. You are the target and he will not rest until he has you dead or alive."

Shane sighs. *Why me, why do all the nutters talk to me?* he thinks to himself.
Robert persists. "Chamuel told me that before Reuben finalises his plan he will come for you."

Shane wonders if he should talk to the prison psychiatrist about this man.

"Hmm, I see you think I'm for the nut house also but soon you are going to have defend yourself, so you'd best be ready. I promised Chamuel that I would protect you with my own life if need be, but you need to be on your guard because they're going to come at us with some mighty-fucking-force, you hear me? Some mighty-fucking-force!"

It would be impolite to throw someone out who has just told you he will die for you but Shane doubts he can nurture another crackpot. Still, he does have questions. "What happened with the fairy and Leo?"

Robert pauses as he thinks back to Leo's attacker. "You mean the gay man, Graham? He was sent by one of the Djinn. Not Reuben though, most likely Levi. Anyway, he was sent to kill Leo. I had been watching him since I came here. The fairy, as you call him, was known to the Arc Hon and so it was no coincidence that I was able to thwart his attempt to kill Leo."

"Why kill Leo?"

"The Djinn are aware that you are the Deliverer and that Leo has been mentoring you. Chamuel thinks they were trying to have you transferred out and perhaps Levi wanted Leo out of the way in an attempt to mess up the plan."

Shane blinks. "What fucking plan?"

"To convince you to side with him."

"Who?"

"Reuben, of course." Robert studies Shane's face, looking for a sign of trepidation regarding this statement. Instead, Shane laughs and falls back to lying on his bunk, closing his eyes.

"Whatever. Listen I am grateful for the warning and all the protection. I will keep an eye out for any ghosts." Shane says no more; he is hoping Robert will accept his promise and leave him the fuck alone. He waits with his eyes closed then opens them to see his wish was granted. The cell is empty.

From the office of Cumisky Casino, Kieran has quickly put together twenty of his best guys for this the mission. Reuben has explained the plan, that his brother will be safely in the yard when the fire takes hold and all his boys need to do is roll up in the ambulance. Right now they are all waiting in a barn less than a mile from the prison. Two are dressed in medic uniforms, the others are fully kitted out in police riot gear.

"You will get a call," Reuben had told him, "and then you move in. There will be hundreds of riot police arriving in similar vehicles. Your men will blend in with all the chaos. They are to go straight to C wing where my guy will act as the commanding officer. They just follow his lead, okay?"

"How can you be certain the fire will spread? What if the inmates don't riot? We could all be turning up looking like the keystone cops!"

Reuben had planned everything meticulously, as always, but he was not about to explain himself to this two-bit hood who was only here so the headlines would be plausible. The fire will be started via a gas explosion. It will be ignited in the lobby of the admin block, a section of the building that was built in Victorian times. With meticulous calculations by Gerome, an incendiary expert who Reuben had planted in the prison months earlier, a device will be supplied to Phil Cumisky, who will drop it down a shaft that leads to the main gas pipe junction, thus causing an explosion. In this old part of the building the flames will accelerate rapidly and reach the main building within minutes, by which time it will be a twelve-hundred-degree unstoppable inferno. The only recourse for the prison guards will be to evacuate the prisoners to the allotments at the rear of the prison. Protocol is that they call ahead to the nearest Met station. The police will then dispatch all available riot police and cordon off the area.

In the confusion Cumisky's men, dressed as both medics and riot police, will grab Phil and whisk him off in the ambulance. As his part of the deal, Cumisky's men will aid Reuben's guy to capture two inmates and kill another. The men will then use the confusion to separately leave the area. Job done.

"Everything will happen exactly as I have planned," is all he offered as reassurance.

Reuben had actually had little to no interest in Phil Cumisky's escape but needed a cover story for his plan to abduct Shane and Leo. These crooks of Cumisky's will be blamed for the prison break and with the high-security wing breach releasing hundreds of the country's most dangerous criminals into the general populace, the authorities will hardly bother to investigate a couple of low-risk inmates who were likely to turn up of their own accord.

He had not let Cumisky know the full extent of the plan, of course: standard practice for the Djinn. As always, Reuben's plan is meticulous and, as usual, his targets will not have a clue what's coming.

𓀀𓀁𓀂𓀃 𓀄𓀅

"Special request for visitor, Mills," shouts the new screw, Boland, into Shane's cell.

"What?" Shane has not had a visitor in all the time he has been in the clink. He has not sent anyone a visiting order either. Puzzled, he asks Boland once more, "What?"
The screw responds by pronouncing each word slowly. "Yooouuu... haavvvve... aaay... vis...it...ooor! Some lady. She has somehow been issued an emergency VO. She either has the warden's ear or she must be special."

Shane suddenly leaps from his bunk, heads out of his cell and sprints to the wing exit door.

"Hold on, Mills," shouts Boland as he struggles to keep up.

It's Sara, it must be, thinks Shane. His heart is beating out of his chest and he is visibly shaking. For so long he hasn't seen those beautiful rosebud lips that slightly crooked smile, that body!

"Come on, Boland, hurry up."

Boland huffs and puffs as he eventually catches up. He opens the wing door. Like a dog out of the trap Shane sprints down to the visiting block. The guards quickly search him and, sensing his urgency, let him into the visitor's room. He is surprised to see that the room is quite big. He is also surprised to see that there are no other cons receiving visits. Mostly though he is surprised and desperately disappointed to realise that Sara is not his visitor. His face shows this disappointment. As his heart sinks he slumps down into the empty chair opposite the only other person in the room.

The young girl can be no older than eighteen with shoulder-length, Celtic red hair, porcelain-white skin, baby-blue eyes, plump lips and an even amount of fairy kiss freckles that are sprinkled across each side of her slightly turned-up, button nose.

"Are you my visitor?" asks Shane as he takes the seat.

Her smile reveals a small gap in otherwise perfect teeth. "Hello, Shane Mills. It's a pleasure to meet you." She runs her hand through her hair, tucking it behind her ears in what seems a slightly flirtatious manner. "My name is Amitiel. I apologise for the unannounced visit but I needed to speak with you. It is urgent and very important."

"Amitiel? That name rings a bell," thinks Shane. "Did Sara mention her? Perhaps she was a work colleague? No, that's not it…"

"Do I know you? Are you Sara's cousin? Have you got a message for me from her?" he asks, more in hope than belief.

"I don't know Sara." The girl smiles apologetically. "I am sorry. Has Leo not told you about me? I am an Arc Hon. I am the Angel of Truth."

Shane has had enough. His hopes are smashed and his heart contracts at what he guesses is somehow Leo's desperate attempt to involve him in this bizarre imagined quest once more. He just wants to see Sara and this was a fucking shit trick.

"Listen, little girl, I don't know how or why Leo has put you up to this but he is a very sick man and I am a very pissed-off individual, so please just get the fuck out of here and forget whatever bollocks you are supposed to say to me."

Amitiel smiles and despite the inner turmoil bubbling inside of him, Shane is calmed by her innocence and her beauty, not the beauty of a Hollywood actress or a catwalk model, rather she has a beauty that is lost to anyone who is no longer a child. Amitiel places her hand on his. It is soft, so soft. Shane means to pull away but is overwhelmed by the comfort her touch brings him.

Softly she whispers, "I must show you, you must see."

A mixture of nausea and elation overcomes Shane and he feels like he is floating. He vaguely sees himself still sitting in the visiting room with Amitiel, her hands cupping his, but he is looking down on himself from a third-person perspective. Then he is no longer in the room but plummeting. Everything is whirling and no logical thought presents itself to Shane. He can see shadows and colours but no solid shapes. He is incapable of controlling any movement as his body is no longer with him. In the distance he feels another presence; it is Amitiel but she is not the same, her form is a silver- and grey-coloured aura, which appears to be shifting in and out of the shape of a wolf. The sensation of falling is followed by the sensation of rising. A voice calms him. It's as if Amitiel is speaking to him but her voice is bypassing his normal audio function and is vibrating in his mind.

"Shane, we have little time and I must help you but first I have to remove your doubt. You must see what I see."

The aura fully morphs into the girl's image and Amitiel comes closer and soon, like a mist, she envelops Shane's consciousness. Euphoria ten times more acute than any feeling he has ever felt is followed by clarity. He feels as if he has returned to the place he once called home.

"How can this be?" asks Shane.

"You are in a state of transcendental consciousness. This is who you are. You are the consciousness. You are not the corporeal appendages of your body. Your body is simply a receptor that you inhabit. I will guide you, do not fear. I must show you so that you know the truth."

Clear pictures begin to form in front of him. The world looks different, he sees it from a bird's-eye view. He watches tribes of ancient men wandering across the plains. In the distance is a great fire surrounding what looks like an idyllic city.

"This is Gheisthelm, it is the home of the Djinn."

Shane can see forms. Not humans, not really even biological, just forms in what seems like a large fire. The flames are not a scary hell-like inferno but a beautiful multi-coloured paradise reminding him of a spectacular firework display, except these sparks are living beings.

"The Djinn originated from a sapient life forms similar to humans they evolved into a race of beings capable of great and wondrous achievements, ultimately they advanced to the realm of metaphysical consciousness. After thousands of years living in this spiritual state several Djinn experimented in crossing back over to the physical world."

At this point Shane's mind is invaded with scenes of huge constructions as thousands of men labour, dragging stone and wooden segments. Others were climbing the bamboo scaffolds that surround a huge temple under construction. As his mind's eye pans out he sees the vastness of this city. He notices the wide streets, which seem to all loop in a spiral towards a huge flat-topped pyramid. The city was bordered by two mountains to the north and east and the sea to the south and west. Dressed in golden garments and a wearing a huge headdress is a tall olive skinned man he looks down from a throne which sits on a balcony positioned high in an impressive ancient palace Shane sees coloured smoke billowing around his head. Next he sees similar scenes of human minions worshipping a man dressed in the most ostentatious garments and beautiful woman who reminds him of Solfrid Gjerde, both have similar mist whirling around them.

"These early visits from the Djinn set the tone, using their great knowledge they set themselves up as god like deities. We Arc Hon decided we need to make contact with the Djinn worried they would eventually subjugate mankind completely, I should explain, we have to follow our rules which forbids us from direct interference we could not actually stop the Djinn but we have instructing from the Demiurge as well, so we negotiated an agreement. They would limit the numbers of Djinn crossing over and in return we would share the secret of Vril, up until this meeting the Djinn that crossed over were limited by the physical form and when it demised they either returned to Gheisthelm or died with it. Crossing over was a complex procedure and needed expansive energy bursts as well as many other logistical requirements. Vril would allow the Djinn to exist as a symbiont with humans, they could transfer the Vril to younger healthier bodies when the host became old or ill. Certain requirements were needed but essentially it allowed the Djinn to stay indefinitely. In exchange they agreed that only the thirteen would crossover to compete in a tournament, plus two of the original Djinn visitors who would act as guides, and thus the game began. It was also hoped that their presence would invoke an Evolutionary leap for mankind."

"Oh so it was for our own good," Amitiel is aware he is using sarcasm but at risk of annoying him more she replies. "Yes in some ways it was, humans had benefited from visit earlier you just witnessed the civilisations Baal, Ayton and Solfrid brought to Mesopotamia, Egypt and the Indus.

"Didn't look like much fun for the humans though did it, so what happened that would make you change your mind, why are you all of a sudden gone all Kofi Annan?"

Once more images spiral around Shane, Hundreds of people dressed in peasant attire stand in a field of dry hay. They are surrounded by soldiers wearing round helmets, two men sit on the hill one wears robes similar to a bishop the other armour made of brilliant polished metal. Shane can hear Amitiel explain that this is Ivan the terrible first Tsar of Russia and his most trusted advisor Macarius the metropolitan of Moscow, Shane sees the clergyman has the now familiar coloured mist above his head. The Tsar waves to his troops who using burning torches set the field alight the fire rapidly circling the field aided by some form of accelerant. Screams cry out as the peasants realise their fate, some cower and cover the eyes of their children some attempt to escape through the flames only to meet the sharp end of a spear. Shane views a mother brake the skull of her own child to save its pain. The two men on the hill fall about laughing at each scene.

A bright light causes pain in Shanes head and now he is witnessing a different scene. A small oriental looking man is working away in an ancient apothecary he seems to be feeding rats and then placing them into small wooden containers inhabited with tiny fleas, through the dark swirl above his head Shane sees a smile on his face he is pleased with himself. The man makes his way outside and approaches a caravan of people dressed in silk garments overlaid with heavy looking aprons. The man gives the box to one of them with a small bag of coins and passes on his instructions. "Release these when you enter Kaffa" the man nods and they set off. The scene jumps and Shane sees the devastation caused by this transaction as thousands of bodies lay strewn over the land. Amitiel explains, "Zeb decided to try to eliminate Simeon Isaac and Reuben by creating the Black Death the worst plague in human history, this was the first example of chemical warfare.

One more vision one I don't think I will have to narrate to you," Shane instantly recognises the place and is very aware of which event is about to take place. "When Levi wanted the Americans to go to war with the nations under Judd's control he hit them in two places their hearts and their pockets. It was simple for him to recruit nineteen jihadist to die for Allah and he soon had them trained and ready to carry out the first attack on US soil for over fifty years. Her was aware the outcry would allow his planned attack under the logo 'war on terror' causing disarray to Judd's fruitful oil income. Shane is spared the vision of the planes crashing into the twin towers and he is now floating above the visiting room looking down on himself and Amitiel bizarrely chatting away amicable and laughing. When he looks around he can see her aura and can hear her once more.

260

"We were guilty of undervaluing human lives and under estimating the contempt to which Djinn held you. I admit we got this wrong we should never have helped the Djinn. Vril has made them too powerful to the extent that they are at least our equal on this plain and know one of them is murdering the others and taking their amulets giving him access to the links created via their Vril soon nothing will be able to stop him and he will force all men into servitude." She seems to mull over her thought before her next comment. "We really fucked up."

"Ya think" Shane really doesn't know whether to laugh or cry, before he has a chance to add his real thoughts he experiences a sudden falling sensation and as if he was never away he is sitting back in the visiting room.

𓂋𓄿𓏏 𓇋𓈖 𓂝𓈖

"So, do you agree, Shane Mills?"
Shane shakes his head as if to clear his thoughts. He looks down at Amitiel's hands; feeling her soft touch calms him. He hears the screw's voice, "No touching, you know the rules."

Amitiel releases his hand. "Reuben is about to try to get to you and the old Jew. He will strike tomorrow. I have reliable information that an armed vanguard will enter the prison under cover of a fire or explosion. The prime target is you. Reuben will have paid guards on the inside to create a reason to lock you up. When the fire starts a riot will ensue. The police, fire brigade and medics will all arrive but some of these will be his men in disguise. They will be tipped off as to which cell you are in and they will come and get you."

Shane's head is spinning. He looks up at the guard who is now looking over at them, seemingly none the wiser to Shane's recent trip through time and space. Amitiel is chit chatting, as if they'd just stepped off a bus together mid-conversation. *Get your shit together, Mills,* he tells himself, mimicking his ritual when he was under fire in

Afghanistan. *Focus, breathe, fight.* He repeats this mantra in his head. It has served him well most of his life and as the guard wanders back over to his post Shane finally accepts all this crazy shit as true. He sinks his head into his hands. "Holy mother of God the old man isn't crazy." He eventually looks up to this Angel of Truth for the next move. "Okay, so what do I do?" Amitiel looks at him puzzled. "I don't bloody know! You're the fucking hero. I'm just the messenger!"

Shane has to laugh at her response. "At least I have the element of surprise now, right? I'm guessing this Reuben won't know that I know?"

She smiles. "He will know nothing." She inclines her beautiful red head towards the guard who is watching them. "He is the guard who has been reporting to Reuben. Reuben will not learn of this visit; I will take care of him. You, however, must prepare for battle. With your permission, I will visit you tonight while you sleep and project a blueprint into your mind." Shane holds his arms wide. "Project away, but a blueprint of what?"

She looks him in the eye. "The sewers. You will need to access them once the fire starts. Escape through these tunnels and I will have someone pick you up at the other end. You will need some sort of lever with you as there is a barred grid blocking your way out, just under the gates."

Shane is not sure he heard correctly. "So, I not only have to find a way to get into the shitty sewer, but I have to find a crowbar in a prison and take it with me, all the while dragging a sixty-year-old Jew along for the ride and with just twenty-four hours to do it? Sounds like a piece of piss!"

The guard shuffles and grumbles, "Time's up."

"Please, sir, could we have five more minutes?" Amitiel says. "I haven't seen Uncle Shane for months."

The guard looks unsympathetic. "It's against the rules."

Amitiel purses her lips thoughtfully. "What if I'm extra nice to you, say in the storeroom, as a thank you?" The guard coughs and stutters as smutty visions pass through his mind. "What do you mean by nice?"

"Well, let's just say you will have a happy ending, I pinkie promise." Her reply is dripping in an overly cute, sweet voice and a very naughty smile. Shane nods, amused, to let him know she will, in fact, give him a good time.

"Okay, five minutes." The guard returns to his corner.

Amitiel's persona changes instantly, reverting back to business. Shane is impressed by her split-second transformation but is shocked by her statement.

"You won't be taking the Jew, just Robert Price."

Shane glares at her. He is pissed off on three counts: one, she's already told him Leo is on Reuben's hit list also, two, he doesn't want Al Qaeda Bob on his team and three, hang on a minute, does he really look like an uncle?

"No way am I leaving Leo here for that cunt, Reuben, to do heaven knows what to." He can tell from the look on Amitiel's face he is not going to like what is coming next.

"Reuben wants Leo alive and for a very important reason. He has obtained a very special book – perhaps Leo spoke of this?"

Shane smiled. He had listened to the tales Leo told him just to be polite but fortunately he had actually absorbed most of them, especially the importance of this book, the ledger that controlled half the world's wealth. "Yes, some sort of accounts for the kings and queens of old, wasn't it?"

"Something like that. The text is in a form of Yiddish that only a handful of people on the planet can read and Leo is one of these. While Leo is alive there is the risk Reuben will use him to access the books secret's."

Only slowly does Shane realise what she is suggesting. "What? Fuck off!"

Amitiel tries to take his hand but he pulls away. The guard looks over and she quickly speaks. "The old man will agree with me. If Reuben captures him he will take him to his fortress in Switzerland and torture him. At some point he will break and then he will turn to Reuben's side. Is that what you want?"

"But why can't Leo come with me instead of the fucking Jihadist? Leo is on our team, he's the one who has tried to educate me about all this and you suggest I kill him?" Shane sits back and folds his arms. "Like I said, you can fuck off."

Amitiel looks at the guard who seems to have picked up on the words 'kill him'. This time she talks to Shane telepathically without speaking.

"You must be calm. You cannot take Leo. He won't make it crawling through sewage on his stomach for two miles, not to mention the combat you will be involved in to get there. He will slow you down and get you caught. Let me explain what will happen when you are caught: Reuben is a sick bastard, you will be subjected to unbelievable pain that no human, not even you, can handle."

Shane thinks quickly. "Okay, you want the black guy, you got him, but we'll be taking Leo with us. I have trained for torture situations and the mind is the most important factor. Trust me, I have the strongest mind you will come across. This is non-negotiable."

A moment of silence fills the room, Amitiel looks at him sternly and pauses before replying. "I will say this, if caught, Reuben will likely tie you to a chair and cut your eyelids off. He will then parade a group of young children in front of you. Then he'll choose a game, maybe Reuben will slowly sexually abuse one, maybe mutilate it, maybe he'll get the children to mutilate each other, commit murder, incest, or even remove and eat each other's eyeballs. If you think you will hold out, then I will go with your plan."

Shane stares into his lap. Being strong enough to resist torture yourself is one thing, being forced to watch innocents tortured because of him is beyond his abilities – if this girl can see this then Reuben will figure it out in a heartbeat. This shit is real and he feels a sudden swell in his throat as a surge of sadness threatens to overwhelm him. He swallows hard, looking up back at Amitiel, his face appearing like that of an innocent child.

"I am sorry, Shane. There is no other way. The old guy will hold you up." She looks genuinely sad. "Now, when I visit you tonight, I hope to have more details of Reuben's plan and we will then counter with our own plan. Shane, you must do all that I ask and you must trust Robert Price."

Shane is not listening, his head is full of sorrowful thoughts about killing Leo.

Amitiel frowns at him. "You must prepare. I will leave it up to you to decide if you tell Leo of the plan or not. But you must inform Robert. Right, now I have to deal with this gobshite of a guard."

Amitiel gives a girly wave to the guard and Shane notices the bulge in his trousers already.

"You're not really going to touch that slime ball, are you?" Shane asks. She smiles "Are you jealous? I need to be sure he does not report my visit to Reuben. Five minutes in the stockroom will ensure of that." She winks at Shane and once more he sees the seductive temptress and a strange feeling he has not felt for a long time stirs in him.

Shane walks back to his cell with visibly less enthusiasm than when he made his way out of it. "How can I leave Leo?" he asks himself. Then, as if recovering from shock, the events that have just unfolded begin to flood back. The things he has seen, the places he has been to. He looks up at the clock and struggles to comprehend that he has only been out of his cell for less than fifteen minutes. In this time he has witnessed the world's history, discovered he is a target for some three-thousand-year-old psycho, been informed that there's going to be a major prison break tomorrow, which is only, in fact, a distraction to cover his and Leo's kidnapping and, worst of all, if he is to succeed in saving mankind, he must first kill his close friend.

"My first visit since I arrived here and what a shit visit it was!" he grumbles to himself.

Shane decides there and then that he will tell Leo everything and between them they will come up with a better plan. He is scheduled to visit him at 14:00 so this time he will do the talking and it will be Leo wondering if Shane has lost his marbles.

♜♖♟

Despite this plan Shane fails to bring it up as the two men sit in the recreation corner of the psychiatric wing playing chess. Shane has lost his first game of chess to Leo for almost twelve months.

"Okay, what's up?" asks Leo.

With a final sigh Shane conveys to Leo what he remembers from his visit with Amitiel, ringing his hands together and shaking his head as he does so, struggling to believe his own words. Occasionally he stands up and walks around mumbling, as if trying to put the pieces together so that they make sense but of course he is preaching to the converted and need not fear any utterance of disbelief from Leo. Still, he was not prepared for the old guy to agree to his own death.

"She is absolutely right," Leo tells Shane.

"For fuck's sake, you're not serious? I am not going to pop you, old man. I'm not going to do it, so get your thinking cap on and help me work out a better plan."

Leo smiles at him. "Shane, I have been expecting death for a long time now and if it was not for you, I would have been dead a long time ago. Who better to send me to God than you?"

Shane is not convinced. "God? You still believe in God? These Djinn freaks *are* the Gods! I've got to tell you the word 'God' has lost a lot of value in my book. In fact, my only thoughts regarding 'Gods' at the moment is 'what a bunch of cunts'."

"You're wrong,' says Leo. "These beings we deal with are advanced but they are not God! I admit my faith has wavered since I met Simeon

266

but now I am once more comfortable with my faith. Besides, either way the girl is right. I cannot make it through sewers and it would not be appropriate for a respectable Jew to wade through philistine shit."

Both men laugh and Leo points out that they can take advantage of Reuben's need for his knowledge.

"We know he is planning some sort of distraction and this will take the form of a major catastrophe, either a fire or an explosion. If the priority is to take me alive then I need to survive this catastrophe, meaning the safest place to be when the shit hits the fan is in this ward. So somehow we need to ensure that both you and Robert are up here, at least when the attack begins."

Shane ponders Leo's tactics. Of course, this could give him an opportunity to get Leo out as well so he agrees. It will not be easy as Shane is only permitted one hour on the psychiatric wing and Robert is not allowed on it at all but Shane agrees that whatever Reuben is planning, he will ensure that there is no danger that he or Leo will be killed. He has the next twenty-odd hours to work the rest out.

Venice

Under the city of Venice runs a labyrinth of canal tunnels. If you know where to look they will take you to an ancient palace, once a meeting place for the Djinn and Arc Hon council, a neutral zone. Today it is both a hideout and a prison. Reuben, dressed in a smart business suit, walks through the pristine white corridors. He enters a room using a swipe key. Inside is a chair surrounded by a cage made up of blue laser beams. Sitting in the chair is Simeon.

"So, my friend, after eighteen months and the best care money can buy, I you finally are looking like you have recovered from that little ordeal?" says Reuben.

The room is occupied solely by the two Djinn.

"Yes, I would thank you for your care had it not been under your instructions that I was riddled with bullets in the first place."

"I have told you I am sorry about that, it is very hard to get decent hit men nowadays. As I said the Jew and you were to simply be captured. Anyway you survived and that is the important thing. Soon I will unite you with your chosen prodigy."

Simeon looks alarmed. "You have him?"

Reuben smirks. "Not yet, but soon, very soon. Unfortunately I expect there to be some collateral damage during his extraction. Six hundred prisoners caught in a huge gas explosion. You can imagine the carnage, especially as they are all locked up, trapped like animals."

Simeon knows he is being goaded. Reuben has questioned him many times about Shane Mills and Leo while he was recovering, unbeknown to him Simeon was able to relay the conversations to Amitiel who in turn would visit Shane.

"Maybe this Leo will be burned to a crisp as well," Reuben adds, smirking. "Tell me what you think of my proposed alliance with this human champion? After all the incessant lobbying and planning you and Isaac persisted in, it's a shame he will have such a short game."

Simeon looks up nonchalantly with a smug smile as he tries to hide his concern. "I don't think you will outsmart him so easily."

Stoke Prison

Phil Cumisky brother of Kieran Cumisky notices the Shane Mills guy looking at him as he sits in the TV area contemplating his escape. Although Phil and his brother are two of the most feared men in London, Phil always feels uneasy around Mills. He had watched him make easy work of the two Jamaicans a few years earlier and knew then that this guy was special. He was thinking of asking Shane if he wanted to work with them when he got out but the guy was very unfriendly towards Phil for some reason. *Anyway,* he thought, *why's he looking at me now? Does he know what's about to happen? Of course he doesn't. How could he?*

Shane would love to smash Phil Cumisky's head to a pulp. He never liked the prick, walking around the prison like he was "the man" just because his brother was a big gangster on the outside. Now though, he also knows this prick is going to start some sort of chaos in order to escape. When Amitiel came to him in his dream last night, she told him what more she had learned.

She was convinced that the guy Cumisky was the one who would instigate the event and subsequent carnage. Shane had asked why killing that prick wouldn't be the best idea, hoping he would then get a reprieve from killing Leo.

"No," she'd said. "If we follow the plan, we will turn this to our advantage. You will be out of here and the authorities will think you perished in the fire. More importantly, Reuben and the other Djinn will assume the same thing."

Shane had expected to be told no but had still racked his brains for an alternate outcome that didn't include him murdering his close friend.

"There must be another way. If you can work out how to get me out of here and you have all this inside knowledge about the plan and who is carrying it out, then you must be able to think of a better idea than me saying goodbye to Leo with my hands around his neck?"

Amitiel had appeared in the dream as the sweet girl he met in the visiting room. She'd smiled and then answered, "I know you do not want to do this but it is the only way. I am aware of the plan because I have a direct link with Simeon who is currently Reuben's prisoner. By goading Reuben and massaging his ego, Simeon has succeeded in encouraging Reuben to brag about his plan.

"If we do anything to show our hand then Reuben will realise that you are being helped by someone with a teleconnection to Simeon. He will soon work out that it must be an Arc Hon and we don't want him or the other Djinn knowing we have sided with the humans. If he does, then we will lose our advantage. He will break the connection and probably kill Simeon, once and for all."

Shane didn't care about this Simeon but knew any advantage in a battle was worth protecting. Amitiel had told him something else.

"Once you and Robert Price have cleared the gates, my associate will get you to a safe house. I will come to you once more but that will be last time until you fulfil the task."

Shane was wondering how exactly he was supposed to do that. He was just one man against this powerful Reuben, but then Amitiel had made it four times worse.

"You are now in the game and although Reuben is the prime target, the other three Djinn must also be taken care of if you are to win."

The dream had then become a vision as Shane was transported to the White House. He saw some faces he did not recognise and one he did. It was the President of the United States of America. He was sitting with a bespectacled geek who was surrounded by the same sort of multi-coloured mist he had seen in yesterday's vision. This one, though, was predominantly red.

"This is Levi. He is very much involved with controlling the American government."

In front of Shane's eyes the walls had crumbled and then been rebuilt. Now he had found himself in a Russian military base where the Russian President and the generals were inspecting a squadron of elite forces. Shane saw no auras on anyone. The vision followed the President as he returned to his Moscow home where there was a tall effeminate-looking young man waiting by the pool. When he entered, the leader of the largest country in the world had a smile on his face rarely seen in his media portrayal. He dismissed his entourage, leaving him with just the athletic, well-groomed, tanned young man. The two men locked in a passionate embrace, undressing each other and showing no restraint, their lust for each other obvious. Shane thought he was beyond shockable but watching the macho Russian President stick his tongue down this young man's throat took him by surprise. He felt slightly guilty at his own discomfort at the scene and looked away as the kiss became groping and the final clothes came off.

"Fuck, who would have known," he'd said, taking one more glimpse and this time spotting the anomaly hovering above the young man's head, a tightly formed yellow cloud. It seemed to move in tandem with the man, swirling around his whole body, then up above, then wrapping around his shoulders. It was wondrous and seemed to be an aura protecting its master. Shane noticed the look of wonder on the President's face. At first he thought he must see the aura as well but then he realised exactly what this look, far removed from his usual solemn public persona, really was. It was love.

"Asher pulls the strings at the Kremlin," Amitiel had commented.

"That's not all he pulls," replied Shane, immediately regretting his immature jibe as Amitiel ignored him.

Finally Shane had witnessed the Chinese delegation arrive in Nigeria. By now Shane had worked out what to look for and he zeroed in on the chauffeur of the Chinese general, a Western-looking man, who was surrounded by a green aura.

"This last one is Judd," Amitiel had told him. Each of these Djinn are your foes. Each must be defeated for you to be victorious. You must play this game as you would play chess. So, for instance, you are the

273

queen, Robert is the knight, and outside these walls are the other key pieces."

"Two rooks, two bishops and another knight?" Shane had mocked, uncomfortable with the comparison.

"Our first mission will be to recruit these others," concluded Amitiel.

"Firstly, I prefer to work alone. Secondly, I'm no queen," said Shane.

Amitiel laughed. "Gender is not important; the queen is the most powerful piece."

"What about the king? You haven't got the most important piece of the game? Your analogy sucks."

"My analogy is just fine," she frowns. "And as for the king, she is coming."

"She?"

"Like I said, gender is not important."

Shane has been lying awake for some time. Amitiel was sure that Phil Cumisky's distraction and the following attack was scheduled for between three and four in the afternoon. Shane would meet Leo for the normal game of chess at one. Somehow or another he needed to make sure he was still in that area for at least two hours and that Robert was there too. He had a plan and explained it as best he could to Robert. Robert just nodded, agreeing to everything. Shane was impressed at the lack of questions. *This guy just follows instructions,* he thinks to himself. *Perhaps he will be a good ally after all.*

If the plan is to work timing will be essential. He will also need both Leo and Robert to follow his instructions to the letter. He is less worried about Robert's part now but fears Leo may crack under the pressure. Shane leaves his cell at 13:50 and heads up to the psyche ward. As usual he is searched before leaving his wing and searched before entering the psyche wing. He sees that the game is already set up and Leo sits calmly waiting just like any other day. The enormity of what he is expected to do weighs heavily on Shane as he struggles to return the smile.

"Are you ready to play our final game?" asks Leo, as Shane takes a seat. Shane is not capable of joviality and remains stony-faced. Leo decides to kick-start the conversation.

"So, have you worked out how you're going to do this?"

Shane looks around before he explains everything to Leo.

𝕸𝖞𝖞𝖆𝖔 𝖆𝖆𝖋𝖔𝕸𝖔

Reuben, as always, has done his homework. He has researched Stoke Prison heavily and has three of the prison guards on his payroll. The main building of the prison was built in 1900. Although a new block was added twenty years ago, the main building has only been majorly refurbished once, which, Reuben was glad to see, was back in the fifties. His plan relied on the antiquated structure of the building making it vulnerable. It was almost too perfect. His only concern now was that one of his informers had failed to report in last night. Still, he had all the information he needed. The plan was flawless.

The new block contains the psychiatric ward, including the solitary cells and also the high-security wing. He wonders if there might be some useful inmates in there. *It would be a waste not to utilise such talent,* he thinks to himself.

The crux of Reuben's plan concerns the older part of the prison, known as C wing, which houses B-rated prisoners. Below this wing is the main service area, which encompasses the gas boilers that heat the whole complex. C wing is a virtual tinder box and a survey carried out only six months earlier, which Reuben has possession of, states that "the Victorian premises are over-reliant on its ageing wooden structure and are a serious fire risk".

𝕸𝖞𝖔𝕸𝕴 𝕴𝕴𝖞𝕴

Phil Cumisky is impressed that his brother managed to entice the screw, Boland, to allow him to smuggle the explosive device. Boland just wanted his little girl back.

The explosive is similar to the shoe bomb favoured by terrorists when planning to explode planes. It would set off a small explosion followed by a fire accelerant disperser.

Phil has also been told exactly which shaft he must drop the device down to cause maximum carnage. He will have three minutes to clear the area and get out to the yard. He's not going to enjoy burning all these other inmates to death and has given some thought to letting a couple of friends know what was going to happen. Ultimately, though, he can't risk his own safety for anyone else's – even if they are mates. Anyway, the idea of being on the outside again with an eight ball of coke in his pocket and some whore bouncing up and down on his dick counteracts any guilt he feels.

The time is now 14:40. He will drop the device down the shaft at 15:00 as agreed. As he makes his way to the drop point he notices the black guy, Al Qaeda Bob, being escorted out of the wing by two guards. "What a jammy bastard," he thinks to himself. "Gonna miss all the excitement."

Phil tries not to look suspicious as he walks but his heart is pounding as random thoughts enter his mind:
What if it doesn't go off?
What if it goes off before it's supposed to?
What if it goes off in my pocket?
He feels drips of sweat trickle from his thickset eyebrows. *Fuck, stop sweating!* he tells himself. *Someone will know something's up.* He places his hands in his pockets and then pulls them out quickly, scared he might hit the trigger. Eventually panic takes over and he decides he has waited as long as he can. Nervously he drops the thing ten minutes early and he swiftly walks away from the shaft and heads for the exit. *Almost there,* he thinks. *Almost home.*

Before Phil can make it to the yard, however, an alarm is activated and the door to the outside automatically closes. Phil is confused and petrified. Guards are running around shouting and screaming. *How could they know already? The fucking thing hasn't gone off yet!*

"Everyone in their cells," shouts the guard as the alarm is blaring.

"I am due to play in the tournament," shouts Phil, trying to push his way out.

"All exercise is cancelled. Get to your cell!" shouts the guard, pulling his truncheon out. Guards are running around all over the block and Phil is being herded along with other inmates back to their cells.

He is filling with primal fear. He's the only one who knows this is about the worst thing they could be doing. In about thirty seconds this place is going to be an inferno! Panicking and desperate not to be locked up in a cell he yells out, "Fire, fire."

Gerald Penavager, a particularly violent screw, reacts to what he assumes is Phil's attempt at rabble rousing by gripping him around the neck with his baton, dragging him to a cell and locking it behind him. Philip's cry is like that of a squeaking pig but it's lost in the chaos of the moment. From the distance an explosion can be heard and the whole ward goes quiet. Another explosion follows and then another as the domino of gas tanks set each other off and rumble through the floor. Finally, as Phil cries to the heavens, C wing rocks and cracks open, the extreme heat melting his clothes to his burning skin, igniting his hair and cooking his insides. His heart gives out seconds before his brain fries. A louder explosion signals the end for C wing and its occupants.

Twenty minutes earlier in the psychiatric ward Shane had just finished his game with Leo. He had a maximum of thirty minutes before the attack and needed to still be here when it happened. His plan was simple: if Leo was so determined to die then he was going to have to work for it.

"Okay, I am going to pass you a shank. You will do that hissy fit thing you do and take it to my throat. I am going to be your hostage and you will demand to see Robert Price. Tell them he can stay on the other side of the security door but that you must speak to him."

Leo's reply is not overly enthusiastic. "I don't have hissy fits and they won't deal with hostage takers, it's their policy."

Shane grabs Leo by the sleeve, pulling him close as he leans in. The serious look on his face conveys to Leo his impatience. Keen to get things started, he explains, speaking precisely and quickly: "As long as you say that Price can stay on the other side of the cage they will have no reason not to because they will not have put him in any danger.

"Once he is up here we will talk shit until Price gets the opportunity to overpower a guard. I will take out fat boy over there."

Shane nods towards the guard by the door just as a second guard enters, who frowns at Shane and Leo so Shane releases Leo's sleeve and smiles. The guard is more interested in talking to his mate though.

"You hear about Brogan down in the visiting room?" Shane's ears prick up, momently distracted from his task by the name of the guard Amitiel had promised to be nice to.

"Yeah, heart attack wasn't it?" replies the second guard.

The guard scoffs. "He was apparently having a wank in the storeroom and his ticker went on him just at the time of arrival, if you catch my drift. Died with his trousers round his ankles and his pecker in his hand. Not a very dignified way to go." There is a second's respectful silence before both guards burst into laughter. Shane laughs to himself; she really did give him a happy ending.

"So where is this shank thing?" asks Leo.

"Oh right, I just need to go to the bathroom and I will bring it back out with me."

Leo pales as he works out where Shane has hidden the shank.

"Run it under the tap, will you?" he requests, as Shane gets up to go to the loo.

Robert Price sits in his cell waiting. He has done as Shane asked and strapped the small jemmy bar to his back. Shane believes the screws won't search him very thoroughly when they bring him up to speak with the disturbed Leo as they will be focused on Leo as the danger. Robert isn't so sure but he has done what has been asked of him.

Mick O'Halloran likes it here on the psyche wing. The fat Irish guard has been at Stoke Prison for almost twelve years and most of the guys are either sedated or in solitary, piece of cake. His mate Kenny even just came by for a chat while he dropped off some paperwork. They'd had a joke about Brogan, the poor bastard. It was weird that Brogan had died from a heart attack only a month after running a marathon in less than three hours. Mick could hardly walk the corridors in three hours but he feels a small triumph as he thinks, "all that fitness training is no good. If it's your time, it's your time." Mick removes a Snickers bar from his pocket. "This is the only marathon I'll be finishing," he jokes to himself.

While he is stuffing chocolate down his throat he notices Shane come back from the toilet. Mick wonders why a man such as Shane wastes time on a loony like Leo. It's a strange coupling, he always thought.

"You fucking cheating bastard!" Leo suddenly screams and Mick almost chokes on his Snickers.

Leo jumps up and pushes the table over. Shane backs up in surprise and puts his hands up in defence. Mike struggles with his baton, half expecting Mills to restrain the old guy himself. But to Mick's surprise he holds up his arms and looks genuinely concerned as he apologises profusely to Leo. Mick frowns. Will he have to call it in? Think of the paperwork!

Mike hovers, unsure, and then blanches as Leo pulls out the shank. The sharpened toothbrush is suddenly under Mills' throat and Mike nearly wets himself.

"Yo, fat boy," says Leo. "Get on the blower and get me face-to-face with that raghead fucking Muslim Al Qaeda Bill!"

Shane is desperately trying not to laugh. "It's Bob. Al Qaeda Bob!"

"Shut up, Mills!" snaps Leo. "I'll call him what the fuck I like!"

Shane is impressed by the old guy's acting skills, although he could release a bit of pressure from the sharp pointy thing he is pressing into his throat.

Mick stutters and stammers as he lifts the intercom and calls for immediate help. Mick looks at the crazy eyes on Leo as he draws blood from Shane's neck. "Tell them to hurry the fuck up!" The prison Governor and half a dozen wardens rally quickly and congregate outside the caged partition, looking in on the unlikely scene of Leo holding Shane hostage. Governor Byrne speaks through the intercom to Leo.

"Hello, Leo. I'm not sure what's going on here but I need you to let Shane go and we can speak about what the problem is."

Leo turns to the Governor and stares with crazy eyes. "I tell you what I want! I want that raghead Muslim cunt Al Qaeda Bob up here right now! I need to know the answer to my question and only he knows."

Shane is both impressed and a little concerned with Leo's performance. "Raghead Muslim cunt" is not a phrase he ever thought he would hear come out of this gentle, well-educated man. Guess that's what prison does to you.

"I can't do that, Leo. You need to put the weapon down. I will make sure you get to ask any question you want but first I want Shane released."

With speed and agility that no one would have credited the sixty-year-old with, Leo spins himself around so he is behind Shane and pushes the shank hard beneath his eye.

"Take it easy!" says a surprised Shane.

"I will take out this cunt's eye in ten seconds unless I get your word that Price will be standing where you are in ten minutes. That's all I ask, he will be on your side of the cage, so he won't be in any danger."

It takes all of Shane's composure not to instinctively react and break Leo's neck. Shane must admit, the old guy is fucking good at being mental as he begins his countdown.

"Ten – I will take his eyes then his life. Nine – I need to talk to the Muslim that is all. Eight – do not try to bullshit an insane man holding a sharp weapon to a man's eye. Seven – Six –"

The Governor holds his hands up. "Hold on, Leo. I need to contact C wing and ask them if Price will agree, is that okay?"
Leo jerks Shane's neck up exposing the large vein sticking out. "Don't ask him, tell him or I'll be cutting this fucker's jugular. You have five minutes and then I'm going to start cutting."

The Governor is talking to C wing, telling them to get Price. One guard, Ray Connor, has a bad feeling about this.

"Are you sure about this, Gov?" he asks.

"If it calms Verdi down, then yes," scowls the Governor. "Price won't be in any danger as long as he's this side of the cage."

It takes approximately five minutes to reach D block from C wing and during these minutes Leo does not relent on his play acting as he roughly pushes the shank against Shane's throat. "Why isn't he here yet?" he demands. Shane wants to tell the old guy to reel it in a bit, his performance is worthy of an Oscar but he seems to have gone all Joe Pesci on him.

"He is coming now," replies the Governor as the entrance door can be seen opening. Robert is escorted by two guards and he looks up, confused at the sight he sees.

"What now?" whispers Leo into Shane's ear.

"Release me and I will get on that side with Robert. You just fake a crazy fit to distract them and we will do the rest."

"Right, we have Robert here now, Leo," says the Governor. "So if you can release Shane then you can ask any question you have, okay?"

Leo relaxes and let's Shane go. Shane does not need to feign relief at getting away from Leo. He follows the Governor's instructions and walks to the cage door, catching Robert's eye. He also notices the guards' hands fall to their batons as they ready themselves to run in and apprehend Leo. The Governor waves to Shane to hurry. The cage opens and Shane jumps out.

"What the hell got into him?" asks the Governor.

Shane pretends to laugh it off to lighten the mood but he's actually focused on the guards' next move. It looks as if they are going to rush at Leo but he knows they will wait until he and Robert are out of the way. Leo suddenly sprints at the cage shouting and banging on about the elves and the fairies. The Governor looks at Robert for a possible explanation but the big black guy shrugs his shoulders. "I ain't got a clue what he's on about."

"Okay, take these two back to their cells." The Governor sighs tiredly as Leo presses his tongue into the toughened glass.

Two guards move to escort Shane and Robert out. Shane keeps one eye on the cage. Timing is everything when it's two against seven, not including mad Leo of course. The guard Connor holds back; somehow a killer like Shane being held hostage by this little old man does not compute with him. At the double doors, just as the exit doors unlock Shane prepares for the cage doors to open. He spins and takes the first guard out with a crack to his jaw. Shocked, the second guard just stares as Robert brings a two-handed heavy blow down on his skull. The three guards who are running in to get Leo turn at the sound of the commotion. Leo leaps on the back of one, pulling him to the floor. Connor, stationed next to the alarm, hits the button and the prison lockdown protocol begins. He then bravely pulls the Governor out of the way of a flying Robert and strikes out with his baton. The lockdown has left him and the Governor stranded between the ward and the main prison but Connor calculates that if he holds out for a couple of minutes help will come. He reaches for his Taser gun and is a second away from firing it when an explosion shakes the whole building. The speeding body of another guard hurtles into him.

Shane has no time for niceties and is dispatching each guard with extreme efficiency. He finishes Connor off with an open hand strike to his temple. Robert is already in the lock-up and has one guard wrapped round each arm and the third around his neck. Shane sees an opportunity to end the fight early as the Governor cowers in a corner. He pulls the Taser from the unconscious Connor and holds it to the Governor's groin.

"Call them off."

The Governor looks down and obeys. "Stop, all of you, stand down."

The four conscious guards follow their boss's command, releasing Robert and Leo.

"Lock them up in your cell," Shane tells Leo.

"What about him?" asks Leo, pointing to the Governor.

"He stays with us."

The Governor begins to preach at them but Shane really doesn't have time for it and silences the man with twelve thousand volts. He shudders to the ground unable to even scream. Robert looks at the Governor then Shane. He laughs, "Nice one." After a couple of minutes Leo returns holding four batons and a set of keys.

"What do we want with all of them?" asks Shane.

Leo runs past him, locking the entrance door. He looks down at the incapacitated Governor. "Why is he here? You need to get going and he will hold you up. And you still have one more task, don't forget."

Leo stands there bravely, waiting. Shane looks at Robert, whose empathetic look tells him he is aware of the deed that needs to be done, that he must kill his friend. Robert indicates that he will do the task if needed as Leo looks forlornly at Shane. Shane has dreaded this moment. He knows that the gesture from Robert is an offer to do this for him. He is tempted but he knows ultimately if this is to be done, then he must be the one to do it.

He looks at Leo's puny bespectacled frame. It won't take much, he concedes. Perhaps a blow to his atlas, the point of the spine that meets the brain. Or maybe a choke lock or punch to the temple. Shane knows at least twenty ways to kill a man quickly. He could simply snap his neck with a powerful hook to the front side of his jaw. Nothing seems appropriate though.

"We are going with plan B," Shane tells Robert and Leo.

Robert wasn't sure what plan A was so he didn't complain and Leo was quick enough to guess plan B would include him escaping with these two and not dying. He wanted to be brave and insist that they stuck to plan A.

"What's plan B then?" he asks.

"We are going out the first class and Governor Mr Byrne here is our ticket out." Shane grabs the groggy Governor, pulling him to his feet and reaching into his hostage's pocket to pull out a short-wave radio. Shane slaps the Governor awake and tells him, "Speak to the control centre, tell them to open all doors in the building." He then turns to Leo and Robert and tells them. "Put the guards' uniforms on, quickly."

Governor Byrne hesitates. "If they open all the doors the prisoners will escape. There will be carnage." Shane speaks with menace. "Did you not hear that explosion? They will all die if you don't evacuate immediately. Now I am not asking, Governor, I'm telling you to give the order. Open all the exits, open all the doors, every fucking last one!" Governor Byrne takes the radio with a shaking hand and calls to the control room. "This is Governor Byrne. Who is in the con room?"

A voice replies over the air waves. "It's me, Parish. What are the instructions, Gov? The place is going to hell, seems like some sort of explosion. The emergency forces are on their way and we have locked down the inmates but Barry and Penavager say that a fire has broken out. We tried calling you, sir. What do we do?"

The Governor coughs. A final glance at Shane's face and he gives his commands. "Emergency procedure Red One. Open all doors, all cells and all exits. Open all gates, tell prisoners to congregate in the Sherburne car park."

Parish looks at his receiver as if he heard wrong. "Sir, could you repeat that?" Byrne repeats it word for word except this time he adds, "Fucking NOW."

"Yes, sir. It's done."

Shane removes the jacket from one of the guards. Robert and Leo are already kitted out though Leo's is too big and Robert's is too small. Shane pushes the Taser close to the Governor's throat. "We are walking out of here as your protection. Before we go out there, Governor Byrne, I need to confess. I am sure you are aware of my case and that I was found not guilty of murder. The jury did not believe that I intended to kill the good doctor as I only hit him the once. Believe me, Governor Byrne, I intended to kill that man and I will kill you too if you make one wrong move."

As the group head out of the psychiatric block, a young screw approaching at pace recognises the Governor. He also notices the men in guards' uniform but does not realise who they are. Assuming these are his colleagues, he begins his report to the Governor.

"Sir, it is chaos down there. The prisoners are running amok, half the floor in C wing has caved in and there are fires in D wing, admin, the gym and the kitchens." The guard stops talking as he tries to name the guards flanking the Governor. In the same split second he finally recognises Robert, he is knocked unconscious by the man's massive fist.

"We won't get far like this," he says, scratching his neck, "seeing as there isn't a single black guard in the place."

"We just need to get to the roof. If I'm right, there will be a helicopter up there." Shane looks at the Governor for confirmation. The Governor nods reluctantly and both Robert and Leo look at each other, hoping the other happens to know how to fly. Governor Byrne has always been proud and quick to boast that Stoke Prison is one of only two prisons in the country with a helipad. It sits at the top of the high-security block. Officially it is for emergency transport of prisoners to hospital. Byrne is aware of the fact that it was financed by the

Americans and was sure its real purpose was to transport political prisoners, mostly Muslim activists who the Yanks wanted to have a chat with without drawing attention. However, he never thought to protest; after all he often uses it to impress visitors like Solfrid Gjerde, whom he had picked up in his personal EC 135T.

Byrne was not a particularly brave man; prison Governors are picked for their management skills mainly he just wanted to see his wife and kids again. He hoped he would live through today but was not worried so much about what the tough-talking but level-headed Shane would do to him, but rather what could be waiting around the corner.

To get to the roof from the psyche block you need to negotiate your way through the high-security wing, which is where the most dangerous inmates are locked up, or were locked up until Shane ordered all the doors open. The Governor considers warning Shane but fears he may make things worse. He decides he must stay quiet and hope they have already fled. And here lies the problem with Shane's plan. He has worked out that it will take ten minutes to get through the prison and up to the roof. The Governor has all the necessary keys and passwords, including the helicopter keys. He is sure that the chaos caused by six hundred prisoners either burning to death or running free will be more than enough of a distraction for the local authorities and law enforcement. However, unknown to him there are two dozen murdering bastards running towards them from the opposite direction and Shane and co are with the Governor, dressed in guard uniforms.

When Shane first sees them coming down the corridor he doesn't worry too much but when the high-risk inmates spot them and start pointing Shane remembers what they must look like. The oncoming group of murdering psychos salivate at the sight of a small group of guards and the Governor. Shane looks at Robert and both men are aware that they will not have an opportunity to explain. In truth, he would just throw the Governor to them but he needs the man's fingerprint ID to enter the helipad area. As expert as they both are in combat they will not defeat twenty-odd of the most dangerous lifers in the UK.

"FUCK," sums up Shane.

Venice underground hideout

"Just about now," says Reuben gleefully, "Leo Verdi and Shane Mills will be in the back of an ambulance on their way to us. Soon I will convince Shane that an alliance between us is the best way forward and I will get Leo to decipher this Yiddish shit that Isaac used to hide all the gold. So after your three-hundred-year campaign to elect a human contender, I will still reap the benefits."

The laughter is genuine. Reuben struggles to control his bladder he laughs so hard. Simeon looks on in disgust, not sure if victory truly belongs to his jailer yet, but more sure than ever that this crazy fuck needs stopping.

"Well, while you're regaling me with your triumph," Simeon replies, "tell me this: what is your plan now? You still need to defeat Asher, Levi and Judd. I must admit you were smart to capture Mills and use him as your tool to defeat the others but still, you must admit, they are in a better situation than you are currently."

"Oh, don't worry, I have a plan for all of them, a plan that is playing out as we speak. You see, they all think they are controlling the superpowers. The one with his Russian boyfriend, Asher, is soon to make an alliance with Judd via the Chinese to trade with them and wipe out the Yanks' wealth. This will weaken them all, they will stretch their economies to the limit. Then once the Jew translates the book I will control the markets and without your interference I will have this entire planet held to financial ransom. You know as well as I do that money is the true power on this earth and this book contains it all.

"Plus I have the church and, thanks to your demise, I also have the crown. Now my beloved Huns rule Europe and most importantly I control over half of the world's wealth." Reuben laughs again. "This game is over! Witness my glorious victory!"

Simeon needs to extract as much information as possible from this madman. He lives in hope that Mills will escape and the more he knows about Reuben's plan the better the chances for the new challenger. He plays to Reuben's ego.

"So, your original idea to create Christianity seems to still be a powerful force. I cannot understand how anyone still believes that crap."

Reuben eyes him lusciously but cannot resist showing him a story he read today.

"This story shows the strength and power the Holy Roman Church still holds over these animals." He pulls out a newspaper and begins to read it aloud to Simeon.

As he listens, Simeon once more doubts the sanity in trying to save these fucking idiots. Reuben reads: *"Two hundred bodies are found in convent grounds".* Reuben scans the rest of the page, reading about how two teenagers who were wandering around the grounds of the derelict building that was once Our Lady of Lourdes convent in County Louth, Ireland, discovered a meshed wooden door lying under the earth. When they fetched a fence post to prise open the door the two teenagers discovered a horrific scene. The door was covering a large ditch that had been dug into the ground. The boys could not make out exactly how many but did recognise that it contained the bones of many young children. The ensuing investigation by An Garda Síochána uncovered seven hundred and ninety-odd skeletons of children, ranging from only a few hours up to four years old. The convent was one of many infamous institutions in the country that unmarried mothers were sent to. The report doesn't explain all the facts, such as that the children died between 1957 and 1963. Some had died soon after birth, some from starvation, others were beaten to death. One was buried alive with the other bodies. His name was Eddy and his mother died at his birth after she went into shock due to a painful cut to her perineum administered by an irate nun who was annoyed at missing Mass waiting for the poor young girl to give birth. As for Eddy, he was a persistent bed wetter and Sister Mary Philomena decided she had had enough of this little bastard.

Of course, this discovery shocked the locals and most of the nation, but the irony of the last line in the article was not lost on either of these Djinn: "Father Padraig Maguire summed up the feelings of all the local community when he said, 'We all need to pray to our Lord Jesus Christ for the Souls of these poor children and the misguided nuns who had been under a lot of pressure causing them to be responsible for such unchristian behaviour.'"

Reuben is in a boastful mood. "This priest said this at a packed congregation at the parish church. Followers of my religion commit mass infanticide and what do these Irish Catholics do? They take their children to church, the very establishment that committed the atrocity, and pray! And you think these fools deserve a champion of their own." Reuben's laughter fills the room once again, a cold deep cackling spewing from his mouth.

Simeon can only shake his head; in a way he knows Reuben is right. Humans are so stupid. They condemn the Nazis and yet follow religions that have been complicit in equally vile atrocities, religions that the Djinn created years ago to control ignorant people, not advanced civilisations. But no matter what evidence there is to the contrary, and with zero evidence to prove any existence of God, they still put blind faith into these pathetic stories. In Simeon's mind Christians are the worst offenders, even compared to other cults like Islam and Hindu. But then Simeon reminds himself of the good and the great humans he has met over the thousands of years he has trekked this world. His influence in their success was apparent but he also was drawn to certain characteristics. His mind drifts back to Voltaire, Susanne Valadon, Byron, and Pascal. He thinks of his personal friends and protégés including Dante, Mozart, Darwin and, of course, dear William. He remembers all of the wonderful women, such as Helen, Elizabeth, the Bronte's, Nell, and Marilyn who were all so

291

beautiful and all of them incredible humans. Simeon is reassured; he is right and Reuben is wrong.

"For all their shortcomings, they have also created greatness that we never reached," he tells Reuben.

"You are so blind when it comes to them. Any advance comes from us; you only have to look at the state of the world. Any place where one of us settled and succeeded has flourished. Only places such as Africa where Daniel messed up, never developed. The same can be said of South America when Naphtali was removed."

"You are a fool if you think these continents have nothing to offer you make the same mistake many western humans do by underestimating these countries they have flourished in their own way". Reuben laughs obviously not convinced but Simeon continues defending mankind.

"What of all the triumphs in spite of our input?" says Simeon. "The art, the poetry, the music? Do you claim these are Djinn influences? Because I do not remember such beauty in our history. Reuben, even you must see they have exceeded us in so many ways. They are not inferiors, they are our brothers and sisters. We all felt as you do when we first set out but things have changed and only you, and perhaps Asher, still regard the humans as animals. For the rest of us the consensus that humans are worthy of ruling themselves has been agreed."

"Simeon, can you not do the maths? Four Djinn are still competing – all of whom do not agree with your 'humans should rule themselves' nonsense. Do I need to say anything more? For every argument you raise in their favour, I can give you one hundred against. Pick a year, pick a day, pick an hour and I will show you an example of mankind's worthlessness. Look here." He snatched the newspaper back. "Yesterday in Africa a group of so-called devout Islamists raped twenty-seven young girls, claiming to be following God's word. They raped these girls because they went to a Christian missionary school. After raping them they removed each girl's clitoris with old scissors claiming their moans revealed that they enjoyed copulation and this was also unacceptable. I would struggle to think up these atrocities

292

myself!" He roars with mirth before proceeding. "Now, you can't blame me for these Muslim loonies. I mean, Benjamin just appeared to Muhammad and told him stories, which, may I add, are nowhere near as credible as the ones I created to start Christianity. I mean, at least I had a real person and faked his death! Benny boy just invades this simpleton's dreams and whoosh, one billion followers, some ready to blow themselves up believing they are forever destined to fuck virgins in heaven."

His laughter becomes hysterical as he struggles to regain his composure.

"I mean, if there was a heaven, do they really think they would be fucking in it? Do they think this God has a few spare bedrooms that they can fornicate in? This world is proof that they are still savages, still the same as the hordes of upright apes that wandered the earth centuries ago. We all know the intellect gene pool has risen because of the Vril we have introduced. I have discovered that this was part of the Arc Hon's plan. We were their puppets. Did you know this Simeon? That our Vril has boosted their evolution? It was a trick played on us by the Arc Hon, when only we, the Djinn, had evolved into the race the Demiurge planned!"

"What do you know of the Demiurge's plan?" scoffs Simeon. "Even the Arc Hon own up to misinterpreting his instructions?"

"Pah! How could humans ever be equal to us? What do they do with this gift we have unintentionally given them? They enslave themselves. You know as well as I do that they are their own worst enemy. Too busy abusing each other to even realise we exist. Slavery, for instance. They think they've risen above it because they had a little civil war in America but in reality there are five times as many slaves today as there were during the peak of the American and European enslavement of the Africans! No one abolished slavery: they just moved it back to Africa, then annexed Bangladesh and South America. Children die in diamond mines and their parents are sent the bill for removing the corpse but so long as the extortion by banks, pharmaceutical companes or clothing shops allows the West to enjoy all the fun of the high street and the kids who are enslaved are across the seas where none of the shoppers can see them, who cares?

"A self-righteous rapper sings about blood diamonds then buys his big ass girlfriend a fucking rock the size of his left bollock! The slaves are now the enslavers. Slaves are the ultimate plan because the aim is always to rule and rule ultimately. Homo sapiens have outgrown their use. 'Gotta make way for the homo superior' to quote the only decent poet of this age. Left to their own devices mankind would be extinct; it is our influence, *our* Vril that has steered them into a path of evolution. But you and those other human lovers complain, 'Reuben's not playing fair. He's hurting the poor little people. Blah, blah blah.' Can't you see that they are the inferior race? Yes, I have experimented a little with them, for their own good I may add, although I may have been a little overenthusiastic on occasion."

Now it was Simeon's turn to laugh. "You think? Do you? We are all guilty of underestimating this race, but you, you went too far. The Jews, the Gypsies, the Muslims! I If they are not of Nordic or Anglo Saxon descent then you treat them as if they are even less than animals. Most humans carry Vril from at least one Jinni and this makes them all our family..."

Reuben reacts with disgust. "They are not *my* family, and in case I misunderstood the game, was it not the purpose to create a clan and set up rule here? The rules no longer apply."

"No, the game began because we were bored and acting like spoiled brats wanting toys. Back then these humans were simple, they were different. Even you must see that. Perhaps the Arc Hon did trick us but humans are now an intelligent species."

A phone rings before Reuben can reply. He picks it up impatiently to find the young boy from the casino is on the other end.

"Plan seems to be working boss, the whole fucking place seems to be going up in smoke. Cumisky and his boys are on site. I am just awaiting confirmation that target one and two are in the truck."

"Trevor, I don't want updates. Just call me when you have confirmation, understand?" The phone goes down and Reuben turns back to Simeon.

"There is one other small matter I need to discuss with you. One unknown quantity in my plans."
Simeon has been waiting for this subject to come up.

"The wanderer," says Reuben.
Simeon smiles and hangs his head. "What can I say, I only know what Raphael told me and probably told you as well."

As agreed, the Arc Hon had investigated the man known as Marco Polo back in the late thirteenth century. Michael suggested that somehow another Djinn had crossed over but this seemed impossible and Solfrid was sure none could without the council's knowledge. Michael then decided he wanted to break protocol and reveal himself to this man to question him. Chamuel, Amitiel and Raphael eventually agreed.

It was not uncommon, especially back then, for the Arc Hon to not meet or see each other for decades, sometimes even as long as a century. The Arc Hon mostly live in human form and although they are advanced beings they rarely use any advanced technology, leaving them bound by the limits of humanity, just like the Djinn, restricted to the current forms of transport and communication. However, the four Arc Hon are linked and they all knew immediately when the consciousness belonging to Michael faded. The remaining three all rushed to what was then a secret base in a church in Constantinople to investigate. They could not detect any sign of Michael nor the man Marco Polo whom they had begun to call the wanderer. It was the first time an Arc Hon had gone missing. Ever. It would be almost impossible to kill Michael as he could possess any human within sight. Yet if he merely captured then the other three would still be able to feel his presence. It was a true mystery.

Over the next couple of hundred years the three Watchers searched high and low for Michael, ignoring their own rules on using advanced technology in the human world. They spanned the earth time and again. Each Arc Hon has at their disposal crafts they call comets. These are anti-matter crafts that can transport matter at super-high speeds. Humans would often mistake them for real comets or meteors but it would be about this time that the many claims of sightings of strange phenomena in the skies began as the Arc Hon became more and more concerned for Michael and less cautious. Still, to this day neither the wanderer nor Michael have been heard of or seen again. The Djinn were also told about this event with the hope they would help with the search. Theories cropped up and soon each of the Djinn claimed to understand what happened. The truth is still not known.

"And you know nothing more," says Reuben suspiciously.

Simeon shakes his head. "It is a true mystery."

Stoke Prison

Richard Yarker leads the gang of high-security prisoners who block Shane and the others' way to the roof. A standoff in the R and A room ensues. The room is a forty metres long with double doors either side. Both groups wait for instruction.

"That's the fucking Governor and some screws! Let's fucking burn the cunts," suggests Jim Brady, a particularly nasty bastard, even for this environment, who had been sent to solitary by Governor Byrne two years earlier and never come out. Now all his praying to Satan has paid off as he faces the prick who put him there.

A chorus of agreed heckles accompany his suggestion and the large group edge slowly forward. Shane notices their hesitation and soon deduces what is holding them back. He is holding a Taser gun as if it is a pistol and hopes with the distance they do not notice.

"So we have a Mexican standoff," Yarker remarks in a terrible Mexican accent. "We need to get past you and, of course, we need the Governor there to aid our escape. You are obviously not here to bring us to safety. So tell me, what is it you want?"

Shane speaks for the group. "We are prisoners too. We need to get to the roof and have no intention of blocking your way. We nicked these uniforms from guards we beat up. Look, have you seen any of us before? Surely you recognise Al Qaeda Bob?"

Two Arab-looking prisoners shoulder their way to the front of the group of inmates, excited to meet the famous Muslim. "As salamu alaykum," the two Muslims greet him.

"For fuck's sake," cries Jim Brady. "Are we going to stand around while these Pakis have a love-in?" He turns to Shane's group. "I don't give a fuck if you're screws or cons, just hand over the Governor and fuck off out of our way."

Shane sees a solution but he needs to convince the tall mountain of a man he knows to be the notorious Richard Yarker to agree to it. He steps forward, his arms held wide to show he is no longer armed. He addresses the group but looks directly at Yarker.

"We need the Governor and actually you don't. It's chaos down there and the gates are open, all you need to do is walk straight out of the front door. But every minute we waste in this standoff is another minute for the backup teams to arrive. So, what do you say? Shall we continue talking or shall we all get our sorry asses out of this shithole?"

Most of the men look to Yarker. He looks thoughtful and is and meets Shane in the middle of the room he nods and is about to answer when someone shouts out, "Fuck you! We will take the Governor and kill you all."

Shane's heart sinks as he recognises this voice: Errol, one of the men he saved Leo from on their first day. The cry is taken up by the second of those men, Garfield Hilton, aka Big Bird, and suddenly a loud angry roar goes up from the inmates and they break into a run at Shane and his group.

Shane quickly instructs Leo to retreat with the Governor at the same time as he swings at Yarker who ducks surprised at how slow the swing was, however the kick too his jaw as his head goes down reveals he has been duped, his jaw splits and his fight is over. Shane falls back, he and Robert brace themselves for the fight of their lives. The next two attackers are unfortunate to lead and are soon dispatched as Shane throws a combination of punches that connect with both men perfectly, sending them into oblivion. Robert decides attack is the best form of defence and charges into the crowd of vicious murderers, aiming directly for Big Bird. He hits the larger man in the midriff, forcing the giant to crash backwards into several others and, like a bowling ball hitting the tenpins, they scatter under the force. The two Muslim men come to Robert's aid as he battles through a swarm of inexperienced kicks and punches. Robert manages to take hold of the unconscious body of a small tattooed skinhead and uses him as a shield and battering ram combined. The three men are fighting back to back for a while until one of goes down and is trampled on as the mob fights to reach Robert. The battle is not well coordinated; sixty per cent of the attack force is focused on Shane who is alone, while the remainder battle Robert and the two Muslims.

Shane is determined not to go down and although massively outnumbered he is still hurling these cons across the room. His strategy is simple: hit, tear, gauge, hit, and bite, gauge, hit. He uses every hard part of his body as he breaks bones with his open hand, his feet, elbows, knees, even his head. Pushing his thumbs in the sockets of one man's eyes he hears the sound of popping followed by screams of pain then a thud as the large, tattooed foe falls wailing to the floor. Still, he cannot possibly defeat all these assailants and eventually a broken chair followed by the boot of Errol leaves Shane on his knees. He fights the urge to curl up into a ball and instead takes out the legs of the nearest assailant using his fallen body as a shield, gaining a few seconds breathing space, before the next attack comes.

Both Shane and Robert are aware that the end is close but both use every ounce of their physical capability to resist the inevitable. Strangely Shane thinks of Amitiel and not Sara as he faces his death. He hears her voice accompanied by the thumping of a dozen angry men pummelling his body. "Hold on, help is coming."

Stoke Prison: civilian staff room: earlier

On the day of the front page news event at Stoke Prison one young man was starting his new job as a trainee. As instructed he reported to the civilian staff manager, George Humphries. George was in charge of the public liaison sector in the prison. These were not prison guards but staff who checked in visitors' bags and such. To be honest George was not pleased that he was given such short notice to induct a new lad today and was even less pleased when he set eyes on his newest member of staff. "Why do we employ such a scruffy-looking kid who has absolutely no interest in what I'm showing him?" thought George to himself, after only half an hour of the induction.

"So, this is the scanner. All bags must go along the conveyor and Diane over there checks the monitor for any suspicious-looking objects."

Diane gives the young recruit a false smile. She is not impressed by the cut of this young man either; even his offer of a boiled sweet does not impress her.

"Right, I will show you to the changing rooms and then you can spend a couple of hours under Diane's watchful eye," says George.

A barely disguised groan can be heard from behind the X-ray machine but just as George enters the changing room he hears the lockdown alarm go off and receives a message in his ear piece. As an efficient team manager he follows protocol and calls out to his civilian team.

"Okay, people, lock down! You know the procedure, treat it like a breach and head to emergency meeting room B." George begins walking out. "Come on, son. Sounds like there is some action going on in the psycho block so lesson's over for now. We have to leave."

George turns, expecting to find the boy following him like a lapdog just as he has done all morning. Instead the young man has gone the other way and entered the main building.

"Fuck's sake!" George cries. "What sort of idiots are we employing nowadays? "YOU! New lad!" He looks to Diane as she gets into her coat, as if asking the new lad's name. Diane just shrugs her shoulders as she picks up her bag. When George next looks the young boy is almost out of sight. George is not comfortable with this type of scenario. His frustration shows as he paces after the new lad, then he suddenly turns on his heel, thumping the wall; procedure is his crutch. "Fuck him!" snaps George, heading for the exit. "The little black bastard can go get himself killed!"

Chamuel hears George's pronouncement as he heads up a long corridor. The commotion caused by Leo abducting Shane means he is not noticed until he is actually standing next to the two guys guarding the area. With no time to waste he pulls out the sub-machine gun from his kitbag and peppers both men, killing one and mortally wounding the other. Chamuel takes the key pass off the dead guard and opens the metal doors.

He is now in the belly of C wing looking up at the two floors that house the prisoners' cells. Guards are busy forcing the inmates into the cells when a sudden explosion rocks the whole building. Chamuel hurries forward, ignoring the screams of several inmates trapped in their cells as a fireball explodes through the first floor. The guards panic, not knowing what has happened. Chamuel makes his way to the link corridor past the recreation area. The heavy steel bars are locked and it seems the key pass does not open these doors. Irritably Chamuel looks around for a guard to help him and he wonders why no one has noticed the young black guy wandering around with a machine gun but concludes they are not really noticing much at all, just freaking out and shouting into their radios as more prisoners go up in flames. Chamuel kicks at the closed door and hopes this is not how it ends, burning to death with a bunch of cons.

The intercom burst into life: "Emergency procedure Red One. Open all doors, open all cells, round up prisoners and lead them to meeting point B2."

The locked door opens automatically and Chamuel smiles, quickly heading away from the panic-stricken chaos and towards the psychiatric ward. He knows it is a good ten-minute walk from here but Amitiel had insisted he go in and help Shane and the others escape. He now regrets the abuse he has given this body over the years and the joint he smoked before starting his new job this morning. When he finally gets to the psyche ward he finds a handful of guards locked in a cell and a groggy Connor on the floor. He puts the gun to Connor's head.

"Shane Mills and the others, where are they?"
Connor points a shaking hand. "They've gone to the roof. They are after the 'copter but they'll never get through D block."

Chamuel drops him and runs off. His chest hurts with the pain that a forty-cigs-a-day habit will give you, let alone the ten joints a day as well. He hears testosterone-fuelled growls in the distance and sees an open door where he discovers a mass brawl going on.

He looks to the side and sees a familiar face. Leo has pulled the Governor into a side room and they are hiding behind a desk. Chamuel taps the window merrily and laughs at the look on Leo's face, then he makes his way to the brawl.

He has no feelings either way about killing these cons but he doesn't want to hit Mills or Price so instead of scattering bodies he fires a volley above their heads. Everyone stops. Shane is not sure if the sight of some little black guy with a sub-machine gun is good or bad. Robert immediately recognises the Arc Hon. Both men struggle to their feet. Six smashed knuckles, four cracked ribs, a broken finger and two missing teeth between them is not too bad a result considering. Leo comes out of the room with the Governor in tow. The

303

remaining cons look at each other and then at Chamuel, confused by who he is and which side he is on.

"Listen you smelly motherfucking-never-supposed-to-be-released bunch of cunts. There is a wide open door here and freedom ten minutes down that corridor." Chamuel puffs. "If you're fit that is; probably more like twenty minutes if not. So what the fuck are you waiting for? Do I need to spell it out? This is a prison break!"

Chamuel fires another volley of shots into the ceiling and the mob jump to it, running out the door. Shane, Robert, Leo and the Governor slowly stand and stare. Leo walks over to Chamuel. "Good to see you again, young man." Robert joins him and takes Chamuel's hand.

"As Salamu alaykum." He greets Chamuel who shakes his head, raises his eyebrows, and turns to Shane.

"I heard something about a helicopter, so shall we go?"

The Jew, the Muslim, the prison governor, an Arc Hon and Shane Mills all head to the roof. Once they get there the Governor plays his role and gets them through the locked doors revealing the helicopter.

At the exact same time that the escaping group reach the roof, Reuben's young associate, Rupert, is entering C wing with six of Kieran Cumisky's thugs. He realises that the plan has not quite come to fruition as he passes the first four cells and can smell the charred flesh inside; these poor souls were caught in the initial blast before the Governor issued the code red to evacuate. Fortunately the body of Phil Cumisky is so badly burned-up that his men do not recognise him. Rupert is not concerned about Cumisky, he takes his orders from Reuben and is only there to extract Mills and Verdi.

Little does he know that right at this very moment the two men are boarding a helicopter on the roof of the prison. Rupert orders the riot police impersonators to search all the cells for Mills. Ray Dowd, a henchman for the Cumisky's, questions the order and explains that his priority is to find Phil Cumisky. Rupert is weary of this group of pricks. Reuben had told him they were only there as a smokescreen to confuse the authorities. He knows Reuben likes to create several scenarios when he orchestrates a plan, leading to unanswered questions and triggering mass conspiracy theories that lead down several blind alleys. Rupert feels secure working for someone who dots all the "i"s and crosses all the "t"s. As such he is now prepared to initiate plan B and the thugs are surplus to requirements.

"You are right," he tells Cumisky's men. "Go find your man."

He must follow Reuben's instructions. If they do not find Mills or Verdi in the first twenty minutes of the search then measures are to be taken to ensure that no one leaves the building alive. He'll make sure no more get out now and any prisoners already outside will be conveniently gathered together in the recreation area.

Rupert says into his radio, "target not found. Commence phase two."

Out in the recreation area three men in fake uniforms stand guard as the prisoners mill around in mild panic and disbelief as their prison turns into an inferno right before their very eyes. Johnny-No-Legs is already suspicious of the men; they aren't acting like normal police. They watch the men with cold detachment as if waiting for something. Of course, they aren't really policemen at all but rather highly paid mercenaries directly employed by Reuben.

One of these men picks up a message on his walkie-talkie and gives a sign to the others situated at the three corners of the prison yard, leaving the corner with the entrance back into the main prison free. As Johnny-No-Legs watches, the men pull out AK47s. At first he thinks he is mistaken but on a second look is convinced that the guards are loading the light machine guns. No-Legs looks confused but does not expect what happens next.

The three men point the guns at the gathered prisoners and indiscriminately open fire. Shocked, No-Legs stands frozen as bodies wriggle and dance, blood gushing from wounds, before dropping to the ground. The sound of alarm and pain rings out as bones and flesh are penetrated by volumes of ammunition. No-Legs feels his side collapse and is careering across the yard, forced by the shoulder of his best friend, Big Pete, who directs them both behind a group of bins.

"They're gonna fucking kill us all!" shouts Big Pete to his shocked friend.

Both men somehow shuffle under the bins and watch on as the imposters slaughter the inmates. A fat guy he recognises as Mad Steve is running right towards the shooters, screaming madly. Each bullet that hits him seems only to spur him on until one enters his eye socket and, like a bull elephant, he is finally floored. No-Legs watches in horror as some inmates freeze in shock, waiting for the inevitable, others use fallen bodies as shields in a desperate attempt to survive and many have tried to rush back into the smoke-filled building but are barred by the rising heat and smoke. With nowhere else to go they are picked off like fish in a barrel.

From their makeshift hideout No-Legs and Big Pete stare in pure terror as the bastard shooters actually herd the men back into the burning prison, no longer shooting at them but more around them. Confusion reigns as the prison guards who are using firefighting equipment inside and attempting to back away from the flames meet the oncoming prisoners trying to escape the gunfire.

Sirens can be heard in the distance. No-Legs can tell from the urgency in the assassins' final moves that they wish to complete their task before the real police arrive. He also notices that the inmates and guards have barricaded themselves inside the burning building, firefighting as they do so, in a mad attempt to survive. Big Pete taps No-Legs on the shoulder and points to the feet of an assassin who seems to be coming their way. The feet stop less than ten feet from the two men. He pulls out a radio and they overhear his message.

"All clear out here. All survivors are in the building. No sign of Mills or Verdi."

Inside Rupert receives the message and presses the detonator.

Outside the shooter makes a hand signal to the other men and they quickly disappear. No-Legs releases the breath he didn't realise he was holding just before the building goes up. The blast explodes out into the yard, debris and dust easily blow away the bins that were their only protection. Coughing and burned, Johnny can no longer see or hear Big Pete. He lies face down, praying the slaughter is over and the slayers have gone. Seconds pass and Johnny looks to his left to witness Big Pete's half decapitated head hanging from his shoulders. He looks up and as the dust settles his heart sinks. An AK47 is pointed right at him, its master smiling like a drunk who just found a fiver.

The only survivors from the entire prison are in the small helicopter that took off two minutes earlier. The Governor watches out of the window in horrified disbelief. "What have you done?" Shane would plead his innocence but he knows there is no point. He debates whether to throw Byrne out of the craft, knowing that if released his version of the story will not reflect well on the three fugitives. Then he remembers that he is likely to be public enemy number one soon no matter what he does, so why bother? Anyway, there has been enough killing.

TV STATION REPORT: ONE HOUR LATER

"Today here in Stoke at one of the UK's largest prisons an unprecedented catastrophe has happened. Reports are unconfirmed as to what has caused the explosion but the emergency services have been attempting to rescue any survivors for over an hour. Early reports suggest that over one hundred prisoners are dead and perhaps as many as five hundred missing. In addition, there are nearly forty prison guards unaccounted for and many emergency staff who arrived just as a second explosion detonated. The police will not let anyone beyond the road you can see here which is approximately two miles from the prison gates. As you can see, behind me convoys of emergency vehicles are coming and going with alarming regularity."

The picture on the TV switches from the anchor to the newsroom studio.

"Can you tell us, Jeremy, what time do we believe the explosion happened?"

"Well, initial reports tell us that the local police station was alerted at 15:15 to an incident, possibly an explosion, in the kitchen area. They then contacted all the emergency services and as a precaution the mobile riot squad was also called. It seems that the first ambulances and fire brigade accompanied by a couple of police cars arrived within twenty minutes. Here the story becomes a bit a little uncertain as the commander of the riot squad has stated his vans were half an hour away at this point. Yet witnesses from the locality have claimed that there was at least one riot van on site before the emergency services got here. Also, reports are coming in that gunfire was heard just before the second, much larger, explosion..."

"Sorry to interrupt, Jeremy, but we have some breaking news. Governor Byrne, who was among the missing, has just been found safe and sound over thirty miles from the prison itself. It seems Governor Byrne walked into Burton town police station, explaining that he had been taken hostage during what he claims was a prison break for three prisoners: Shane Mills, Robert Price and Leo Verdi. We will get more on that report as soon as it's confirmed."

Venice – Present day

Reuben has been watching quite contently up until he hears that last statement. He looks at Simeon, confused and angry, but the smile on Simeon's face cuts him dead. So many thoughts are running through Simeon's mind but mainly he is relieved that the human champion managed to escape. He wonders how this has happened, though, as they obviously did not follow the plan. If they had, no one would have suspected that Shane had survived the explosion, never mind hold him and Robert responsible for it, making them the most famous people in Britain right now. Then how did he allow the prison Governor to slip through his hands? Human kindness? Simeon ponders that the change of plan was probably a result of Shane's reluctance to kill Leo. Amitiel had expressed her concern in this matter. Good old Leo. Simeon has mixed feelings about the survival of his friend, happy he may still be alive but also concerned. Simeon does not know if these issues are signs of weakness on Shane's behalf or perhaps signs of strength. Either way, he cannot help him now. His beautiful plan to give them new IDs and have both of them transported to a safe place is in tatters. Still, at least they got out. He looks at Reuben who is still struggling to work out how his perfect plan went so wrong and now Simeon is the one who laughs uncontrollably.

𒐊 ☐🜍 ☐𒐊

Shane fairly competently navigates the helicopter through the English countryside; the army was a good source of a true variety of skills. They have a hair-raising five minutes while Shane hovers only ten feet off the ground and tells Robert to throw the Governor out into the field.

"Are you fucked-up or somink?" the small black guy shouts at him, still brandishing his sub-machine gun.

"What do you want me to do? Kill the guy for no reason?" replies Shane.

"No, I want you to kill him for a very good reason: he's the only guy who can tell the world that you are out and on the run!"

"Well, I won't kill him," frowns Shane. "I am not going to start killing innocent people, not for you or Leo or this Simeon dude I've never met. I don't kill people just for the sake of it or to protect my own hide, okay?"

Chamuel looks at Leo then Robert. "So, this is the great white hope? Man we is all fucked!" Chamuel is still sulking as Shane contemplates their next move.

"We best land soon," shouts Robert over the din. "We don't want air traffic to trace us once Byrne spills the beans." Shane nods in agreement and sets the craft down with a jolt in a field full of cows. Chamuel wrinkles his nose. "If I get cow shit on these trainers there is going to be trouble, yo hear me?" Shane looks at Leo and Robert. "Does he ever shut up?" The two men respond together. "No."

The Pitts 2146

For two hours Chamuel has been using his large repertoire of late-twentieth-century popular culture to entertain his fellow travelling companion. His main objective is to get her mind off the unfortunate loss of Adam. So far, he thinks it is going rather well.

Ember has no idea what the man she is travelling with is going on about but from his heavy laughter at the end of each anecdote she assumes he is trying to be funny. She has never heard of Mr Bean or Samuel L. Jackson and what he is doing puffing out his cheeks and saying some crap about the Godfather heaven knows. Not that she is even listening. All she can think about is Adam.

"Look, where are we going?" asks Ember when Chamuel pauses in between impressions.

"Patience, you must have my young Padawan," says Chamuel in his best Yoda impression.

Ember stops.

Noticing her clenched fists, Chamuel stops too. "I am sorry, truly I am. Everything that has happened to you lately must seem totally bizarre and pretty damn scary to boot, but I promise you it will all become clear soon. It will still be scary but at least you will know why. For now I can explain the first part of the mission if you think it would help?"

Ember bristles at the word "mission". Surely one had to accept a mission before being expected to complete it. She shakes her head in disbelief. "Just tell me where we're going."

"We have to get to the Hispanic part of the city. Fortunately these sewers service the whole of the Megatropolis above and there is a gateway ahead that I am hoping the authorities will not be monitoring."

"What is in the Hispanic sector? Is there a safe house there or something?"

"There is no safe place for you now," Chamuel says apologetically. "If the Host is aware of who you are then he will willingly tear his own beloved city to shreds to find you. Believe me, he has a track record in such things. We can only hope to stay one step ahead of him. To do that we need to see what is on this disc and to do that we need to find someone with an old-fashioned DVD player. I know a guy who knows a guy…"

"Don't we need vaccinations to enter that area? We are taught that there are rampant issues with disease in this sector. Plus our chips won't work…" Ember looks down at her redundant device. "Oh yeah."

Chamuel laughs. "Okay, we have a long journey ahead of us, so why don't we conduct a small investigation into what utter fucking rubbish you were taught in school."

Ember feels pleased for the first time in hours. Always keen to impress people with her knowledge, Ember decides she will join in this conversation. *"Finally, a chance to prove my worth,"* she thinks; no longer will she be seen as the foolish spoiled brat. She knows this stuff, and she knows what *actually* happened, rather than some of the crap that other kids were taught. She silently thanks her father for taking the time to educate her properly.

"Well, to be honest I learned more out of school than in," she tells Chamuel.

"That's good and what is your chosen specialist subject?"

"Er, history is my favourite subject, well… I suppose specialising in pre-rapture."

"Okay, you have the next ten minutes to answer questions on events prior to the rapture. I will give you a starter for ten. Who was the leader of the Diabolicals?"

"Ffft, that's a bit easy. Shane Mills."

"When was the first mention of the Diabolicals in the media?"

"Mmm, that would be around two or three years after the prison break. They led an Islamic terrorist group into Cyprus, capturing British army bases. The news reporters there nicknamed them the Diabolicals because of the slaughter and carnage they caused to the beautiful island and its people."

"Okay. When did the Host first appear to the world and in what form?"

"Easy peasy. The miracle of Juarez was the first report of the Messiah's return."

"Go on."

"An American news reporter witnessed the miracle during a visit to Mexico. He saw a holy man preaching peace on the border town of Ciudad Juarez. The local drug cartel had taken objection to his preaching and the large following he had. The reporter claimed that he saw the man being dragged off the steps of the church and taken to a square where he was to be publicly executed in front of his followers. The leader of the bandits pointed his gun into the Host's face and pulled the trigger but nothing happened. He then took a second gun from one of his men and checked it was working before pointing it at the Host and pulling the trigger. Once more, nothing happened. The Host was said to be praying for the man's forgiveness while this all went on. He smiled each time the guns failed to fire and blessed them. After five or six attempts some of the bandits began to kneel and pray. Eventually the leader also kneeled and prayed, crying while he did. The Host wiped away his tears and told him, 'From today you will be my envoy for peace. Go to your people and tell them this war is over. They must be ready to fight in another and this time, they will fight for God.'"

"Wrong."

"Excuse me! That is exactly what happened." Ember stares at Chamuel, determined to prove she is right. "Trust me, I have read everything there is to read about the coming of the Host and how he saved the world from destruction."

"Wrong."

If he is trying to antagonise her, it is certainly working. Ember squeezes her hands into fists. "Oh, this is stupid. Are you just going you say 'wrong' to every answer I give? And, I am sorry, but what would you know? I mean you're not much older than me and you're black... by which I mean you don't get the right education because you're not Aryan... Oh, you know what I mean."

"You think because I am black and I didn't have access to all them fancy books that I don't know anything?"

"Well no, but you don't know everything..."

"Wrong."

"Whatever." Ember can feel her rebellious inner teenager rising to the surface and is on the verge of letting it loose on this idiot. Her education is the one tool she has and now this guy is saying everything she knows is wrong? Feelings of anger and fear of the unknown bubble in her tummy. "There you go again, you just keep saying wrong without saying why."

"The books are wrong," shrugs Chamuel. "Yes, there was a miracle at Juarez but Reuben Lupas, the pretend Host, was nowhere near there when it did happen. The whole thing is a twist on the truth and you need to swot up on the truth real quick. I see I will have to educate you. Anyway we are here."

"Where? I can't see anything?"

Chamuel takes a small cube from his jacket and it independently rises from his hand. A beam of light emanates from it and soon Ember can see what looks like a huge steel door at least ten metres high with a mass of bars and locks criss-crossing its dimensions.

"What is that?"

"That is the only exit out of the Pitts that the Mackies won't expect us to leave by."

Ember can see why they wouldn't be expected to leave this way. Several gun drones sit on top of the gate, all prepped to fire. In a fit of sass she points to them, waiting for Chamuel's response.

"Well sure, it looks like we are not supposed to go this way. You would have thought that there would have been a sign," he says jokingly, much to Ember's annoyance. She decides Chamuel is the fool and it's him who needs educating, not her.

"Those things are gun drones," she says sagely. "They activate by sensor. There must be an e-line or something that sets them off if passed. We have got to go back, and carefully."

"You're not wrong," says Chamuel. "Well not about the e-line, anyway. Only problem is we already passed it, back there when you was busy with the made-up history."

"What!?" Ember looks up to see the six drones rumble out of their holsters and take off towards them. She hears a volley of shots and instinctively ducks, covering her head. The shots continue as she huddles, sure of a quick, messy death. But she doesn't die. Instead she can see that the cube floats between them and the drones, the light coming from it cascading down around them. The bullets stop dead on hitting the light and seem to be suspended in mid-air.

"The miracle of Subterrainia! Where's a reporter when you need one?"

This time his joking doesn't annoy her as she stands up amazed and in awe. Exhausted of ammunition the guns have stopped. The small cube averts its attention to the large metal gateway. The cube moves around the service of the door emitting digital clicks. Ember watches in fascination as the large bolts and locks slide and turn one after each other until the door stands unlocked.

"Are you ready, Ember Jones, to *Live' la Vida Loca*?" Chamuel attempts a few steps of flamenco then with a grand gesture, motions for her to step through.

The lake at the end of the east pipe

Adam feels his lungs are about to burst. He is powerless to resist the strong arm that holds him as he is dragged further and further into the dark depths, which he now accepts will be his grave. Too traumatised to even be scared he simply submits to his fate, allowing the darkness in as he feels life ebb away. Not the most unpleasant feeling he has ever experienced, he has to admit, as the veil of death seems to bring with it a feeling of peace and tranquillity.

"WAKE UP MAN! For fuck's sake! Lisalotte, I think you killed him!"

"Excuse me? I saved his life! Those stupid monkeys are starving. He would have been ripped to shreds and chewed like a piece of bark!"

Adam can hear voices. He feels as if someone is standing on his chest and he dare not open his eyes. Then a hard push on his solar plexus forces him to jump up as he heaves and evacuates what seems like a gallon of soiled water.

"See. He's fine."

Adam sits up. He looks around and makes out a heavy-set man with an unkempt beard sitting next to a small but shapely female with long dark hair and not many clothes on.

"Who are you? Where am I?"

"You're okay, you're safe. Well, you are for now. I am Nelson and this is Lisalotte. She was the one who pulled you under to save you from the Humanzees."

Adam looks at the tiny slip of a girl and considers contradicting that this girl was the creature that overpowered him so easily and pulled him down through the lake, but then a glance at her back reveals what he can only describe as a shallow shark-like fin.

She gives him a stern look before addressing him.

"The words you're looking for are 'thank you'."

He colours, embarrassed. "Thank you." He then looks at the man. "Did you say Nelson? You don't mean Alex Nelson?"

Adam doesn't need an answer as he notices the rota blade attached to the man's arm that replaces his severed hand. Even under all the hair he recognises the face of one of the most wanted criminals in Jinn City; a man accused of murder, theft and high treason and the leader of a band of terrorists known as the Sons of Abraham.

Not many know the truth. Nelson was actually born and bred in the Caucasian section of the city. He grew up just on the wrong side of Utopia Gardens and his father was a respected clerk who worked in the Temple as a quantity surveyor. On Nelson's twelfth birthday he waited for his father to come home to see what present he was getting but by nightfall he still hadn't come and when he heard his mother's tears, Nelson realised something was wrong.

He never saw his father again and the family received no explanation for his disappearance. Nelson soon learned that this was the norm and questions should not be asked. He watched as his mother grew sicker and sicker, suffering from a broken heart and the frustration of never knowing what had happened to the man she loved. It took her four years to wilt from a strong beautiful woman to a frail shell of herself. Only on her deathbed did she dare utter defiance against the establishment that had taken her love away and had not even seen fit to mention why.

"Why? Why did they take him? Where is my love?" she cried as she lay dying in the small living room of the apartment. She had tried to stay strong for her son but the pain was too much and to be held in such low regard as not to even deserve an explanation of what had happened was the worst pain of all. She actually envied the wives whose husbands were publicly executed for poor performance or attitudes. At least they had anger and sorrow. At least they had the truth and not false hope. Mrs Nelson died a painful death. Not physically painful but mentally unbearable.

Nelson hated the regime for what they had done to him and his parents and how insignificant he was to them. He made up his mind that one day they would regret their actions and more, their inactions. Nelson managed to hide his hate and, while posing as a loyal citizen, joined the external guard, or J soldiers as they were better known. These were the brutal troops that patrolled the city to round up and kill any non-chipped renegades and even the odd Humanzee or other mutation who dared to leave the Pitts.

It took four years of watching and partaking in the murder of thousands of innocents before Nelson got his chance to escape and form the Sons of Abraham. It was during an operation into the Oriental District that his sixty-strong company of J soldiers were ambushed by a large group of raiders who had been forced up from the Pitts by hunger. The attacking group outnumbered the J soldiers six to one but they were only armed with stones and makeshift bows and spears against some of the best weapons technology had created. In less than an hour ninety per cent of the raiders were captured. The J soldiers did not actually take prisoners and Captain Andrew Page was no exception. He lined them all up and instructed his most accomplished machine gunner to first take their knees out, let them bleed for a while, and then kill them. Nelson had looked down the sights of the XXX53 as the two hundred-plus survivors lined up, mostly disfigured, all wretched and often mutated. He felt total empathy with their plight and had waited a long time for this opportunity. He noticed that between him and them was the remaining external guard, including his captain. They were all looking forward, expectant of the imminent entertainment, with their backs to Nelson's gun. A slight twinge of guilt at shooting his comrades in the back was soon overridden as his mother's dying words sounded through his head.

Nelson cut through the fifty-six men like a knife through butter. They all fell to the floor, bodies in pieces with no time to ask why, just time to die. Now he had to worry about the men and women who he had five minutes earlier been battling. They looked at the bodies in amazement, grateful but confused. Nelson walked away from the XXX53 and addressed the ragtag group.

"I am Alex Nelson. I am an enemy of the state and I wish to join your militia."

The men and women did not even know they were militia. They thought they were just hungry people tired of dying a slow death. Now they were alive and, thanks to this Alex Nelson, they were armed and dangerous. But that didn't mean they trusted him. His next act, however, confirmed his commitment as he took the machete he had sharpened every day from his belt and, kneeling down, placed his left hand on a tree stump. The confused men and woman watched in strange fascination as with one swoop he lopped off his own left hand. He had fallen then, the pain and shock pulsing through his body, but he pulled out a bottle of white spirit and poured it over the stump, confirming this was a planned act. Not only did this extraordinary act ally him to this mutilated band of brothers but it also set him free from the hated regime by removing his chip. Alex bonded the group of misfits together and was soon accepted as their leader. Survival and the odd triumph had given them hope. Under Nelson's guidance they became a hardy group and a force to be reckoned with. High-profile robberies and kidnappings had secured them plenty of food. They grew their arsenal of weapons with every raid and although many lives were lost, a steady line of inhabitants from the Pitts tried to join the SOA.

Nelson, a shrewd operator, also knew that picking the right personnel was the key to survival and that treachery would be their downfall. He hand-picked every member of his band of thieves and made sure they were not only loyal but beholden to him. Lisalotte was his prized recruit. He had rescued her from years of pain and misery when he raided the "Laboratories for Human Advancement" in Old Town. Nelson was aware from his days with the J soldiers that these were gruesome places where experiments were conducted to create human/animal hybrids. She was the most unique and successful specimen to date of an Aquasapian. He would smile to think how cross they were to lose her.

Also amongst his men was Tiberius, who had been treated with a combination of myostatin gene manipulation embryotic and stem cell treatment, as well as been dosed with human growth hormone and steroids from the age of three, resulting in an eight-foot powerhouse who was also, unfortunately, in constant agonising pain. Only Nelson could actually go near him. Then there were the others like Randolph, a more human Humanzee, two less successful Aquasapians, a bunch of radiation victims and many more victims of experimentation or just cruel mutilation. All had suffered at the hands of this elitist regime and none were loyal to the so-called Messiah. All would die for Nelson. Unbeknown to them, they would soon become the pivotal part of a real revolution.

Ember and Chamuel at the entrance of the Hispanic sector

Chamuel and Ember emerge from the tunnel exit and into the Hispanic sector via a service area for an underground train station. They follow the light and find it opens out into the densely populated and colourful Nuevo Favelas. As far as Ember can see there is a maze of multi-coloured shacks stacked upon each other, stretching high up a steep hillside. Tiny dirt-track streets zigzag through the wooden and breeze-block houses, connecting the population to bars, bakeries and street grocers. Ember is once again reminded of the divide in society as she witnesses the poverty-stricken children playing barefoot as their parent's mill around, keeping a watchful eye. Child abduction is the most prevalent crime in this area. Chamuel takes her arm and guides her to a small hut that houses the local tram station. Ember eyes the vertical track of the tram with awe. It travels straight up the hillside, stopping at several plateaus before ending up at the Plaza de Michel that overlooks the whole district. As they rise Chamuel is aware that they have said very little to each other since exiting the Pitts.

"So, what do you think of Reuben's great design?"

Ember doesn't respond. She is not sure what she thinks. She has no doubt that this place reeks of deprivation and poverty but is also amazed at the vibrant and colourful atmosphere radiating throughout.

To fill the silence Chamuel decides to act as a tour guide. "Of course, the name favela has become a name for all the non-white areas but this is what the original slums looked like back in late-twentieth-century Brazil. It is typical of Reuben's sick sense of humour that he had the Hispanic urbanisation built this way for the Latino people. You didn't get a chance to see much of the Oriental District but that too is designed to remind the people where they come from and where they belong. Reuben is nothing if not a traditionalist. He planned long and hard to have everything reflect the era before the war for the underprivileged. That's why there is a void in technology on these streets compared to what you are used to. He was clever enough though to make sure they had just enough not to want to lose it and end up down the Pitts. He learned the hard way that those who have nothing to lose can be the most dangerous enemy."

Although Ember thinks of herself as a free-thinking and liberal Aryan, she is not comfortable with direct attacks on the Host. Still, she is beginning to wonder and must admit to herself that her empathy towards the non-Aryans in the city is growing stronger the more she witnesses their lives. She desperately wants to discuss these changing feelings with someone and her heart sinks as she thinks of the two people who she could have shared them with: both lost to her. She likes this crazy Chamuel but he has not won her confidence yet. Still, he is making an effort, so maybe she should take advantage.

"If the Host is as bad as you say," she says, "why did he save all these people? Why not just allow them to die in the rapture and be done with them? Surely he would prefer an Aryan-only world?"

"Good question, and one you will soon know the answer to."

"Oh my God! Will you ever actually answer a question?"
Chamuel looks a little shocked. "Oh, okay, well I can give an answer but it's not a simple one-answer question."

"It'll be one more than you normally give."

"Now you're starting to sound like your mother and before you ask, yes, I did know your mother. But in answer to your first question, Reuben believes he has won a game. A game that was played over thousands of years, a game for dominance. His reason for keeping all the non-Aryans, and the Aryans for that matter, is simply because who would he dominate over if they were all dead?"

"And that's the reason?"

"No, but it's one of them. The other is one you need to learn yourself and once you see this," Chamuel taps his breast pocket where he'd placed the disc, "you will have some idea why."

Ember sighs. "Can you at least tell me where we are going?"

"We are getting off at the next stop, actually. You are going to meet one of the most amazing women ever born: smart, beautiful and quite deadly. Donegal Gillespie."

"Strange name."

"Well, around these ways it is. Her father was of Irish descent, her mother Italian, so she was either going to end up as a nun or a gangster. Fortunately she opted for the latter."

The Sky Dome, Jinn City, 2146

The Sky Dome hovers two thousand metres above the centre of Jinn City. It contains the central hub for the security forces and from it almost three thousand video cameras from around the city are monitored as they scan the streets below. It's also the base for eight thousand gun drones and houses six Aircopter gunships that regularly patrol the streets. The Dome has only one controller who has total command over its utilities and uses them to keep the people of Jinn in line, and Solfrid very much enjoys her position of power.

The most powerful woman on Earth has many titles in the New World Order: High Priestess, the First Minister of the Council, Commander in Chief of all military forces but the one she cherishes the most is Prime Enforcer and Protector of God's Law.

After the failings of Procurator Conrad and the brutally inept Mackies to capture Raphael's two accomplices, and Freya's incompetence during the original operation, Solfrid has decided to take matters into her own hands. She tells Reuben of her plan to draw the youths out from hiding and then she summons Procurator Conrad to her office in the Dome.

Conrad expects the worst and prepares himself to do whatever he needs to do to save the most precious person in his life. He is accompanied on his trip to the Dome by Freya Mortensson and two of her guards, sparking a worrying suspicion that he may now be viewed as more of an enemy of the state than an upstanding official. Things can change quickly in the hierarchy of Jinn City and Conrad has seen many others disappear overnight after losing favour with the Host. He is also aware that neither Freya nor Solfrid are likely to support him if he has lost the trust of Reuben.

As soon as he arrives at the entrance to the Sky Dome he is rushed up to the office, which sits right at the top. As he enters the room he can see hundreds of screens all scanning the city, focusing on any possible exits out of the Pitts. Seated at the large cube-shaped glass desk are the two Mackie brothers. Standing behind it with her back to them is the distinctive figure of Solfrid. She is looking out to the city below through one of the large glass windows that make up the four walls of the room. Even with the severity of his situation Conrad feels the awe of the vista from here.

"So," says Solfrid. "You all failed to find her and rumour has it she has now left the Pitts."

The two Mackies look at one another and mumble something, Conrad looks at them inquisitively.

"That's not possible," Colin Mackie says. "The girl could not have left the Pitts, not without one of our spies hearing of it and surely one of your drones would have seen her? I mean, I assume they are all working, right?" Colin is nudged by his brother to shut up.

Solfrid waves them away and turns her attention to Conrad and her voice softens.

"We need to bring her home, Conrad." She sounds so sincere that Conrad allows himself to accept her concern as genuine, but only for a moment.

"She is my little girl," he says quietly. "No one wants her home more than me."

Freya expresses her disagreement by expelling a loud grunting noise. "You have had your chance, Procurator, and I must say I question your loyalties in this matter. How did a young girl who has never left the confines of upper Djinn escape a whole legion of police and your own security force? Hmm? Someone must have helped her." Freya's look leaves Conrad in no doubt who she is blaming for this knowledge.

Solfrid turns and walks back to her desk. "You may all go, except Conrad. Wait for me in the debriefing room and I will join you soon."

"But I thought we..." begins Freya.

"To the debriefing room, please."

Conrad recognises that "please" as the most loaded and deadly in Jinn City. Fortunately for her, so does Freya.

"Yes, Your Worship." As soon as she leaves Solfrid indicates for Conrad to sit.

"It is a bad situation, Conrad. Freya is not the only one who expresses concern about your loyalty."

"What of you, Solfrid? Do you question my loyalty?"

"No. I know how loyal you are. My only worry is *who* you are loyal to."

There is a minute's silence as Solfrid looks out to the city, her back to Conrad. A small gun drone appears in what Conrad assumes is an attempt at intimidation.

"You love your daughter dearly. I understand that. I'm sure you often think of the day she was born, the day your beloved wife gave birth to her."

Suddenly Conrad felt nervous, and for good reason. He had never told anyone of Ember's true origins; after all, there had never been any reason for anyone to suspect anything. But for the first time since this crazy situation started he realises that her origins and the events may be linked. He also guesses that Solfrid must have made the same connection, but how? She couldn't possibly know the truth, could she?

"So," she smiles. "Tell me all about the day she was born." Solfrid adopts a more sinister demeanour as she sits on the edge of the cube desk and looks hard into his eyes, her own like the diamonds.

Conrad is aware of her ability to get into his mind. SHE KNOWS. She will know if and when he is deceiving her. SHE KNOWS. He feels torn, can't think straight. He needs to act fast. SHE KNOWS. Why is he here, discussing an innocent beautiful girl, whose life he has cherished since he first set eyes on her? SHE KNOWS. He dare not lie to Solfrid, she will know and may then guess the truth. SHE KNOWS. They both know he will never put his Ember in harm's way.

As he looks into the eyes of the High Priestess he feels as if he is falling under a spell. She is one of the divine who came to save us all. She is the Protector of God's law, sent by the divine creator himself to prepare the Aryans for their ascension on the coming of the Nibiru.

He realises he really has no choice left if he wishes to tell her nothing. Although he had been expecting it, he now knows he will definitely die today. The plan will most likely include severe torture. Perhaps his slow death will be made public so as to entice Ember out. No matter, he will not betray her, not ever. Once he makes this commitment he feels calmer. Solfrid leans closer as if attempting to pierce Conrad's mind, the narrowing of her eyes indicating that she recognises the planned disobedience so he must act quickly. He must act now!

With a sudden explosion of speed he leaps from his seat and grabs the gun drone. Conrad is very familiar with these and knows this model well. He quickly switches the controls to manual and directs it towards the large eastern window. Solfrid suspects he is trying to assassinate her and dives for cover behind the cube-shaped desk, pulling out her dart gun in one fluid move. She readies to neutralise Conrad but the rapid gunfire persuades her to keep her head down. Conrad is not interested in killing Solfrid, however; that won't save Ember. Instead he keeps firing at the window until the safety glass finally shatters and he can see the clear sky outside. There is a rush of cold air that gives him the impetuous to fulfil his plan. He runs at the opening.

Solfrid realises his true intentions and rushes to fire the dart, hitting him right between the shoulders and paralysing him within seconds. Conrad feels distraught as his legs suddenly stop obeying him. Helpless, he topples but the opening is still coming nearer as his inertia carries him the last couple of feet. He seems to totter at the edge for a split second with the whole city laid out below him. And then he is falling, just out of reach of Solfrid's desperate grasp. The sensation of the fall is dulled by the immobiliser but inside he is smiling as he sees Solfrid's contorted face.

It is such a long way down from here. Unable to flap his arms or even close his eyes he just tumbles and spins. His whole life doesn't flash before him, just the most significant day of it; the one that changed his life forever.

♪♪♪

It was seventeen years ago, late on a Monday night. His wife, Katrina, began screaming from the kitchen and he'd jumped sleepily from bed and ran into the room to find her huddled on the floor, crying, clasping her blood-soaked nightdress. He knew what had happened and the devastating effect it would have on them both. They had tried for years and finally she was pregnant; to lose the child now was more than they could cope with.

Dave Hughes, the family doctor and a close friend, lived next door. He attended the house and assured Katrina that, although it was a traumatic experience, physically she was fine. He suggested she rest and then register the loss in the morning. The next day the distraught couple headed for the office of birth and deaths. Conrad did not feel able to drive so he and Katrina bravely boarded the loop. His poor wife was only just functioning. Her mind was broken, his heart shattered, her hopes crushed. Thankfully she had fully expelled the miscarriage but for no reason she could think of, except that she couldn't just flush it away, she had placed the tiny foetus in a sealed bag and put it in the garage freezer. The thought of leaving it there consumed her with sadness.

As the train carriage had pulled away they noticed a young girl sitting opposite them, crying uncontrollably while holding a large bottle of clear liquid. Although caught up in her own grief Katrina approached the girl and asked if there was any way they could help. Conrad remembers his thoughts on how compassionate his wife was;

331

her own heartache not stopping her from trying to comfort this child. The girl was barely fourteen and was pregnant and the father of the baby was the master of the house she worked in. She was a Caucasian girl living and working in an Aryan household. She didn't exactly protest his advances but how was she expected to keep her job and her home if she had refused him?

After she discovered that she was carrying his baby she went to him but he went crazy. He threw her out, promising to kill her, the child and her family if she told anyone it was his. She was not capable of raising a child, even if by some miracle she survived until the birth. Who could she turn to? How could she go back to her family like this? How would she survive with no credits? And the unspoken horror was, what if the baby looked Aryan? She'd be stoned for sure. She was so desperate she had stolen a bottle of gin and was hoping to get rid of the baby herself.

"I think we must have met by fate," Katrina had said to the girl. "Just this day I have lost my very much wanted baby and you have one you cannot care for. Surely the solution to both our problems is clear?" She had looked at the girl and then at Conrad who appeared clueless. "God has brought us together today. He has given us all a second chance." Katrina's face shone with faith as she took the young girl's hand. "We will look after you and your baby."

The plan developed quickly. The girl would stay at their house but tell no one of her pregnancy. They would not register the loss of their own child and, with the right planning, and a few props there was no reason for anyone to discover that this was not the child Mr and Mrs Jones had been expecting. With the help of their dear friend and medical professional, Dave Hughes, they would be able to care for and deliver the baby safely without any intervention.

After the birth no one ever questioned that Ember was theirs. The young girl, who never told them the father's name, gave birth and left, not even taking any of the money they offered her. The only thing she asked was that the child be called September and that they love her as if she was their own.

Everything just seemed to fall into place, even the unfortunate accidental death of bachelor Dave Hughes assured that the story could not possibly come out. Then tragedy struck when Ember was only eight years old and Katrina passed away. Conrad was left to bear the secret alone. A secret he had never revealed and was now taking to his grave. His last thought before he hit the ground was of the girl they had met on the train. She was like an angel that had come to save them from despair. She even had an angelic name: Amitiel.

The Nuevo Favelas, Hispanic Sector, 2146 AD

In the Nuevo Favelas of the Hispanic sector, the girl who Conrad had raised as his own sits on the steps of a small alleyway. She is deep in thought about her daddy and hopes to see him again soon. Chamuel has gone into the brightly coloured building opposite. The sign hanging above it names it "Gillespie's Bar". Chamuel has asked her to wait outside while he checks the place out. She can hear quite loud conversation coming out from the open windows. In fact it could be arguing so Ember decides to move closer and listen in.

"Of course I wanted to contact you but you know how it is, honey."

"Don't ye be callin' me honey! You wee cheating, lowlife, useless excuse for a goblin or whatever de feck you are!"

The level of sarcasm coming from the female voice as she chastises Chamuel is even obvious to someone as unfamiliar with this form of wit as Ember. Curious to see the woman who is belittling Chamuel she moves even closer to take a sneaky peek.

"Fuck's sake, woman, why you gotta get all up in my face?"

Ember can see the back of Chamuel and just make out the figure of the woman. She hears her hysterical, if somewhat ironic, laughing.

"Chamuel, why do you insist on talking like some auld time black actor from a gangster movie? You do know you not really black, don't ya? It's not your body, ya little skitter ya."

Ember is not sure what that means but at least she can now make out this feisty woman's detail. She has jet-black hair tied back in a plat, with curly wisps falling from her brow across her deep brown eyes. Her skin is olive, like that of her Italian mother no doubt, but her strong jaw and athletic body probably come from her Irish father. Even from this brief glimpse Ember can see she is a formidable-looking woman. She is wearing a khaki shirt tied at the middle and exposing ample cleavage. This and worn brown leather shorts remind Ember of some image she saw in a book once, or was it a comic?

"This cloud spinning round ya head, this is you, my darling wee black Leprechaun."

Her tone is still strong but Ember recognises a shift in Donegal Gillespie's aggressive stance. Now she has her hands gripped to the lapels of Chamuel's jacket and before he manages to answer her comment she pulls him to her and begins what can only be described as "not in front of the children"-type kissing. Ember, embarrassed and a little grossed out, backs up and hits her head on the shutter. She wonders if they heard her. The next words Donegal says suggests she did.

"So, are you going to introduce me to the child?"

"Of course, once you stop molesting me."

Ember waits expectantly as the two exit the bar. She feels awkward and a little intimidated when Donegal looks her up and down. Then, from nowhere comes a warm smile and a hug and Ember relaxes slightly.

"Well, look at you, poor wee thing, Chamuel did you drag this poor girl backwards through the Pitts?"

"Well, actually..."

"Ack! Don't tell me, I don't wanna know. You come with me, girl. Let's get you fixed up."

Ember had not even thought about her appearance over the last day or so. She had stepped out of her front door yesterday morning wearing her favourite jeans and a baby-blue soft wool jumper. As always her hair would have been immaculate as would have been the minimal make-up on her soft flawless skin. When Donegal takes her up to the bathroom upstairs she wonders who the dishevelled little urchin is, standing in the corner. She can hardly believe it. Noticing her shock, Donegal reassures her.

"Don't ye worry, we'll get ya cleaned up." She runs her hands through Ember's hair. "We best get something done with this as well. You will stick out like a dot on a domino around here."

The water is lukewarm and she has to roll around to get fully wet but still, it feels so good. She blanks out everything that has happened and for a few short minutes she allows herself to relax. Once she is clean, Donegal applies a black dye to her hair, making sure to apply it to her eyebrows as well. Ember does not argue but draws the line at the suggestion that she should cut it short.

Donegal knows that the poor girl has not yet accepted that she will never return to her old life and decides not to make an issue of it. When they eventually return to Chamuel, he is setting something up in a back room. He looks at Ember and stands back, impressed by her metamorphosis into a local girl, her hair now long and dark and her summer dress a colourful floral pattern of yellow and green. Even her light skin has been darkened.

"Hola chica," he remarks in his best Spanish. Ember feels the flush of embarrassment and tries to change the subject. "What are you up to in there?"

"I am setting up equipment for you to watch this disc."

Ember's face collapses, exhaustion getting the better of her. "I don't want to watch it," she says definitively.

"Ember... you must."

"Why don't you watch it and then you can tell me the good bits."

"It is for you and you alone. Now, we might as well get this over and done with. Everything is ready. I will put this on then we will leave you to watch it."

Ember looks to Donegal who gives her a reassuring nod.

"Don't stress, we will be just outside."

Once alone, Ember, as bemused as ever, watches the screen flicker. A voice startles her and then she can see the most infamous man to ever walk the earth looking directly at her through a fuzzy screen.

"Hello, September, my beautiful little girl," says Shane Mills.

Ember recognises the Antihost from all the paraphernalia she has seen with his picture on. Also she recently watched VR footage of this evil psychopath slaughtering women and children. She struggles to match this smiling kind man – calling her by her full name, which not even her daddy does – with the image she is used to seeing.

"I don't know what you know of me," says Shane. "But I can only guess that history may have painted a certain image of me that is none too favourable. I hope you can bear to listen to my message to you.

"What seems like a long time ago know before I made this recording I was imprisoned in a place called Stoke Prison. Previous to my incarceration I had led a life that was pretty insignificant compared to what happened afterwards. I was, what you would call, a bit of a rogue. I had allowed myself to be led astray. But not long before I was banged up my life began to actually come together. I had met a wonderful woman and I'd allowed myself to believe I could be happy."

Shane stares into the camera as if he can see Ember. Ember is baffled and uncomfortable that the Antihost is telling her about his domestic problems.

"Anyway, it was not to be. I've spent many hours wondering what could have been if only Sara never went to that flipping gala night… but, anyway, I eventually realised that these things are not within our power and that somewhere someone or thing is pulling the strings and manipulating everything that ever happens. I am telling you this because I assume that you have just been torn away from what you thought was reality. I don't want you to waste time thinking 'if only I hadn't done this or done that', because you see, my darling, whatever you did, this message would still have been at the end of it."

Ember is not sure how she feels about this man who is talking to her so frankly and calling her "darling". Internally she is fighting the warmth that seems to be flowing through her as he speaks. She knows who he is, she has studied what he has done but she cannot fight the feeling of belonging that his image is invoking in her.

"I am so sorry that I, the very person who should be protecting you, am the one who is about to turn your life upside down. If everything

338

has gone to plan you will have lived a very privileged life up until now. I hope that your adopted parents were good to you."

Ember sits down with a bump, struggling to control her breathing as she contemplates what Shane is saying. As if he notices her discomfort he suddenly shifts in his seat.

"Sorry. I am making a mess of this. I should explain first exactly who I am to you and how this has all come about. As I said, I assume history does not paint me in too good a light. I am not here to plead innocence, I am anything but innocent. I am, however, an important piece in a very complex game. Hopefully chess is still played in your time and if so, I would be the queen on the board."

Shane shakes his head, still uncomfortable with the gender.

"And you the king."

Ember is also uncomfortable with the analogy but more out of confusion than association.

"For many years I have raged war against the enemy force that is the Djinn. I had first thought my mission was to defeat Reuben and the others myself but recently I have learned that my mission was to pave the way for you. I am sure by now Reuben, Solfrid and probably Levi have revealed themselves to mankind. They will most likely have presented themselves as god-like saviours. Let me just say, these murdering pricks are no gods! They are a bunch of self-serving bastards that must be wiped from this planet!" Shane checks himself as he feels his outrage may sound crazy to a teenage girl, years in the future. "Sorry, I shouldn't swear. Let me go back to why I... erm..." He is struggling to find the words. "Why we, when I say 'we' I mean... sorry, I really am no good at this shit."

Ember observes a tear running down his face. Can this be the sadistic maniac that she had read about? Books on him were actually not allowed to be read by underage students, so bad were his deeds. Yet what she sees here is no monster. Ember feels a pull to him. She doesn't know why and yet she does know why. If she is honest, she knows exactly why.

"The main thing to know is that you are a product of love. I am your father and, although I will never meet you and you will be born long after my death, I want you to know that I love you just as much as any father has ever loved a daughter. Your mother will be watching over you, literally like an angel from the heavens. Her name is Amitiel and she… she…" Once more Shane struggles for the words. He wonders how to explain that her mother is in fact an Arc Hon and yet still the love of his life and the most amazing, beautiful creature imaginable. "Your mother…" He smiles. "She is not of this world. She was sent here to watch over us all. She was supposed to only watch but she broke the rules and, along with others of her kind, she has helped me and the revolutionaries known as the Diabolicals…" Shane realises he is jumping ahead again. "Sorry. I can imagine this sounds very strange to you. I guess finding out you are adopted is shock enough for most people but then to hear that your parents are an evil historical figure and an super sapient your mind must be boggled!"

This is an understatement. Ember feels like she has slipped into a kind of coma. She can hear the words and see his face but nothing is real, and yet it is also very real. Something causes her not to doubt what is being said. Amitiel. Even if she knows it sounds crazy, she has always been drawn to the Angel of Truth. Even though she has only ever seen pictures, she has always felt a presence.

"Like I said, you were created from love. We both love you. I tell you this because I don't want you thinking you were a product of necessity." Again he pauses for an awkward moment. "Reuben and the other Djinn are very powerful; I know because I have been fighting them for so long. It is obvious that no mere human can defeat them. The Arc Hon were a match for the Djinn but they have been betrayed by one of their own and now their capabilities are reduced."

Ember cannot keep up. She wonders if she missed something. Shane reassures her.

"Don't worry, if you don't follow all the babble I am coming out with, I will explain everything one step at a time. First though, I must reiterate: you are the first ever offspring of both a human and an Arc Hon. This makes you very special and very powerful. I pass on some pretty special genes if I say so myself, and as for your mother, well she's basically a fucking angel."

Shane hopes his sense of humour is helping Ember to take it all in. If he could see her he would be uplifted. Ember smiles at this man's attempt at humour, the feelings of empathy are growing stronger and the closeness is now undeniable. Could it be that she feels a fondness towards the most infamous mass murderer who ever lived? What does that say about her?

"Unfortunately, one other thing I am passing on is the burden of fighting the Djinn. You see, my sweet little girl, you must help lead humans out of the darkness. You must free the slaves and wipe the Djinn from the face of the planet and back to their own dimension."

The picture flickers and Ember's heart misses a beat. Oh no, it's damaged, she thinks. Panic ensues and she readies to call Chamuel but to her relief, the image returns and her new-found father is back on the screen.

"There is so much to tell you. First let's just get the facts straight. I want to tell you what really happened. I will start from when we escaped from prison, Leo and Raphael, Chamuel and myself. All the news channels blamed us for the prison break, saying how Robert Price and I had masterminded the killing of six hundred innocents in the process. Thanks to Reuben and his PR machine, I became the most wanted and evil man on the planet. Ultimately though, this plan backfired on him because it made me realise I had nowhere to go but onwards. I was already damned so innocence was no longer an issue. It was also just after escaping that your mother reappeared to me and told me about the recruits I needed to find. I am sure you know these as the Diabolicals."

Ember has an involuntary shudder just at the name of the group who history depicts as the inner circle of evil, all infamous for their part in the massacres and the final war.

"Well, let me tell you these 'Diabolicals' were the bravest men and women I could ever have had the privilege to have met." Shane holds up a group photo. In it stands himself and Robert Price. There's also a tall black woman with thin sharp features standing next to a man wearing a cowboy hat and a long leather coat. Unlike a typical cowboy, this man is East Asian with long dark hair and an athletic build. He is leaning on the shoulder of a middle-aged red-headed woman; attractive if you are into domination. The third woman in the photo is South Asian. She has short cropped hair and a beauty that resembles a pixie. The last person in the photo is a short wiry-looking Arab who wears a fez.

"These people are my family," says Shane warmly. "They are your family too and each and every one of them loves you and hopes that you are well. I know there is a lot to explain and I only have the length of this disc to do it in so I will stop rambling and get to the point. You know by now at we have been defeated but that is not quite true. This is merely the next step in my strategy. I know I am not the one to defeat the Djinn, they are too strong. They have the control of men's minds and have built up their strongholds over thousands of years. We need something, or someone, who can match the Djinn. We have help from the Arc Hon, Raphael, Chamuel and Amitiel, but they are restricted in what they can do and they fear some entity called the Demiurge more than they fear Reuben. Anyway, while I slept one night I had a dream. It was you Ember, you came to me and told me what to do, what needed to be done."

Ember is looking at the face of a loving father, a sincere and caring man.

"I reiterate that you were not a product of necessity, conceived out of a plan to overthrow the overlords. I would never have used you that way. You came to me and told me what to do. The battle we waged is now almost over. Most of America is uninhabitable, Africa is burning and Asia, well, quite frankly Asia is finished."

Ember holds her hand to her chest. Her emotions seem tied to his and she feels sorrow on realising the 'Antihost' is choked by his words. It is clear that he is building up to some heart-breaking revelation and she feels his anguish.

"Defeat, it seemed, was inevitable, and then you came to me. I understand that you are confused now. I must admit to not being too sure myself but you told me to tell you straight so I will try. As a hybrid – sorry, I hate that word but it's the one you used. Anyway, as a hybrid you will have access to many of the channelled powers that the Arc Hon possess but you won't have the restrictions that they operate under. You also gave me instructions on the last push, an event you told me is known in history as the October Massacres."

Ember holds her breath, even the madness of the situation cannot prepare her for discovering that she is somehow involved in history's darkest days. What was he saying? That she somehow planned the genocide of whole ethnic group: an event that superseded her birth by decades?

Ember's mind has flipped into some sort of protection mode, telling her this is crazy, she is being hypnotised or something. He is not her father. She is not some sort of hybrid *thing*! She needs this to stop. She runs at the machine, randomly hitting buttons, shouting at the box.

"Shut up! Shut up! My father is Conrad Jones! I am a normal girl and I WANT TO GO HOME!"

Eventually she manages to hit the right button and the madness stops. She falls to the ground, crying uncontrollably. She wants her daddy to hold her and make it all right. The tears become more intense when the image she wishes to bring to mind is not of Conrad any more, but of Shane Mills.

H.Q

After dumping the helicopter and traipsing through endless fields, Shane and the group of escaped prisoners spot a small farmhouse. The farm is in a secluded part of Northamptonshire, forty miles north of London.

It is the home of the Wilkinson's, a retired couple who bought it two years ago under the false impression that living off the land in beautiful countryside miles from the nearest city would be a utopia. Jackie, the wife, was bored and tired of the hard work and tedium of the place. She had not told her spouse, Dave as she was embarrassed about it after all the years they had planned their dream retirement. If she'd had the courage to tell him she may have learned he shared her feelings and was also bored to tears. Either way, the boredom was about to end.

"We just need a vehicle and some food," says Shane. "So we're in and out of this place like lightning. There may be children, so let's try to be civil."

Chamuel laughs at the instructions Shane has delivered. "You mean don't forget our please and thank yous?"

Shane, still unsure who the little black guy even is, looks him up and down before telling him, "Listen, I didn't thank you for your help back there and we still haven't been introduced but I am sure you can appreciate that there is a time and a place for us to get acquainted once we are safe. For now though, I am assuming leadership of our little group and I hope that is okay with you."

The statement is tinged with overtones of violence. Robert considers warning Shane off confronting Chamuel but is taken back as Chamuel replies.

"Yes, sir, Massa, you is de boss. I just trying to lighten the mood. Sorry me is a bad Chamuel." Chamuel slaps his own wrist.

Shane accepts this and looks at Robert and Leo, checking if they are okay with his assumption of leadership. Nods from both men reassure him. They find a vantage point while Shane and Chamuel trek across the fields to a small mud track that leads to the Wilkinsons front door.

"So, what? We just gonna knock on de door and hope they offer two rough-looking men the use of their jeep? That's assuming of course, our pictures aren't all over the TV by now, what with the Governor telling everybody that we kidnapped him and blew the entire fucking prison up."

Shane does not respond to Chamuel's constant yapping. He knows when to react and when not to and has already got the measure of this man... or whatever he is. Chamuel continues regardless, but not until they are in sight of the front door does Shane speak.

"Okay, I will do the talking. You try and concentrate on not freaking the poor people out, tiendes?" Then he rings the bell.

In all the time David and Jackie have lived on the isolated farm they have only heard the doorbell go twice. Once when the Jehovah's Witnesses came to call on a nice sunny afternoon and then again when a fed-up young man selling frozen fish turned up looking very lost indeed. This time when the bell goes David is watching the news and swearing at the TV about the prison incident.

"That'll be the fucking Muslims. Al Qaeda or ISIS no doubt. Well, I hope all the liberal bastards who blurt on about Guantanamo and how bad those bastards are treated are happy now."

Jackie looks at him disapprovingly. She would class herself as one of those "liberal bastards" and she knows David is looking for a debate on the subject but she isn't in the mood. Although she can't let his idiotic statement go without some comment.

"How can a breakout in a UK prison have anything to do with the happenings in Guantanamo?"

They hear the doorbell before David can reply. Both look a little worried. The worst thing for David about the isolation of living out here was the fear of been held up and robbed. Still, he goes to the door while Jackie tries to see who it is via the window. David peers through the spy-hole. He can make out two figures, they look fairly rough and one is black. This concerns him. He shouts through the door, "Hello, can I help you?"

"Hi, I'm sorry, but we broke down up the hill. It's my radiator. Could I possibly get a jug of water from you?"

Shane had been planning to case the farm before taking any action. First he wanted to see how many people he was dealing with and then he needed to know if there were any children. He does not want to cause any more stress than needed and, although prepared to take hostages, he really hopes that there were no elderly or youngsters.

It seems rude not to help so David Wilkinson opens the door and then immediately regrets his actions as the two men give him calculated looks; the white guy is particularly fierce-looking. David stutters his words, betraying his anxiety.

"Th... there is an outside tap by the barn. You can use the bucket next to it if ye... you w... want."

David knows that this is not two innocent travellers and that he needs to play it cool. Problem is, he isn't cool and both Shane and Chamuel realise this too.

"Thank you, sir. I wondered if you might have a landline we could use as well. I need to call ahead to a garage." Shane looks past him, noticing a woman standing in the hallway. He estimates they are both mid to late fifties; this should rule out young kids. These people are not typical farmers so he guesses this is their retirement home and he doubts they would have elderly parents here with them. He decides to make a move. David's heart beats wildly as he feels the strong arms take hold of him, throwing him into his own hallway. Shane does not want to hurt him but this is an emergency.

"How many are in the house?" he shouts at the cowering David

"It is just me and my wife. We have some money upstairs and some jewellery. Take what you want, just don't hurt us."

Shane is always surprised how easy it is to make a grown man cry. He does not want to be the bully but he has no respect for victims. Jackie has frozen, scared and angry. Mentally stronger than her husband, she wants to both run away and attack these bastards at the same time but what can her pear-shaped frumpy body do against these men?.

Chamuel orders her to sit down and pulls down the large curtains. He disappears and returns with a couple of belts. Shane drags David to the chair next to his wife and pushes him into his seat. A nod confirms he wants them both tied up and Chamuel expertly complies.

"We will not hurt you. We need your car and the money you so kindly offered."

It takes around ten minutes in all to commandeer the Wilkinson's' Land Rover and six hundred pounds, along with some clean clothes. They secure the couple in the pantry, leaving them gagged and tied up. It would be far safer to kill them both but Chamuel doesn't even try to convince Shane of this. Calculating that the Wilkinsons will be tied up for three to four hours, Shane is confident they have enough time to find somewhere safe.

From the passenger seat of the Land Rover Shane says, "So Amitiel had a plan for us, somewhere we could hide. Do you know where this is?" Shane is hoping Chamuel is going to show them a secret HQ where he and the others will be able to rest up and plan their next move. Instead he can hear the Arc Hon laugh.

"Are you for fucking real?" says Chamuel from behind the wheel. "There *was* a plan but you decided to do your own thing, remember? So now, instead of utter confusion and chaos masking our escape we have the prison governor, plus Darby and Joan back there, who will be contributing to our notoriety and of course, more importantly, our fame. So in answer to your question: is there is somewhere safe for us to hide? No. Unfortunately David Beckham has more chance of not being recognised by the day's end.

"We need to use the precious couple of hours that it'll take for the media and the authorities to put things together, and before your photos are splattered all over the news and before Al Jazeera put out a two-hour special on the life and times of 'Al Qaeda Bob' to get us back on track to the original plan." Chamuel looks at the three men with exasperation. "Luckily for you lot, these Djinn are kinky about underground tunnels and none more so than Simeon himself."

The men look at Chamuel, waiting for the inevitable long and curse-filled explanation. They get one.

"I always wonder why humans go around questioning how the Egyptians built the pyramids and how did them druids move massive stones all the way across Britain to create Stonehenge? There is always someone who thinks he is on to something that will explain what is really happening and that all is not as it seems. Yet no one, and I mean no one, asks how the fuck did the Victorians build a fifty-mile stretch of underground railway back in 1853, and more to the point, why? I mean, it's not like there were a heap of cars causing congestion. In fact, there were six. So, why build an underground? There wasn't even any fucking electricity worth utilising that could run a train down there and if you're going to tell me they had steam trains underground, forget it! No, this was Simeon's doing. I have to ask myself, is there a conspiracy theorist that deserves the name when they miss things so obvious? With all the technology and know-how you have nowadays, you would still struggle to complete such a task. So let me explain, Simeon was pulling all the strings during the time of the British Empire. He was the king-maker and the builder of Great Britain. Like all good Djinn, he has his own fetish. Isaac loved art, Reuben loves inflicting pain, and Simeon, he loves building shit. And as I said, all the Djinn love a good tunnel."

Chamuel holds his left hand out. "Djinn love a tunnel." He holds his right hand out and the others shout for him to grab the wheel again.

"Simeon loves to build big stuff. Result? Miles of underground secret passages and loads of other shit running underneath us from Oxford to the capital. Only a handful of people have ever known about this. So, we are going to Simeon's secret tunnel network, a sort of advanced version of the Christians' catacombs back in France. He had it built when he was first disqualified by the Council and, more recently, he had it all kitted out when he decided he was going to help you, Shane. He is a very resourceful Jinni, even us Arc Hon didn't realise the extent of his labyrinth. I promise you, if we get there you will be impressed. IF WE GET THERE."

Gillespie's Bar, Nuevo Favelas, Hispanic District, 2146 AD

Donegal knocks on the door. "Hey, Ember, are you okay?" She can hear how upset Ember is, crying and mumbling to herself.

"Akk, ya poor wee mite, come here."

Ember shuffles out and is grateful for the tight hug. She feels torn-up inside but knows she must go back in and watch the rest of the recording. Over Donegal's shoulder she spots Chamuel standing in the corner. He says nothing, just turns and leaves.

"It's a drink you'll be needing." Donegal releases her grip and walks behind the bamboo bar. She takes a bottle from under the counter and pours two generous shots.

"I don't drink," says Ember, settling onto the bar stool and lifting the glass anyhow.

"Trust me, if you're gonna be spending time with that one out there and his like, you will need the sauce."

"Thank you." Ember drinks it down in one gulp then coughs and splutters as she attempts to keep it down. Donegal necks hers too and pours one more for each of them. "I am guessing there was some bad news on this thingy-me-bob he's given ya?"

"Well, yes and no," she sighs, trying to make sense of it herself. "I just found out my daddy's not my real father, and that my real father died a long time ago." She takes the second drink, handling this one a little better.

"Well, we all need our daddies. Mine was a good man, bit of a drunk, not the tidiest, but he loved his family and he was my best friend 'til the day he died. Didn't leave me much, just this place, and the debts that went with it, but I still wish he was here." She pours two more. "Have you watched it all? I couldn't help overhearing you trying to turn the thing off, sounded like there was more."

"There is but I'm not sure I want to see or hear any more." Ember feels she can be honest with this kind-hearted woman but they both know it isn't so much a case of "wanting to see more". She simply isn't sure she can physically or mentally take any more.

"Well, ya dunna have ta. Just take it and fling it out da window. It'll fly across the favelas from up here."

Ember sighs. "I can't do that, and to be honest the damage is done. Perhaps I should go back. Get it over and done with?" She looks down at the glass, realising she feels a little strange.

Chamuel comes back into the room. He is unusually quiet. She is grateful for his silence. They nod and share a faint smile before Ember jumps down and returns to the viewing room.

"She is very young, Chamuel," says Donegal, running her hands through Chamuel's tight curls. "I don't know what you have her watching in there but I am guessing you have plans for her. I hope you know what you are doing."

He holds her around the waist but for once has no cocky retort. "Not exactly."

"Well, we could be waiting out here a long time so best we keep drinking, as me old daddy would say."

They do wait a long time. The message runs for over two hours. No more crying is heard though, no more shouting at the screen. The first indication that it is over is when the door opens. Both wait expectantly as Ember reappears. Donegal is pleased to see the young girl looking radiant, with a glow she had not seen in her earlier. She turns to Chamuel, about to comment, but notices that he is staring at Ember as if he has seen a ghost. Donegal follows his stare and is sure he is looking just above Ember's head.

Chamuel is entranced. He was prepared for a change in Ember after she saw the message but he is amazed at what he can see. Swirling above her head, a thick silver cloud glistens. The cloud takes a shape and Chamuel knows he has seen this aura once before but even so, he cannot explain it. The great white shark swims between Ember's arms, around her torso, up along her legs then back across her shoulders. Chamuel mouths the words as he is thinking them. "It can't be."

Venice

Reuben has calmed down or so it seems. He paces around, staring at the floor. Simeon is grimly expecting a very slow and painful death to balance the distress he has caused his fellow Jinni. Finally Reuben speaks. "Touché, old friend. It seems you have managed to get the human out safe and sound. I should thank you really, it would be no fun to win so easily."

Reuben walks around the smug Simeon like a hunter circling its prey. "I suppose you want to know my next move. You know, so you can message whichever one of those cunts, who are supposed to WATCH and not interfere, is helping you."

Simeon is not surprised that Reuben has worked it out. Of course, someone would have to be an Arc Hon for Simeon to be able to link with them. He doubts Reuben will be able to work out that in fact all three remaining Arc Hon have decided to ally themselves with the new challenger. They will still follow certain rules but for the most part they are no longer Watchers; they are players.

"Well, actually, I *am* going to tell you... no, I am going to show you what my next move is and you, dear friend, are going to link with your Arc Hon friend, and then they will show it to Shane Mills himself."

Simeon is curious and a little concerned about what strategy Reuben is about to play now. A strategy that he is so confident will work that he wishes to willingly inform his adversaries about it.

"I won't be aiding you in any way," says Simeon. "If there is something you want Mills to see, then it'll be my task to make sure he doesn't. You should know, old friend, there is no pain that you can inflict which will cause me to compromise the challenger."

When Reuben looks up, he smiles a smile that Simeon recognises as one of confidence. Whatever he has up his sleeve must be good, Simeon concludes. He waits to hear the smarmy retort that he expects to come from Reuben's mouth but instead he hears another voice, a female voice. Solfrid.

"Oh, I think we can manage to change your mind, my dear Simeon."

Shit, he thinks, of course the bitch was helping Reuben all this time. She was probably the one who told him how to eliminate the others. In fact, she probably helped him do that.

"Why?" he asks.

"What did you think this game was all about? Do you really think it was all just a distraction for the Djinn collective, something to relieve the boredom?" She laughs at the quizzical look on Simeon's face. "Oh, you did think that, and of course you swallowed the bullshit too, about us ultimately helping the humans reach enlightenment. God, can you imagine these savages living on the same plain that we occupy? No, this game will establish the Djinn once and for all as the true and rightful overlords, both in our world and this pleasure-filled physical world. We are GODS to these humans! We shouldn't be skulking around in the shadows. We should be sat upon the thrones ruling them! And I don't just mean the select few that the all-fucking-mighty Arc Hon allow to take physical form, I mean all of us. The thousands who seethe in envy from our dimension. There has been a shift, Simeon. The Djinn want the life we always should have had. We *will* cross over and we *will* rule!"

Simeon has never trusted Solfrid. She was the first Djinn to take human form and he knows she has been corrupted by the pleasures of the flesh ever since. However, she is ranting about an impossible task here. Even the Arc Hon could not possibly transfer the thousands of Djinn to the state she expects.

She smiles at him. "You wonder what I am talking about, how this could be possible. Let me show you."

Simeon's mind merges with hers and he sees the universe outside of the physical barriers.

"In approximately 150 years the Age of Aquarius begins and the Demiurge returns, hoping to find his calculations have proved correct and that a utopia has occurred. The alignment will coincide with the event of the Nibiru cataclysm, which heralds his arrival. These events and a controlled nuclear fusion via our new toy, the Hadron Collider, will cause a power surge that will enable a mass crossover. We will farm human bodies for future possessions, allowing the Djinn to exist as infinite beings in the physical world. When the Demiurge sees what we have done, he will accept this is now our planet and that his plan has failed."

Simeon scoffs. "Another oracle. How would you even know what his plan is? Even the Arc Hon wonder what the plan is. So you come up with your own interpretation? That is just the same as the humans with their deities, their Quran or Bible."

The harsh slap from her hand leaves a welt across his face. "Never compare me to these vermin!"

Simeon prepares for another blow but she calms down, as though the next thought that has entered her mind has caused her to become serene. "I will tell you how I know what his plan is, shall I? Better still, I will show you."

Inside his mind a vision appears, showing the image of Michael, the Arc Hon who has been missing for centuries. He sits in the realm known to Simeon as the corona, the world between worlds. The vision shows Michael speaking with Reuben and Solfrid. Simeon witnesses the whole meeting from a fly-on-the-wall position.

"I am delighted that we are close to completing the plan," says Michael. "Soon the world will be lost to chaos what with the Muslim Jihadists, the crazy Jews blowing each other up, and of course that nasty virus we will release in Africa. Soon we begin the Solution under your leadership, Reuben. You will become the saviour with grateful followers."

"Yes, and then we can prepare for the Nibiru to reappear from its Occultation and blaze the path ready to combat the Demiurge's return!"

Simeon is surprised by Reuben's unusual tone; one of reverence and subservience. Everything clicks. Of course. Reuben is just another player. And even Solfrid is just an underling. It is Michael who is the mastermind. It has always been him. Centuries, perhaps millennia, of planning at work.

"And what if he is displeased with the results of his experiment?" asks Reuben.

Michael is smug. "Oh, he will be displeased but what does he expect? He cast us down here, his loyal servants, sentenced to watch over these inferior beings, while he left. But now we know the truth. The Fallen One has told us all; that the humans are his chose people and we Arc Hon and you Djinn are just second-class citizens, only here to guide and help these savages. Well, by the time he has returned this will be my... sorry, *our* world, and we will be ready for him. I wait in anticipation to see how he reacts to finding these hominids that he loves so much utilised as mere slaves and body vessels for the use of the rightful rulers, the holy trinity of the Arc Hon, the Fallen One and the Djinn.

Things are now finally clear to Simeon and his questions are being answered, except now he has a new question. Who is the Fallen One?

Somewhere in the British countryside

Located in the north of Buckinghamshire lies an area of rolling agricultural landscape known as Aylesbury Vale. Shane sits up front in the stolen Land Rover that Chamuel drives. He wouldn't class himself as a nervous passenger normally but he is concerned that Chamuel's erratic driving will bring attention to the group. He assumes that the media will by now have photos and video images of him and the other two splattered all over the TV. It is nearly three hours since the prison break and perhaps two hours since they released the Governor. Perhaps Chamuel had a point, getting out of this predicament would be a lot easier if the authorities were presuming they had died with the rest of the prisoners. Still, they may be lucky and get to this Simeon's underground place before the story really breaks.

He feels a pang of guilt towards the Wilkinsons who they left tied up in the farmhouse but he knows if Chamuel had had his way they would be dead, so at least he doesn't have their death on his conscience. Shane looks into the back seats and notices both Leo and Robert are looking at each other and gripping the seats.

He decides to comment. "You need to slow down. You're drawing attention to us."

The speedo reads 110mph. Chamuel tuts but he does slow.
"Yeah, well, we gotta get to the tunnels before you and the twins back there are poster boys for worldwide terrorism," he retorts. "Anyway, we're nearly there. In fact, we need to ditch this vehicle."

Chamuel swerves off the road and drives through a small wooded area, coming to a sudden halt. Leo and Robert are so relieved to get out of the car they don't question what is next. Shane does.
"So, where are we going now?"
Chamuel smiles. "We are going to gaol."
"Again?" sighs Leo.

Chamuel smiles. It was clear to Simeon that he was a target after he was eliminated by his other Djinn for his radical views towards the humans and so he prepared a retreat, a secret haven with an entrance hidden in the local gaol. He favoured a place called Aylesbury Vale, where he'd had many followers through a Freemason lodge he'd set up there. He had a house built there in the 1700s, calling it Claydon House and by the mid-1800s, he was building underground tunnels into London. Under the premise of building a modern transport service, he orchestrated the commissioning of not one, but many tunnels. The first one, all the world knew about but the second one, only a soon-to-be deceased MP and eleven thousand black slave-workers. He also had a gaol built, which contained the entrance. Today it is a museum but the entrance is still there for those who know how to find it, hidden in the same cell as always.

Shane and his band of renegades pass into the museum unnoticed as the skeleton staff are busy watching the news on TV.

"Would you just look at that big black chap? He's got murderous eyes if I ever saw them. Typical Muslim. It was clearly his plan," says Ivor the curator.

"They don't know who it was yet. Isn't the fit Mills bloke Irish? Maybe it were the IRA?" adds Eliza, who has worked on the door here for forty of her fifty-nine years.

"I heard the old guy with glasses is in with the Italian Mafia and it was a revenge hit that went wrong," says the youngest staff member and the others all mock him for such a ridiculous idea.

If the three staff members could be bothered to look at the monitor that watched over the entrance and hallway of the museum, they may have noticed that the four people entering the prison cell exhibit are in fact the same four people they are scrutinising on their TV screen. Luckily for the staff, they did not notice.

The cell stands as it has these past three hundred years, only now it's an exhibit, kept as it was to give the visitors a realistic experience of life in gaol back in the day. Chamuel sneaks over the barrier and counts bricks, up then across. Shane gets the Indiana Jones theme in his head.

Under the stone bench attached to the wall a small opening appears.

"Well it still works, sheesh... how nobody ever found this, I don't know!" Shane hopes it is going to get bigger as he doubts he could squeeze in through it as it is. He looks at Robert and knows he definitely won't. Chamuel pushes the brick harder and the opening grows a few centimetres more.

"You first, big boy," Chamuel instructs Robert, who lies down and rolls into the black opening. He sticks for a moment but after a helping foot from Chamuel he disappears into the darkness. Next Leo puts his glasses into his pocket and, kneeling, enters the hole head first. Soon his feet are swallowed up.

"Ok, once I release this brick, we got sixty seconds, so get on your belly, soldier boy and start shuffling. Shane ducks under the bench and pushes his body into the dark, damp hole. Soon he is in a narrow tunnel and he can hear the other two shuffling ahead of him.

"Get a fucking move on!" he hears from Chamuel, whose silhouette fades as the opening closes behind him. Shane wonders how Robert managed to get through as he himself is struggling to move in such a confined space. The incessant griping of Chamuel behind him drives him on and soon he reaches another opening and he can make out Robert's outstretched arm pulling Leo out and up onto his feet. Shane reaches the end and is relieved to find a lighted, spacious room awaits them.

Chamuel exits last, still moaning. "Man, you need to wash them feet soon as we find some running water."

The modern room is lit by florescent strip lighting that turns on and off via a sensor. It reminds Shane of the interrogation rooms back in Afghanistan with its bright lights. A large secure door seems to be the only way forwards and the three men wait patiently for Chamuel to produce a key. Chamuel walks to the door and simply pushes it open before turning to face the three humans.

"Seriously? You three are the saviours of the world? The world is fucked." He laughs to himself and walks through the door.

They follow him into a long white-washed corridor, leading to a red-walled corridor, which leads to a lift with a metal shutter gate that needs pulling up and down. They all enter the lift and, after what seems to be a one-floor descent, the doors open into a huge room resembling an empty hangar.

"So he had it all kitted out, did he?" says Shane sarcastically.

Chamuel does not reply; instead he continues walking until he reaches the far side of the huge room where there is a small door. Inside they find a person-sized clear tubular chute.

"What's that?" asks Leo.

Chamuel smiles. "Transport to London."

The group stands on a small platform looking into this spectacular-looking network of clear tubes. "This is the lay-line system. It makes it possible for blocks of meat like you three to travel at real speeds, instead of faffing around at snail's pace."

Leo looks apprehensive. The trip here in the stolen Land Rover at breakneck speed was fast enough for him; he is sure he is going to dislike this form of transport even more.

"Right, who's first?" Shane steps forward and Chamuel opens a sliding door to one of the tubes. Leo observes, "It looks like an air tube system, the ones which cashiers would use to send money up to the offices."

"Okay," Chamuel tells Shane. "Step in, place your hands on the blue spots and feet on the red spots so you are assuming the missionary position, if you can remember how that goes."

Shane follows the instructions like a good soldier. He can feel the anticipation coupled with excitement. Even in the elite company of paratroopers, Shane was classed as an adrenaline freak and he loved speed. He doubted this would match his first skydive or the first outing with the air force when he was allowed to take the controls of a Typhoon jet but still it was a pretty big buzz.

"Okay, you ready?"

"One question, what's at the other ennnnnnnnnddddddd?"

Nothing. Not skydiving, not rolling a Typhoon at plus 5G, *nothing* prepared him for the feeling he was experiencing at this moment, as if he was plummeting to the ground with a huge weight tied around him. He hurtles through the tube, somehow avoiding contact with any sides as his body speeds through. And yet, despite the mind-blowing speed he feels no G force. The trip lasts no more than twenty seconds and without any warning he comes to a sudden stop. He hovers inside the tube briefly then drops the small distance to the floor. There is a swoosh noise as a door opens to the side. Shane quickly pulls himself clear and out of the way of the others arriving. He steps into another large hangar-sized room, only this one is not empty. Not by a long shot.

The noise of Leo arriving and stumbling to his feet does not distract Shane from the awe he feels at what he can see. Soon Robert arrives via the lay-line tube and last comes Chamuel, who looks at his fellow travellers as they all stand silently staring into the room.

"What did I tell you, fucking impressive, innit?"

Simeon had worked tirelessly converting his old HQ into a modern-day war room. The room, easily the length and breadth of a football pitch and fifteen metres high, is filled with objects whizzing around: hundreds of floating pods, each no bigger than an upright vacuum cleaner and not that different in shape, except these are like transparent bubbles with coloured forks of light flashing around inside them. These pods keep stopping at small stations attached to the ceiling and the walls and then detaching themselves randomly before setting off again, whizzing around till they find another station. The lightning emanates from a spinning core of energy, which Shane notices resembles a marble in size and shape; in the centre of the space there is a square glass room the size of a large sitting room. This is the command centre, which contains all the controls and various monitors.

"This is the God computer," says Chamuel. "The most advanced and wonderful technology you philistines will ever see. Come on, let's get in the little room and I'll show you how it works. These are organic bots, they collect data from the minds of all the little minions that are channelled with Simeon through his bloodline, data from nearly one hundred and fifty million minds spread throughout the world."

He looks to Shane, waiting for his comment, but only receives a blank expression.

"Information and knowledge are the strongest and most powerful weapons you can possibly harness," he explains. "This facility will allow you to process all the information available direct from Simeon's line of humans." Again blank expressions. Sighing, Chamuel moves to a small control panel. The screen is liquid and ripples to his touch. Give me a name of anyone on the planet but not someone you are personally attached to. A celeb or someone like that."

Robert says, "Cyril Regis."

Chamuel looks at him. "Who the fuck is Cyril Regis?"

"He is a legend! He played for the Sky Blues back in the..."

"Never heard of him or the Sky Blues but let's go with it. He still alive?"

"Ehh, I think so."

Chamuel shakes his head then puts his hand further into the liquid screen and the pods outside seem to become more erratic. Leo looks on in amazement. He wonders how many there are. Hundreds? Thousands? How do they not collide?

Chamuel points to a floating cube where a three-dimensional picture appears, "Is that Cyril Regis?" he asks Robert.

Robert screws his eyes up trying to make out the grey, balding, black man standing in a bank queue.

"Yes, it could be. Yes, it is. He's a bit older than last time I saw him, but yes, that's him."

Chamuel continues, "Cyril is standing in the NatWest bank on Dudley High Street. I won't go into details about him as I doubt anyone but Jihad Joe here cares but we could find out where he lives, who he lives with, if he is married, having an affair, if he was gay, if he had a secret love child, etc. etc. I'm sure you get the point." The picture evaporates when Chamuel takes his hand out. "The Djinn have used instruments like this to influence and persuade humans to do their bidding for centuries. They have bribed, blackmailed and corrupted you saps into following them and carrying out their wishes.

"Of course, they don't need a huge rig like this as they can link directly into any linked human's mind, but Simeon is a very clever Djinn. He has created this device so as to give you, Shane, the ability to gain the same insight as your opponents. It doesn't do exactly what they can do and I'm not sure your tiny brain will be up to controlling all the information it will download, but in some ways it's even better than Vril-linked mind communication. We won't sweat the small stuff now though; we will get the instruction book out later. Let me show you around the rest of the place."

Chamuel is dancing around, excited by his role as guide to this place of wonderment. It reminds Leo of Willy Wonka as he jumps around, springing from one end of the room to the other, pointing to various weird and wonderful gadgets. Leo half expects to see Oompa Loompas on the other side of the door as they enter yet another large room. At least that would explain the boiled sweets, he smiles to himself.

They enter a new room. This one is only half the size of a hangar and has doors stationed all around it and a balcony, which also has doors all around it. The layout and doors could be that of a futuristic prison, thinks Shane.

"Each door is a lay-line," says Chamuel, "capable of transporting you in seconds to a choice of over two hundred locations within London. Now, let me show you the armoury and the living quarters then we can all get a well-earned rest so we can plan the tactics for tomorrow."

Shane looks for the usual smile on Chamuel's face but there is none. They pass into a room full of modern and not so modern weapons, all orderly stacked. Both Shane and Robert are impressed, Leo not so much. Finally the living quarters, which resemble the on-board facilities of a submarine, very snug with small sealed chambers containing single beds and nothing else. These pod-like sleeping chambers are just a tad bigger than a pulldown sun-bed and big man Robert remarks that with all the room down here, such claustrophobic sleeping arrangements seem unreasonable.

"Oh, sorry your fucking highness," snaps Chamuel. "Not good enough for a cave monkey? Would you rather you were up in the Kashmir Mountains counting stalagmites, is that it?"

Robert whispers to Leo. "He is the most racist black man I ever met."

"Tell me about it," sighs Leo. "Try being a Jew in his presence."

Chamuel opens one of the sleeping pods. "They are small, but trust me, they serve two very important functions, one is sleep and the other, well, actually, let's get around to that later. Right, finally through here is the kitchen, fully stocked. Everything runs off the national grid, so don't worry about the bills. Any questions?"

No one wants to hear Chamuel's sarcastic reply so no one asks anything.

"Good," says Chamuel. "Now I gotta go back up top get some nice threads, I might even get me a new identity a fit non-smoker without the duck features. I suggest once you girls finish exploring... you get some sleep. Especially you, Shane. You gonna need your sleep, tomorrow's a big day."

"What's happening tomorrow?"

Chamuel shrugs his shoulders. "I dunno, you're going to tell me. Don't worry, it'll all become clear tonight. Now just get some rest. I will have a drink for you boys while I'm up there in the West End. Well, except for the Muslim of course and the Jew. Anyway, I will have a drink for you, Shane."

As he leaves Leo holds his arms out in disbelief: "Jews drink!"

As tiredness overcomes them, Shane realises very quickly how comfortable the pods actually are. A low hum does not disturb him but in fact relaxes him until he drifts off into a deep sleep.

He is not surprised that his dreams are vivid and that he is meeting with Amitiel in a large country house. Cream teas are being served by an eight-foot-tall butler and a tiny but beautiful French maid. Amitiel sits on the large garden lawn. She is wearing a formal and conservative unfitted dress with beaded edges. She looks very cross. Shane kneels beside her.

"You decided to ignore the plan and do your own thing did you?" She pulls out a copy of *The Times* which looks like it is from the 1920s. A picture of him and his two colleagues next to a sketch of Chamuel brings a smile to Shane's face, seeing the duck features.

"What can be so funny? Are you fucking insane?" she frowns, only getting crosser. "Please don't tell me that of all the billion saps to choose from Simeon has picked a fucking idiot?"

Shane is both taken aback and offended by her outburst and gets defensive in return. "I am not an idiot but I will not be involved in killing defenceless people! That is me, okay? I don't like bullies and I won't be one."

Unimpressed, she gestures wildly. "If there was a Lord God, I would beg him to save us. This isn't the playground, Shane. You're not on a mission to avenge Chloe. This is a battle to save your species. Your opponents will not show any weakness, believe me, and they will thrive on your weaknesses so don't reveal them."

The tiny waitress pours Shane some tea and takes the lid off a silver platter full of cream-topped scones. They look delicious but Shane has always looked after himself and never indulged in such fattening foods.

"You can't put weight on in a dream," Amitiel assures him.

Shane tucks in and, dream or no dream, they are the best things he has ever tasted. Once he has room in his mouth to speak he adds. "Anyway, we are safe now. We've made it to Simeon's bunker and I'm sure I was never going to remain anonymous for long, so what is done is done. Let's move on and discuss the next stage."

Amitiel gives him a curious look. She no longer seems cross, more sympathetic. "You think you are safe? I'm sorry but you will never be safe again. As for that bolthole of Simeon's, I'm afraid it's for one night only. First thing tomorrow you must leave with Chamuel and find your first recruit."

Shane is pissed off to hear he will be leaving the luxurious HQ and wonders why he was given the grand tour in the first place.

Amitiel pities his grumpy face. "You needed to rest and the other two can run the operations in the meantime. For you, the plan is to recruit the other five humans necessary to fulfil the task, then you can return to Simeon's house and use it as your base. Now, let me introduce you to your first recruit." She hands him the old newspaper again and shows him an article on the back. A short wiry Arab wearing a fez is looking over the body of a general in the Iraq army; the title reads, "Is this the mastermind behind the Islamist nation propaganda videos?"

As Shane reads on, the article explains how the most recent terrorist group to rise out of the Syrian conflict is known as ISIS and they are successfully recruiting thousands of foreign fighters and gaining support all over the world due to a very well-run internet publicity machine. It seems that for the first time, the Jihadists are getting truly savvy with information technology equal to that of the West and they are having remarkable results, not least the conquest of many cities within Iraq and Syria. The columnist goes on to say that the use of IT specialists has advanced the cause of these Islamists more than any oil, money or state sponsorship has in the past. It finishes by claiming that the man spearheading the propaganda coup is the man in the funny hat, an Egyptian called Abasi Kubba. It is rumoured that he is not even a fundamentalist himself but more a paid consultant who is acting as the Saatchi and Saatchi for the Jihad.

"Well," says Shane, taking a deep breath. "He looks like a cunt and reading this, he sounds like a cunt too. Why do I need him?"

"For that exact reason," smiles Amitiel, "because he is a cunt. Now how about you just go along with me on this one, hey?"

"Okay, so where do I find him and how do I get him to join us?"

The ground disappears and they are floating above a desert camp just outside a dusty Arab city. Shane had almost forgotten he was in a dream and takes a moment to gather his thoughts again. Amitiel points to the camp below them.

"In two days Abasi will come here to receive his payment for services to the newly crowned caliph. Unfortunately for him, this group is running out of money so they can't afford to pay him. Instead Abasi will be tried and beheaded for treason within five minutes of arriving here. That is, if you fail to rescue him."

Shane knows he won't like the answer to his next question. "So where is this? Where are you sending me?"

"This town is in Iraq and you have less than forty-eight hours to plan and execute your rescue. This is why you need a good night's sleep. You need to ask Chamuel for access to Simeon's toy. It will get you there quickly."

"Gee, thanks, what is this toy? No, don't tell me. So what? I rescue him from this army of mental murdering bastards and then we come back here?"

Amitiel smiles the same sympathetic smile. "No, then you both go to China."

Venice

Back in his prison cell in Venice Simeon reflects on the vision of Michael, Reuben and Solfrid's meeting. He feels even more determined. It is clear to him that Michael, the Arc Hon everyone had thought disappeared centuries ago, is behind all the missing Djinn and many of the evils mankind has faced. He understands Reuben and Solfrid are part of this trinity but as hard as he tries, he cannot imagine who this Fallen One is. Perhaps before he renewed he may have heard of him; Simeon had recalled most of his previous lives but the renewal still took a toll and there are many things that are not so clear. Simeon thinks back to when he was a real human, one who had no memory of the Djinn...

♙♟♟♙

He was born late in the year of 1883. At first his young mother, Susanne, wondered if she could cope. Only she would know who and what Maurice really was. Worried she wouldn't love the child like a mother should, she often left him with her own mother as she returned to her wild ways in Bohemian Paris.

Maurice was a happy child who loved his grandmother and life in the Montmartre district of Paris; although he did not have a father he was not short of male role models in his life, such as famed artists Renoir, Toulouse Lautrec and Pierre de Chavannes, any one of whom could have been his natural father.

All that Maurice had been and all that he expected to be changed the day his mother died, when he received a wooden box containing letters from his father, amongst other things. Maurice was fifty-five years old and was about to learn that he was not insane, as everyone thought. In fact the truth was far more bizarre.

– The Power of the Coming Race, several postcard paintings and parchment sealed with wax. The letters were placed in order and it was on reading the first that everything began to become clear. An epiphany of sorts, but one he had created himself before he was born.

Dear Maurice

What I am about to reveal to you would shatter the strongest of minds and you most likely are convinced yours is fragile. Do not worry, you are not crazy and certainly not fragile of mind. I know you will read this and think to yourself, who is this man telling me what I think and what I am? Well, the reason I know how strong you are, Maurice, is because you are me – I am you. Not just our genes or our bloodline; we are one and the same.

Simeon was right, his revelation did not shatter Maurice's mind. After reading every letter from back to front several times over a two-day period Maurice accepted everything his former self was telling him. To him it explained all the pain and confusion that had led him to drug and alcohol dependency and the frustration of memories that he realised but could not hold on to: like building a house of cards on a windy day. Even after reading the letters he still could not remember his real life but in the notes were various instructions on transcendental meditation and other forms of spiritual access that Simeon promised would help. The book he left himself had no author on the cover and one of the notes explained that Simeon had revealed secrets to its actual author who then used artistic licence to produce one of the best-selling books of the time. Simeon was still unsure of why he had included this book, but knew of its coded messages, perhaps the fallen one is mentioned in there, he thinks to himself. I must revisit the book if I ever get out of here.

Under the pretence of becoming religious, Maurice/Simeon disappeared from public life and became a recluse. What he was actually doing was completing his transformation back to Simeon and planning his next move. Mostly he prepared for the coming human champion. Maurice died in 1955 but Simeon was reborn as a thirteen-year-old boy, the son of a very grateful member of the secret society of the "Grande Loge de France."

⚶ 𝅘𝅥 ⚭ 𝅘𝅥 ⚶

Simeon is drawn away from his memories as Reuben enters. He is followed in by Solfrid, two lackeys, and a naked woman. Reuben parades the dazed woman in front of Simeon.

Reuben is smiling, obviously pleased with himself. "Let's see what soldier boy is made of, shall we?"

Solfrid places an astral band around her head, a device used by Djinn to project their visions directly into cerebral cubes. It does not take Simeon long to work out what they plan. He can guess who the woman is and that they have worked out that wherever Chamuel has taken Shane, it will have the receptive technology. Solfrid will simply send what she sees out to all such receptors around the globe with the likelihood that Shane will be able to see it. Simeon is worried. This will not be easy for Shane. The only consolation is that his London base is near impenetrable and even if they manage to force Shane to reveal his location they will not be able to get to him.

Unfortunately, Simeon was only ninety per cent right regarding Solfrid and Reuben's plan.

𝅘𝅥𝅮𝅘𝅥 𝅘𝅥𝅮𝅘𝅥𝅘𝅥 ⚭ ⚶

Back in Simeon's hideout, Shane is explaining to Leo and Robert over breakfast that he is off to Iraq when the visual cube lights up and a computerised voice announces an incoming call. An image appears.

The three men look up, bemused to see a blonde man in a high fashion smart suit looking down at them.

"Hello, dear Shane. I feel we already know each other but it would be impolite not to introduce ourselves properly I feel."

Shane watches intently, wondering if this means he has been located already. He remembers Amitiel telling him how ruthless Reuben is and decides they would be dead by now, or worse, if he did know.

"My name is Reuben Lupas, which I'm sure you know. I have a gift for you here and because I know you are an honest man, I am going to make you a deal."

The naked woman is pushed into view. She is emaciated, very thin and badly bruised but Shane recognises Sara immediately. His heart stops, his head spins, every fibre of his body tenses...calm. He needs to be calm. He needs to be able to operate and think straight. He repeats his mantra in his head.

Looking up, he takes a deep breath, waiting for the ultimatum.

"Now, while you have been away some of my friends have been taking care of the lovely doctor here, but as you are now out, so to speak, it is only right that you are reunited, don't you think? Oh, and there is someone else I want you to meet."

The image pans to watch a nurse come in. She is leading a small boy by the hand. He is no more than three years old. He wanders into the room rubbing his eyes sleepily. Sara gives out a sob and squats down, holding her arms out to the child.

"Say hello to Shane Junior. I mean, I guess he is your son but I suppose he could be the result of that sick Dr Cameron's forced fuck," Reuben laughs. But Shane can instantly see that this is his boy: the hair, the jawline, the skinny body – so like him at that age.

"Sorry, that wasn't funny," Reuben says, all serious. "Of course he is yours. Look at him, he is the spit of you. Now don't fret, we have been looking after him also. Come here, Shane." Reuben holds his hand out but the boy wobbles and ultimately stays in his mother's weak arms. Reuben's face quickly flows from humoured to irritate. "COME HERE!" He shouts and the startled boy begins to cry; Reuben snatches his hand. Poor Sara. She is mouthing words of comfort to him as tears soak her face. The boy holds out his free hand, reaching for his mummy, his tiny face terrified. Reuben pulls him away harshly, wagging a finger at his naughtiness before rubbing his hand into the boy's curly blond locks like a good uncle before calling the nurse to take him again. Sara doesn't even comment, she simply slumps to the floor. Shane has to reign in his imagination over what horrors she may have suffered.

The image focuses back on Reuben's face. "Here is the deal." He looks at his watch. "You have one minute to swear your allegiance to me or Sara will have a very painful death, as your son watches. Not a lot to ask, I mean, you could lie and swear allegiance with your fingers crossed, but that's okay, I will trust you. So, one minute, starting now."

Shane stares at the image, his jaw dropping open in stunned despair.

"Don't," says Robert, reaching out for his friend. "Don't watch. There's nothing you can do."

The image pans back to Sara as she is yanked to her feet. Her once beautifully toned body is now a shallow, quivering wreck. She doesn't even try to cover herself, suggesting she is well used to this treatment. As the three horrified men watch from the safe confines of Simeon's base, one of the lackeys starts slapping at her with a brush, smearing a clear liquid onto Sara's naked body, especially enjoying her more intimate areas. She recoils but it is hopeless. Once finished he walks her to the middle of the room.

"Forty-five seconds left," says Reuben.

Shane stands. His breathing getting shallow, his clenched fists wobbling through inaction.

Two chains are hung from the ceiling and the lackey ties Sara up so that she dangles limply. He uses a pulley to drag the chains higher up until her arms are fully extended and only her toes touch the floor.

"Thirty seconds left," says Reuben as he and the others back away behind a glass partition. The little boy looks worriedly between the nurse and his mother.

"What is he going to do..?" Leo starts in utter shocked bewilderment but stops with a glance at Shane. He puts a fist to his mouth and turns away, not wanting to cry and steal any attention. He is worthless and stupid. He should be dead, not this innocent woman.

"Twenty-five…" sings Reuben.

The image turns to look at the lackey in full body armour on the other side of the room, his hand resting on a door handle. Behind the door there are snarls and growls. Shane feels his legs go weak suddenly and leans on the table. He tries to shout out and agree to Reuben's request but the words stick in his throat.

"Twenty, nineteen, eighteen…"

Robert is stark still. "Just tell him you'll do it," he whispers. "Swear allegiance. Lie."

Leo looks to Shane. He wants to agree, "Tell the sick son of a bitch that you'll swear loyalty, tell him anything he wants to hear," but he knows Shane can't. Reuben really has done a number on him. Shane's one true weakness. It's not that he won't tell a lie, it's that he physically can't, no matter what. So if he agrees and swears allegiance, then he really will belong to Reuben and they will all be lost.

"Seventeen…"

The door opens and a pack of dogs drag another lackey into the room, pulling at their leads. The dogs are mixed mongrels, some small, some big but all hungry, growling, snarling and building into a frenzy at the smell of the animal fat that is covering Sara's flesh.

Shane frantically looks to Robert then Leo, unable to act, unable to cope.

"Sixteen, fifteen, fourteen…"

Many scenarios present themselves in Shane's mind. He imagines storming in and rescuing her. Blowing them all away with guns. Even swapping places with Sara. None of these are even remotely possible of course. Just fairy tales.

"Ten…"

The dogs are now too much for the handler and he is being pulled closer and closer to the chained-up Sara. She has been remarkably calm up until now, maybe they have threatened her too much before or maybe she was thinking Shane would rescue her, he thinks, suddenly mortified. Now though, the reality of the situation is dawning on her. Even restrained as she is her body bucks and jerks as instinctive primordial reactions take over. Shane's eyes are latched onto her terrified tear-strewn face… Her beautiful innocent face. He can't let her die! Not like this! Not in front of their child! He can't! What was he thinking taking this long to decide?

"Five, four…"

"I'll do it! I'll swear my…."

Chamuel arrives just in time. He's been standing in the doorway, his mouth hanging open. Even though he has known Reuben all these years and thought nothing he could do would any longer surprise him, he is surprised, horrified, beyond comprehension. Still, as Shane begins to speak he snaps back into focus. However horrific, one grisly death is not worth an entire species. Chamuel runs and wrestles Shane to the ground, stopping him from finishing his declaration.

"One, zero. Really?" Reuben looks at Solfrid to check if she has received any message from Shane. She shakes her head. He looks at his watch once more.

"No? Gosh! Oh well, sorry, Sara." Reuben nods and the dogs are released.

It's a good thing Shane is on the floor. Robert helps to keep him there as the screaming starts. Leo alone is left to stare at the images in a sort of stunned trance. Instantly the dogs are tearing into the only woman who Shane ever loved, literary ripping her apart. The first beast has hold of her soft inner thigh, shaking his head viciously until a strip of meat pulls away. Two bigger dogs fight for the flesh around her rump. A brindle-coloured bitch puts her front paws on Sara hip to catch a mouthful of breast.

Sara knows she is screaming but she can't hear anything. The initial intense, unbelievable pain has passed into a sort of numbness now as her body is yanked and shaken. Her breath is shallow, her heart slow; as her vision begins to darken around the edges she stares at her little boy screaming hysterically as the nurse calmly forces him to watch.

As Shane rages blindly on the floor Chamuel in his new adult body picked for strength and agility, with Roberts help holds him down giving him something to fight against, Leo has finally snapped back into himself and is desperately looking for some way to turn the bloody thing off. He cannot find anything and he looks back at the screen as the pulley is released, Sara's body dropping to the floor so that the dogs can properly begin to feast.

As the screams stop Shane finally relents and as the two men release him he curls in the foetal position, arms over his head, lost to pain no one can save him from. The savage attack continues on screen and Reuben laughs loudly coming into shot.

"Well, that was entertaining," he says. "Phew! Just to let you know this is what awaits you too, and all your loved ones. In fact anyone who sides with the human champion, Shane Mills, or takes up against me, will endure pain that they never imagined possible." Reuben's jollity dissolves into a serious stare. "Understand this, Shane Mills, you are just a human. I understand that these Arc Hon are forcing you into something I am sure you have no interest in getting involved in, so why don't you just accept defeat now? Save us all the bother and I will allow you to get on with your life. I'll even reunite you with young

Shane here. The crying toddler is passed into his arms. Reuben points towards them. "Look into that pretty woman's eyes," he tells the child. "Say hello to your daddy."

The child stops crying and stares; his expression is scared and confused, looking for his daddy.

"I hope you are still watching, Shane," says Reuben. "Your little boy here seems to be very upset and I think he needs his daddy. Now I am disappointed that you refused to save the woman who loved you so much. But I am hoping you won't be so cruel regarding your very own blood. Look at those sad, tear-filled eyes, Shane."

Chamuel and the others now regard the images with detachment, an emotional barrier to save their sanity.

"I really don't want to hurt this child, but needs must and all that," smiles Reuben.

Shane pushes himself off the floor. He stares at the little boy who he never even knew existed until a few minutes ago. Shane's mind is close to breaking point but the face he is looking at now forces him to come back from the brink. He needs to save this child, but how?

"So, what will it be Shane?" continues Reuben. "Do we have to go through all that drama again or do I just cut his throat now?" One of his lackeys passes Reuben a wicked-looking knife. "I am quite tired now after the previous excitement, so this time shall we call it thirty seconds? Same deal, just a few simple words."

He places the blade close to the child's throat.

Shane stands there expressionless. He looks to the new Chamuel, saying nothing but letting him know he should not get involved this time. Chamuel relents and decides he can do no more. Robert can watch no longer and leaves as he hears yet another countdown. Leo follows.

"Twenty-five, twenty-four..." Reuben suddenly halts his countdown. He frowns. His attention has been distracted by something else, something behind Solfrid. The image rotates as she also turns around to see what Reuben has seen. Now Chamuel can see too: a bright light independent of any form hovers behind Solfrid. In seconds it grows from a tiny twinkle to a bright blinding glare. Shane, as bemused as everyone else, seems to be staring into thin air. He can't see anything. He looks at Chamuel who is also staring.

"What is it?" he asks.

"It is an aura," says Chamuel. "One I don't recognise. It has no physical host but it's growing, it has taken shape, it's a..."

Chamuel stops. Shane turns to see his eyes flicker then completely glaze over as if he is frozen. Shane looks back at the image to see that the Djinn there are also frozen, not even a twitch. If he looked hard he would see there was no evidence even of breathing. The nurse and the two lackeys fall to the ground. Then young Shane toddles into the frame. He is looking up at something but Shane cannot see what.

"What is going on? What are you looking at?" Shane shouts, not knowing who he is asking.

Chamuel still stares with no expression, his body rigid. Shane looks back to find the boy is following whatever he is looking at. The door swings open and the boy leaves. Shane is certain his child actually disappears as he exits. The door slams shut again and, as if waking from a sleep, the Djinn reanimate. The image on the screen pans back to Reuben.

"What the fuck just happened?" he asks.

Solfrid cuts the connection and the screen goes blank.

𒈦𒀭𒍣𒁉𒀭𒍣𒊭

"What happened? What just happened," asks a panicked Shane as he catches the stumbling Chamuel.

"I have no idea... the aura it, it was as if it possessed me and the others. I could see but couldn't move, but how I don't know. I wasn't in the room. I'M A FUCKING ARC HON! Nothing can do that to me!"

Shane grabs and shakes him. "Whose aura was it? I must know, it took my child!"

"I don't know! I recognise every aura, Djinn or Arc Hon, but this I have never seen before. I cannot explain how it exists without a physical form. I don't understand."

Shane is losing patience. "You must know something. What did you see? I could see nothing but the child seemed to see it. What was it?"

"It was white, no, silver... it was an aura the likes of which I have never seen before. Quite magnificent. I don't think it will harm the child. I felt its empathy."

"I saw the auras of some of the Djinn. Not a white one, though. You must know whose it was."

"It wasn't a Djinn aura, it was an animal aura. A shark, a magnificent great white shark. Djinn don't have animal auras, only Arc Hon do."

Two days later

Shane readies himself to leave the base. He now has two quests: he must defeat these Djinn bastards and he must find his son. Amitiel visited him once more last night and explained that although she had not witnessed the scene with his son, she had felt the presence of the aura at the time. She was of the same belief as Chamuel, that this aura showed great empathy with the child and so believed that somehow it was connected to him, and, therefore, most likely to Shane too. The rest she could not explain. She had no idea who or what it was. She did know, however, that she also had a strong connection to the aura. A feeling she had never felt before.

Shane was more than ready for the fight. He was angry, he was determined, but more than anything, he was focused. By introducing him to his child, Reuben had inadvertently created a foe ten times stronger and more committed than before. He had his list from Amitiel. He would recruit them all and together they would wage war on these bastard Djinn. He may have lost his first battle with Reuben but now he knows his opponent.

This is not over, this has just begun.

Epilogue

Hagga village, northern Nigeria. Four hundred Boko Haram rebels stealthily approach, heavily armed and under orders to abduct all women eligible for marriage and to kill everyone else. The villagers are not aware of the fate that awaits them as they sleep.

One man is awake, though. The strange white man came into the village that morning. He just wandered in and sat by the tree that is set in the village centre, saying nothing. Most of the villagers have seen white men before but not like this one. His clothes are not Western and his hair is a huge matted mess. The village elders had approached him, suspecting he was with a TV crew or on some life experience programme, like the German who came last year. The white man did not speak however; he just sat there, waiting. All day he sat under the tree, the children teased and giggled, the women gossiped, some pointed and laughed. But still the man just waited.

As night came, the village went to sleep and the man stayed under the tree. When the four hundred rebels are less than half a mile away, the man stands up. He wanders from the tree, out into the one road that leads in and out of the village. He waits. Soon he can see the dim lights of the burning torches held in the hands of bloodthirsty, battle-hardened men who are ready and prepared to rape and murder in the name of their God and creator, Allah.

Well, they are about to meet their maker but his name is not Allah.